Praise for Elizabe

The Book of

"Tender and transcendent, *The Book of Secrets* is about the truths we hide, the consequences we face, and the particular comfort we can find only in a good book. Elizabeth Joy Arnold has written a beautiful and haunting ode to the power of words, and how they shape our lives."

—SARAH ADDISON ALLEN, *New York Times* bestselling
author of *The Peach Keeper*

"*The Book of Secrets* plunges the reader into the strange and intense world of the Sinclairs, a family bound and pulled apart by the forces of imagination and religious _____ of Chloe Tyler, trapped in this _____ Arnold paints a fascinating pic-_____ s that offers a complex medita-_____ e of truth and on the power of

E LAZARIDIS POWER, author of
The Clover House

ld heart-wrenching story about the secrets that can both hold a marriage together, and drive two people apart. Reading *The Book of Secrets* is like walking through a dark labyrinth: Just when all hope is lost, you step out into sunshine."

—CARLA BUCKLEY, author of *Invisible*

Pieces of My Sister's Life

"This well-observed story is vibrant and rich with the subtleties and nuances of family life."

—*Publishers Weekly*

"The perfect summer beach book or engrossing book club discussion novel. Its contemporary characters jump off the page and stay with you even when you've put it down. The plot, while taking surprising twists (like life itself), touches universal nerves, with its emphasis on the strains and joys of family relationships."

—Trenton *Times*

"Poignant, heart-breaking, and at times highly emotional . . . The perfect book club read."

—Fresh Fiction

"Elizabeth Joy Arnold's debut is the perfect book for a day at the beach or a rainy weekend indoors—a guilty-pleasure, fast-paced read that begs to be devoured in one sitting, despite its length."

—Bookreporter

"In prose both elegant and direct, Arnold delivers a piercingly romantic, highly readable tale of mystery and loss, longing and redemption, as haunting as the last dusk of summer."

—Book Page

Promise the Moon

"Exceptionally well written and outstanding character choice will make this book a must-read."

—Coffee Time Romance and More

"When a book brings out the tears like *Promise the Moon* does, there are really no other words to explain how incredible a read this is. Elizabeth Joy Arnold deserves great praise—and RRT's Perfect 10 Award."

—Romance Reviews Today

When We Were Friends

"Arnold pens a dramatic story about ordinary people in extraordinary situations. Her characters are our neighbors and friends, just trying to get through life the best way they know how. Readers who like words that paint a picture will enjoy this story, as the images leap from the pages. Once you start, you will not want to put this book down."

—*Romantic Times*

"*When We Were Friends* packs an emotional punch where it is sometimes hard to choose sides between what is right and what is morally wrong. Author Elizabeth Joy Arnold has written a story that ropes you in from the get-go and keeps you hanging on till the last page, with a storyline so moving it is hard not to enjoy and embrace this book."

—Coffee Time Romance and More

The BOOK *of* SECRETS

The BOOK of SECRETS

a novel

ELIZABETH JOY ARNOLD

BANTAM BOOKS TRADE PAPERBACKS
NEW YORK

F ARN

A Bantam Books Trade Paperback Original

Copyright © 2013 by Elizabeth Joy Arnold
Reading group guide copyright © 2013 by Random House, Inc.

Published in the United States by Bantam Books, an imprint of The Random House Publishing Group, a division of Random House, Inc., New York.

BANTAM BOOKS and the rooster colophon are registered trademarks of Random House, Inc.
RANDOM HOUSE READER'S CIRCLE & Design is a registered trademark of Random House, Inc.

ISBN 978-0-553-59253-5
ebook ISBN 978-0-345-53866-6

Printed in the United States of America

www.randomhousereaderscircle.com

9 8 7 6 5 4 3 2 1

Book design by Diane Hobbing

I dedicate this book to all the brilliant authors who have kept me up till the wee hours, made me see the world—and myself—differently, and inspired me to become a better writer. Every day I look at the book spines on all my overloaded shelves and remember the worlds behind them, and feel full.

Books can be dangerous. The best ones should be labeled, "This could change your life."

—*Helen Exley*

The stories of childhood leave an indelible impression, and their author always has a niche in the temple of memory from which the image is never cast out to be thrown on the rubbish heap of things that are outgrown and outlived.

—*Howard Pyle*

Love never dies a natural death. It dies because we don't know how to replenish its source. It dies of blindness and errors and betrayals. It dies of illness and wounds; it dies of weariness, of witherings, of tarnishings.

—*Anaïs Nin*

A book should serve as the ax for the frozen sea within us.

—*Franz Kafka*

Loneliness the clearest of crystal insight into your own soul; it's the fear of one's own self that haunts the lonely.

—*Keith Haynie*

PART I

The CHRONICLES *of* NARNIA

1

SITTING in our bookstore at night, I can hear the stories. Or not hear them so much as feel them: the neat, round softness of Austen with its improbable, inevitable love affairs; the sprawl of Dickens with its meandering threads tying into coincidental knots. All the books have colors and shapes not just from the stories written but from the stories of the authors who've done the writing; from Steinbeck's realism to Murakami's cubism, a regular art museum of voices.

It's different from the stores that sell new books, I think, with their splashes and shouts for attention. Because here when I sit at night in the worn armchair by the fireplace, I can also hear the stories of people who've held these books. Some of the first editions must have been read by generations; I imagine women in their petticoats and men in breeches looking for escape from sadness or dreariness. The books have seen plagues and wars—back when wars were still romantic—have been read by candlelight and oil-lamp light; it's all written there in smudges and stains if you just know how to look.

And hidden behind it all? Is our story. Our once upon a time.

So. Once upon a time there was a girl named Chloe who lived virtually alone, in a cottage by the woods. Until her eighth birthday when she woke to find her mother already gone to work, without a good morning, a kiss, a birthday wish. Chloe had been forgotten. So, being a headstrong girl, she gave herself her own birthday present, skipped school for the first time of many, ate Lucky Charms (minus the marshmallows), and then biked out into the neighborhood to explore.

And there at the end of Bayard Lane, playing in the yard of the biggest house in the state, perhaps even the world, were two girls in pastel dresses and a boy in a pressed white shirt. They were the perfect family, too beautiful to be real, and of course the truth was that what Chloe had seen wasn't actually real at all. But by the time she figured this out she'd already been in love with them for years and it hardly mattered. Because it was here with these magical children in this world so different from her own that Chloe's real life began. On her eighth birthday, she was born.

Every day she came to play with her new friends as the weeks passed, and then the years. In time she'd marry the boy, give birth to and lose a son, open a store, and begin building an empire. Until the empire began to crumble and the boy grew haunted and disappeared. No fairy tale, no happily ever after; Chloe was alone again.

And in the new silence, the echo of untold stories was deafening.

Secrets. It was one of the ways we were a good match, because Nate loved secrets and I loved his surprises. We both believed one needed to be shocked out of one's expectations in order to fully feel life.

The bookstore was both a surprise and a shock. He'd bought the house over twenty years before with the money his mother had left him and his advance for the book he'd just published. But I'd had no idea he was even thinking of moving from our apartment until the day he walked me blindfolded to the front door and pulled away the scarf. "Welcome to your new life!" he said.

And there we were in front of a Victorian mansion, all crumbling scalloped shingles and tall windows, two of which were boarded with plywood. It was an aged beauty queen, now with no hair, bunions, and missing teeth, and at first I had no idea what he was implying by bringing me there. We'd talked about opening a store, but only in vague "someday" terms, and one does not surprise one's wife with houses in the way one might surprise her with roses. Unless one is Nate.

He opened the door and led me through what felt like a thousand walk-in closets, with scarred wooden floors and faded, peeling wallpaper, and an overpowering smell of stale black tea. "We'll set up the store downstairs," he said, voice rushed like a kid trying to explain the wonders of a video game or Harry Potter movie to someone he knows is much too old for it. "We'll line the walls with wooden shelves floor to ceiling, attach sliding wooden ladders. And I realize right now these little nooks look like toilet stalls, but we'll shelve them too, so finding the books there feels like a discovery, ancient treasures."

He led me down the front hallway to show where we'd put the cash register, and a "reading room" for customers to page through the rarer books, searching for signs of foxing or bookworm holes. He'd already imagined it in minute detail: the cushy chairs with tufted ottomans, round end tables with green glass lamps, paintings of authors most wouldn't recognize but that would give the most bookish patrons some self-satisfaction. "Look at that fireplace!" he said. "I think there's marble under there if we just strip off that paint. We can light fires in the winter and set greenery here in the summer, put velvet armchairs here and here so people feel like they're actually sitting in someone's old library." And then he led me upstairs to show me how we'd build a separate entrance in back, break down walls to turn a bathroom and two of the spare bedrooms into an open kitchen and living area. He made me see it all.

But Nate was a gifted storyteller. "Leave out the parts that people skip," that's a quote from Elmore Leonard when asked how he made his novels engaging. And Nate skillfully left out the debt that would take us years to tunnel up from, the months of hand-chapping, back-straining labor, the stink of the chemicals used to strip the floor and walls. The tedium of sanding fifty yards of dentil molding, bleaching out a century's worth of grout stains and spackling a century's worth of plaster cracks; Nate didn't mention any of this, just made me see the magic of his story. And yes the magic was there, under it all. He didn't lie, just left out some unromantic narrative detail. And in time our house, our bookshop, they did become our fairy tale. His story came mostly true, until the ending.

The note was on the kitchen table. I'd returned after a round of errands and the gym to find the shop unexpectedly closed; it was just six, and on weekdays we stayed open till eight. But I was only vaguely worried. It had been a hard year for both of us, and Nate had been fragile over the past few months, perpetually seeming on the verge of . . . I don't know what. Breaking down, I guess, although those words sound way too simplistic and cliché. What do you call being perpetually on a knife's edge? Feeling like your body has crystallized, so that something as innocuous as a "Do I know you from somewhere?" from a stranger who's seen your story on the news can shatter you into sharp, serrated splinters? I'm a woman who loves words, but there are times there are no words.

Maybe Nate had just needed to get away, lie down and immerse himself in a book or the National Geographic channel, someone else's world. And seeing the store closed, I thought I might have just the remedy.

We'd gotten a FedEx that morning, the first American edition of *Alice's Adventures in Wonderland*: octavo, red cloth and gilt edges, original dark green endpapers, meant for a Mr. Ernie Howell, who'd requested it for his ten-year-old granddaughter. Its pages were yellowed and stained, its spine sunned and frayed. And his granddaughter would probably think it was gross, thanking him politely before stowing the book in a back corner, having no concept of its true value. Ninety-five hundred dollars plus tax, to be exact. The cost of history, but to me putting a price on history felt crass.

We'd read the story together as children: me, Grace, Cecilia, and Nate on the Sinclairs' brocade sofa, hanging off Mrs. Sinclair's shoulders so we could see sketches of the hookah-smoking caterpillar and Cheshire cat teeth. And now for the few days the book was ours, Nate and I would sit together, turning pages and remembering.

On my walk home I'd been listening to my iPod, the Beatles, and thinking of how we'd spend the night, I was tempted to dance to the music. I *would've* danced if there'd been nobody around to see, but instead I just walked to the rhythm, adding extra steps where warranted, tiny hops on my toes. Almost happy. Tonight we'd congratulate each other over wine for our find, and maybe then we'd make love; it had been a long time. A very, very, very long time.

But Nate was gone. And in his place, seventy-four words.

Someone, I don't remember who, said that life is like a beautiful melody with messed up lyrics. I never really understood that until just now. Something's happened very suddenly, something truly "messed up," and I need to go back to Redbridge tonight. I tried to call your cell but it must've been off. I'm not sure when I'll be back. It may be awhile, but I'll call as soon as I know more.

—N

And that was it. At the time, I didn't even wonder about how strangely it was written, the clipped sentences, the quote he'd chosen to explain his leaving or the vagueness of the word "awhile." The only thing that had scared me was his return to Redbridge.

It was the town where I'd spent the first twenty years of my life, and so you'd think I should have twenty years' worth of memories, as many good as bad. But instead all I could see was the nightmare of those last few weeks, a movie on an infinite loop perpetually goring and twisting. I tried not to let myself drift back further to life with Gabriel, the memories like slashes: watching him learn to walk by staggering between library shelves; at the park throwing a ball two-handed that inevitably ended up behind him, wearing a look of bewilderment followed by self-congratulatory applause. Even the places Gabriel had never been part of, like the front steps of the grammar school, or twisting trails through the Redwoods, were places I'd imagined taking him someday. And I couldn't stomach the thought of seeing them again, knowing I never would.

We hadn't been back since my mother's funeral, and even then we hadn't gone to the Sinclairs' home, where his sister Cecilia, and now Nate's father, lived. We talked to Cecilia every month or so, got updates on the meandering threads of her gratingly uneventful life. But Nate hadn't seen his father for almost twenty-five years. Was one of them sick? Well that must be it, what else could it be? But then why hadn't Nate just written that in his note?

It wasn't till after I'd taken a shower that I thought to check my messages to see if he'd given more details and listen to the tone of his voice, make sure he sounded like he'd be okay. But although he'd said my phone had been off, I found it was actually still on, no messages. And when I checked missed calls to get a sense of when he'd left, it turned out there hadn't been any. He hadn't tried to call me.

And why not? Despite everything, we were still each other's stabilizing force. Something happened to set one of us off balance, and we needed the other to get back on steady ground. Had things between us really changed so much?

No, he must've dialed a wrong number without realizing, left a message on someone else's phone. And as soon as the thought solidified in my brain I grabbed onto it, became sure that it was true.

Because I was still living inside the fairy-tale shell he'd constructed to safeguard his secrets. Yes, Nate was a gifted storyteller.

Once upon a time there was a young man who'd loved a girl so deeply, so truly, that he left his family to be with her. Defying the wrath of his father and the imprudence of commitment at such a young age, they held hands and made a vow of forever. And they lived happily, or at least as happily as possible considering the circumstances. Until, they did not.

It started last Christmas. We had a number of odd traditions, me and Nate, the way I'm sure most couples do after years together. The bizarre Buddha bobble-head doll a customer had left in the shop, which we periodically, randomly, hid in places we knew the other would find him. The way, when eating potato chips, Nate would silently hand me each folded chip he found like it contained a secret love note. And then there was our Christmas Eve marshmallow fight. It had started fifteen years ago when I teased him about the string of toasted marshmallow hanging from his chin, the way he couldn't eat anything gooey, pizza cheese or caramel sauce, without leaving a strand of it dangling from his face like a strange, lone whisker. He responded by pelting a marshmallow at me, so of course I'd pelted one back, and soon the living room was littered with them. Since then, every Christmas we bought marshmallows to roast in our fireplace and to throw, laughing like adolescents, often ending the night by making love amidst the sticky ruins.

But last year Nate had been preoccupied, in one of the moods that hit him sometimes where he seemed scraped raw, everything on the surface. Usually these moods only last a day or two, but this time he'd been edgy for almost two weeks. So to lighten the mood, after studying the burn marks on the marshmallow at the end of my tongs, I'd held it up for him to see. "It's Jesus's face!" I said.

He'd forced a smile, then squashed the marshmallow between his thumb and forefinger and studied it. "Now it's a sheep."

"We could've made a fortune off that, you jerk, eBayed it or kept it in a bell jar and charged admission."

To which he'd responded, "Joel's getting out of jail this week."

I'd stared at him silently, a fist knuckling against my ribs.

"I'm sorry, I didn't know how to tell you. I mean I realize this wasn't the right way, but I thought you should know."

"How?" My voice was pitched too high. "I don't get it. How could they let him out?"

"He had twenty-five years to life, Chloe, and it's been twenty-five years. He's going back home."

"But . . . Cecilia's in your home. You mean he's staying with Cecilia?"

"Because he doesn't have anywhere else to go. She called me a couple weeks ago, wanted to know how I felt about it, and I just told her it was all up to her. It's not for me to say who she's allowed to live with."

How could Cecilia stand to even be in the same room with their father? It felt like the worst betrayal, this woman who'd once been my best friend now agreeing to live with the man I despised most in the world. All the times I'd fantasized about strangling him, shooting, stabbing, suffocating, by all rights he should've died a slow and agonizing death alone, but Cecilia was agreeing to take him in?

"How could you tell her it was up to her? It's good he doesn't have anywhere else, he should be out on the street!" I'd strode into the bedroom and slammed the door shut, and when I emerged hours later into the dark house, needing to talk and cry and be held, I'd found Nate—who long ago had sworn off alcohol—lying unconscious on the sofa, reeking from the bottle of whiskey I later found empty and buried in the trash.

Since then we hadn't talked about it, although it was there behind every conversation, my hostility at him seeming not to care enough. I assumed it must've happened, that his father was now out of jail and living with Cecilia. But I didn't ask, didn't speak to Cecilia when she called and, without consciously meaning to, I stopped talking to Nate about anything real.

That summer, for our twenty-fifth anniversary, he'd given me a silver bracelet engraved with the words *that fine fixed point,* a quote from one of my favorite poems, by Jean de Sponde.

> *What could be more immovable or stronger?*
> *What becomes more and more secure, the longer*
> *it is battered by inconstancy and the stress*
> *we find in our lives? Here is that fine fixed point*
> *from which to move a world that is out of joint,*
> *as he could have done, had he known a love like this.*

It was an attempt to start us back on the upswing, I guess, as if a written reminder of what we'd had would be enough to make me forget all I blamed him for. I'd thanked him, slipped the bracelet over my wrist and wore it that once and never again.

And now he'd left home without telling me why, like I was a neighbor informed only so I'd know to water the plants or feed the pets. He didn't call the day he left or the next or the next, even though I tried his cell phone several times, left countless messages. I didn't want to call Cecilia's number because I didn't want to risk having to speak to their father, and so I kept calling his cell, increasingly desperate. Until Saturday afternoon, when I was looking for information on a missing set of Victor Hugo. And realized why he wasn't answering his phone.

"What do you mean you don't know if they've been ordered yet? I asked for them six weeks ago! Maybe I should've stayed on top of it, asked to see photos before I paid, but I trusted him! It never takes this long."

The man in front of me, Lester Jarvis, was red-faced even when he wasn't upset. With the flush, his unfortunate body shape, and his tendency to dress in clothes that probably hadn't fit him since ten years and fifty pounds ago, he looked disturbingly like an overstuffed sausage.

"I'm sorry." I clicked on one of the tabs of the complex book-keeping system our friend Daniel had let us illegally copy last year. Was I supposed to search for Lester's name? The collection of books he'd ordered? A date?

I tried typing in *Victor Hugo,* which resulted in a startled pop-up window: *String not recognized! Numerical value expected!* "I'm sorry, it's just Nate always handles these things, and he's been away. I'll go ahead and look for another set." And pay for it how? I knew what this meant, that of the three thousand dollars left in our bank account, more than half must have come from Lester Jarvis's down payment. Which meant that technically, until the books were in his hands, that money still belonged to him. And the books would cost thousands, so even after getting the rest of his payment there'd be nothing left. Maybe less than nothing.

He studied my face. "What's wrong, Chloe?"

"Oh nothing. Just, you know . . . tired."

"Fatigue is a side effect of a full life," Lester said. He paused, then nodded as if pleased with the phrase. "Although me, I'm only tired from insomnia." He held my eyes, like he was expecting something. (Sympathy? A sleep-inducing massage?) But then, maybe seeing something in my expression, he turned away. "Funny thing, insomnia, you'd think it would give me time to accomplish more. But it's sucked the motivation straight out of me, and it seems like all I do these days is eat and read. Speaking of which, I'm going to browse. I'll expect the books by the end of October, Chloe. I've got a bibliophile friend coming to visit from Sacramento, and the Hugo's part of my scheme to fully convey to him my vast superiority."

He headed across the room to a section that held mostly hard-boiled mysteries, and I watched him from under my bangs. It always astonished me how one could never guess by a person's outward appearance what sort of books they'd choose for leisure reading. I would've pegged Lester Jarvis as a reader of poetry. Or gay erotica.

I turned back to the computer and clicked on the remaining tabs, trying to figure out which might show the books that had been ordered, or requested but not yet ordered. But there were too many buttons and boxes and drop-down menus, and I shoved the mouse away, my frustration always so close to the surface now that all it took was a nudge for it to show its teeth. My eyes on the tweed casing of Lester Jarvis's behind, I dialed Nate's number, willing him to answer. And heard his ring tone.

My eyes sprang wide and I twisted my head frantically left, then right, almost expecting to find Nate crouched in a corner, as if he'd perhaps been hiding there unseen the whole time, waiting for an opportune moment to jump out. The phone stopped ringing, went to voice mail, and I hung up and dialed again, following the sound out to the hallway and into what we called the "reading room," with its long mahogany table, wingback chairs, and glass case with our most valuable books. There, slung over one of the chairs, was Nate's Nike jacket. I fished into his pocket and pulled out his cell phone.

I stared at it blindly. He'd left his phone? The glass case was cracked open, I noticed suddenly, and the key to the case was thrown on the table beside it. When we never kept it open. Not only because it would've been as foolish as leaving thousand-dollar bills in an unlocked case, but also because the case was temperature and humidity controlled and needed to be closed to work properly.

"Chloe, where are you?" Lester Jarvis's voice from the next room. "Can I pay or would you rather I walk out with these?"

I shut the door and used the key to lock it, my throat tight. I walked back to the register, where Lester's arms were cradling Raymond Chandler and Lawrence Block, rang him up and watched him leave the store, then reached for the phone and called Daniel. When he answered I hesitated and then said, "Listen. I need help."

Daniel showed up an hour later with a bottle of pinot grigio and the fixings for burritos, and spent an hour showing me the most useful ins and outs of the system, including the page where Nate should've noted Lester's request. "So it's not just that he didn't order the Hugo collection," I said, "he didn't even note that he *needed* to order it, or that he'd already been paid."

"Crazy, right? He's usually so OCD-ish about keeping track of everything."

"I told you about his note," I said. "You think he knew even back when Lester ordered the books that there was something going on with his dad or Cecilia?" The thought occurred to me briefly that maybe I shouldn't be inviting Daniel into this particular corner of our lives. Or not a corner but a thread, intertwined with the millions of other threads of our past, mangled spaghetti. Daniel had only seen the outer fringes, and Nate wouldn't want him knowing more, but my brain was scorched. I needed help.

"I want to show you something," I said, and pulled out Nate's phone, paged back through his dialed calls. "I wanted to see if he'd tried to call me the day he left, maybe gotten a wrong number and left a message on someone else's phone. But he didn't call anybody that day, just Cecilia. Who had called and left a message a half hour earlier. Listen."

I opened his voice mail, paged back through all my frantic messages, and then on speaker played the message Cecilia had left. "Nate, it's me. Please listen, I'm so confused . . . Oh crap, I don't even know how to talk or think about this. There's too much to leave in a message so please call as soon as you get this, because I'm scared there's not much time." The phone clicked to silence.

"You haven't called Cecilia to ask her?" Daniel said.

"Well, I'll have to now, I realize that. I'm just trying to come to terms with the fact that he's been hiding something from me. Here, look." I paged again through his dialed calls. "He called Cecilia's home six weeks ago, and then again the following week. When he *never* called there, it was always Cecilia calling him since he didn't want to chance having to speak to his father."

"You think something happened six weeks ago that he didn't tell you?"

"Maybe even longer ago." I looked up at Daniel. "He's been so . . . I don't know, strange. Distant. Things've been weird between us over the past few months, you know that."

Daniel touched my hand with the back of his finger and I stared intently at the computer screen, the blinking cursor, as if it might beat out a Morse code message. Tell me how life had turned around this blind corner. S-O-S-H-E-L-P-M-E.

"Look," he said, "let me make you dinner, and maybe you can call Cecilia, try and talk to him. It's crazy to start guessing what's going on when you don't even have a hint of an idea. So just call and then we'll figure out how to deal with whatever it is."

We? I took a step backward. "I shouldn't have brought you into this," I said. "This is between me and Nate; I'm sure he wouldn't want you involved."

"It's between *Nate* and Nate at this point, isn't it? And everything that affects you . . . well, it affects me too, obviously. Don't you think I see how the past few months have been for you? You've been miserable lately, and him leaving like this, running away with whatever secret he might be keeping, don't you realize it's just a sign?"

"A sign of what!" Had I led Daniel to believe I considered my marriage broken beyond repair? He didn't understand, but how could I blame him when I didn't understand myself either? For twenty years I'd felt alone, at times even when I was with Nate, even when I knew I was in love with him and him with me, and that had made the aloneness so much harder. Because it wasn't physical, wasn't something that could be moderated by attention and care, it was strictly internal, separate from him and our relationship, something only I could see. Being alone in my aloneness.

And in the midst of that had come Daniel. I'd met him eight years ago when he was considering acquiring an indie bookstore in downtown Truckee, and he'd come by the shop to make sure we weren't going to be direct competitors. Which we weren't at all; the store he was looking at was more of a discount warehouse. And after seeing we were as far removed from that vibe as Joan Didion is from Joan Rivers, he'd cemented his decision to buy the store and taken Nate and me out for a celebratory dinner.

From the first conversation I'd felt like I knew him, saw it all from the cramped ranch where he'd live with an adored Labrador mutt, to the five newspapers he'd religiously pore through on Sundays, to the socks he wore until they disintegrated into threads, to his affection for nieces or nephews he wished were his own. And it turned out that, except for the mutt, all of this was true. He was the kind of man who lived life with a quiet contentedness, watching the world go by around him, somewhat bewildered but accepting of whatever came.

The three of us became great friends, commiserating over the death of indies and the challenges of keeping one's chin up when one's net profit was lower than one's grocery budget. He was handsome, in a Jude Law way, intuitive and creative and an all-around good guy and, it turned out, in love with me.

Which I'd learned eight months ago when we drove together to a bookseller's convention in New York. We'd been at the hotel bar when James Taylor, "Fire and Rain," started to play over the speakers and I immediately started singing—badly—along. He smiled at me, eyes darting to the couple seated next to us. *Totally wasted,* he mouthed to them, and I swatted him. "And abusive," he added, then turned back to me. "You're, like, the most uninhibited person I've ever met. Everything you're feeling, you just express it and the hell with what other people think. It's a great way to be."

"Except that you can't take me out in public," I started to say. But he'd gotten a melty look in his eyes, the conversation stopped, and he touched the side of my jaw and smiled and . . . I kissed him. I was drunk, but probably not drunk enough to justify it. It was just that melty look, and the bar had been candlelit, and my favorite song was playing and the kiss had been, I guess you could say, instinctual. One kiss, that was all it was.

But then of course there was a new edge to our friendship that made me start looking at the underbelly of my relationship with Nate, questioning everything. I knew Nate had secrets; we'd adored each other for most of our lives, but still there'd always been this barrier between us, subtle as a gauzy scarf or a haze of smoke, made up of the things we kept from each other.

And the more I looked at those secrets, the more conspicuous they became, from a gauzy scarf to a fortified concrete sound barrier between us. We never fought, never even spoke harsh words, but I'd stopped trying to dig beneath that surface. We kissed hello and goodbye, exchanged I love yous that had begun to feel perfunctory, made each other tea, let each other cheat at Scrabble, and talked about the shop, the news, the books we were reading, but never about ourselves.

And then . . . two months ago. Nate was away at an auction and Daniel had come by the store, told me about his brother's leukemia diagnosis and broke down in my arms. And holding him had ripped a seam inside me.

I'd made love to him here in the shop, on this green velvet couch, watched by Salinger and Vonnegut and Martin Amis. More passion in it than I'd shared with Nate in months, but the wrong kind of passion, something I felt only when Daniel looked into my eyes, like that look was a contagious rash. Impossible to refrain from scratching until he left, when I'd think back on it and try to remember how it felt, rekindle the intensity, but could evoke only the way our passion must have looked from the outside, the words I'd said, the intertwining of our limbs.

An hour after he'd left that day he called me to say that he hated himself, could never do this again. But I was the one who'd gone back to him. Had gone twice more over the past two months, triggered by loneliness and maybe a reckless desire to stir the waters, figure out if there really was anything under their cloudiness. In the hours I spent with him, I remembered how it felt to be in love. And I still had no idea what that meant, or what was real anymore.

Now I turned away from the computer screen and looked into his face. So different from Nate's, equally handsome but almost boyish where Nate's was angled sharp, his hair sandy blond where Nate's was thick brown. In a way, Daniel was the person Nate had been when we first fell in love, intelligent and perceptive without being wary, open and honest to a fault, wonderfully, painfully innocent. Nate had put up barriers, but I could see into Daniel, could mold his face with my words like he was a blancmange. Awful to have so much power, but also shamefully exhilarating.

"When there are parts of each other's lives you aren't willing to share," he said now, "it's almost always a sign of something broken."

"Daniel," I said softly, carefully, as if care could keep the blancmange from falling. "I know how I've made it seem but there's a lot more going on here; I don't know how to deal with any of this."

His face hardened, anger instead of devastation, which was a relief. "Then what are you going to do when he comes back? Just keep going with this double life? You get the best of both worlds, but what do me and Nate get?"

A double life. Of course that was how he'd been seeing it. Eating dinners with Nate, having to pretend he didn't know the shape of Nate's wife's breasts. Why hadn't it been worse for me? How had I been able to sit in this same spot with Nate, looking at this couch and knowing what had happened there? Because I'd tried my best to make myself believe sex with Daniel was only a comforting distraction rather than actually "making love." I somehow had imagined that might be more forgivable.

"You're right," I said. "Of course you're right, it can't go on like this when he comes back." The room had grown dark around us. It was late September, the time of year when the sun set disturbingly quickly, day to night within minutes, the only light from the streetlamps outside and the blue glow of the computer screen, and I suddenly felt penned in by the dark. "But I can't even think about that right now," I said. "I'm worried about Nate, and I'm terrified for myself, and that's all I have room to feel at this point."

Daniel's face twitched. "Right," he said. "I shouldn't have suggested it." He stood quickly, and handed me the notes he'd scrawled with instructions and tips on the database. "I should go then, let you start trying to find that Hugo."

"Don't go, Daniel, we didn't even have dinner yet."

"I'm not all that hungry actually. I only brought stuff for Mexican because I know you like it, so I'll leave you the groceries. I'll take the wine though, if you don't mind. I'd been looking forward to it." He kissed me dryly on the top of my head, then went upstairs to the kitchen. A minute later he returned, wine bottle in hand, flashed a smile at me, and walked out the front door.

I wanted to call after him, say I was sorry, but sorry for what? For loving Nate?

I looked over at the tall shelves by the doorway, the Poe collection with its red embossed spines, which Nate and I had bought at a flea market two years ago. We'd paid five dollars per book when it was worth easily ten times that, and after the purchase we'd raced with bags in hand to the car, laughing, as if we were scared of being caught and forced to return them.

I remembered walking hand in hand with him as we searched for treasures: a turquoise hand mixer, lace doilies to place on the end tables in the shop. A Chutes and Ladders game identical to the version we'd played as children, which we played again that night for nostalgia's sake, realizing from the first moves how ridiculously monotonous it was and overdramatizing our ladder-elation and chute-devastation for effect.

Now I stood and walked to the books, arranged them first alphabetically by title, then pulled them off the shelves again to arrange them chronologically by original pub date. I aligned the spines perfectly, obsessive-compulsively, trying to keep the thoughts at bay. Wishing that Daniel hadn't left. Wishing I'd found the right thing to say, as if there could be any right thing. But more than anything, wishing that he hadn't taken the wine.

After closing up the shop I went upstairs to the bedroom, and sat on Nate's side of the bed by the telephone. Propped on his nightstand was our wedding photo, the only photo we had, Nate in a suit with no tie and me in a white jacket and skirt, framed by a giant Christmas-light-strung heart.

We'd gotten married in Vegas, the idea of a Vegas wedding so tackily ridiculous, completely unlike us, which in a strange way had made it irresistibly romantic. We looked so happy in the photo. We'd laughed through the whole ceremony, in hysterics over the canned organ music and the overearnest reading of the vows. Everyone must have thought we were drunk and twenty-four hours away from an annulment. But really the hilarity, the explosiveness of our glee, was just a release from the hell of everything we'd so recently been through. We'd needed that night so we could begin to live again.

As we proceeded back up the aisle, Nate had slipped a cold hand into mine and squeezed. I turned to meet his eye and he put on an overly solemn face and under his breath said, "I think we need to do this every year."

I'd looked up at the mural on the ceiling, two Pillsbury Dough Boy–shaped cherubs blowing snub-nosed gold horns. And I'd thought, *Every year*, played the phrase again and again in my mind, and started to laugh.

In a movie this would've been the impulsive sidestep that led us on a madcap tangent to our ordinary lives, whirlwind trips to the Mediterranean, petty crime sprees and close escapes, taking us such a distance from our past that we'd be able to look away from it. But in actuality it had led us to this, a quiet, middle-agedness, but one that was overhung by shadows. A husband who left without explanation.

Now I turned on the bedside light and lifted the photo, traced a finger across Nate's rounded cheek and then my own. We'd been so very young, only twenty and twenty-one, broken children. Memory was so very strange, the way you looked back on the distant past as if it was you who'd done the things you did and made the decisions you made, wondering if you'd gone temporarily insane when really it was just that you'd been a completely different person.

If I'd been an outsider, looking down on this couple, what would I have told them? Would I tell the girl to go to college as she'd always planned, to find her own future rather than molding her life to someone else's? Warn the boy that there are no such things as fairy tales, especially when one is too broken inside to create them? Maybe, but of course it wouldn't have mattered; we would have married anyway.

I reached for his pillow and buried my nose inside it to see if I could still smell the scent of his aftershave, his shampoo. Inhaling here and here and here, even pulling the pillowcase off to inhale its insides, but any scent it might have once held was already gone.

I set the picture down, threw the pillow back onto the bed, and reached for the telephone.

2

CECILIA and I used to be the best of friends. Our personalities were so similar, our favorite activities jumping headlong out of trees or lifting damp logs in the hopes of finding new species of beetle, and for years we'd been closer to each other than we were to either Grace or Nate. But time and circumstance seemed to have muted her. She'd been married soon before we left Redbridge and then divorced within two years, gone back to her childhood home. I couldn't imagine that she wouldn't feel bitter about how her life had turned out, but instead she just acted resigned.

Not that I'd talked to her in a while. When we'd first left she called us daily, worried after all we'd been through, wanting to make sure we hadn't shattered into microscopic shards. But over the next few months she'd gotten more and more entangled in her volatile marriage, all her energy spent digging in her heels so as not to be bucked off. She called less and less frequently and then, for the first years after her divorce, hardly at all. As the pain—or perhaps the embarrassment—over her situation began to wear off, she started calling a bit more frequently. But soon she'd become mired first in depression and then in the church, after which she stopped asking to speak with me, and it was only when I insisted to Nate that I got to spend any time with her. Since their father had returned home last year, I'd stopped insisting.

I hunched forward on the bed as I listened to the phone ring, feeling expectant and uneasy. It took eight rings before anyone picked up, and I spent the time trying to work out what the hell I'd say if Nate's father answered. Pretend to be a telemarketer, maybe. Or scream.

But it was Cecilia who finally picked up the phone, sounding winded and vaguely anxious. "Chloe," she said. "I thought it might be you."

"Could I talk to Nate?" I said, then shook my head quickly to erase the words. "I'm sorry, that was rude. How are you?"

"I'm doing okay, and it wasn't rude. I'm sure you're worried about him."

"So he's there with you? It's just I haven't talked to him since he drove out there. He left me a really vague note, and I kept trying to call but it turned out he actually left his cell phone here."

"He did?" She paused. "Well, I wish you could talk to him now, but he's gone out."

"Gone out?"

"For groceries and a few odds and ends we needed. He's been taking care of problems with the house because things've started to fall apart over the past few months."

"So . . . you asked him out there to fix them?"

"Well, I guess that's part of it. With everything that's been happening here I haven't had time, and somebody has to watch Dad."

"Watch your dad?" I felt a flicker of dread. "What is it, Cecilia? What's going on?"

"Nate didn't tell you any of it?" A beat of silence, then, "Dad's sick."

There was something strange in her voice, a tone I couldn't quite place. "Is it . . ." I said. "Is he . . . ?"

"Deathly ill? No, not at this point, but he does need to be taken care of."

"I heard the message you left Nate on Wednesday. You said there's not much time? What were you talking about?"

"Oh. Well, I was talking about my dad. Because we've known for a while now, and at first Nate didn't want anything to do with it. But I keep telling him that even though Daddy's mind is slowly leaving, his soul's still there. Disease can't rob a man of his spiritual prosperity."

I gave a choked laugh and Cecilia said, "Right, I can see why you'd find that ludicrous. And Nate did too, of course in his mind Daddy doesn't have a soul, but in the end I think he realized he needed to see him one more time, just to finally say whatever he needs to say before it's too late."

I stared fixedly out the window at the flagstone path we'd laid years ago, now filmed with moss and edged with crabgrass. "So what's wrong with him?"

She paused, then said, "It's dementia, Chloe. Alzheimer's."

I felt a swirl of horror. "What?" How long had Nate known? Why hadn't he told me?

"In retrospect it's been going on for a while now, even before he came home. But over the past few weeks it's been getting much worse, and I'm scared to leave him alone now."

The thought of Joel Sinclair having Alzheimer's horrified me. Not the horror of what this would mean for him; he deserved this and much worse. But one didn't think a man like Joel could be vulnerable to such a thing. He felt to me more like an energy, if that makes any sense, more an *essence* than a person with a body that could be weakened by such a human disease. Plus, I knew what this would mean for Cecilia. Nate might be willing to help now, for Cecilia's sake, but I didn't know how long he'd be able to stand staying with his father. Soon he'd be back home and Cecilia's life—what she had left of it—would be consumed with caring for a man who didn't deserve care.

"I'm sorry," I said softly.

"Yeah, thanks. Just taking it day by day, for now."

"But have you figured out what you're going to do long-term? There has to be somewhere you could put him. Like, you know . . . a home."

"Chloe, no. I'm sorry, that was Nate's first reaction too, but I don't want him locked up again so soon. Maybe in a few months, I don't know. But for now, at least for as long as Daddy knows where he is, I'll keep him here. Nate's been taking care of things I haven't been able to, I'll only need him for a few days." She was talking strangely fast now, nervously, as if trying to fill empty spaces—an underlying awkwardness—with sound. "We've been so busy, which is probably why he hasn't called. He's actually started cataloguing all our books, trying to see how many of them are worth something because Mom's money's almost gone. I should've used it to build a future, like Nate did, but I was stupid. I made some bad investment choices and the recession almost wiped me out, so we can really use the money. I adore our books, but most of the time they just sit there collecting dust."

What was it like for Nate, living with his father? Were the ties of blood so strong that they'd pulled him back and strangled him into forgiving? I should be there for him, I knew that, but I also knew that to go into the house when Mr. Sinclair was there would kill me. Or, even more likely, lead me to kill him.

But I could at least be there on the periphery somehow. I thought of a night years ago; Nate had been traveling and I woke from a dream about Gabriel, two years old but talking to me in an adult's voice, asking why I never came to visit. The old guilt came back with its claws and teeth, and when I called Nate, sobbing, he'd thrown his clothes in a bag and stayed on the phone with me till his cell died three hours later, driving through the night. I'd woken the next morning to find him sleeping in bed beside me, cocooned protectively around me, his shoes still on. It was one of the memories I'd revisit whenever I was angry or hurt, an attempt to hem our fraying ends.

What if I drove out there and stayed in a nearby motel? I'd go into the house only when Joel was away, turn my mind off and do whatever I could not to think about what might have happened in those rooms. It would be better than sitting here, thinking of Nate with his father. Hating him for it.

"I want to drive down there to help," I said, "at least for a few days. I'll just close up the shop and I can come out and help you with the house, the cataloguing, whatever you need." I suddenly imagined the house I'd loved so much as a kid, the warm colors and elegant antiques, thick Persian rugs and damask draperies, which I'd tried to model our bookstore after. And immediately I felt a sense of childish excitement that stomped its little feet over my trepidation. All this time I'd been too terrified to even contemplate the idea of returning, knowing how memories had drowned me five years ago when I'd been back to bury my mother. But now I wondered if it would feel like coming home.

But Cecilia answered quickly. "No, Chloe. Thank you, that's amazingly generous, especially knowing how this all must seem to you. But you better not. I guess you could say we're trying to focus on tasks instead of emotions at this point, and having you here, I think that'd just make it harder."

"Right." I felt a hollowness in my stomach, something close to disappointment. "What about Grace? Does she know?"

It took a long time for her to answer, and when she did her voice sounded suddenly broken, so much behind it. "I've tried leaving messages with the convent over the past few weeks; she was closer to Daddy than any of us and she was the one he'd want to see most. But I don't even know if she's gotten them. Like the letters and messages we've left over the years, she's never acknowledged any of them, and I don't know if it's because the Poor Clares are so strict about enclosure that they don't even pass on messages, or whether she's just completely ignoring them because she doesn't want to be reminded of what she left. All I can do is pray that she's found peace, whatever that means for her, over everything that's happened."

We hadn't talked to Grace since she'd gone into seclusion the week after Cecilia's wedding, twenty-five years ago. But surely she'd be able to sense how hard this all would be for Cecilia. Weren't some needs on earth more important than her own need to have isolated herself from them? "I'm sorry for everything you're going through, Cecilia. I'm glad Nate's there."

She was quiet a moment, then said, "Thank you."

"How's he doing? I mean how's he holding up being back there, around your dad?"

"It's tough." Her voice shook slightly. "He's hurting, I'm sure much more than he's willing to show me, but you know Nate. He's amazingly strong."

"I know he is." I thought about the years after we'd lost Gabriel, the way he'd flinch when I broke down, like I'd just torn off my shirt at an inappropriate moment. And then he'd hold me, whispering that he was there for me, when all I really wanted was for him to cry too. Yes, he was strong, but there was such a thing as having too much strength. When you're hurting, the "strength" of the people who try and comfort you just feels like a wall, your pain bouncing off against them. What I'd needed was to see my pain reflected in someone else's face; it would've felt so much less alone. But without that all I could do was bury myself inside the shroud of my grief, pull it around me until it was all I could see. "Listen," I said, "could you have him call me?"

"Okay, okay, I'll ask him to."

"Thanks, Cecilia," I said, and I wanted to say more, to tell her that I missed talking to her, or to at least ask her to tell Nate that I loved him. But the fact he hadn't told me what was going on with his father, had been up there for three days with his family without wanting to talk to me, it all made me feel so isolated from him. Like he was judging me a less important part of his life. Instead I just said, "Take care of yourself," and hung up without waiting for a reply.

I paced to the kitchen, staring at the junk strewn across the table, trying to still the steel wool prickling under my skin, my feelings so huge and so wide-ranging that I had no idea how to decipher them. Not that I was ever the greatest housekeeper, but since Nate had left I'd let the house become even more cluttered, piling dishes in the sink, even though the piling had become a precarious balancing act and the kitchen had now taken on a smell reminiscent of rotting flesh. I'd thrown mail across the table unsorted, as if that would somehow spirit away the unpaid bills; the living room was crowded with old pizza boxes and candy wrappers, and books I'd abandoned after the first few pages. I reached for the electricity bill and flattened it on the table. In a week the gas bill would come due, and then property taxes. How were we going to afford them?

I shoved the bill away and walked back down to the shop, turned the computer on, and started searching for editions of the Hugo. I found a set at a store in Manhattan: original brown embossed cloth with moderate wear to the spine ends and edges. Five thousand dollars, which meant that, assuming Nate had asked Lester Jarvis for a ten percent commission above the expected value, almost all the money in our bank account had come from the down payment.

I'd have to put this on a credit card; it would probably take us months to pay off, and after interest we'd lose money on the deal.

I was about to shut the computer down, frustrated nearly to tears, when I noticed the store was selling a second-edition copy of *The Scarlet Letter* for $1,000. We had a first edition, in good condition, and after a quick search I found an auction where a first edition had been sold for $18,000.

I stared at the number. Placed my finger over it.

If Nate was willing to sell just this one book, we'd have enough to get the store back on its feet, do more advertising, fill some of the shelves that had been almost depleted. I pulled my finger away slowly and then, without any real intention behind it, I grabbed a notepad and flipped on the lights in the narrow, windowless hallway and the back reading room.

I reached into my pocket for the key I'd found earlier on the table, and used it to unlock the door of our glass holding case. Inside, along with the Hawthorne, were:

- A 1540 edition of Homer's *Odyssey,* speckled Italian calf with marbled boards

- A signed, limited first French edition of Saint-Exupéry's *Le Petit Prince*
- *The Lion, the Witch and the Wardrobe,* by C. S. Lewis, first edition, original green cloth in pictorial dust wrapper, with color frontispiece
- An 1891 limited edition of *The Picture of Dorian Gray,* copy number 113 out of 250, signed by Oscar Wilde

Nate bought our collectibles at auction, usually, or estate sales, although there'd been times he found the books at yard sales or flea markets for a fraction of what they were worth. It always seemed like theft to me, but Nate had a significantly less stringent view on the morality of retail advantage. "They sell for what it's worth to them," he'd say, "and I sell for what it's worth to me."

Most of the rarer books we picked up were requested by customers who commissioned Nate to find specific editions. But these five books were pulled from his mother's library years ago, on the last day he'd entered the house. Nate refused to sell them, claiming they added atmosphere, showing people that Classics Corner wasn't just a used bookstore but an *antiquarian* bookstore. Really, though, I knew their main value to him was sentimental.

He kept the books in the UV-shielded glass case, each in its own separate Mylar sleeve. When he found new customers who might be interested in such things, he'd bring them into the room and give them white cotton gloves so they could page slowly through the books, admire them and, by association, admire him. Or maybe I was being unkind.

The books in the case were all he had left of his mother. There were days I'd found him alone, paging through the books and smiling with some remembrance. Because they represented Sophia to him, like her voice was traveling through some space-time portal to live on through the printed words.

I slipped on the gloves he kept by the case and pulled out the books in their sleeves. I stacked them on the mahogany table and started inspecting them, noting signs of wear on my notepad. Not that I'd ever sell them, of course not, but if things got desperate in the coming weeks it would be nice to know there might be a thumb, a set of five thumbs, to plug into this continual leak. I'd approach Nate carefully, feeling him out, and if he didn't snap at me for just broaching the idea, then I'd show him the books' appraised value. My closing argument: *Which has more value to you, the books or our store?* The implied clause hanging off this question would be, *Or me?*

This is what I was thinking when I opened *The Lion, the Witch and the Wardrobe,* remembering the four of us acting out the story, rehearsing for our first theatrical performance. Grace as Aslan, since she liked playing the "good guys," Cecilia and I as the White Witch's servants, holding her down so Nate could tie her wrists and ankles. Grace directing us, bossy as always; Nate whispering in first Cecilia's ear and then mine, and then the three of us racing into the woods, bent double with laughter as we listened to Grace howl. Grace had thought she was the leader, but Nate was the one who always got his way, manipulating so subtly that the manipulations were invisible.

Nate's mother, Sophia, had read to us from this copy. I'd leaned against one of her arms as the adventure came to life, focusing on the echo of her voice, and her dissonant smells of coffee and deodorant. And now as I opened the front cover, for that second I understood why these books had been so precious to Nate, every page a memory taking me back to a time things might've turned out differently.

I understood it until I turned past the first page, and realized I hadn't actually understood anything at all.

This wasn't the copy from Sophia's library. It was a recent printing, under ten years old, one of those books made not for actual collectors but for the spray-tan version who liked to decorate shelves with embossed spines. At one point the original had been in Sophia's library, but Nate had replaced it with this shell.

The inside of the book had been hollowed out, leaving only a half-inch frame of cutaway pages. And in the hollow was a Moleskine notebook, and a lock of fine reddish-brown hair tied with a pale blue ribbon.

I lifted the hair, held it in my palm. Nate's hair was darker, almost black, and my own was a reddish shade of blond. Whose was this? I closed a fist around it, gripped with a sudden dark certainty. The hair belonged to another woman. Maybe Nate had found out about Daniel and turned to her as an eye-for-an-eye thing, or maybe it had nothing to do with Daniel at all. Maybe he'd met her and fallen in love, and that was the reason for the ever-widening distance I'd felt from him over the past several weeks. I dropped the hair and opened the notebook, turned the page.

And stared.

It was maybe a hundred pages long, filled with Nate's handwriting, the words in some language I didn't recognize, not Latinate but a language with oddly placed consonants and vowels like Gaelic, or maybe Nordic. I leafed through the remaining pages and found they were all covered in nonsensical lettering, paragraphs of carefully lettered print.

This made no sense. Why would Nate have gone through the trouble of learning a new language? Was it just so he could keep me from understanding what was written, in the event I found the notebook? What was it he didn't want me to see?

Ondece arthe Garebri werele whafota woum chider fuldreln whobiserth nadaym cesele brawertione wepewtere shadusani wedism hundyo aund welucre yolThide snostough tory holids amembo riessout soomey outhinc gouthald lothappo kenebad tock theatmit whewn theheny weyore surente graway ofrowm lonn!

It was like he was writing in tongues.

I stood and brought the book to the computer, and searched on the first word, *Ondece*. Nothing. *Garebri* and *werele*, also nothing. This couldn't be a real language, but then what the hell was it?

I went back to the hollowed copy of *The Lion, the Witch and the Wardrobe*, studying the inside flap and the only intact pages, the title page and frontispiece illustration, as if they might hold clues. And there, tucked inside the dust jacket, were two slips of folded newspaper. I unfolded one of the pages.

The article was about Joel Sinclair, from last year when he was released from jail. I looked a long while at the photo, Joel gazing warily, perhaps confusedly, at the camera, a prison official's hand at his shoulder to guide him. A thick book was tucked under his arm—the Bible, I guessed; it looked like it might be the same ancient King James version the Sinclairs had studied from, with its brown leather cover and the wine-red ribbon bookmark that would dangle at Sophia's knees while she taught us the stories. Joel looked so much older, so frail. And his eyes, once clear as a mirror, eyes that seemed continually assessing and calculating, here seemed muddy with fatigue.

I tried to see the evil in Joel's face, the sort of deadness one can see in the eyes of men who've committed the most soulless of crimes, but in this picture he just seemed broken. RELEASED AFTER TWO DECADES OF CONFINEMENT, the headline said, PASTOR JOEL SIN-CLAIR NOW PROCLAIMS INNOCENCE.

Reading this, I crumpled the paper and threw it into the trash. Damn him. And damn the Alzheimer's, which would allow him to forget everything he'd done and forgive himself, and was apparently allowing Cecilia to forgive him too. It almost felt like he'd chosen the disease himself.

I opened the second article. The page was badly yellowed, almost orange at the edges. The photo here was of the Sinclairs' home, police with evidence bags climbing down the front steps. My stomach wrenched and I quickly dropped the page, jumped to my feet, and then paced out to the hallway. Why had Nate saved the articles? How could he have stood to keep these tangible reminders, the way parents saved articles of their children's sports or scholastic achievements? The articles, the strange language, the lock of hair, what did they mean? Were they connected in some way or just separate secrets he hadn't wanted to show me?

Down the hall and back, down and back, focusing on the muscles in my legs in an attempt to shake away that last image of the Sinclairs' home. The house had years ago begun falling apart when Sophia had grown too sick to care for it. I'd forgotten that until this moment, seeing it in the photo, the chipped paint on the front porch and siding, and the weed-choked garden. I hadn't truly seen it at the time either, maybe had blocked it out as a self-protective mechanism, the deterioration of the house I'd loved so much. Or maybe I'd just been too distracted by falling in love with Nate to notice anything. It was, in retrospect, symbolic of the crumbling of the entire family, which I'd also refused to see.

I didn't think of the past often; Nate and I never talked about it, pretending to each other and to ourselves that our lives had begun here in this house, this town, a quiet, easy life fully separate from our beginnings. The few times I did let myself remember, my mind seemed to judder awkwardly across the surface of my teens, only landing further back on the house, Nate, Grace, and Cecilia as I'd first known them. So stately, both the house and the children, mysterious and magical. I'd been eight years old when I met them, still young enough to believe in magic but on the very edge of not believing. And yes, I had found magic that day. A day that changed everything that came after.

My birthday.

Once upon a time, there was a little girl.

PART II

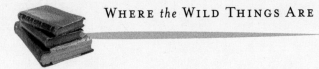

WHERE *the* WILD THINGS ARE

3

I lay in bed, pointing and flexing my toes, tracing my fingers in figure eights over my kneecaps, looking for differences. What did it mean, really, to be a year older? Oh I knew in actuality I'd only grown up by a day, but there was a new *feeling* to being eight, an eight-year-oldness that made everything seem fuller and stronger, like I'd crossed from one sort of childhood into another. Losing my sevenness a forever thing, like losing my baby teeth. My toes had now been alive for eight years, my feet, my legs, belly button, and arms; maybe they didn't look different but they *felt* different, like I was finally becoming solid and fully in the world.

I'd say this when Momma came to wake me, how I felt like I had changed. And my mother would smile, maybe sit on the bed and tell me that yes, I had indeed changed, pointing out a new mole or muscle or half inch in height that I hadn't yet noticed.

And then she'd tell the story of when I was born, her voice all soft, remembering. How I started squalling as soon as my throat had been suctioned enough to allow for it, kept squalling as I was cleaned and weighed, kicking in protest when my father had held me. Until I'd been put into my mother's arms, where I sighed and immediately fell asleep. "It's like you suddenly felt reassured that entering the world hadn't been a freaky mistake after all," she said. "You knew we belonged to each other."

I opened my eight-year-old eyes, smiling at the pointy-fanged purple fish I'd painted last month on my door and waiting.

And waiting.

After a minute I ran my fingers up my chest to see if I could feel any difference. Like Sabrina Harris who was already wearing a bra, and pink lip gloss that she carried inside a silver rhinestone purse. But no, nothing happening there at all, which was both a disappointment and a relief.

Amazing to think my body would someday create them out of nothing, that it would know what to do. They must be in there somewhere, seeds buried deep, waiting for the chance to burrow up from under the fence of my rib cage and bloom. I thought of my mother's heavy, pale breasts, their crisscrossed blue veins. Not flower seeds then, but more like some kind of fruit or vegetable, like butternut squash.

I looked over at the clock on my dresser, and my eyes popped wide. It was 7:45! And the house was so quiet, too quiet, no sounds of breakfast making or morning news watching. Momma hadn't come to wake me for school, which must mean it was one of her bad days.

I pulled the covers up over my head.

The phone started to ring, but nobody picked it up. It stopped and then started again, and I slipped out of bed, blinking in the light, and padded barefoot down the hall. Momma's door was open, her bed unmade, her Scooby-Doo nightshirt and undies in a pile on the floor. A knuckle of pain nudged into my stomach and I ran to the kitchen, where the knuckle became a knife. Because there on the kitchen table was a bowl and a spoon, a box of Lucky Charms, a glass of juice, and my vitamin. And a note. I picked up the phone.

"Well, it took you long enough! You weren't still asleep, were you? Just calling because I realized I forgot to set an alarm for you, and I wanted to make sure you're not lazy-bumming it. Bus'll be there in five minutes."

I looked at the far wall, unblinking. "Where are you?"

"You didn't read my note? I got a call while you were asleep to work early shift. Sons of bitches, but at least I'll get the overtime. Did you brush your teeth?"

I stared at the wall, nodded at it. "Uh-huh."

"Good. Lunch money's on the bar, so don't forget it. You better get out there now, 'kay? And bring your coat because it's supposed to get cold this afternoon."

"Uh-huh," I said again, and how I felt was like my head wasn't quite connected to my body, like it could go flying off somewhere without me, out the door, over the hills like a birthday balloon. It could be that this all was a dream.

"So I better go before Merrick gets on my ass. Love you, honey."

"Love you," I echoed, but Momma had already hung up. I sat at the table, looking down at my bowl. Ran my finger inside it, round and round, round and round.

Two years ago I'd had a party at McDonald's. Mara and Jodi and Allison came, and Momma had bought an ice-cream cake, we'd played in the PlayPlace, there were presents, and then we went to see *King Kong* at the Garden Theater. That was probably the best day of my life. But then Mara moved away to a different school, and Jodi and Allison weren't my friends anymore. In fact, nobody was really my friend anymore and I knew why, had read it on the report card Momma had hidden in her sock drawer but that I found anyway. Mrs. Milton had said I performed exceptionally at math and language arts, but that I had some issues with social skills. Which I knew what it meant, that people thought I was weird.

I picked up the note.

> *Got a call late last night saying they needed me to work double shift. Bastards! I slept about 2 hours last night! I'll try and call before you leave to say good morning, but till then give yourself a hug for me. And have a fantastic day!*
> *XOXOXOXO, Mom*

I crossed my legs up on the chair and looked down at my lap. Then picked up the note and read it again, and then folded it in half, in quarters, and got up to throw it into the trash. Just as I heard the rattle of the school bus. Eyes wide, I rested my palms on the windowsill as I watched it drive away, holding my breath as its taillights disappeared. And then, slowly, I smiled.

I did an ice skater's twirl in my socked feet and a dancer's leap back to the table, where I flicked my finger again and again at the cereal box until it fell down. Lucky Charms were blah. I just ate them because Momma thought they were a special treat, *Look what I bought!* which made it impossible to express my true feelings. But really they had no flavor except sweet, and the marshmallow bits squeaked between your teeth when you chewed them and turned slimy after a minute in milk, like boogers or tiny knobs of flesh. But, one had to make do. I poured a bowl, picked out all the marshmallows, and ate the rest, chewing meditatively.

When I was done I studied the bits, sifting through them with my index finger, then went to my room for my sea glass collection and a piece of red construction paper, which I folded in half, then brushed with rubber cement into the shape of a heart. I started gluing the marshmallow bits, which turned out to be a lot harder than one might think when considering whether it was a task worth attempting. The glue dried too fast so that I had to peel it away with my fingernail in long, rubbery worms—satisfying as peeling a scab—then spread the glue again.

But I was pleased with the result when I was done, a marshmallow heart. I shifted through my sea glass collection, separating brown and green and white. My collection was one of my favorite things, new pieces from every trip to the beach. Glass might not sound interesting but you just had to think of it right, trying to imagine who the glass had belonged to and how far it might have come. Maybe pirates drinking beer in the South Pacific, maybe wine bottles poured by Japanese ladies in kimonos, or eyeglasses from a man drowned on the *Titanic*. Maybe one of these bottles had been drunk by my father, who knew? Mom said it wasn't likely, but I had hundreds of pieces from hundreds of bottles so it was definitely possible.

I gave the heart two green sea glass eyes, an orange vitamin nose, and a brown sea glass mouth, then opened the card carefully and wrote, *Happy Birthday Chloe!!* inside. After which I stuck it on the refrigerator and stood back to admire it. But where I'd been sure such a card would immediately make me happy, instead I felt a twistiness at the top of my chest.

What was Momma doing now? I really didn't have much of an idea what her days were like, "managing the floor" at a factory where coatings were applied to propellers. Just knew that she had one of the most important jobs in the world, seeing as how those coatings kept thousands of planes from rusting and falling down. I imagined her in a field surrounded by airplane parts, maybe shooting them in the air to see if they would fly. Probably she was having fun.

I looked at the card a minute, then pulled it off the fridge and stuffed it into the trash, after which I brought my juice glass into the bathroom and stood in front of the mirror so I could watch myself chugalugging.

When I was done I tried on a smile, but it didn't feel real, one of those smiles where I needed to pay attention to the muscles in order to keep them from falling. I put down the glass and decided not to brush my teeth, thinking of the whole day now spreading long and blank in front of me. Crazy to think I could choose to do anything with no one to tell me no, like being a grown-up. Maybe I'd keep working on the banker's-box-and-coffee-can spaceship I'd started last week, or I could practice tricks from my magic set, or make chemistry experiments from food and art supplies. The possibilities were endless, but really none of them felt exceptional enough for the first day of eighthood.

I leaned forward, staring at my reflection, then opened Momma's makeup case and put on blue eye shadow, purple lipstick, blush. I pulled out the mascara and examined the tube, then drew two black lines across each cheek and a black spot on my nose. I stared a long time in the mirror, admiring one side and then the other, then went to Momma's bedroom where I stripped off my nightgown and pulled on a yellow sweater-dress. I fastened it with her macramé belt, stuffed two pairs of stockings inside the top for boobs, and then put on all her bead necklaces.

Here I was, a warrior princess, loved for my beauty and kindness. And every year my whole kingdom celebrated my birthday by surrounding our village and joining hands and singing the birthday song, after which they wheeled out a cake big enough for everyone to share, tall as a tree, red velvet with white icing. I'd climb a ladder to blow out candles, make a wish for every person in my kingdom to win the lotto and become rich enough to never have to work. After which they all would cheer and then hand over my birthday presents, little things mostly, lots of them handmade, but I'd give them as much grateful attention as if they were paint sets or scooters.

Now I practiced a kind smile and a curtsy, then slipped on black spike-heeled pumps and hobbled to the full-length mirror.

Where I burst out laughing because I'd forgotten about the mascara lines, which made me look nothing at all like I'd expected. I twirled in a circle, then kicked off my shoes and raced to the living room where I turned the stereo on full blast. Queen, "Bohemian Rhapsody," which was excellent, and so I danced barefoot through the living room. Jumping onto the couch, running across it and leaping off the other side, a ballerina, a fairy spinning round and round so fast that if anybody looked, all they'd see was a yellow blur. Maybe it was possible to blur so much you disappeared, looking like UHF channels on TV. Momma would come home and wonder where I was, and the answer would be that I'd spun myself into infinity.

But then the next song came on, "Breaking Up Is Hard to Do," and it sucked so I turned off the stereo. Which is when I heard the phone ringing, so I ran to the kitchen to answer.

It was Angela the attendance officer from Chester Creek, wondering where I was, so I said, "Hello, Angela. I'm sick."

"Sorry to hear that, sweetie. Could I talk to your mom?"

I hesitated. I was quite good at lying, it was one of my top three talents next to wheelies and gin rummy, but that didn't mean it was something I especially enjoyed. I slowly pulled the boob stockings out of my dress and set them on the table. "Yes, except she's in the bathroom. Puking. We're both sick."

"Oh gosh, okay, could you just have her call the school when she can, then? You feel better soon, okay?"

"I'll try," I said and then . . . then I didn't want Angela to go. So I added, "I have a fever and I'm real stuffy? And plus, it's my birthday." But the phone line went dead. Today was the day of people hanging up on me when I had something important to say.

If you lied and nobody heard you, did that count? If you spun around till you disappeared and nobody noticed, did that mean you'd never existed at all?

The lies to Angela made me feel all prickly, so I galloped through the house, trying to shake that prickliness away. And when that didn't work, I jammed my feet into my sneakers, ran outside to grab my bike from the front porch, and then raced down the street.

The rule for biking was that I was allowed to ride to the top of the hill, then back down to the house again. But after all, that was a rule from when I was seven. Things had changed. And when I got to the end of the road, I couldn't stop. I just couldn't. Like the girl in "The Red Shoes" whose feet kept dancing until she was almost dead, I was the girl in The Yellow Dress whose feet would keep riding until the Executioner cut off my legs, which would then ride alone without me over the fields and into the forest. This was not my fault; the legs had a life of their own.

Up Lasser Hill and past Garrity Pond, my heart pumping and my muscles burning, my mother's necklaces swinging heavy against my chest, and I could go anywhere. To Washington, to British Columbia, to whatever was on the other side of British Columbia. Down the hill and past the farm, waving wildly at the fat cows who watched me back with narrowed, disapproving eyes.

There were only a few roads in Redbridge. There was the main road, which led straight up through the Redwood Forest all the way to Oregon, and we lived on the side of this road in our little brown-shingled ranch house. After our house, before you got to town you'd pass Blakely Campground, the Treetop Motel, and a gift shop where they sold handcrafted redwood-stump tables and redwood wall clocks, redwood candle holders, and redwood salad bowls.

Most of the other roads branching off 101 were actually just unpaved driveways leading to one or two hidden houses. Some of these were huge summer homes built by rich people who wanted to get away from San Francisco or L.A. The smallest homes were also hidden, single rooms with slate roofs, lived in by people who just wanted to get away from life.

I loved these smaller roads. I'd only dared to trespass a handful of times past the Private Property signs, on foot rather than on bike so the snapping of twigs wouldn't give me away. It felt like being sucked through outer space to an alien world, whose only residents were trees. High as the moon, looking down at me but also up into the sky, protecting. Sometimes three or four trees grew together at the base where they'd leave a small cave just the perfect size for hiding, and I'd sit inside, arms wrapped around my knees, feeling both tiny and—when I looked up at the dark roof above me—also huge, like I'd become one of the trees myself. Invisible and invincible.

Now on my bike, I passed a dirt road I must've seen thousands of times by car but at that speed had never noticed. Unlike most side streets, this road had a whole name to itself, Bayard Lane, and I stopped to peer down it but it curved fifty yards ahead, disappearing into the trees. So I got off my bike and walked it down the road, listening to the swishing wind and the sound of gravel under my feet. Around the curve, walking slowly, reverently, until I reached a gate: iron painted reddish brown to match the trees, a small metal box with a blinking red light covering the latch. I looked through the gate and, still seeing nothing of what lay behind it, I wheeled my bike around it, farther up the road.

Which was when I heard it. The unmistakable sound of children playing.

4

"How deep are we now?" A girl's voice.

"Don't keep asking that!" A boy. "This'll take at least a week."

"More like ten years." An older-sounding girl. "Except you'll be dead before then because Daddy's going to kill you."

I hid behind a holly bush watching the children. Two girls and a boy, all dressed like they were at church, playing in the backyard of a huge white house. The older girl, wearing a red frock with a rounded collar, sat cross-legged under a large maple sewing the dress hem of a baby that lay unnaturally still by her knees. The boy and the younger girl both looked around my age, her in a pale green dress and him in a sky-blue sweater and pressed chinos. They stood inside a hole that reached nearly to their waists, the boy digging with a garden shovel and the girl with a large plastic cup. As I watched, the boy pulled off his sweater, used it to wipe the sweat off his face, and then set it into the hole. He whispered something in the girl's ear, which the girl responded to by widening her eyes and grinning wide enough to show a missing molar.

They looked too pretty to be real, all of them with their glossy chestnut hair and alabaster skin. Even the house behind them looked unreal, with its wide wraparound porch, tall windows, and trellises overrun with roses and morning glories. Only the younger girl didn't seem pulled straight from a painting. Beautiful, maybe the most beautiful of the three, but her curly hair had escaped from her ponytail, her dress was spattered with mud, and both her knees were scabbed. Even she seemed to be on another plane of existence, and I was suddenly certain that I could step out from behind the bush and jump into the hole beside them and they still wouldn't be able to see me.

The younger girl galloped over to the girl with the baby and knelt beside them. "I want to learn how," she said.

"No way, Cecilia, you're filthy. You'll wreck the dress."

"I won't, see?" She spat on her palms and wiped them on the grass.

"That's so gross," the older girl said. But she handed the baby to Cecilia.

Or no, it wasn't a baby at all, but a doll. The most real-looking doll I'd ever seen, with its golden blond hair, eyes that opened and closed, tiny curled fists, and a lacy white christening gown. And I wanted it.

I wanted it more than I could remember ever having wanted anything. In a way it felt like all of this had always belonged to me, the doll, the house, the children, and I suddenly knew I'd never be happy again until I owned them all.

"See, it's easy, just up and then down, and when you come up again you have to hook the needle through the last stitch." She sounded kinder now, mothering, as she leaned over Cecilia's lap, helping her aim the needle.

Cecilia glanced over at the boy, who was now watching her, his arms crossed. She bit the side of her cheek, then turned back to her sister. "I think I got a better way to fix her," she said slowly and then, without warning, she jumped up and ran to the hole.

"Cecilia?" The older girl dove at her, landing flat on her belly. "Cecilia!"

Cecilia bent to lay the doll in the hole, and as I watched in horror the boy raised his shovel.

"Nate, don't you dare!" the girl screamed, and my heart stopped. How could they possibly be so cruel, so beautiful but so *evil*? Burying the baby doll in her pristine white dress, well it was like burying an actual *baby*. And as the boy dumped the shovelful of dirt onto the doll, I couldn't stop myself. I screamed.

All three children turned to stare at me, and I clamped my hands over my mouth. For a full minute nobody spoke until Cecilia said, "Who're you?"

I shook my head, hands still over my mouth. The boy looked down into the hole, then gave a half smile. "It's okay, we didn't really bury her. Come look."

I walked slowly toward the hole, somewhat stunned that they'd actually been able to see and hear me. This felt like stepping into a fairy tale, and I was scared of dirtying it somehow.

"See, she's safe," Nate said. The doll was lying on the sweater he'd removed earlier, and the dirt from the shovel was piled beside it.

"You're both idiots," the older girl said, jumping into the hole to rescue the doll before she turned back to me. "So seriously, who are you? And what're you doing spying on us?"

"I'm nobody," I said. "I mean I'm Chloe Louise Tyler. I'm Chloe."

"I'm Grace, and this is Nate and Cecilia. Never met anybody called Chloe before. How come you're not in school?"

"Because." I squared my shoulders. "Because it's my birthday. How come you're not?"

"We don't go to school, that's why. Not real school." She shrugged as if this was something that should be obvious, not warranting further explanation. "Cool that it's your birthday. How old are you?"

"Eight." I felt the number, round and weighty on my tongue. It didn't feel like something I fully owned yet. "I'm eight."

"So am I!" Cecilia clapped. "Or at least I will be next month. I'm seven and eleven-twelfths. And Nate's nine and a half, and Grace is eleven. What're you supposed to be, anyway? An Indian? A Zulu?"

"She's a cat," Nate said. "You're a cat, right?"

I touched my cheeks, only now remembering the lines I'd drawn on my face.

"*Why're* you a cat?" Cecilia said.

I searched for a response but came up with exactly nothing. Nate tilted his head, watching me, but it must've become clear I had no answer, because he said, "Why not? Cats're cool."

"That's true," Cecilia said. "Did you know they can jump seven times their height? Which for me would mean I could jump twenty-eight feet, onto the roof. It'd be like flying, don't you think?" She smiled. "Don't you talk?"

"You're freaking her out," the older girl said. "She's scared."

Nate watched me appraisingly. There was something about him that made me nervous, something about his eyes, the way they fixed probingly on my face, like I was a painting and he was trying to count the freckles on my cheeks or the strands of hair in my bangs, so that he could exactly reproduce them later. "Don't be scared," he said. "You want to help us? It'll go faster with three people. Grace won't do it 'cause she's afraid of worms."

"Am not. I'm just not stupid enough to bust my back digging a hole that isn't going to lead to anywhere except mud."

"Scared of worms *and* mud." He turned back to me. "We're digging a tunnel to London so we can ride a hovercraft and hopefully talk to C. S. Lewis. We have some questions."

London. I didn't know anything about London except that it had a queen, who I'd often dreamed of meeting and perhaps being adopted by.

"Like I told you, they're idiots," Grace said, and then she bent to whisper in my ear. "In actuality he's dead, but our mom can't stand to tell them."

"Who's C. S. Lewis?" I said.

"*You* know," Nate said, "the Narnia books. I have to ask where all the kids went after Narnia was destroyed and what it was really like. Mom says it's like heaven, but who knows? He should've wrote another book about it, I think. And Cecilia wants to ask him what Turkish Delights are."

"Grace thinks it's just a kind of candy," Cecilia said, "but there has to be more to them than that."

"Enough talking, okay?" Nate said. "You going to help or what? You could use that serving tray by the tree."

I reached for the silver tray. "I'll help," I said.

"Good, then. If we ever get there you can ask him something too, so you better think out your question now."

I jumped into the hole and dug the corner of the tray into the dirt. It was harder than I'd expected, rocky and stiff as clay. I struggled to lift the tray, then said, "Actually, I don't know exactly what the Narnia books are."

Silence. They all stared at me, then, "Seriously?" Nate said.

"It's okay, don't make her feel bad," Grace said slowly, in a tone that did make me feel bad. "We can tell you the story if you want."

"Mom's read them to us I don't even know how many times," Nate said. "Mostly because they have to do with God, but don't worry if you're not into God stories because you'd have no idea unless somebody told you."

"There's seven of them," Grace said, "and they're all good but the first one's the best." She sat cross-legged on the grass and spread her skirt to cover her knees. She smiled at me, then turned to smile at Nate and then Cecilia, in a way that felt like she was drawing us all in to tell a secret. "It starts with four children, Peter, Susan, and Lucy, and also Edmund, who's the one you have to watch out for."

"First you'll hate him," Cecilia said, "but you'll like him okay by the end."

And so, Grace told the story, the greatest story I'd ever heard. And this was how I spent the rest of my morning, digging toward London and listening to Grace, with frequent interjections from the others of tidbits she'd left out. A mysterious uncle, a closet that led into the woods, the white witch and talking beaver, the lion that ruled over them all. Soon I'd completely forgotten about the shoveling, absorbed in this other world, glancing shyly now and then at Grace, Nate, and Cecilia, all of whose eyes were on me as they relayed the story, their faces animated and anticipatory like the faces of grown-ups giving gifts.

And suddenly it was over. Grace had just started talking about Narnia's winter snow melting when a bell rang from the front of the house.

"Duck!" Nate whispered loudly, pulling me down into the

hole. He and Cecilia climbed out and Grace rose and called, "Coming!"

"Don't you tell *anybody* about this hole," Nate said, "or we'll get seriously creamed. But you could keep working on it if you want. Mom might maybe let us out again by five."

I bit back a smile, something hot glowing in my chest. There'd been a change building inside me all morning, I could feel it. All my life to this point had been shapeless, just drifting from day to day. But now all at once I felt like I'd found my place in the world, the blurriness cleared. Like finally I knew where I belonged. I peeked over the edge of the hole to watch Nate and Cecilia join hands and sprint with Grace toward the front of the house. And then I picked up the shovel he'd dropped and continued to dig, my head swimming with fauns who served tea, a witch who turned people into stone, and portals to other, better worlds.

5

I kept working on the hole well into the afternoon, until my palms were torn and my shoulders sore and the hole started filling with water. I looked down at my ruined, squelchy sneakers. If we were really going to make it to London, it appeared we'd have to swim there.

Actually, I was a little skeptical about the whole London thing. With Grace, Nate, and Cecilia around me, I would've been willing to believe almost anything they'd told me; there was something about them that made it all seem possible. But now that they were gone, my real life, and my stomach, were calling.

I pulled myself out from the hole and jogged to the woods where I'd hidden my bike, jumped onto it, and started toward home. Nate had said they might be out again by five, and I'd do anything I could to come back then, but I knew Auntie Eva would be expecting me home, and that upsetting her was not a good idea.

Auntie Eva was not my real aunt, just a babysitter who pretended aunthood as if that would give her some kind of claim, or maybe make it easier for me to love her.

I did not love her.

Not only did I not love her, I also didn't like her much. She'd always felt like a permanent fixture, like the furnace or kitchen faucet that required attention only when they caused problems. And she didn't seem to like me much either. For years she had used every possible excuse to compare me, unfavorably, to her grand-children. *My Isabella, she cleans not only her own room but also the dishes!* or *My Bobby, when he was in kindergarten, he was already playing chess!* And these comparisons—along with my mother's admission that she'd chosen Auntie Eva solely because, at two-fifty an hour, she was the cheapest sitter in the neighborhood—had always made me feel grossly inadequate. Like I was the sort of child only worth two-fifty an hour.

I leaned my bike on the front porch and entered the house. The TV was on, *General Hospital* just starting, so I knew Auntie Eva would be trapped on the couch for at least the next hour. "I'm home!" I called, and dashed into the kitchen where I grabbed a bag of Oreos and began jamming them into my mouth as I started toward the stairs.

"My God in heaven," Auntie Eva said.

I turned slowly to the living room, my mouth full of cookies, and Auntie Eva widened her eyes and slapped a hand on her bosom, then slapped again like she was trying to restart her heart.

I quickly swallowed the cookies, wiped off my mouth, and said, "I fell. In the mud."

"What is that dress? The necklaces? Your face!"

Watching her, something curdled inside me. All morning Grace, Nate, and Cecilia had treated me like someone interesting and fun, looking at the person I was under my weird clothes and makeup and judging me worthy. But Auntie Eva was like all the kids in school who only cared how different I was, and seeing the disgust on her face, I felt a punch of anger. "Mind your own business!" I said, racing upstairs, and then for good measure, "You suck!"

I ran into the bathroom and locked the door behind me, something hot and jagged in my chest. I rested my palms and ear against the door, listening for footsteps, expecting Auntie Eva to come after me, but the only sounds came from the television and my own heavy breath. I stuffed another Oreo in my mouth and started the shower, then walked to the mirror. I chewed slowly, studying my reflection, my tangled hair, the mascara and mud smears on my cheeks. And I smiled.

I was in my bedroom working a comb through my wet hair when Auntie Eva knocked on my door, then opened it. "Do you have something to say to me?" she said.

I eyed her blankly.

"What I'm meaning is, wouldn't you like to apologize?"

The answer to this was no. But I raised my chin. "I'm sorry I said to mind your own business, and that you suck."

Auntie Eva watched my face, her eyes narrowed and head raised like she was trying to figure out whether I had pooted, and then her head dipped a quick nod. "I accept your apology. And I have something for you." She strode back to the hallway and retrieved a khaki-green sweater, which she handed to me. "Happy birthday," she said, sounding more indignant than indulgent.

I slowly reached for the sweater. I recognized the yarn; Auntie

Eva had been knitting with it for the past two weeks, without giving me any sign what it was for. I slipped it over my head and walked to the mirror, frowning at my reflection.

The sweater was all wrong, the color of dog poop, scratchy and too small and bunching under my arms, the sleeves falling an inch short of my wrists. But I loved it. "It's excellent," I said, "thank you." I turned to Auntie Eva and hugged her, stiffly at first, but when I felt the soft width of her body, smelled the overly sweet scent of her perfume, I pressed harder against her, burying my face against her boobs. "I love it."

"Well." Auntie Eva stiffened. "Well, it doesn't look so good on you as I'd hoped, with your coloring."

And the moment was over.

I pulled away. "Could I go and play with some friends I know? They invited me over for five o'clock."

"Your mother, she knows them?"

"Oh sure." I flashed a bright smile of innocence. "Their names are Grace and Nate and Cecilia, and they live just past the farm."

She stared at me. "The Sinclairs?"

"Maybe," I said, then seeing in her eyes something that looked almost like awe I said, "Yes, that's who."

"Well, how did you manage to get in with them?"

I was about to explain to her how easy it had been to just walk around the gate, but then realized that wasn't what she'd meant. "You know them?"

Her face stilled, a moment of contemplation before she said, "No one knows them really. Except them *matto* church people, and even they don't really know." Which didn't make much sense.

"They're totally nice," I said. "And pretty."

"Just because a family has pretty on the face doesn't mean the family is right in the head," she said cryptically. She narrowed her eyes, and for a horrifying moment I was sure she'd forbid me from going. But then she said, "You'll be back before dark, yes?"

"I will be!" I was briefly tempted to hug her again, but thought better of it. "I'll be back before dark," I said.

They weren't in the yard. I looked in dismay at the muddy footprints I'd left earlier across the perfectly green grass, tried rubbing them out with my foot, but my sneakers were still filthy so they only made the smudges worse. I finally got down on my knees and rubbed each of the prints away with my fingers.

When I was done, I walked toward the house and sat on the bottom step, waiting, glancing at my watch, running my thumb against my palm, testing out the sores I'd gotten from shoveling to see how much I could make them hurt. After ten minutes, when they still hadn't appeared, I rose and tentatively crept toward the front window.

Inside was a long, dark wood table, a chandelier above it so big I could've crawled inside it and set up a lemonade stand. The walls were a deep, one-day-old-scab red, covered with paintings of haloed angels and saints. On the far wall was a thick wooden crucifix, Jesus with his head slung low, crying silent wooden tears.

On the other side of the door was an even larger window, and I crept to it and peered inside. There they were, Nate and Cecilia sitting on either side of a woman in a long, high-collared corn-flower-blue dress, heads resting on her shoulders. Grace was on the red Persian rug at their feet, meditatively twirling a strand of hair around one finger.

The room was huge, filled with late-day shadows from the

bookcases lining each wall. There were tons of roses, probably cut from the garden, stuffed into large, brightly colored vases. And oh, the books! Hundreds of them crammed on the shelves, maroon and navy and black, short and tall and thin and thick. And where normally this wouldn't have impressed me, now I wondered which of these books held the Narnia stories.

"In due time came the telegram," the woman said, "announcing that Pollyanna would arrive in Beldingsville the next day, the twenty-fifth of June, at four o'clock." She was reading from a small gold hardcover book with her eyebrows raised, trailing her finger down the page to mark her place. "Miss Polly read the telegram, frowned, then climbed the stairs to the attic room."

I leaned closer, pressing both hands against the window as I listened rapt to the story, the girl arriving at the train station in red gingham and meeting her prickly Aunt Polly, who didn't like ice cream or conversation. Brought to the dusty, fusty attic room without carpets or pictures but with a beautiful view from the high window, punished with a meal of just bread and milk, but still playing her Glad Game because she happened to like bread and milk. I wanted to be Pollyanna, able to find a flip side to every awful thing. It gave me hope that there might be unseen angles to my own awful things, and I lost myself inside her story, her life that was so much worse but also so much better than mine.

Until a disaster happened. One minute I was on my feet listening, and the next I'd slipped into the story like it was a soft, warm bed, forgetting I had a body and the importance of bracing that body's legs. I stumbled against the window with a thump.

All of them turned to face me and I quickly dropped to my knees. I hunched there, my breath heavy, heartbeat loud in my ears, then slowly I raised my head. To find them all at the window, staring down at me as if I was something two-headed and six-legged they'd found on the bottoms of their shoes. I stared back at them and scuttled backward on my butt.

A minute later the front door swung open. "No point hiding now, you know," the woman said, smiling. "We've already seen you. Who are you? Come introduce yourself."

Nate walked up beside her, leaning on her arm. He met my eye but didn't speak as I pulled slowly to my feet. "I'm Chloe," I said, to my sneakers. "I live down the street."

"Pleased to meet you, Chloe. I'm Mrs. Sinclair and this is my Nathaniel."

Nate raised his hand in greeting, not giving any sign of having already met me.

Mrs. Sinclair scanned the yard behind me. "Where are your parents? Do they know you've come to visit?"

"Yes . . . I mean my aunt knows. And she said it was okay."

She tilted her head as if considering my answer, then said, "So, Miss Chloe, do you often listen in at people's windows?"

My heart was still racing, a mustache of sweat flushing my upper lip. I shook my head silently and Mrs. Sinclair smiled. "Don't look so terrified, I promise I won't call the police. You here selling something, or just listening to the story?"

I hesitated. Which would be more excusable? "The story," I said finally.

Mrs. Sinclair raised her eyebrows, looking surprised. "Really! Well, then, I guess you'd better come in to hear the rest."

I widened my eyes and Mrs. Sinclair smiled. "Come on, we only have about an hour before you'll have to leave." She backed away from the door. "Could you take your shoes off first please? Mr. Sinclair gets upset when he sees tracks."

I looked down at the gleaming hardwood, thinking of the worn lima-bean-green carpet in my own home. How wonderful to have a house you had to remove your shoes to walk inside. Like at Found Treasures Gallery with its sparkling crystal vases and bejeweled music boxes, where you could look and wish but never touch. I quickly pulled off my shoes, and then seeing the grayness of my socks, pulled them off too. Then followed Mrs. Sinclair and Nate into the library, the plush rug soft as confectioner's sugar under my bare feet.

As I entered, Grace strode from the window grinning, her hand outstretched. "I'm Grace Sinclair," she said, "and this is my sister Cecilia. Pleased to meet you."

I glanced at Nate, then took her hand. Had I dreamed this morning after all? Why would they all pretend not to know me? Maybe I'd imagined them into existence, like might happen in one of the storybooks on these shelves, a girl who needed friends so bad she dreamed them into life. But then Cecilia winked at me, and my insides settled. "Pleased to meet you," I said softly, then winked back.

"Enough gawking." Mrs. Sinclair sat on the couch. "Chloe's here to listen to the story, so you better all come sit back down, because we're running out of time."

Nate sat on the far end of the couch and gestured to the spot between himself and his mother. "You can sit here," he said.

I padded across the rug and sat stiffly next to him. He leaned to whisper in my ear. "You won't tell, right?"

His breath smelled like red licorice, a safe smell. I shook my head, eyes wide for emphasis.

Thinking back later that night, all I'd remember was the weight of Nate's arm against mine, the heady scent of the roses around us, the feel of pressing up against Mrs. Sinclair and the deep, soothing sound of her voice. Sitting there, I felt a continuous drum roll of excitement that kept me from really comprehending the story behind Mrs. Sinclair's words. Focusing only on the story around me, through a wardrobe into this world that didn't have even the slightest resemblance to my own.

Until a clock chimed from somewhere in the house and Mrs. Sinclair tilted her head, counting the chimes. Then jumped up. "Oh shoot, shoot, I haven't even started dinner. And Cecilia, look at your hair! Grace, fix her hair, would you? And then both of you come help me in the kitchen. Nate, you better finish your memorizing because your father's going to want to hear your verses tonight." She clapped her hands, striding from the room. "Hurry!"

"Upstairs," Grace told Cecilia, and the two of them left as well. Without even glancing at me, Nate pulled a thick leather-covered book from the shelf and brought it to a rolltop desk, where he sat to read it. And just like that, I had disappeared.

I watched him a minute, then said, "Well, I better go."

He turned to me, seeming surprised I was still there, thought a minute, and then said, "Come back tomorrow."

"Tomorrow?" I said, and then, "Okay. I could do that." I bit back a smile as I walked out to the porch and stuffed my feet back into my socks and shoes, glancing back through the window to see Nate hunched over the desk, mouthing words.

What was Mr. Sinclair like that they seemed so scared of him? I didn't know much about fathers and nothing about my own, although I envisioned a mix between Mike Brady and Hawkeye from *M*A*S*H* but with my overly straight reddish-blond hair and my too-short nose. I certainly had never thought a father was anything to be scared of.

I jumped onto my bike and pedaled home, cheeks stinging from the late-day cold. Momma's car was in the driveway, and suddenly I hated the idea of entering the house, seeing the messy tables and dirty floors, the fake-wood furniture. And Momma, her eyes bagged like her eyeballs were weighing too heavy on her cheeks, her skin already smelling prickly from beer. Was this how the Narnia children had felt when they came back home, stuck in a place they were realizing they didn't belong?

Inside, the house was all quiet. There were two kinds of quiet, the good kind and the bad. Sometimes Momma was caught up in what she called her "self-improvement" projects, journal writing or painting, or the reading of books with titles like "Adversity, Begone!" But this, this was the bad sort of quiet.

"Ma?" I called softly, looking into the living room.

Momma was on the sofa, eyes rimmed with pink, mousy ponytail loose and crooked. Holding my Lucky Charms birthday card. She jumped up when I entered. "Oh sweetie, I'm so sorry, I'm so sorry!"

I stood there stiffly, not sure how to react. Momma seemed more upset realizing she'd missed my birthday than I had been myself, realizing she'd missed it. "It's okay," I said carefully, "I didn't care."

But this just made Momma cry out like she'd been sucker punched. "It's not okay! I know that." She knelt in front of me and set both hands on my shoulders. "I just was so busy this week my mind was pulled away to less important places. But I have a gift for you, *look*!" She pulled the earrings out of her own ears, large, silver hoops.

I stared at them, then took them from her, turned them over in my hands. "But they're pierced."

"Well, right, sure, I know. But that's actually my real present, is I'm taking you out to get your ears pierced. We can get dinner somewhere, burgers at Chelsie's maybe? And then we'll get your ears pierced at Gold Palace, and if you don't like these I'll buy you whatever earrings make you happy. Maybe pearls? You'd look so sweet in little pearls."

I thought about this, frowning. I was almost embarrassed to say what would really make me happy. I knew what kind of look Momma's face would get, one of the *I just don't know where you might have come from* looks she gave me at least once a day. Me and Momma were opposites, and the older I got, the less I told her about anything that really mattered. But I steeled my shoulders and said it anyway. "Actually," I said, "actually . . . You ever hear of the Narnia books?"

How late was I awake that night? Well into the next morning surely, till not just the story but also the curves and crosses of the letters came alive and swam dizzyingly in front of my eyes. This was the story Grace had told me, but with texture so I could smell the forest and hear the children's voices. Having found it felt like destiny.

One day a week my class was taken to the school library, allowed to check out any book we chose. They treated it like it was a privilege, like they were giving us a dime and letting us choose between licorice and Pixy Stix. But I'd always just plucked a random book from the shelves—Dick playing ball with Spot while Jane played house, as bland and uninspiring as multiplication tables—tucking it into my knapsack where it would stay until I returned it to the library again.

But this book, it was a completely different species. I remembered how it had been first learning to read, how the squiggles of print finally organized themselves slowly and painfully into words, then pieced together into sentences with meaning. Now, for the first time, the squiggles were releasing actual worlds, a woman in white fur and a golden crown sauntering into the room beside me, a man called Father Christmas—who was actually Santa—on his sledge, which was actually a sleigh. All of them surfacing from the page so real that when I finally closed my eyes, I was amazed their lives didn't continue around me. A whole world somehow tucked back into the book, waiting for me to set it free.

I woke late, Momma shepherding me out of bed only twenty minutes before the bus. I sat up, my eyes landing on the three books from the series I'd stacked on my desk, each as inviting as a wrapped gift. How was I possibly going to be able to stand something as colorless as school when I had new worlds to discover?

I ended up bringing a book into the bathroom, sitting on the toilet seat to read with the shower running in the background. I read during breakfast, the cereal spooning and chewing as automatic as the digestion because I was elsewhere, rescuing Edmund who was now imprisoned in a dungeon, locked in chains.

I read on the bus, and in class whenever I could sneak the book open on my lap. Scribbling random numbers into columns of math problems so I could hand in my paper and read again. Sitting on a bench at recess, for the first time not caring when I wasn't invited to join in jump rope lines, or when Mr. Shane slapped my math quiz on my desk with its red-penned frowny face, all of it only a mirage behind which the story continued, two girls and a boy and Chloe Louise Tyler, trekking through the woods to find their brother.

That afternoon, I returned to the Sinclairs' expecting to find out more about Pollyanna, or continue our dig through the earth. But when I got to the house and peered in the library window, I saw Mrs. Sinclair lying on the couch with her eyes closed, a hot water bottle clutched against her belly. Grace was sitting next to her with a hand on one of her legs, her face pale and mouth set.

As I stood there wondering if it would be wrong to ring the doorbell, Grace's eyes shifted and she saw me. She didn't startle, just rose and walked toward the door, stuck her head out, and said, "You'll need to be quiet."

I pressed my lips together and nodded, and Grace stepped back from the door. "Nate and Cecilia are upstairs. I'll take you." She closed the door behind me and pointed at my shoes, and I slipped them off and followed her.

The upstairs hallway was wide, sweeping in both directions. Iron sconces hung on the walls, and a scattering of end tables held graceful stone statues in flowing robes and vases filled with brilliantly colored flowers. Grace gestured toward a ladder that extended from a hole in the ceiling. "You're not scared of climbing, are you? They're in the attic."

I tried to imagine what the attic was like. My only experience with attics came from two late-night movies, both involving ghosts. But I said, "I'm not scared," and to prove it I scrambled up the ladder, then turned back to Grace. "You coming?"

"I can't. I have to . . ." She waved her arm at the stairs, then descended without saying more. Grace, I thought, did not act like she was eleven. Really she acted more like she was forty.

I turned back to the attic and peeked my head through the ceiling. The room smelled cloyingly malty, like Whoppers. It was dim, lit only by small windows at either end, beams of light laced with swimming dust fairies.

"I knew you'd come back." It was Nate's voice.

I squinted in the darkness and finally saw him crouched with Cecilia next to a box taller than both of them. Or no, not a box, it was a house, a dollhouse, huge and Victorian with canary-yellow shingles and red shutters. I felt myself drawn to it involuntarily as I tried to think what to say, finally coming up only with, "Wow."

"It's our grandmother's," Cecilia said. "But she's with God now, so she can't play with it anymore. We're not supposed to play with it either since it's not a productive use of our time, but we do anyway."

I swung the rest of the way into the attic and crouched beside Cecilia, staring inside the dollhouse. And staring.

Every room was furnished with intricately detailed miniature tables, chairs, dressers, and beds. There was a living room with red velvet couches, Tiffany lamps, a tiny phonograph; a kitchen with open shelves filled with miniature loaves of bread, bowls of fruit, and wheels of cheese; and a nursery with a cradle, rocking horse, toy chest, and a jack-in-the-box the size of my thumbnail. Inside the cradle was a white mouse.

In fact, looking closer I saw the mice were everywhere, propped against kitchen shelves, sitting at the dining table and in armchairs, smoking little pipes or reading little newspapers. I reached for one, a pale gray mouse in a green velvet dress, gingerly petted it with my index finger.

"That's Dorian," Cecilia said, leaning forward so I could see the band of her underpants above the waist of her skirt, gray with rippling elastic. It made me think of the time I'd seen a Santa in McDonald's, eating a cheeseburger.

Cecilia picked up another mouse, this one with a thin blue tie. "She's married to Spencer. You can play with them if you're careful." She handed me Spencer, then glanced at Nate. "Can I tell her?"

Nate watched my face expressionlessly, and then his lips tightened and he gave Cecilia a short nod. Cecilia leaned close. "The thing is? They're alive."

I looked down at the mice in my hand, waiting for the punch line. When there was none, I decided to laugh anyway. "Alive!"

"I'm serious, Chloe, it's a miracle. They move around when we're not here. It happens all the time, we put them in one room and they *always* end up somewhere else."

"They do not," I said, but I studied the mice, their blank-staring black glass eyes, and felt a shiver. I set them back carefully where they'd been.

But then Nate said, "It's the truth!" and stared fixedly at me in such a way that I could tell he, or he and Grace, were responsible for the mouse-moving. "Last week we put Anabella with her blocks on the living room rug, and when we came up today, look where she was." He gestured at the tiniest mouse, the one in the cradle. "And we'd left Dorian in the kitchen cooking, but when we came back she was reading."

From the overly enthralled tone of his voice I could tell he wasn't making fun of Cecilia for believing but encouraging it, wanting her to believe in magic for as long as possible. Probably that was why he'd been digging to London yesterday, not because he actually thought we could do it, but because he wanted *her* to think it.

So I picked up one of the books in the living room, opened it—it had actual pages—and looked at the zigzags of pretend writing inside. "Toy mouse writing must be different from people writing," I said, "if Dorian could read this."

Cecilia took the book from me and studied the pages, and I watched her, wondering how it happened that people stopped believing in tooth fairies and fairy godmothers and dolls that came alive. Did you just suddenly, all at once, know none of it was true? Or did you stop believing one thing at a time? Me, I didn't think I'd ever believed there was magic at all.

But as we started playing with the dollhouse, inventing stories for the mouse family to live through—a missing mouse baby, a mouse heart attack, and, my idea, an invasion of killer mouse aliens—thinking of how easily Nate and Cecilia had stepped back to let me inside their life and how it felt in a way like I'd always belonged, I realized I could almost imagine myself changing my mind.

I started visiting the Sinclairs every day after school, running home only to grab a snack and my bike and then racing off to see them. Auntie Eva, maybe feeling guilty about being paid to sit in an empty home, started greeting me at the door and trapping me in random conversations about her bad back or what doctors had said about her bad back, or the people she knew who had died or married or "God help them!" divorced that week. And I'd stand there shifting from foot to foot, my face making whatever expression I thought she'd probably expect, waiting for the tiniest pause so I could excuse myself and run.

Because my time with the Sinclairs was so very precious, so much to cram into the few hours we had. Some days I'd join in their home-schooling lessons, all of us listening to Mrs. Sinclair discuss Bible stories or history, Egyptian rituals or Roman emperors or the Crusades. All of it so far removed from life in Redbridge, California—where the only drama came from turkey hen battles over roadkill—that it couldn't be real, and was therefore excellent.

I watched the news with Momma every night, and she'd talk about the stories she wanted me to understand. "The most important lesson anybody can learn from the news is that his life isn't quite so bad as he thinks," she'd say. But Mrs. Sinclair didn't talk at all about Watergate, Bloody Sunday in Ireland, the plane crash in the Andes where people ate each other to survive. They were stories that had shown me the world, the people we were supposed to trust, our *foundations* were shaky. But when Mrs. Sinclair got shipments of textbooks for her lessons, she weeded through them, tearing out sections she didn't want to teach. It seemed wrong to me, illegal almost. But the children all did well on the standard-ized tests they had to take to measure their progress, and nobody seemed to care that they'd never learn about the Vietnam War.

And I wouldn't tell them.

I'd decided this early on, after a particularly bad day of school, a day that ended in detention. Ashley Lane's fault. "That's my shirt!" she told me when I walked in that morning. "That's one of my old Izods we gave to Goodwill!" She pointed out a little beige spot on my cuff and turned to the girls at her table. "I made that stain!" she said, which prompted the others to run through my entire wardrobe, claiming even the items I knew had been bought new, until finally I kicked Ashley, hard, in the groin. Awesome for a minute, knowing the power of myself, until a teacher was called.

I'd needed to tell the Sinclairs about it, share the weight of my world. But when I approached their house that afternoon I saw Nate and Grace in the yard putting on a puppet show for Cecilia, Raggedy Ann and Andy getting into mischief in their mistress's pantry. ("Mischief," "Mistress," "Pantry," even their words sounded fancy!) Watching the dolls overturning fake cookie jars and syrup pitchers, and Cecilia's belly laughter, I knew I needed to protect this world, my only safe place. And so while I was there I pretended there was no hurt, no tragedies, closer than hundreds of years ago.

I say this even knowing there were darker things under the surface of their lives, things I saw but didn't fully understand. The days I'd arrive to find one of them kneeling on the gravel driveway, head bowed. Ignored by the others until they rose an hour or more later with divots from the stones on their knees and shins, any questions I asked ignored. The day Grace, Cecilia, and I baked oatmeal cookies, Nate had been upstairs all afternoon and when I suggested we bring some fresh from the oven, Grace set a hand on my shoulder and told me, almost conspiratorially, that it was a day of fasting for him and he wouldn't be allowed to eat.

And then there was the afternoon Nate and I were squatting by the stream collecting tadpoles in large glass jars. He lifted his jar into the sky to study the light reflecting through the greenish haze, and I'd seen two dark scabs crisscrossing his left arm. "What happened!" I said.

He'd pulled his sleeve down to cover them. "Nothing. It's nothing."

I touched his arm, gripped by a horrified certainty. "Your dad did it," I said.

"He did not! He doesn't hurt us, Chloe, this was just something I tried, an experiment."

"*You* did that? But why would you hurt your own arm? What does that mean, an experiment?"

"It was just a way to stay with the Spirit last night, and it works, Chloe, even better than I thought it would. I know you wouldn't get it, but Satan takes hold of my mind and I—" He flapped an arm in the air, fiercely, like he was trying to slap a bug or fling off mud. "—think things I shouldn't. So this drives the thoughts away, that's all. 'If thy right eye causeth thee to stumble, pluck it out and cast it from thee for it is profitable for thee that one of thy members should perish, and not thy whole body be cast into hell.'"

"Pull out your *eye*?"

"Well, I'm not actually going to pull out my eye, am I? I mean

I would if I had to, but this is just a knife cut and it doesn't even hurt anymore. It's a way of joining myself to Christ and his suffering, Chloe. He went through the worst suffering to redeem us and this is like, I don't know, a crumb of suffering when he suffered a whole loaf."

I stared at him. My mouth felt dry. Nate dumped his jar of tadpoles into the stream and stood. "Your world's different from mine." His voice was prickly and toneless. "Just forget I said anything; I told you that you wouldn't get it." And then he turned away without looking back.

I'd wrapped my arms around my waist and sat there looking down at the stream, watching the freed tadpoles wriggle frenziedly away. I'd thought of the Sinclairs' faith as something that made them wholesome and pure, part of the fairy tale of their life. And I'd been jealous that they had it to lean on, Bible stories to guide them, and a father with a direct line to God. But every fairy tale has dark undertones, witches or evil stepmothers, wolves or trolls. And I was so blinded by what I wanted the Sinclairs to be that I hadn't been able to see what might be hiding underneath.

Of course I'd known from the beginning that they were full of secrets. It felt amazing being enveloped into their closeness, the way they were always touching, spontaneous hugs, arms slung around shoulders, holding hands as we all charged from place to place before collapsing on one another in heaps. And I was almost surprised each night when I was asked to leave before their father came home. Their father, I knew, was one secret they weren't willing to share. Much as part of me wanted to believe they were almost like stories, freezing in place when I left them and continuing only when I returned to their home, I couldn't help noticing their inner life, the little glances they gave one another, the whispers and frightened looks they exchanged at unpredictable times.

I knew it shouldn't hurt, and in a way it was their mystery that made them who they were. But still, the secrecy worried me because I knew the fickleness of friendship. So I did what I could to keep them interested in me, acted like myself but even more so. Because it seemed like they were drawn to the very parts of me that the girls in school seemed repelled by: the way my mind was always so crammed with words that they leaked from me sometimes when I was only trying to straighten them in my thoughts; the way I sometimes spiraled through funnels of overly exuberant laughter, unable to return for minutes at a time (the tail end of a note Mara Shockley had passed me last spring: ". . . and plus you laugh like Betty Rubble!" she'd written, then added a frowny face), and cried too easily not only when I was hurt but when one of the Sinclairs fell or bumped or twisted. I was pretty sure it was their first impression of me, looking feral and pseudo-feline, that had made them invite me into their world, and so I cultivated my true self, my love for recklessness and overdramatization, and my adrenaline-fueled spontaneity.

Days went by, weeks, April, May, and into June. Time did a strange dance for me that spring, both a tarantella blur of sameness and the intricate procession of individual moments. Until summer vacation began, free from what I'd started to think of as the broken parts of my life. Summer vacation, when I finally met their father.

6

"I'M bored," Nate said. It was eleven o'clock, during what I'd come to think of as our recess. Every morning the children were given time to play on their own while Mrs. Sinclair did her embroidery or napped. And as the days grew warmer, the duration of this recess started stretching into hours, Mrs. Sinclair calling us for lunch later and later in the day.

At first I'd thought it was her way of giving the children a summer vacation, but soon I started wondering whether there was something else going on. As the days passed she seemed more and more sickly, her eyes on the bad days smudged with gray, her face crumpled and pale. I didn't ask because the children didn't seem to want to talk about it—in fact they didn't even seem to have noticed anything might be wrong, and so I pretended I didn't notice either. I'd fallen in love with Mrs. Sinclair, her softness and kindness and her impromptu hugs and encouragement so different from my own mother, the type of mom I'd always wished Momma knew how to be. And part of me knew it would be best to pretend even to myself.

There were no lessons when she wasn't feeling well, so instead we'd work on building skyscrapers from fallen twigs, or robots from dead appliances, and other similar momentous projects destined to alter history; all of which, like the tunnel to London, were abandoned as soon as they failed to meet expectations. This morning we'd been taking turns aiming rocks and acorns at the slack-jawed orange flowers on Mrs. Sinclair's hibiscus, pretending they were the faces of our current favorite evil leaders, Maximilien Robespierre and Vlad the Impaler. Cecilia was the best at aiming; she was best at pretty much everything we tried despite being the youngest, and the others had gotten fed up and cranky about it.

Suddenly Nate pulled himself up onto a tree branch, and smiled down at us with the look of someone issuing a proclamation. A Robespierre sort of look. "I have an idea," he said. "We're going to put on a play, write the story, and make the costumes and the stage set."

Cecilia gathered the flowers she'd knocked to the ground, and stuck one in her hair. "Write a story about what?"

"I know," I said, a knot of excitement in my chest. "We should do the Narnia books." I'd been through all the books twice already, and the stories felt as real to me as my own bedroom. I'd focused all my strength on believing, standing with my eyes squeezed shut in front of my closet and then opening the door and entering full of that belief. Finding only my clothes and the back wall, but this, putting on a play, would be the next best thing to finding the wall had suddenly disappeared.

The others seemed to feel this too, all of them jumping in with an opinion on what we might and might not include. We'd condense the story so we could have bits from all the books (leaving out only *The Last Battle,* which we all agreed should never have been written in the first place), have six acts, each ending with a cliff-hanger. We'd use stuffed animals and puppets for the smaller creatures and we'd play everyone else, asking Mrs. Sinclair to play the White Witch.

We plotted the story, outlining it with a Sharpie on a drawing pad, and then we cast the parts and assigned the portions of the script we each would write. I'd be in charge of the prequel book, *The Magician's Nephew,* and I loved the idea of creating the creation, the beginnings of the magic, Polly sneaking across rooftops with Digory to discover his uncle's secret study, the shiny yellow rings that led them into other worlds.

It was after we'd all brought notebooks from the house, to begin creating the script, that Cecilia posed a conundrum. "Who's going to be the audience?" she said. "Did you ever hear about a play without people to watch it?"

Nate thought a moment, then said, "Your mom, Chloe, she can come see us."

I felt a sour twist in my belly. I didn't want Momma coming there. All these weeks, I'd managed to keep these two worlds separate, telling her almost nothing about the Sinclairs. And while I was here I could bury my home life in a dim back corner of my mind, pretend it belonged to some other girl. "My mom can't come," I said. "She works pretty much all the time, but how 'bout your dad?"

They glanced at each other, and then Grace said, "He wouldn't like it. We won't let him know. But it's okay, we don't need an audience. The important part of a play is doing it, not watching it."

I turned to her, studying the forced nonchalance on her face. Understanding for the first time that they must think of their father the way I thought of school and my own mother, as belonging to a separate world. A part of our lives we could pretend, for a few hours, did not exist.

POLLY: We better go before your uncle catches us.

DIGORY: Wait, Polly, listen, do you hear a funny sound? It's a humming kind of sound, and it's coming from this box of yellow and green rings. [Listens to the open box]

POLLY: Ooh, I can totally hear it. And plus, Digory, look, in the corner. [Points to the shadows] I think it's a ghost! I see its white head!

Every day now we worked on writing our play, an activity Mrs. Sinclair seemed to wholeheartedly support, fitting time for it around her lessons, proofreading our scripts and offering suggestions. She even bought material to use for our props and costumes: glitter and beads, cotton batting and tinsel and Christmas icicle lights for Narnia's endless winter. We worked in the yard when the weather was nice and in the basement when it wasn't, a damp dusty space filled with sheet-covered furniture and old wooden trunks I imagined held long pearl necklaces and eighteenth-century gowns.

As the days passed, our anticipation grew, an unspoken excitement that sped up our conversations and made us twitch Tourette's-like when forced to sit still for Mrs. Sinclair's lessons. We'd scheduled our performance for the second Tuesday in July, and with a deadline in place we set to work memorizing our lines. Along with the more minor characters, I was playing Polly, Susan, Jill Pole, Aravis, and Doctor Cornelius the dwarf. A nice conglomeration of characters, I thought, but taken together all the memorization was overwhelming.

I whispered my lines at home as I walked from room to room and washed dishes and lay in bed at night, and shouted them as I biked to and from the Sinclairs' home, until in time they seemed as reflexive as the alphabet song. We started dress rehearsals, first with scripts in our hands, and then tucked into our shirts to be pulled out only if we needed them. Even Mrs. Sinclair had memorized her lines, and she spoke them laden with emotion and great arm movements that made us all smile, while secretly embarrassed for her.

And then finally came performance day. In our dress rehearsals we'd never acted through the scenes in order without stopping. We wanted to save that for our performance; since we wouldn't have an actual audience, we wanted something to make that day special. But this worried me, knowing there was a chance we might forget our place, might even forget which characters we were supposed to be playing. And I was up all the night before running through the scenes and transitions in my mind, so filled with expectation that my body felt swollen.

The next morning I felt too feverish to eat, so I dumped my cereal in the trash while my mother was dressing and then dashed out the door without even saying goodbye. But as I started toward my bike a window opened and Momma called to me from her bedroom: "You're off to see the Sinclair kids so early?"

Momma had no idea how often I went over there or how long I stayed, and it was clear Auntie Eva hadn't told her either, maybe not wanting my mother to see how she'd been basically paying $2.50 an hour for someone to watch our TV. Momma had suggested that we should invite the Sinclairs to dinner to reciprocate their hospitality, but she'd never followed through with this, and I'd grown comfortable that she probably never would.

"Just to play," I said. "Not for any other reason."

Momma was quiet a moment, then said, "Is there something you're not telling me?"

"What? No! It's just we've been working on something, a kind of project, and today we're going to finish it."

I knew we were veering dangerously close to the truth, that she'd wheedle me closer and then insist on following me to the Sinclairs' to see our play, and then what? She'd probably laugh and call us cute, in private drop the term "hoity-toity" when referring to Mrs. Sinclair, her favorite word to describe any adults whose work didn't involve the creation of practical objects. And that? That would ruin everything.

But she only said, "A project!" her voice indulgent. And then, "Well, get to it then, and I'll see you tonight. I'm thinking of roast pork for dinner." Her window slid shut, and that was it.

I slowly walked to my bike and straddled it, looking up at the window. I hadn't wanted her to know about the play, it would've killed me to have her there, but . . . part of me wanted her to *want* to know. And that was the thing about having two lives, keeping them secret from each other. The harder you tried to separate them, the more you were also split in two.

By the time I got to the Sinclairs', half of the yard had already been transformed. I stood in the driveway staring at it all, dazed. It was beautiful: icicle lights draped from the branches of the tall oak, cotton batting surrounding the roots. By the tree was the cardboard panel we'd cut out and decorated to look like a carriage, behind it the castle we'd built from three old doors and glitter-covered foam cones. At least from a distance and askance, and blurry-eyed, it looked exactly like I'd imagined. Narnia.

"*There* you are already," Nate said. He was carrying the burlap sacks we'd use for the desert of Calormen, laying them end-to-end. "You can help bring stuff up from the basement. That's where Mom is now."

But when I entered the house, I saw Mrs. Sinclair sitting on the bottom step holding a damp dish towel to her face. She startled when I entered, then quickly straightened and dropped the dish towel. "Must be the hottest endless winter on record!" she said.

I sat next to her silently. After a minute I rested my head on her arm. We didn't speak but something passed between us, a kind of understanding. She, like me, could be two different people, living in two completely separate worlds.

Finally she said, "I'm so glad I can do this with them." Quietly, like she was speaking to herself. And although I didn't quite understand the unspoken meaning behind her words, I could feel it. The implication of some kind of end.

I crouched behind the bushes, the exact spot where I'd been when I first met the Sinclairs, watching Nate approach—his cheeks smudged with dirt—and waiting for my entrance. But instead of saying his line, Nate glanced back at the others and then ducked behind the bush with me. He gave me a quick kiss on the cheek. "For luck," he whispered, and then his face flushed and he turned quickly away. I watched him a moment, then smiled and touched my cheek, feeling a trill of excitement-slash-stage-fright.

A minute later Nate peeked over the side of the bush. "Hello, I'm Digory," he said. "Who're you?"

I smiled widely at him, my mind completely blank for a moment before the line came to me. "I'm Polly and your face is dirty. Were you crying?"

"So what if I was? You'd be crying too if you used to live in the country with a pony, and if you had to come and live with an aunt and an uncle who's crazy!"

And so it began, the story of Polly and Digory. To Charn and the sleeping kingdom, Queen Jadis and Aslan and a magic apple that could cure Digory's mother of an unnamed but deadly illness. When we'd first read through the ending I'd written, bringing home the apple, all of us sat silently for several minutes staring at the grass. And then Grace had gotten up and walked away.

I was wearing one of Cecilia's dresses, too tight on me but still nicer than anything I'd ever owned. Cecilia, as Frank the cabbie, was wearing a pair of Nate's pants rolled at the ankles, her face painted with an oil pastel mustache. Mrs. Sinclair, as Jadis, was wearing a gold crown and a large white sheet wrapped as a toga. Grace, as Aslan, wore half of a fur stole around her head, the other half tucked into her pants as a tail, and a shirt Mrs. Sinclair had made from a fuzzy yellow bath mat.

Being there with them, playing through the scenes, felt like being in love, in love with the Sinclairs, with the story and the script we'd written, every rhinestone and brushstroke we'd pasted and painted. I wanted to dance, that's how happy I was. The act was going so well; Cecilia did stumble on a couple of her lines and Nate snickered when Grace tripped over her tail, but I hardly noticed, I was so caught up in living through the story that had once been only in my head. The props we'd built became real; five cellophane disks, a row of folding chairs, they were transformed to the pools in the Wood Between the Worlds and a palace room of sleeping, waxlike people. Cecilia's old wooden rocking horse grew wings and became Strawberry the flying pony, and a cardboard drainage tube we'd pinned with candy became a toffee tree.

And when Grace began to sing about the beginnings of Narnia, I could see new grass and wildflowers grow under her feet, animals emerging from under the ground to walk across the lawn two by two. "Creatures," she said, "I give you yourselves, I give to you forever this land of Narnia." She set her hand on a stuffed bear, her face solemn. "I give you the woods, the fruits, the rivers, I give you the stars and I give you myself."

I hugged my waist, the joy like a fireball inside me as I watched the new stars start to sing, the new sun rise. And then . . .

"How special." A man was standing at the edge of the lawn, dark-haired with a square chin and full lips and the prettiest gray eyes I'd ever seen, like cat's-eye marbles. He was dressed in a suit that was part white and part cream, a combination that you'd think should've left the cream seeming dirty, but on him it seemed elegant and purposeful.

"Joel . . ." Mrs. Sinclair said.

"Did you really think I wouldn't notice?" he said. "I'm not blind. I do see what's going on in my own home." As he spoke he turned to Grace, who'd wrapped her arms around her body. He stepped closer, his expression unchanged, eyes roaming across her bare shoulders. "How old are you, Gracie?" he said.

She glanced at her mother as if for confirmation before she whispered, "Eleven."

"Eleven. And is this an appropriate way for an eleven-year-old girl to dress?"

Mrs. Sinclair reached for Grace, and Grace huddled against her side. "It's my fault, Joel," Mrs. Sinclair said. "It was my call, not hers."

"Oh I realize that. 'Course I realize that, I know Grace and she never would've dressed like this on her own."

"That's true, Daddy, I wouldn't."

Nate gave her a look. "Poor Grace, she was threatened at gunpoint."

Mr. Sinclair ignored them. "But they're old enough to take responsibility for their own appearance and conduct. What would the congregation think if they saw this? And you with that . . . sheet!"

"They'd think we were having fun." Mrs. Sinclair's voice was soothing, conciliatory, but with an undercurrent of irritation. "They'd see we were playacting. That's what children do."

Something unreadable crossed his face; it looked almost like pity, or maybe kindness, but then he said, "Do you think this play-acting is a constructive part of their upbringing? Does it nurture their moral education? Intellectual?"

He had such a strange way of speaking, his words so formal, his voice not especially loud, but somehow powerful. And even though I didn't quite understand him, I felt myself drawn to him, standing straighter and taller like the words were tugging and un-folding me.

As if this newly straightened spine had made me more visible, his gaze turned to me for the first time. "Who's this?"

Nate, who'd been standing next to me, took a slight step away. Mr. Sinclair held a hand to me and I hesitated, then took it. His fingers were warm, callused, completely enveloping mine. He didn't shake my hand, didn't even squeeze it, just held it gently. "Do you have a name?"

"Chloe," I said softly. "Chloe Louise Tyler."

"Hello, Chloe Louise Tyler," he said, still holding my hand.

"She's a friend of the children's," Mrs. Sinclair said.

"A friend." He stretched a smile that I couldn't even begin to interpret. Maybe amusement. Maybe the opposite of amusement. "And why didn't I know this friend existed?"

His eyes were on mine like he expected me to answer, but I felt like I'd lost my place in this conversation, like it was happening in some secret language. I opened my mouth but had no idea what to say so I closed it again.

"Why don't you go home now, Chloe Louise Tyler." He gave my hand a squeeze, then dropped it. "Do you need a ride?"

I swallowed, shook my head. "Bike. I have a bike."

"That's good, you're an industrious girl. Go on, then."

I looked back at the stage set we'd worked so hard on, which now all looked like exactly what it was, badly painted cardboard, chipped scrap wood, and old, worn toys. Grace, Nate, and Cecilia stared back at me, not seeming scared exactly, more ashamed and resigned.

I backed away toward my bike, suddenly very conscious of the tightness of the dress Cecilia had given me, the way it bunched under my arms and only zipped partway. As I reached the bike I turned back to see the children silently gather our props, Mrs. Sinclair walking with her husband toward the house.

In retrospect there was something almost beautiful about the moment, the silence, the way they bent and carried. Beautiful in the way a funeral procession can be, or maybe the end of a funeral when the casket is left behind. I watched a minute longer before I got on my bike and rode away.

It would be many months before I saw them all again.

PART III

A SWIFTLY TILTING PLANET

7

WE think we know our friends, our lovers, but really all we know is pieces of them. Fragments we learn by watching, sharing time and place, listening to their stories; over the years there are more and more of these fragments and we can draw lines between them, fill them with what we imagine is truth. But of course we only know what they show us; lines we think jig here may actually curl somewhere else altogether. The lines we draw aren't always real, and often have more to do with our own selves.

Even after many months, the fragments the Sinclairs were willing to show me were so convoluted and widely spaced that I'd had no idea how to connect them. I tried, and as I learned more about their home life I was able to come closer to understanding. But I'd always known there were whole dimensions I'd never seen.

I could probably say almost the same thing after nearly four decades with Nate. I'd tried to imagine myself living his childhood, what it would have done to me, the lines it would have forged, but in the end this had probably only helped me understand myself.

I retrieved the newspaper article I'd crumpled and thrown in the trash, the photo of Joel Sinclair. I studied his face, now the texture of a rusted pipe. Maybe it's natural to want to be able to untangle the thoughts and reasoning of suicide bombers and serial killers, try to put yourself in their heads as if that could help you understand *why*. And when you finally realize you can't understand, you try to convince yourself there's nothing there. That these people are more reptilian than human, never loved a wife, a parent, a child. Were incapable of sympathy and never had any desires beyond the most base. No lives outside of whatever they'd done.

But I've come to realize all people are so much more complex than that. And trying to understand Joel Sinclair, even before he'd lost his mind, was impossible. He wasn't soulless, that was the thing. There was goodness in him; he'd gone out of his way to care for the people in his parish; he'd loved his children despite how he sometimes treated them, and they'd all loved him. It was true they'd seemed afraid of him, that's all I'd been able to infer when I was a kid, but I later realized that overshadowing this was their wish to please him, to make him see that they were worthy.

Of course he'd changed after Sophia's death, and it was that person, the person he'd become, who I hated. He'd become mired in whichever stage of grief the anger is, that anger intensifying and boring through him like a tapeworm, devouring whatever humanity had been left.

But who was he now, weakened by years in jail and the disease taking his brain? The neurons that had fired to make the decisions he made, had they only been formed after Sophia died? And were they still there or now deadened by plaque? It didn't matter, of course. I'd always despise him. But maybe understanding would help me forgive Nate for being there now.

That Narnia summer, I'd only understood enough to be

scared. I'd gone back to the Sinclairs' the day after the play, Cecilia's dress slung around my neck. But when I rang the doorbell, Sophia answered and ushered me outside, where she set her hands on my shoulders, looking into my face, and then pulled me into her arms. "Oh Chloe," she said.

I felt a wash of trepidation and kept my eyes closed, head buried against her, feeling strangely adult like I was the one comforting her. Hoping this was only about the ill-fated play, her regret.

"I'm sorry, sweetheart." She pulled away and set her hands back on my shoulders. "But I think it'd probably be best if you don't come by anymore. Besides, don't you have friends from school you've been neglecting? I'm sure you do, so wouldn't it be nice to spend some time with them instead?"

Her words were like a slap. Or no, like ropes, a noose cutting off my breath. "No!" Sudden tears flared in my eyes. "I don't have any other friends!" I said.

"Well, of course you do." She swept my bangs off my forehead. "I'm sorry, Chloe, but you can't come back here." She looked down at Cecilia's dress still around my neck, then said, "You can keep that if you want."

These words only tightened the rope. Looking back, I think she might've wanted me to keep the dress because she'd had some sense how precious it might become to me, how I'd end up pulling it from my closet day after day, studying the lace cuffs and the neatly stitched hems, the one sign I had that the past few months were more than just a dream. But at the time I'd only been sure she now considered the dress contaminated in some way. Thought *me* contaminated.

I'd pulled away from her and said, "I *do* have friends, actually," and then I turned away. Tried to convey an anger I didn't feel by striding purposefully across the lawn back to my bike.

I hadn't gone home, though. Instead, I walked my bike down the driveway and into the woods, hid with it behind a circle of trees. And hours later when Mr. Sinclair's car pulled down the drive, I followed it, staying always just out of sight. Watching as he stood and set both hands at the small of his back, stretching as he looked out across the lawn. The look on his face was pure contentment, maybe self-satisfaction at the life he'd built. The look of a man who has fought a hard battle and knows he's won.

I don't remember much about the rest of the summer and fall. What did I do without the children to play with? I'd never been one of those kids to whine the word "bored"; there were just too many things that interested me, too many adventures to dream up, too many pictures to paint or Lego towers to build and destroy. But that summer I couldn't find anything that seemed worth doing.

Nothing, that is, besides reading. I'll probably never again feel as intensely about books, read as desperately, and fall as deeply in love with stories and characters as I did that summer. Now when I read, I'm continuously trying to bring back that same immersion, fall in love again, and I judge every book against that impossible ideal. The books I love now aren't necessarily those that are written best, they're those books, like *The Thorn Birds* and *Clan of the Cave Bear*, that bring me closest to that magic.

Every Saturday I demanded my mother bring me to the library, and she—bemusedly—obliged. The children's librarian now knew me by name and seemed excited to see me every week, setting aside books she thought I might like. I fell in love with Roald Dahl and Laura Ingalls Wilder. Never-Never Land, "open only to children and imagination." Its hints of darkness: "Children are gay and innocent, and heartless," I read, and felt an immediate thrill. Every one of the stories resonated inside a different part of me, teaching me things about myself I hadn't known.

After each book I was bursting to tell the Sinclairs, feeling as much a sense of pride over having discovered them as I would have if I'd written them. It was almost physically painful to hold the stories inside. To be pulled out of these worlds where I lived night and day and not be able to talk about them, it was disorienting, made the real world seem less real. How could the people around me not see that I'd been spending my day in nineteenth-century Kansas, or in the pit of a giant peach? It was like I was the only one living in the real world, and they were skating blindly over an opaque surface above me.

It was Madeleine L'Engle who finally broke me. I'd devoured *A Wrinkle in Time* within two days and it enchanted me, horrified me, confused me, such a tangle of feelings that I had no idea what to do with. Meg Murry was me, her fatherlessness, her aloneness and inability to fit in, the way she'd been teased for being strange. The Black Thing and travel to Camazotz to rescue her dad, the evil IT who lured and imprisoned Meg's mind. In Camazotz, as in Narnia, children could make a difference, they were counted on, tested, and succeeded, had weight in the world.

The profoundness of this, and the horrifying deliciousness of the story, rattled inside me desperately needing something else to echo against. And as I sat in bed the night after I'd finished, it was Mrs. Whatsit's words that struck me, the way she'd compared life to a sonnet. "You're given the form," she said, "but you have to write the sonnet yourself. What you say is completely up to you."

And so, the next afternoon, I wrote the next line of my sonnet by going to the Sinclairs'.

Nate, Grace, and Cecilia were outside on the lawn in front of three large sheets of poster board laid end-to-end. As I watched, Grace dipped a large branch in a pan of green paint and swept it in spirals over the posters. Nate and Cecilia knelt across from her, arms filled with pinecones, twigs, and fallen leaves. They began to set them on the poster, beside Grace's paint-swept lines, standing to study the effect and then kneeling again to rearrange.

The image they were creating seemed strange, almost mystical, and I found myself drawn to it the way one feels drawn to music. I stepped toward the holly berries on the bush where I'd parked my bike and began plucking them one by one until my hands were full. And then I approached and set a berry at the edge of Grace's painting.

Nate saw me first. He stared at me a moment, his face blank, and then slowly he smiled.

I smiled back and we stood there dumbly grinning at each other, until Grace raised her head and followed the direction of his eyes. Her eyes widened. "What're you *doing* here?"

"Chloe!" Cecilia said, galloping toward me. She wrapped her arms around me and I dropped the berries, laughed, and hugged her back.

"You can't stay," Grace said. "You're going to get us all in trouble, including Mom."

My stomach twisted. "But why!" Cecilia's arms were still around me, her shoulder digging against my chin as I spoke. I pulled away. "Why, Grace? I didn't do anything!"

"Daddy thinks you're an influence," Cecilia said. "But *I* don't."

"Don't feel bad," Nate said, "he just doesn't like kids outside the church is all. Nothing about you in particular."

My palms were damp, maybe from nerves, or maybe just berry juice. I wiped them on my jeans, wanting to feel indignant but instead I just felt lost, and slightly queasy. "I don't care," I said. Sounding lost and queasy. "I don't care, I didn't come here to play, just to give you something." I reached into my back pocket and pulled out the paperback, which was somewhat bent from its cross-town bike ride. I didn't know what to say next so I clarified the obvious. "It's a book."

Nate took it from me, studied the back. I stepped closer so I could read the description with him, and immediately felt my eyes fill. He smelled like clove soap and boy-sweat, the same way he always smelled, and the scent made me homesick. I wanted to lean closer to his neck, maybe eat it. "It's so much better than this makes it sound," I said. "I mean there's no way to explain the story, you just have to read it."

"We have to ask Daddy," Grace said.

But Nate was looking at me, holding my eyes. On his face, a quiet determination. "Things were funner when you were here," he said, the first glimmer he'd given me—really that anyone in my life had ever given me—that I'd been missed while I was gone.

I biked home after this, deciding to wait at least a week before returning, to give Nate a chance to read. But just five days later I was sitting in the kitchen with a bowl of puffy Cheetos when I glanced out the window and saw Nate standing at the door. Not knocking, just waiting. I jumped up and opened the door. "You read it?" I said.

His hair was windblown, his face flushed and clammy from the exertion of running the two miles between our homes. "We all read it." He shoved the book toward me and I swiped the cheese dust from my fingers before taking it. "We have to talk about it, and you should be there. Plus this says there are two more books?"

"There are!" I said. "I'm reading them now!"

"Well, you need to bring them when you're done. Don't tell *anybody* you're coming, okay? We've told you where and when." He nodded at the book in my hands. "It's a code we made up last month and we'll use it with you from now on. Cross out the words from the book and you'll understand it." And then he turned and ran back up the street.

I'd stood watching him, wondering what he could possibly mean, until I flipped through the book and found the folded note.

Friti wadasy atath darreke band sytorthe mycre neight inkher.

I stared at it, turned the note over, turned it back, and then stared some more. "Cross out the words from the book," Nate had said, and suddenly I understood. I took a pen from the junk drawer, set the book beside the note, and began to cross out the letters from its first lines.

Friti ~~wadasy~~ atath ~~darreke band sytorthe mycre~~ ~~neight inkher~~

Friday at three, by the creek. I grinned and hugged the pen and the note against my chest.

After this we started using the code as a way of setting up secret meetings, leaving the notes in an old toolbox we hid under the holly bush, intertwining the letters of a message with the words from a book. Impossible to decipher unless one knew which book had been used to encrypt, so that even if Mr. or Mrs. Sinclair figured out the mechanism, they'd have no idea how to go about applying it.

The artifice was largely unnecessary especially since, as we learned soon, Mrs. Sinclair had known all along about my visits.

Accepting them at first without acknowledging them, but then—as we became more careless—gathering the children to reprimand them, not for letting me come over but for our recklessness. After that she actively worked with us to make sure Mr. Sinclair never found out I'd been there, mapping out his schedule and finding us secluded places in which to play. So we didn't need the code, but using it had added an irresistible undercurrent of danger to our meetings. We were undercover agents, KGB spies; the same theme repeated in so many of the books we'd read, of child heroes breaking arbitrary adult rules to save the day.

The code.

Sitting in the reading room, I stared down at the Moleskine notebook Nate had hidden. Is that what he'd done here, written in the code of our distant childhood, assuming I wouldn't remember? And it was so obvious, how could I not have remembered till now? It was like I'd tried so hard to forget the horrific parts of the past that the memories from before Gabriel were no longer instinctual; my mind put up a protective shield that I had to actively walk around.

I rose slowly from the table and, feeling a corkscrew twist of fear in my chest, I made my way into the heart of the bookstore.

Nate had a unique filing system, rarely bowing to the convention of shelving alphabetically by category, separating literature from romance, mystery from spirituality from true crime. He wanted customers to browse, and in their hunt for entertainment or knowledge to find new authors or interests they might not otherwise have discovered. Shelve *Like Water for Chocolate* next to cookbooks so that someone searching for recipes might find an author who'd also been obsessed by food. *Sophie's Choice* near World War II history;

James Michener surrounded by travel books, and science mixed in with the science fiction. Confusing to every new customer, frustrating, although if they asked for a specific book Nate could find it within seconds. And the readers who knew the store seemed to love it, sometimes spending hours wandering, listening as the spines called their temptations. *Become a Mohican, a musketeer, a mafioso!* they said. *A boy paddling his raft down the Mississippi, or a ferry boat captain motoring down the Congo!*

Now I searched for *The Lion, the Witch and the Wardrobe* on the shelf next to mysteries and then British history, before finally finding a copy in the Travel section, between *Off the Beaten Path: A Guide to Unique Places* and *Dove,* the story of a sixteen-year-old boy who'd sailed around the world. I used one finger to rock it forward, away from the other books, tilted it horizontal. Stared at it and then pulled it from the shelf.

I brought the book to the mahogany table where I'd set Nate's notebook, and laid them open side by side. I copied the first coded words onto my notepad, hesitated, then began striking out the first letters *O-n-c-e-t-h-e.*

~~Ondece arthe~~

Dear. "Okay," I whispered. "Okay."

How long had it taken to encode this whole notebook? It was a hard process, figuring out how to intertwine the letters so that the encoding looked like actual words, pronounceable without long strings of consonants and vowels. This must've taken him days, weeks, and why? Why the hell use such a ridiculously convoluted means of writing whatever he had to say?

Garebri werele

I held a finger to the copy of *The Lion, the Witch and the Wardrobe*, slowly crossing out the next few letters on my notepad: *r-e-w-e-r-e* Then dropped my pen. The second word in the notebook was Gabriel.

My mouth washed with the bright coppery taste of blood, and I touched my lip where I'd bitten it, looked blankly at the horribly jewel-toned smear on my finger. I shouldn't be reading this; I couldn't read it, so I tossed the notebook back into its cutaway shell, slapped the cover closed, and strode upstairs. Without even taking off my shoes, I huddled in bed, shivering, pulling the covers tight around me as if that could keep me from cracking in two.

I didn't sleep that night, just lay there strangled by the darkness, my thoughts not complete trains with beginnings, middles, and ends, but random epileptic bursts, spatterings of disparate images and voices: my childhood, my pregnancy, Gabriel in the baby tub I'd laid across my mother's kitchen sink. The empty toddler bed that I'd kept for months after in his room, still refusing to believe he wouldn't return.

Finally I rose and walked into the kitchen. I filled a tall glass with water, drank it in breathless gulps. And then, from the pocket of the jeans I was still wearing, my cell phone started to ring. I startled, then pulled the phone from my pocket. The call was coming from an unlisted number, and it took me a minute of staring wildly at the phone buttons before I remembered which to press. I brought the phone to my ear. "Hello?"

"Chloe, I'm sorry to call so early." It was Nate. "But I knew you'd probably be up already, and I wanted to make sure I caught you before you opened the store."

"It's okay, I was up." My voice shook and I swallowed quickly, tried to steady myself. "God, Nate, do you know how I've been worrying? How could you leave without telling me what was going on?"

"I know, I'm so sorry, really sorry, it's just I wasn't thinking straight. Cecilia had called me weeks ago to tell me how sick Joel was, and then she called a few days ago insisting I come up here without telling me why, so I just assumed the worst. I guess I went a little crazy."

I couldn't tell how he sounded. Apologetic? Dismissive? I needed a facial expression.

"I should've thought more how this would feel to you, I realize that. There's just so much going on and I'm not thinking straight . . ." His voice trailed off and I heard the strange throaty humming sound he made sometimes when his mind was somewhere else, unreachable, as if pulling away from me involved actual physical, mechanical movement. Then softer, "It's so crazy being here. It's like as soon as I stepped in the door everything came back, the good, the awful . . . Mom. Maybe this is why people believe in ghosts. It's so different now, the house is run-down, and my dad and Cecilia too, and I can see those changes but they're less real than the house and all the people who were here before. Christ, I just wish you were here."

"I would've been." I tightened my grip on the phone. "You excluded me; you didn't tell me Joel was sick when you'd known for weeks."

He didn't speak for a minute, and when he finally answered his tone was stiff. "Would you really have cared? I mean I didn't even think *I* cared until I saw him and realized that some messed-up part of me did. And I knew that however you reacted, even if on the surface it seemed like the right reaction, there'd be something completely different going on behind it. What would you have said if I'd told you I was coming here for him?"

"That's not the point!" My voice broke and I pressed a fist to my mouth, bracing myself before I continued. "The point," I said, "is that when you're going through something that's tearing you apart, coming to me should be like an instinct for you. I'm supposed to be . . . I don't know, a steady force that can absorb some of your pain, something to grab onto. But you never show me anything!"

He exhaled loudly, exasperatedly. I leaned back against the wall and squeezed my eyes shut as he spoke. "I'm tired, Chloe, not just physically, I'm emotionally drained. You have every right to be angry, I don't blame you, but there's nothing left inside me to absorb the anger. When this is over and I come to terms with everything that's happening, then I can handle you lashing out, but for now can you please just try and understand?"

Nate had always excelled at making me feel like I was overreacting, even when he didn't explicitly mean to. He had this perpetual serenity about him, a stillness that made me feel like a fly butting against a window trying to enter. I wanted to tell him I'd found his notebook, almost hit him with it like a slap, but I realized that I couldn't. The letter he seemed to have started to Gabriel, and whatever else was in the notebook—a diary, I suspected—were the most intensely private parts of Nate. To have looked at them, when he'd gone through such elaborate machinations to keep me from looking, was an unforgivable invasion of that privacy. I felt my head momentarily spin, trying to reorient, then said, "Okay, tell me this, did you order books for Lester Jarvis recently? He came back to ask about a set of Victor Hugo."

"Ah."

"Ah what? We only have three thousand dollars in savings and he already gave us a deposit. How did that happen? Where the hell has our money gone?"

"I was going to take care of it, Chloe."

"You were going to? He was expecting the books already!" I tried to sound irate, but really I just sounded tired.

"I'll do it when I get back. Or you could try and find something that'll work for him, just don't pay more than six for it. You know where to look."

"We don't have six thousand dollars, Nate! Didn't we have more than that last month? Where did it go?"

"There were expenses I wasn't planning on, that's all. We can increase our home equity loan if we have to and just be a little more careful about what we spend. Look, it's early, I'm guessing you probably haven't been sleeping well either, and this isn't the kind of conversation to have over the phone. I promise I'll deal with all this when I get back, but tell Lester I'd already ordered a copy and it's en route, would you? I love you, Chloe."

And then he hung up, without waiting for a reply. The air around us heavy, vibrating with things unsaid.

Downstairs, I emailed the Hugo bookseller, asking for photos of the exposed corners, the inside boards, and any damaged pages. Then sat at the computer, staring transfixed at the empty screen. After a minute I grabbed a polishing cloth from the desk drawer and strode through the shop, dusting all the surfaces, shaking out rugs. But the flurry of activity didn't help. There was something gripping at me, a sort of desperation, like Nate's notebook had arms reaching ribbonlike to tie themselves around my legs and stomach, pull me closer.

I wiped my hands off on my jeans. I knew I should shower and change, brush my teeth, open the store. But the ribbons knotted round my lungs pulled tight, and I stared down at the polishing cloth, then dropped it and went to the reading room.

I sat at the table, opened *The Lion, the Witch and the Wardrobe,* and pulled out the notebook. Sat a moment with it in my lap and then opened it and began copying and crossing out letters.

> ~~Ondece arthe Garebri werele whafota woum chider fuldreln whobiserth nadaym cesele brawertione wepewtere shadusani wedism hundyo aund weluere yolThide snostough tory holids amembo riessout soomey outhinc gouthald lothappo kenebad tock theatmit whewn theheny weyore surente graway ofrowm lonn!~~

Dear Gabriel,

What a wonderful birthday celebration we had. I wish you were old enough to hold memories so you could look back at it when you're grown! At the park with your mom, one of those tempera paint blue-sky days, making wishes on dandelion fairies (and yes they are real fairies!). Building pebble fences around anthills to protect ants from intruders, I'm not quite sure you understood that's what we were doing, but you're such a studious, intuitive boy that I have a sense you did, and that you approved.

I wish we could have more days like this. But even though I haven't spent enough time with you to impress on you how much I treasure the minutes we do have, I know your mother's been showering you with enough attention to make up for what you haven't gotten from me.

That's part of why I'm writing this letter, I think. Because I

know when you're older you'll probably look back on the first years
of your life and feel betrayed that I didn't play more of a part in
them. So I'm writing this to make sure you understand how hard
this has been for me too.

I'm sorry for how your life started out, living in that drab
house, all the secrets. But it's all for you, I hope you come to
understand that someday.

And soon we'll take you away from here, I promise. Your mom
and I have imagined what sort of home we'll build together, wood
fires in the winter and vegetable gardens in the summer, a
Goldilocks sort of home where the beds and chairs and porridge are
all just right. I close my eyes and I can see it. Right there. Clear as
hope.

> *Love,*
> *Dad*

I leaned forward in my chair, lips pressed between my teeth, trying to hold back a sob that escaped anyway, a keening like a rusty hinge. *Oh no, oh Nate.* He must have written this twenty-seven years ago, in the first year or two of Gabriel's life, expecting the day would come when Gabriel would be able to read it. And soon after, Nate must have realized that he never would.

But he'd saved this notebook, had kept writing inside it and hidden it here, inside a book from his own childhood. How could he have been able to stand keeping it, working daily beside this letter full of hope? But of course the idea of throwing it away must've felt even worse.

Was this whole notebook filled with letters? What else was hiding here?

I closed the notebook and was about to slot it back inside the shell of *The Lion, the Witch and the Wardrobe* when suddenly I realized. I pulled out the lock of hair Nate had hidden, a curl of reddish-brown hair tied by a blue ribbon. It was Gabriel's hair.

Such thick hair he'd had, haloing his head like a dark aura. I'd hardly been able to stand the idea of cutting it; it would, in a way, signify the end of his babyhood. But my mom had started making comments about needing to buy him bobble bands, so I finally relented just before his second birthday, half in tears, collecting all of it in a sheet of tissue paper, later acknowledging my own ridiculousness by throwing most of it away. Except one lock, which I'd combed out, tied in a ribbon, and tucked into a photo album.

The day after we learned what had happened to Gabriel, I'd sat with the album studying the minute details of each photo, each blue fleck in his irises, each dimple in his curled hand. Here dancing at a folk concert, arms outflung as he twirled in circles; here cuddled in my lap, playing with my face, touching my nose, my mouth, as if he was trying to memorize my features—in the same way I had been while looking through the album—knowing there'd be a time he wouldn't be there to see them. Chasing after bubbles, stuffing sand into his mouth, not enough photos and I'd hated myself for not having taken more. Wanting a photo for each day, every minute, like that could make up for the minutes without him. I'd finally turned to the end, the pocket where I'd saved random photos waiting to be sorted, and that's when I saw that the lock of hair I'd saved was gone.

I'd searched the shelf where I'd kept the album, pulled off all the books, even looked behind the bookcase, frantic and in tears. I must've asked Nate about it, so why wouldn't he have told me he'd taken it? *Why* would he have taken it?

Now I ran the hair across my palm, then across my lips, inhaling just in case there were any traces of Gabriel left. It was so brittle now, the color dulled by time. Not really Gabriel's hair anymore.

I remembered the evening after we'd first been brought in for questioning, sitting in the kitchen with Nate and my mother, all of us too nauseous to do anything more than stare into our coffee mugs. "It's like Kafka," Nate had said. And now thinking back, I had no idea whether or how he'd expanded on this statement. Like *The Trial,* where we'd been forced to stand judgment with no clue what we might have done? Or like *The Metamorphosis,* where we'd woken one morning inexplicably transformed? I tried to play through the conversation, but my mind kept stuttering over that one line, *It's like Kafka; It's like Kafka,* like one's brain gets stuck on a single refrain line to a song one doesn't really know. Maybe he'd just meant that this all felt unbearably surreal.

How could this still be so close under my skin? Something I could be distracted from sometimes, maybe more often than not, the way one can be distracted from a low-grade headache. But then something would happen: I'd see a woman holding her toddler's hand, or even just pass bags of diapers as I strode down a store aisle looking for tampons, and *bam,* a sledgehammer to my skull and I'd realize the grief had never left me after all. Just as strong in that moment as in the first days after Gabriel disappeared, when the disbelief-slash-terror had slithered and then plummeted into terror-slash-despair.

I could hardly remember the months after we knew he wasn't coming back. My only memory was of the reaction from other people, tentative at first, wondering if it was still necessary to start conversations with how're-you-doings, if it was okay to smile, talk about everyday mundanities. But over the weeks beginning to exert a subtle pressure, an obvious hinting that it was time to move on, focus on work, watch sitcoms, reciprocate invitations and favors. Everyone suffers tragedies, and life must go on.

At some point in those months Nate must've created this book, both of us hiding our grief from anyone who asked, from each other, even from our own selves. How many years had I been hiding?

I stood quickly and walked back to the front desk, where I sat at the computer, stared at the swirling screen saver a moment, and then checked email. Daniel had written, the subject line simply: *Apology.* Did this mean he was apologizing, or did he expect me to apologize? I studied the word, as if the curves and angles of the letters might be hiding some deeper meaning, then clicked on the reply email from the Hugo seller.

After studying the photos he'd sent, I forwarded them to Lester Jarvis with a note telling him it was the collection Nate had ordered and summarizing what the photos showed. I hadn't done this right; Nate sometimes pored for days over options, comparing and haggling. But the collection was in good shape, the price—as far as I could tell—reasonable. And Lester was desperate. Desperation, the barbed hook prized by everyone with potential clients, from attorneys to exterminators.

I rose and walked to the door, out into the dense fog of the late morning, the air heavy as damp sheets. I strode down the front steps and then started to run; running, the only drug I'd ever sought, substituting the emotional pain for physical pain, becoming only pulling muscles and seizing lungs. Now in old Keds and the jeans and sweater I'd worn for two days, hair and clothes soaked and skin clammy within three blocks, almost luxuriating in the pure, unadulterated grossness of it.

Old Town Truckee had been renovated over the past several years to satisfy an influx from the Bay area: new shops and galleries, old homes refurbished to look new and new homes refurbished to look old. But our part of Truckee was somewhere between sleepy and downtrodden, its stores vacated by the sinking economy, the only entertainment of note a seeming overabundance of churches and two diners where old men passed whole mornings at the bar in front of ESPN Classic and the same cup of cooling coffee.

On weekends, especially in the fall, the streets held as many meandering, probably lost, tourists as residents. To them I probably looked half insane, or maybe they'd view me as safari goers might view the local wildlife: Boondocks Woman.

I ran the route I usually took, which ended in a steep hill that on clear days rewarded one with a view of Donner Lake, named after the pioneers who'd eaten each other. But today I could barely see the houses on either side of the road. I stood a minute, staring into the nothingness as I caught my breath, hunched with my hands on my knees. Wishing I could just walk into the fog and dissipate into the minuscule water droplets. I undid the band holding back my hair and let the hair fall over my face, my breath slowing. Then stopping.

Soon I was fighting against my straining lungs and pressed my hands against my nose and mouth until my throat started to gulp for air. I exhaled and squatted with my eyes closed, palms flat on the damp gravel until I was sure I'd be able to stay upright, then turned and started the run back home.

At the house, a middle-aged couple, both with similar wheat-grass-textured hair, stood at the door, studying the store hours. I considered turning away, perhaps hiding behind a bush, but . . . we needed the money. I approached them. "I'm Chloe Sinclair, the owner," I said. "Did you want to come in?"

"Oh? Oh . . ." the woman said. Then glanced at her husband, who quickly added, "Oh no, just browsing." Immediately blushing as he realized this wasn't the correct dismissive phrase. "We can see you're busy," he amended, and then the two of them flipped identical shoulder-height waves before descending the steps and continuing down the street. It seemed Boondocks Woman was too much for them.

Inside, I took a long shower. It felt like I hadn't showered in a week, and I turned the water overly hot, disinfecting. Emerged pink and prickly, overcooked meatish, toweled off briskly and dressed and then walked downstairs. Back to the reading room. That barbed hook of desperation; the harder one tried to twist free, the more deeply it embedded.

I stared at the notebook a full minute, glared at it like it could be intimidated away, but then opened it to where I'd left off.

Adessar ~~ogon~~ abastheyr ~~hielad~~ ~~satod~~ ~~ayidyogo~~ ~~uodnigh~~ ~~attoret~~ ~~thewop~~. Fiess veojur santred ~~gotumene~~ ~~dufrompast~~ ~~alittiler~~ sponart ~~theyfweh~~ ~~adirstni~~ tod celeght ~~brathete~~

Dear Gabriel,

Today, you are two. I've just returned from a little party we had to celebrate, me and your mom and grandmother, the only people who know who you really are.

I wonder whether you still have the presents I brought you tucked away somewhere? They were the complete set of Pooh books (first edition), and a tiny baseball cap. Your mom gave me a look both pitying and angry; both "You don't have a clue about two-year-olds" and "How can you not have a clue about your son?" But you're a Sinclair child. You'll understand soon how precious the Pooh books are. And as for the cap, well, I guess I want you to be the sort of boy I never got to be, the sort who collects cards from bubble gum packs and knows the ins and outs of rules and stats. I think it'll make your life easier.

Everything about your life is going to change soon. It'll get harder in a way, I know that. But also, I think, better.

Your mom probably wouldn't want me talking to you about this. She's done what she can to make a haven for you, shield you. But I look at how I was brought up, and was it good for me? Entering the real world was a shock, I was completely unprepared. Why, when we think back on childhood, do we always think of it as so innocent anyway? I think children's book authors are more astute than parents, they know it's the bare truth that'll appeal to kids. Even in the Pooh books, although nothing happens to the animals worse than getting their behinds stuck in front doors, you can get some sense of the cruelty of life. Eeyore is the symbol for this, his misery and desolation. We laugh because it seems so excessive, but deep down part of us understands.

To tell you the truth, I'm not quite sure why I've written you these letters. I lie in bed every night and imagine all the fatherly advice I want to give, and then day comes and I realize it doesn't really add up to a cohesive picture. Loose threads for the future that I want so much to be able to tie together and hand you like a braided rug.

This particular rug is more of a badly sewn patchwork quilt, but I'm thinking if I write to you only on your birthdays, a year should be more than enough time for me to gather and braid the most important threads. We'll make this our secret, a father/son thing. When I'm done tonight I'll disguise this so that no one else can read it, hide it someplace only you will know to look. (Do you love code as much as I used to? It gives words a sort of weight and magic, I think.)

I'll show you this book as soon as you're old enough to decode and understand. Tell you everything I wish my own father had known to tell me.

But now you are only two, and the only wisdom I can give you
is to try and always see the world the way you see it now. The
world revolves around you, Gabriel. You are the center.

Love,

Dad

I closed the notebook and bit down hard on the side of my cheek to keep myself from crying or gouging out my eyes, both of which seemed equally necessary. Then opened it again to reread the letter slowly, slowly. My insides felt swollen and gummy, like I'd swallowed a can of caulk. All the anger at Nate I'd felt throughout Gabriel's life, all the blame, but he would have made such a wonderful father if he'd just been given the chance.

Where I'd been terrified to see what he might've been hiding from me, now I was suddenly hungry for it, sensing all I didn't know, the spaces left by whatever parts of his life he hadn't been willing to share. It felt raw, like something that had been torn from our marriage long ago, left it bleeding. I'd thought I had grown used to those holes, living around them without continually noticing their presence in the same way I'd thought I had grown used to grief. But tear too many pages from a book and the binding threads start to wear, to lose their hold on all that's left. And now, the missing pieces felt essential.

I hesitated, then turned the page. And found one line, not in code:

Today, you are three.

I stared at this, each of the words a separate claw swipe. *Today.* *You. Are. Three.* Gabriel, of course, was never three.

I traced my finger along the lettering in the notebook, Nate's rounded H's and J's and E's. I missed Nate, I missed him. I missed him. And why was I only realizing that now for the first time?

I reached slowly into my pocket for my cell phone. *I just wanted to hear your voice!* I'd say, the sort of thing that would've tilted the world under me if Nate had ever thought to say it to me. It suggested that the torn seams inside could be stitched neatly back to wholeness just by hearing a certain unique timbre and inflection. It suggested something vital.

But, we didn't talk that way with each other. And now there was *this* between us, my excavating of his secret. I did so much want to hear his voice, but for reassurance more than adoration, reassurance that he'd hidden things from me as loving protection, rather than distance. And the desperate undertone of this would probably infect my words, wring the life from them, so instead I set down the phone and turned to the next notebook page.

The first sentence of coded text contained both letters and numbers:

> *Diwa soyobor niufenetheor geye ivar1ee6
> 3meor2id oyonu heta tehecime fo tyrof wheyora
> tivek dofaneg?*

I set a finger under the next sentence of *The Lion, the Witch and the Wardrobe,* struggled a moment, then pulled my finger away.

There was something wrong. Crossing out letters from the next sentence left me with an unintelligible mass of letters. I paged to the next chapter in case he'd skipped ahead, tried letters from the foreword and each of the remaining chapters, feeling frantic, like I was chasing the wisps of something quickly slipping away.

But none of them worked. It seemed he'd used some other book to encode it.

8

ALL afternoon I tried to figure it out, treating the new page like an acrostic, searching for common letter combinations, *the* and *was, tr* and *sh*. I'd never been a puzzle person. Nate spent Sundays on the *New York Times* crossword, maybe to feel productive or distract himself from thinking about anything more real than a seven-letter word for sledgehammer. But I'd never understood how anybody could have the patience to sit for hours slotting letters and numbers into boxes just for the satisfaction of having done it. And now I was lost. Maybe this was some other form of code altogether. I circled the numbers 1-6-3-2. Could they be a key? Some way of translocating letters in the alphabet, substituting one letter for another?

Finally at six that night, dizzy from the intricate surgical dissection of letters, from disappointment and from not having eaten since breakfast, I gave up. I threw my pen across the table and rose, miming frustration in an attempt to feel something, but really just feeling broken.

Upstairs, I slipped in a CD of *La Bohème* and raised the volume as high as it would go, then squirted canned cheese on water crackers and crammed them into my mouth. Not truly inside of myself, this woman eating neon paste, but watching her from above. An artistic image of despair, titled "Mastication." This was the sort of person I was becoming without Nate, the kind who ate cheese that tasted like salted Softsoap.

Nate and I had seen *La Bohème* at the San Francisco Opera ten years ago, sat through the whole thing holding hands. I'd glanced over at him several times and seen him with his eyes fixed, program clutched at his chest, wearing the same expression I remembered from his childhood back in the days he'd prayed with his mother. Like he was actually hearing words from God.

I closed my eyes and imagined sitting there with him beside me, the press of his fingers, the music surrounding and filling us. I'd fallen back in love with him there, watching his face, the stage lights brightening his eyes and shadowing his cheeks. And toward the end of Act 4, as Mimi, minutes before her death, had sung with Rodolfo about their former happiness, Nate rested the side of his head against mine and we sat like that till the curtain call. When he finally pulled away to stand and applaud, I had felt the loss of it like a slap.

Now, when the canned cheese cramming started making me gag, I threw the box and can into the trash. Sitting at the kitchen table, I pressed my hands against my eyes as if that had even a remote chance of helping, then pulled them away again when the lack of distraction only made things worse. Without fully thinking what I was doing, I turned off the CD player, pulled out my cell, and dialed the Sinclairs. Cecilia answered. "It's Chloe," I said.

"Oh! Oh . . ." she said. "I guess you're wondering why Nate didn't call."

"He did call, actually. This morning." Had it really been only that morning? "He didn't tell you?"

"He called you! Well good, that's great. No, we've hardly talked today. He's been so busy, you know, cataloguing books."

I frowned at this, at the odd forced cheer in her voice. "Still cataloguing?"

"Well yes, sure, there are so many of them. You remember Mom's library. It could take him, I don't know, a week maybe."

I stared at the kitchen table, a ring of dried coffee perhaps a week old. Perhaps Nate's. "Is there something else going on, Cecilia? You're not telling me something."

"What? No, there's nothing. I mean I'm a little frazzled, we had an episode today where Daddy soiled himself in church, started pulling off his clothes, and his body, well, it's something nobody's eyes should've been subjected to. Church these days is always so hard anyway, everybody staring at us, the hate and horror; nobody's even willing to sit in the same pew, so this lovely moment was just icing. That could be what you're sensing."

I tried to keep myself from picturing it, feeling a swirl of embarrassment and disgust and dark pity, for all of us. "Can I talk to Nate?" I said.

Silence, then, "Gosh, I'm sorry, Chloe, he went to bed already. And he was so tired I really don't want to wake him up."

"It's not even seven o'clock!"

"I know, but I don't think he's been sleeping well. And with all the work he's been doing, it's just so exhausting."

"All that cataloguing of books, right. Listen, I need you to get him. Tell him I insisted, that it's an emergency." I had no idea really what I'd say to him. I only had some vague thought that with just hearing his voice my mind would untangle, that by studying the words he chose I'd be able to filter out whichever book he'd chosen for his encoding, like his dialogue might be a code for the code.

But after a long pause Cecilia said, "Oh hell."

I felt a twist of fear. "What do you mean, oh hell?"

"I'm sorry, don't hate me."

I sank into the chair next to the coffee ring, tried to focus all my attention on it, the everydayness of it, as if it could ground me, a totem, a mantra.

"Because I have to tell you something. Chloe, I was lying. Lord forgive me, I've been lying this whole time and I'm awful at it, Nate should've known that. I'm so sorry, Chloe, but the truth is that he isn't here. He left three days ago."

"What? What the hell do you mean?"

"He wasn't here when I talked to you yesterday, and when he called you this morning he was calling from somewhere else."

"But where did he go? If he's not helping you, then why isn't he back home!"

"I don't know, he just left suddenly without saying where he was going. Said there was something he had to do and he asked me to lie to you if you called, tell you he was out or too busy to talk." Her voice trailed off, wearily. But when she finally continued there was a thickness to her tone, tears or anger, maybe both. "That's all I know except that he said he'd be back here within a week, which is this Thursday. I'll make sure he calls you then."

There was something she wasn't telling me, I knew that, something hidden I sensed like a staccato beneath her words. She was a bad liar, yes, but from the edge of anger in her tone, anger that, for some reason, felt directed at me, I knew she had no intention of telling me the truth. "I'm coming down there," I said.

Silence, then simply, "You don't want to be here, Chloe."

"I'm leaving tomorrow. I should be there by one or two." And then I slapped the phone shut and stood to stuff it into my pocket.

Nate wasn't in Redbridge? Then where the hell was he? Could it just be that he was so upset by seeing his father that he'd needed to get away? Couldn't stand coming home to a woman he knew despised this now broken man he'd once loved?

But no, Cecilia had said there was something he "needed to do." So what was it?

I walked fitfully through the house, dodging clothes and shoes worn and discarded, traipsing across leaves fallen from an under-watered ficus. All the times I'd sensed the sharp angles inside of Nate, angles he hid from the outside world, even in childhood they'd been there. But taking up far more of him in the years after Gabriel's death, when a question I asked would be met with a certain stillness and there'd be a weird flicker behind his eyes, a kind of crystallization like he was focusing inward, on some invisible world under his skin.

I strode through the hallway and down to the dark shop. Without turning on the lights, I walked into the main room, the room we called Great-Aunt Edna's Library because that's how it felt to us, like the library of someone's antiquated tea-with-cream-drinking great-aunt. And I stood there with my hands at my sides, feeling the press of books around me.

Cliché to say these books felt like my friends, but at times, the lonely times, that's exactly what they were, my only and best. They were my shelter; I could enter and tuck myself against the margins facing in, forget my loneliness. All of them from memoir to metaphysics, but especially the books I associated with events in my life at the time I'd read them, and held as close and personal as the events themselves. Books I'd loved and shared with Nate, books he'd loved and shared with me, standing here with them I felt every day of our thirty-seven years together. Each book echoed against specific segments of my past, each with its own mark on our history, marks as palpable to me as photos in an album.

A. S. Byatt's *Possession,* which I'd read in a long swoon ten years ago, then handed off to Nate and read again, lying beside him in bed while he turned the pages, glancing at his face to see his reaction to my favorite sections and twists. Updike's Rabbit series, all of which we'd reread over twenty years ago when *Rabbit at Rest* came out, following Rabbit through love and loss and acceptance and the progression of the decades. *In Cold Blood,* which had chilled me, the spare style as well as the story, which I'd only been able to bring myself to finish the year my mother died, using the horror of it as a temporary escape from pain.

And then the book Nate had written, his fairy tale to Gabriel, drafted in the months he'd spent away from us and then revised and submitted for publication as an attempt at healing after we learned Gabriel was gone. The book had been on best-seller lists for years, but each time his publisher tried to convince him to write sequels, he'd put them off. This, he'd said, was the only book inside him.

Those years his novel was selling were the best in our marriage. The store was thriving, we hosted theme nights and holiday parties and book clubs, we had extra money for advertising and taking chances because people actually *read* books in those days. We brought people in to improve the renovations we'd tried to take on ourselves five years before, replacing pine shelves and oak flooring with cherry, opening up fireplaces and installing antique sconces. We took trips to New York and Vancouver, and then Nate surprised me with a literary tour of the UK, from the Pennines where the Brontës lived to Beatrix Potter's Windermere, through Austen's Mansfield Park and Northanger Abbey.

It was such a heady time, felt like everything was still ahead of us, so we were able to focus our attention on looking forward, instead of on keeping ourselves from looking back; this wonderful life we felt was due us and therefore destined. I remembered that Thanksgiving, we'd just decorated for the holidays and Nate lay with me under the tree holding my hand, both of us looking up at the lights. "They're like stars," he said, then turned to me. "Make a wish."

"For what?"

"You need me to tell you what to wish for? That's kind of sad."

"Why sad? It just means I'm content."

"Are you?" He paused, then said, "You know what I've been thinking? What if we get really rich? What if the store takes off so well we can open franchises? Or what if the book turns into another *Neverending Story*? We were pretty well off when I was a kid, Mom never talked about it but I think she inherited a million or more on top of the house, and I know what it's like to be able to afford extravagant stuff. But it's never really been *my* extravagant stuff."

"We'd probably live just like this if we were rich," I said. "Don't you think?"

"Like this, plus diamond tennis bracelets and summer homes in Capri." He brought my hand to his mouth and spoke against it. "But yeah, I guess there comes a point when you have so much already it's almost scary. You're on this tall tower made up of precarious pieces, a best-selling novel, a successful business, a beautiful home and beautiful wife, and you imagine losing them like a Jenga game, pull out a block and everything topples down."

What had I said to this? Did I tell him he was all I needed, rich or poor, one of those cliché answers that make one groan but are secretly reassuring? Probably not, because it would've felt like I was betraying Gabriel, my only real wish and need. But I should have said it. Because at that time in our lives I was finally starting to find the beginnings of, if not happiness, at least fulfillment. And he deserved to know that.

There was a sound from outside now, the crack of a breaking twig; I watched headlights dilate as they approached, watched the taillights fade. And then I turned back to the hall and walked to the reading room.

I lifted Nate's notebook and ran my fingers across the page, scrutinized the letters as if time—or new knowledge—might have deposited some key that would help me see them with new eyes. Which it didn't, of course. The man who'd written the text was himself as indecipherable as Arabic or Mandarin, so how could I ever hope to understand?

Maybe I was thinking too hard. Maybe the numbers were just a date used in a book, part of the encoding meant to be crossed out. Maybe something important had happened in 1632, some battle I wasn't aware of, described in a book I wasn't aware of. After the Mayflower, before the Great Plague . . .

Oh this was ridiculous, too hard for me. I should go up to bed, maybe bring a novel, mindless chick lit about headstrong single gals finding success and love in the big city. Or no, an old favorite, *The Little Princess*, which I could wrap around myself. A bear hug sort of book. Oh I should, I should, but instead I walked to the front desk slowly, like I was navigating an unsteady floor or trying to balance a plate on my head. I sat at the desk and turned on the computer.

The first thing I found was a novel by Eric Flint actually titled

1632, part of an alternate history series, where a West Virginia community traveled back in time to the seventeenth century. But the book had been published just a few years ago, and if he'd been writing each year on Gabriel's birthday he must have encoded this text well before that. I needed something published before the nineties.

There were several battles in 1632, of Wiesloch, Rain, Lech, and Lützen, part of the Thirty Years War, but none seemed especially relevant. There was a 1632 Code of Federal Regulations, rules about flammability standards for mattresses; Vermeer and John Locke were born and Maryland was founded ... Oh, this was pointless. For all I knew it wasn't even text used for encoding but actually part of his letter to Gabriel. I set my elbows on the desk, heels of my hands against my eyes, and exhaled. Okay, I thought, Okay.

I switched browser tabs so I could check my email, and when I saw the unread message from Daniel I stared at it a minute, and then picked up the phone.

"Bookdrop, can I help you?" His voice was brusque, no-nonsense; it was one of the things that appealed most to me about him. He was so grounded in the everyday, so practical, his life governed by To Do lists. Exactly the opposite of Nate, and there was something so soothing in feeling like I knew him completely.

"Hi," I said. "It's me. And I miss you."

"Chloe." His voice softened. "You read my email."

I hesitated, then said, "Thanks for sending it."

"I meant what I said, completely. I woke up this morning and I felt like such a complete, jealous, son-of-a-bitch tool, it made me want to bludgeon my own head. This has been such a hard time for you, I know that, and I just want to make sure you know I'm your friend more than anything else. Everything else is just the icing. Or not even the icing, the little candy confetti on top of the icing."

"Thanks, Daniel. And I promise you, it's more than confetti. At the very least, it's those fireworky kind of birthday candles."

"Ha, that almost turns me on. So how're you feeling? Did you talk to Cecilia?"

"Yeah, I've talked to her twice." I touched the computer screen, wiped away a scrim of dust. "And Nate called this morning, they told me some of what's going on."

He waited, then said, "And?"

"There's really not much worth talking about, although I know they're keeping things from me. His dad's sick and that's supposedly why he went out there, to help Cecilia out. But he's apparently left Cecilia's home and she won't tell me where he went."

"Seriously? When's he coming back?"

"I don't know for sure, a week, maybe more . . . It's so ridiculous, the whole thing. Why won't they tell me? Do they think I'm going to come after him or something?" I thought of Daniel sitting now in his brightly lit shop, music in the background, the bright jazz he liked. All the books laid faceup on rectangular tables organized by category and price, and I wanted to be there with him, stack and sort alongside him like we were toddlers playing a nesting game. Could I forget all this while I was there? What if I left here forever? If I moved in with Daniel, someone who loved me the way it seemed Nate had forgotten how to, could I repress the past thirty-seven years the way I'd managed to repress much of our childhood?

As if he'd read my mind, Daniel said, "Listen, I'm about to close up here. You want me to come by? Or you could come over if you need to get out of there."

For a second I considered it, imagined showing him the notebook, the relief of having someone to talk to. But I knew that would only be using him to vent my frustrations. Having Daniel here now would feel like an intrusion, and having him mired inside all this would taint him. I needed him wholly separate from this in the same way in childhood I'd needed my home life separated from the Sinclairs. It was probably best for both of us if I didn't see him until whatever was going to happen with Nate had already happened, until I decided for sure how I wanted to live the rest of my life. "I'm sorry," I said, "but I'm beat and I probably look like hell right now. I just called because I wanted to hear your voice." The words I'd wanted to say to Nate but had known would feel wrong; spoken to Daniel they felt not only true but also benevolent, like I was handing him a gift.

"Okay, that almost makes up for not wanting to see me."

"So keep talking, okay? My mind's in a bad place and I need distraction. Just . . . tell me about your day or what you dreamed last night, or your recipe for sangria, I don't even care what. Just talk."

So Daniel started to tell me about the book he was currently reading, a collection of interviews with defectors from North Korea. I tried to lose myself in the stories, the strength of the people inside them and the deep undertones in his voice. But as he talked I found myself scrolling again through search pages, skimming titles casually now, giving them no more attention than I would skimming sales in a grocery circular. Until I saw it.

I was born in the Year 1632 . . .

"That's it," I said, my brain doused by the memory of a beach, a nearly full moon, a confession. Of course.

"That's what?"

"*Robinson Crusoe.* I mean, obviously," I said, then, "I'm sorry, I have to go."

"What's going on, Chloe?"

"I'm sorry, Daniel, I'll call you." I hung up and stood.

It had been one of the first "adult" books we read. As we'd grown older it got harder to find books we adored. I spent hours scouring the children's section of the library, but all the books had begun to feel derivative, showing me people I'd already met, lands I'd already visited. I was hungry for more knowledge, more understanding of how the world worked. And where I'd once loved how kids' books showed the extremes of "good" and "evil," now I wanted more, reasons behind actions, complexities that those books didn't even try to touch. The stacks of books filling the rest of the library started to feel like secrets being kept from me.

These days adolescents aren't faced with that same impasse; they can transition through the world of YA, progress gradually from the more childlike to the more adultlike. But there weren't any real YA books at the time; publishers seemed to think teenagers were incapable of reading. So seeing my frustration, Mrs. Webb, the children's librarian, led me to the adult classics, thinking they were safest for young eyes. Which of course depended on one's definition of "safe." A crazy aunt locked in an attic, a spinster dressed in a wedding dress and one shoe with all her clocks stopped at twenty to nine, a governess in a gloomy English mansion caring for a progressively bizarre girl and boy; these were the worlds I'd been missing, the twisted people on twisted adventures that I'd longed for without even truly realizing they were what I longed for. *Robinson Crusoe* was tame by comparison but we loved it despite its politeness, the adventure of a man taming nature. The stuff of daydreams.

Now I walked through the store, searching, looking in literature and then nature guides, and finally found the book in the History section, between *Walden* and a text on the Civil War. I pulled it out and brought it to the reading room, my heart jittering so fiercely I wouldn't have been surprised if it jackhammered its way out through my ribs.

Why would he have switched to using a different book for his code? My guess was that the tone of his notes had changed; he'd gone from writing letters to Gabriel to writing to himself after Gabriel's death. *The Lion, the Witch and the Wardrobe,* the story we'd reenacted in the summer we met, and *Robinson Crusoe,* a story we'd reenacted on the night of our first kiss.

Had using it been comforting somehow? The book had given us one beautiful night in the midst of what had been one of the darkest times in his childhood, a rose growing out of a sewer, not really eclipsing the fact that it was fed by sewage. But maybe most memories of childhood bring comfort, even when they're fraught with pain. Not just because we're nostalgic, but also because they're part of who we became, something we understand—or at least think we do—more completely than we can ever understand our own adulthood. Maybe the understanding is what we're nostalgic for.

It was the best and worst of times, the prettiest and ugliest. I'd tried not to think back on that spring, but when I did, the main flavor of my memory had been fear.

We were fourteen when Mrs. Sinclair was forced to start on dialysis. I'd known she was sick, but I kind of imagined it must be with some romantic-seeming eighteenth-century sickness, consumption or diphtheria. But no, Sophia had suffered her whole adulthood from lupus, an ugly disease with the ugliest of names. And when we were fourteen, the ugliness began to envelop every part of the Sinclairs' lives.

PART IV

IT BLOWS *a* MOST
DREADFUL HURRICANE

9

WATCHING someone get sicker is like seeing the video of someone doomed, flailing in the ocean while being pulled slowly from shore, deeper, deeper, gradually disappearing. Needing to rescue them but unable to do anything but watch.

Mrs. Sinclair had been weak for as long as I'd known her, suffering from intense head and muscle aches, napping several hours a day. She spent most of her pain-free hours with us, homeschooling, reading, and crafting, but as the years went on her time grew more and more fragmented, she lost attention easily, was no longer able to hike with us through the woods, or even spend much time on her feet at all.

Every afternoon as I biked to the Sinclairs', I repeated the healing prayer Grace had taught me, over and over like a chant: "In the name of Jesus, drive out all infirmity and sickness from her body, turn this weakness to strength, sorrow into joy!" And sometimes it seemed to work, I'd find her on the lawn with them gardening or teaching or smiling as she watched them play, but other times the lawn would be empty. And because I'd been warned against coming into the house without them leading me, in case Mr. Sinclair was home unexpectedly, on those days I wouldn't see them at all.

The dialysis meant that Mrs. Sinclair was at the hospital three days a week, and when she was home she was so tired and nauseous that she wasn't really there at all. Her belly grew pregnant with retained fluids, like an opened umbrella under her shirt. She made jokes about it. They weren't funny.

Even when she was in wrenching agony, the pinch in her face seemed more anguished regret than anguished pain. And in response, Grace, Nate, and Cecilia surrounded their mother whenever she was home, as if guarding her from something. Death, I suppose. You could hear it, the worming squelch of the invading inflammation, and underneath that, throughout the Sinclairs' home, a low hum of fear.

At first they all kept up with the housework Mrs. Sinclair was unable to do, but after a while it seemed beside the point. Surfaces hazed with dust; as we traipsed shoeless through the house the bottom of our socks turned increasingly darker shades of gray. Mr. Sinclair stocked the refrigerator with pounds of lunch meat and sandwich bread and under-ripe tomatoes, and this was their lunch and dinner. The meat grew steadily slimier and gamier, but was almost never thrown away.

Even our games grew darker. Debating hypotheticals, the Would You Rather game: Would you rather gouge out your own eyeballs or cut off your own legs? Be mauled by a bear, face destroyed and ugly but alive, or eaten quickly by an alligator? Find a body that had been decomposing underwater or one only recently decapitated? Debating the pros and cons of each, helping one another imagine in intricate, grotesque detail how these scenarios would look or feel. We were good at imagining the unimaginable.

And then there were the plays. For years, ever since the squelched Narnia play, we'd been acting out the books we read. These plays were nowhere near as elaborate as our Narnia production. We condensed the stories, no stage set, and only the barest of costumes (brambles in Nate's hair when he played young Heathcliff, a ribbon around Grace's neck when she played the doomed Beth March). Always the stories we chose, either consciously or unconsciously, included a character who died young. Always that character was played by Grace.

Sometimes we wrote the scripts, but usually we just winged it. Improvising felt more natural, immersive. If we really knew the characters, understood their motivations, the lines and reactions came as naturally as if they were our own. With no effort at all we could make ourselves cry.

In time, though, we stopped acting through the whole story, focusing only on the best parts. We dared each other to duels with long, curved carving knives, or set large signal fires à la *Lord of the Flies,* which we only just managed to contain. Playing Finny and Gene, climbing a tree by the deepest part of Briar Creek, and jumping. The deepest part, but this was a *creek,* not a river, not nearly deep enough to be safe. And of course that's what we loved about it. The jump required precision, three feet off-center in any direction and we might meet Finny's fate, break a leg, or die, or break a leg and then die.

When I was eleven or twelve I first came up with the idea of dares, giving each other badges for completing them in the way Girl Scouts collect badges for sewing or field sports, wanting something tangible to mark our bravery. Together we made the badges out of kraft paper circles and colored pencils, depicting ourselves in precarious situations. I collected my badges inside my old Baby Tender Love, popping her head off daily to dump them out and admire them, my medals of honor.

The games continued for years, much longer than they probably should have. Now we were old enough to know better, and past the age when collecting homemade badges should've held any appeal, but we continued, maybe out of boredom or a need for distraction. Or maybe because we were searching for the exhilaration and enchantment with life that we'd had in childhood and now sensed was ebbing, perhaps even already lost.

The most dangerous of these games was at the train tracks, our Anna Karenina dare. The badges were orange twist tie tracks glued to black paper, a small circle set over them wearing wide, scared Sharpie eyes. The badges were horrible-looking, reflected the utter fear of the situation, and I sometimes lined them side by side along my leg, wondering how many times a girl could avoid death before God threw up His hands and gave her what she seemed to be asking for.

The train passed at five-ten, and so at 5:05 we'd lie on the tracks, holding hands and waiting. Sometimes we'd hear the whistle from somewhere behind the line of trees, sometimes we had no warning until we felt a rumble in the tracks. There was an overpass about fifty yards from where we lay, and we used that as a marker. When the nose of the train shot past it we'd grab each other and scramble away, just in time.

I say "we," but really after a while it was only me and Nate playing these more dangerous games. Cecilia, we felt, was too reckless, and Nate had decided that Grace was too old, was sure she'd only meet our suggestions with narrowed eyes and Don't-you-dares.

Me and Nate. Before this I'd never spent much time alone with him. I felt closest to Cecilia because we were the same age and our personalities were so similar. And besides the fact that he was a boy, something about Nate scared me a little at the same time as it intrigued me, his intensity, the way he'd look at me sometimes, unblinking, a questioning sort of look when I had no idea what that question was or whether he expected me to answer it in some way.

But in the hours we spent alone those weeks when I was fourteen, talking about God, dreams, books—of course books—feeling out the shape and meaning of life without fully understanding that's what we were doing, I got to know him.

And then on a wet spring afternoon, hiking to the tracks through ferns waterlogged and drooping like hooked fish, Nate said, "I've stopped believing."

I waited for him to go on, but he just shoved his hands into his pockets and walked faster, like he was trying to get away from the words.

"Believing . . ."

"In God, or at least in the Bible. Maybe I never really believed it."

In all the years I'd been with the Sinclairs, I'd never discussed my own beliefs, which had become, in the end, nonbeliefs. It hadn't always been that way; Mrs. Sinclair tried hard to teach me faith with her Bible lessons, and I grabbed onto it like I was drowning. All children believe in magic and I was perhaps more firmly entrenched in fantasy than most, reaching for that all-powerful force that could perform miracles, add music and color to the desolation, could save us.

But that all changed the fall I turned ten, when Mrs. Sinclair pulled me aside and sat me on the couch. "I've been wanting to talk with you for a long while," she said, "but I wasn't sure if it was my place. I mean I know it's *not* my place, actually, but I'm bring-ing it up anyway because I want to feel like I've tried." With this odd preamble, she knelt in front of me to take my hands. "I know you weren't raised in the faith, Chloe, and you've probably never even stepped inside a church."

I had, in fact, stepped inside the First Lutheran Church the year before, on a trip downtown with my mother. Mom needed to pee, and it was the only bathroom one didn't need to be a customer to use. Waiting for her, I'd stood a long while gazing at the tall stained glass window, Christ watching stoically back, naked except for a blue loincloth. I'd wondered if, wherever He was now, He was embarrassed at being depicted in His underwear. And I wanted to tell Mrs. Sinclair about this, but knew in the current context of this discussion that visit wouldn't be relevant.

"I'm hoping," she said, "that you might want to visit our church on Sundays. Maybe not every week, but often enough that you could see if it's something you feel drawn to. Your mom should come too, we'd love to have her there!"

I remembered my mother's reaction after the first time she'd met Mrs. Sinclair. "Her dress!" she said. "She's trying to eradicate any indication she might have boobs! Dress, shoes, and that hair . . . What, is she auditioning for *Little House on the Prairie*?"

If Mrs. Sinclair was anyone else, my mom would've thought her style was weird maybe, but in an amusing way. But there'd been something darker than that in her tone, a derision. Probably from jealousy—I'd sensed it even then—resentment that I spent more time with Mrs. Sinclair than with her.

I imagined my mother in church mimicking the way the Sin-clairs prayed, the way they shouted certain words like *Lorrrrrd* and *Jeeesus* and *fiiiire*. I saw her throwing her hands in the air, throwing her head back and screaming, wriggling her hips like her body was being overcome by the Holy Spirit, and felt my face flush. "My mom can't," I said, "she's busy Sundays. But maybe I could try."

"For me, being surrounded by tens of people praying is one of the quickest, most immediate ways to really feel God. He's like a blanket around your shoulders."

I tried to imagine this, God as a blanket. It seemed an almost insulting image, like saying He was a stapler.

"See, I've always thought you'd come to us for a reason. I guess you know I haven't told Mr. Sinclair about your visits?"

Of course I knew, from the elaborate mechanisms we all went through to conceal any suggestion of my existence. Everything I created and didn't want to bring home was stuffed to the bottom of outdoor garbage cans; dishes I used were promptly washed, dried, and put away, and under the guise of trying to time dinner, Grace made nightly calls to the church office for an estimate of when Mr. Sinclair would be home. So I knew they were ashamed of me, that I was, as Cecilia had relayed years ago, "an influence."

"Keeping that kind of secret probably seems wrong to you; I'm essentially lying to my husband. And yes, of course normally it would be wrong, but I want you here because I think God brought you to us for a reason, His way of helping you find and come to love Jesus. Does that make any sense to you?"

I nodded mutely. I'd thought she wanted me there because she loved me.

I remembered the times over the past two years that Grace had patted my shoulder, told me how good it was that I'd become their friend. And suddenly everything took on new meaning. "If I go to church," I said, "if I go every week, would that mean Mr. Sinclair won't mind me coming here?"

Mrs. Sinclair had looked down at my hands in hers, squeezed them, and then looked back into my eyes. "Chloe," she said softly, "this is a lot more important than Mr. Sinclair, don't you see? If you don't come to faith in Christ while you're alive, then you won't be allowed to join Him in heaven when you die."

That night, lying in bed, thinking about all of this, a hole opened inside me and gradually God started leaking out. Even though the mystery of the Sinclairs' faith was part of what attracted me to them, I'd finally realized it was actually at the core of our separateness. The belief and understanding was in their hearts, they'd been born with it firmly planted there, whereas after years of trying to wrap myself around it and pull it inside, in the end I'd only been able to touch the periphery. I'd told Mrs. Sinclair later that Momma had forbidden me from going to church but that I still wanted to learn. In part to make her happy, keep her from thinking she had failed, but also because I no longer fully trusted her. I was scared she might tell me to leave and never come back.

"You're the only person I'm telling about the not believing," Nate said now. "You can't tell anybody else."

I knew what this meant to him, the immensity of this confidence. All his life Nate had looked at every event past and present, every plan for the future, through the glasses of religion. So this meant that everything would change, everything that his world was based on. And it meant I was the only one in this world he trusted.

"Think about it," he said. "I think probably everybody has this feeling like their life isn't enough. Like there's things they want that they can't even put a name to. Think about the books we used to love best. They're about people on earth who find some kind of doorway into another world where you can talk to animals or meet unicorns. You read those books and your life gets bigger, but you realize the book's going to end eventually and you'll still be stuck in the real world. That's why people invented heaven, to convince themselves they won't always be stuck in this world that isn't enough."

"Also people want to believe bad guys are going to be punished eventually," I said.

"Exactly! Bible stories are just like Greek myths or like fairy tales. So fine, I understand that. People like listening to stories, but by the time you grow up, you realize stories are just words. You don't really believe the stories are true unless you're crazy, and that's what religion is, a craziness."

I reached for Nate's hand, held it as we walked on. Showing him I knew how hard the admission had been. And I could feel the new understanding pulling like a string between us.

"Real people's lives don't have happy endings." His voice sounded distant, toneless. "Dad pretends it all has meaning, and I pretend alongside him because I know it would kill him if I questioned everything he's based his life on, but I don't know if he even believes it anymore. He can try citing the Book of Job, say it's only because God's testing us so He can reward us in heaven. But why would He do this to my mom who believes with all her heart and hurts for everybody but her own self? That 'test' is just another word for pointless cruelty. And all I can say is I hope there isn't a God, because if there was I'd hate Him. If He called me up now and asked if I was worthy of heaven, I'd kick Him between the legs."

I squeezed his hand. Feeling what I knew was an entirely inappropriate sense of happiness. It was wrong, and I didn't really understand it, but there it was.

Until he spoke again. Said something that would haunt me for days. "It makes you wonder what's the point."

"The point?"

"Of dealing with all this crap. It makes you wonder what's the point of living. And Grace, Grace—" He stopped short then, pulled his hand away as we reached the clearing, approaching the train tracks, and pressed the back of his arm to my chest to keep me from going farther. "I've figured it out," he said, "why we're doing this, all the dares."

I ran a finger along my palm, feeling the warm sweat he'd left behind. I'd thought I knew why: for the rush of it, the way my heart hammered rapidly and then, in the last seconds, plunged through my feet. A reminder that I was not just living but ALIVE, and the feeling was a red-tinged, jagged-edged imitation of joy.

But Nate said, "It's like strength training before a fight. Our insides are stronger now than most people's."

What fight? I thought, but didn't ask.

"Like this." He took hold of my hand again and stood with me overlooking the tufts of rye grass and pink sprays of milkweed along the edges of the overpass. For a full minute we stood there, and then he said, "Just do what I tell you, okay? Do what I say and don't question it." He nodded at the tracks. "I want you to look at the spot on the tracks where we usually wait, and think how a train's going to be passing over it. Really picture it, all those people inside looking out, their briefcases and knapsacks on their laps, how heavy the walls are, the seats and floors, all together I bet it weighs thousands of tons. The train's driven over that same exact spot where our heads have been." He turned to me. "So okay, here's the question. On a scale of one to ten, where ten's the most afraid you've ever been, how scared are you?"

"Seriously?" There were too many possible numbers on that scale. I didn't think fear had that many gradations. But I shrugged and said, "Four," a more or less random choice.

"Four," he repeated, walking us to the edge of the track, our toes touching the front rail tie. "Okay, now imagine two people, not us, lying here. And the train's getting closer, they're screaming but they don't get up, and then they stop screaming." He looked at me. "How scared are you now?"

"That's sick, Nate."

"It's not real, just something to imagine. Like the fake people in our Would You Rather game."

"Would you rather I kick you or barf on you?" I said, but I rolled my eyes to the sky, a pseudo-annoyed concession. "Okay, seven."

He gave a sharp nod and said, "Perfect." As if there'd been an actual right answer. "Now think back to when you were just imagining the weight of the train. Does that still feel like a four?"

I studied his face, realizing where he was going with this. He thought you could bench-press with fear, build up your fear muscle so that over time, subjecting yourself to heavy enough terrors, you'd grow calluses, a shell. Fear throws a right jab, left hook, unexpected knee to the groin, and even if you can't fight back you still win.

"C'mon." He knelt on the tracks and directed me to lie beside him, our heads against a wooden tie. He swiveled to face me, hesitated, then said, "Listen, we're going to do this different. What I want is for you to not move, even when you see the train, okay? Just trust me."

I stiffened, tried to pull away, but he grabbed my hand tighter and snaked his other arm under my back. "I want to try something, Chloe. I promise I'll get us both out of the way if you promise not to move."

Around us the air was heavy with fog, muffling the timpani rattle of cicadas. We were probably going to die, but none of this felt real so it hardly mattered. I held my breath, feeling his arm under me, the wiry muscle. He put our joined hands on my stomach, and I felt suddenly like I was being led in a dance, the rumba maybe, bracing to be dipped back through the earth.

"Scale of one to ten?" he said.

"Eight," I whispered, and he squeezed my hand tighter.

"Now," he said, "here's what you do. Focus on that fear, open it and wrap it around yourself head to toe, like a blanket. Keep it there when the train comes and you'll see how the rest of you goes away, your heart stops beating and your brain stops thinking, and all you are is the fear. You're strong."

Nate had done this before, I could sense it. Had lain here alone on the tracks, maybe each time letting the train get closer, taunting. Afraid of pain, the sudden stunning impact, but probably not afraid of death. And now he'd brought me here because he sensed death didn't frighten me either.

I stared blankly up into the sky, white mottled with gray like it was growing mold. Maybe heaven was up there, maybe just the planets and galaxies and black holes we were told about but would never see. Or maybe there was nothing. "Six," I said, and I thought I could feel him smile.

The train. I could feel it before we saw it, a humming expectation, and staring up at the sky, that's what I tried to wrap myself inside rather than the fear, that low hum as Nate's arm tightened around my waist, maybe in preparation for saving me, maybe to keep me from saving myself.

"Okay," he whispered as the rumbling became a rattling, the train lights and then the engine appearing through the shadow of the overpass. "Okay, okay, okay," he said as his body stiffened around mine. I thought I could feel the air compressing between us and the train, the air and time and his arms compressing, the Doppler effect, molecules becoming thick as ice and I was suddenly aware that I couldn't move. I had only a few compressed seconds to ponder this, but as I did I realized it was strangely comforting. Maybe this was how everyone felt just before death, a letting go.

How close did the train get? Certainly within fifty feet, maybe within twenty. All I knew is that I could see it at a startling angle, the stained yellow paint at its front, the rusty gray gears underneath, that I noticed it was high enough off the tracks we probably could have slid right under if we'd been parallel to the rails, perhaps only losing a nose. That was the thought I had as Nate suddenly threw himself on top of me and I was sure he was pinning me down, against the tracks. Our bodies would be mangled together; whoever prepared us for the funeral wouldn't be able to sort out whose legs and fingers were whose. They'd have to guess and they'd probably get it wrong. Forever after our families would come to our graves and cry over my arms and his legs, my ears and his chin.

That's what I was thinking, only vaguely concerned, when Nate gave a roaring cry, yanked me to my seat, and dove.

Across the far end of the tracks, rolling down an embankment through the wet grass, the train squealing like it knew it had lost, careening above the rails where we'd just lain, the sound of the engine loud enough to rattle inside my skull, then slowly fading. And then, silence.

Nate was lying on top of me, breathing heavily. I stared up through the mop strings of my wet hair, not sure if I wanted to cry or laugh or both. Feeling the solidity of Nate's body, more solid even than the earth. He pressed his cheek against mine, held it there, breath heavy in my ear, then slowly lifted his head.

For a full minute he stayed like that, gazing into my eyes, unmoving. And then he touched my cheek with his thumb, his whole face softening, questioning.

I looked back into his eyes, feeling my breath catch. *Yes,* I think I wanted to say, but instead I just said his name, *"Nate,"* maybe too loud, maybe in a way that sounded like a warning.

A flush stained his cheeks and he stiffened and rolled onto his back. Only the backs of our hands were touching, until he pulled his hand away and folded his arms over his chest. Both of us lying there, looking up at the sky, unspeaking.

On a scale of one to ten, a one hundred.

10

I didn't go back to the Sinclairs' for over a week. Pretending to myself that it was because there were finals to study for, term papers to write. When in actuality I spent much of my time watching soaps, at first amused by the ridiculousness of the story lines, but soon getting sucked into the tragedy and romance of it. And, I met Holden Caulfield.

It was a fluke; the book was on a reading list along with twenty other titles, provided in my English class as options for our last paper. I'd only chosen it because it was shorter than the other choices, and considering Mr. Perry's assignments the rest of the semester (he held deep respect for the swampy sludge of Melville and Milton), I didn't hold out much faith in his ability to select books that were actually readable. But—as all teenagers do—I fell in love with Holden. Because I *was* Holden, lonely, looking for something but trapped inside my own head, all too aware of the phoniness of the world. For the first time I saw how an author— with the same black-printed letters and words one found in newspapers and on street signs—could express the mysteries of the mind and the heart just by using those letters in new combinations. And, like all teenagers, I thought my ability to relate to those mysteries was entirely unique. The Sinclairs lived the kind of childhood Holden dreamed of, where nothing ever changed, pure innocence that would go on that way forever. And I came to realize this was part of the reason I was so drawn to them.

Thinking of this, I knew I needed to introduce Holden to Nate. But the more time I spent away from the Sinclairs, the more awkward my absence felt. What would I say when I saw him? Should I meet his eye or just talk to his chin? Could I really pretend everything was the same? I felt like I was wearing the weave of my emotions on the outside of my skin. Everything I saw—an old couple walking hand in hand down the street, a feral cat desperately circling our garbage cans—chafed them and left me raw.

I thought about how it had felt to have Nate touch my cheek, the searching look in his eyes, and I wanted to go back, be there again by the side of the tracks, cup my hand against his face and tangle my fingers in his hair and apologize for making him think whatever he must be thinking now, tell him it was only that I'd been scared.

Before that day, in the time we'd spent alone, whenever I'd let myself wonder what it might be like to kiss him I'd felt an instant punch of terror. So I'd only allowed myself to think of it analytically rather than emotionally, the way I'd wonder what it might be like to orbit the earth in a rocket. But now at night, every night, the only time I let my guard down, I dreamed of it.

It was a week later that I saw him at Sandler Park, a pure coincidence that felt like it must be fate since I'd never seen any of the Sinclairs there before. I'd brought a sandwich on my bike, planning to eat on a hike around the pond. But when I parked the bike

I saw them immediately, Nate with Cecilia and their parents on the pond trail only a couple hundred feet ahead. Stunned, I sat on a bench and watched, riveted as if they were a TV show, eating without tasting.

They could've been any other family, Mr. Sinclair reaching to help both Cecilia and his wife cross a wide puddle, smiling indulgently at Nate and Cecilia's animated conversation. Cecilia bent to skip a rock across the pond and Mr. Sinclair raised his eyebrows, reached for another rock and flung it and then bent for another and handed it to Nate, saying something that made Nate laugh. They continued this way, a family competition as they walked around the pond, and I found myself almost disappointed at their ordinariness, that Mr. Sinclair would wear normal clothes and hiking boots, that after the cold pond water splashed Cecilia's dress he would drape his cardigan around her shoulders, like any other father might do for any other child. That they would all actually walk together in a public park, playing a perfectly ordinary game.

Where was the man they all seemed so scared of? The man I'd seen the afternoon of the Narnia play who'd fascinated me, mesmerized me—I'd had this sense he knew things that I couldn't even dream of, but had I just invented that person based on the few things I'd been told and the mysteriousness of not having been told much? It seemed like I must have exaggerated his power, or maybe even completely fabricated it, in the way I'd constructed my own versions of Jadis and Mrs. Danvers and Captain Hook. This man I was watching looked like the kind of man I'd always imagined my own father must've been.

I watched Nate, the ease with which he jogged ahead and threw, feeling a molten heat in my stomach. What were he and Cecilia talking about? Had she and Grace wondered why I hadn't been around that week? And if they'd asked Nate, what would he have said? He wouldn't be talking about me in front of his father, I knew that, but I still imagined him now whispering to Cecilia to ask for her advice. In some kind of code, perhaps. Hoped she might know me well enough to understand and explain.

As they rounded the pond and walked closer, I quickly rose and threw my sandwich crust to the geese. But as I turned to get on my bike I saw Nate watching me, his face still. Our eyes met and I froze, then raised my hand in a quick, childish wave before swinging my leg over my bike and riding away. I pumped my legs as hard as they would let me, racing across the parking lot and down the street, wishing I was running instead or that I had a wall to punch, something to stop myself from imploding. I knew I was being stupid, this was just Nate! I'd known him since forever and nothing about him had changed. Except of course that the relationship between two people is a creature all on its own, and that Nate-Chloe creature had grown extra legs, tentacles that squeezed and shaped everything around us. And I didn't know whether those legs had made us stronger or carried something vital away.

The next morning, he came to the door. My mother answered in her faded blue Hello Kitty robe, still with raccoon-eye indentations from her sleep mask. Watching from the kitchen table I could see Nate's face flush, in what I took to be embarrassment for her rather than for himself. I wanted to grab her by the arm, duck and run.

"Nate, right?" she said. "Gosh you're all grown up since I last saw you. Come on in, you want some breakfast? We have Cheerios or . . ." She glanced at the table. "Actually all we have is Cheerios, I need to shop. But you're welcome to them."

"It's okay, thanks. I already ate." He stepped inside, then saw me and stepped back again. "Should I come in?"

I was pretty sure the question was directed at me. Not, *Is it okay to come in?* but rather, *Are we okay?* But my mother answered, "Of course!" and swept her arm toward the table.

Nate sat tentatively across from me, not meeting my eye, instead surveying the kitchen: dirty cracks in the linoleum, sink half full with grayish standing water, dark crumbs pocking the table like a rash. I now wanted to grab the entire house and duck and run.

But instead I wracked my brains, came up with something semi-safe to say. "How come you're not in church?"

He gave a one-shouldered shrug. "Everybody else is there, but I told them I had a bad stomach."

"Getting out of church by lying about illness?" My mother seemed amused. In fact the whole idea of religion amused her. She compared churchgoers to lottery players: *The odds are one in a million that prayers will help them hit the big time, but they trust superstition more than science and statistics.* "My heavens," she said, "what would Jesus say!"

Nate looked immediately stricken, and I glared at her. "She thinks she's funny."

"Oh look at your face, Chloe! I remember being fourteen when everyone who wasn't fourteen was a complete embarrassment. I'm sorry, I'm sorry, I know when I'm not wanted so I'll let you two be." On her way from the room she squeezed my shoulder and bent to whisper, "He's grown up so pretty!" in my ear.

I swatted at her but she'd already turned away, so my arm flailed ridiculously. To hide it, I raised my arm to tuck my hair behind my ear. Was Nate pretty? I'd known him from an age where boys were alien creatures, interesting maybe, in the way a Martian would be interesting. But now I tried to look at him as if he were a stranger, the way I sometimes studied my own reflection, cataloguing—my square jaw, high forehead, wide mouth—to see how the pieces worked individually and together. And for the first time I noticed the signs of stubble at Nate's chin (Nate shaved!), his pink cheeks and thick dark hair, green eyes and ridiculously long eyelashes. Yes, that was exactly the right word for Nate after all. *Pretty.* I felt myself blush, and looked away so he wouldn't see it.

"I saw you at the park yesterday," he said.

"Yeah," I said tentatively, "I was going for a walk."

"I've missed you."

I didn't know what to say to this. Of course I'd missed him too, but saying that would just feel like a one-dimensional facsimile of something that had hundreds of dimensions. All I could think to say was, "I'm sorry."

"No, I'm sorry. I mean really sorry, that's what I came here to tell you. All week it's been killing me, Chloe. I can't stand myself sometimes."

At first I thought he was referring to those moments he'd lain on top of me, studying my face, maybe-probably about to kiss me. But then I realized he must mean he was sorry for almost killing me. "It's okay," I said, "I thought it was kind of cool."

He looked into my eyes as if assessing something, and then all at once he smiled. "That was the closest I ever got to dying," he said.

I lifted my spoon, balanced it on the rim of my empty cereal bowl and seesawed it up and down. "Do you want to do it again?"

He paused, contemplating, then said, "No, I'm done with that."

"Okay," I said, not sure if I felt relieved or disappointed. Both, really.

"And I feel like I should tell you this too, that everything I said about not believing, I shouldn't have said it. I've been looking too closely at things, I guess I was trying to figure them out in my own head, and I went too far."

Was he scared of divine retribution? Was the idea of playing with the thoughts so terrifying that he'd forced himself to suppress them? "You didn't go too far, there was nothing wrong with you saying it."

"No, I should've put it like this, and I realize it sounds bad. But I don't know if I believe in my father's God. Some of it's true, I'm sure of that, but I think . . . sometimes the ideas in his head get twisted."

I thought of the man I'd seen yesterday walking with his family, found myself imagining the mundane, human things he must do, like blowing his nose, cutting his toenails, peeing. This man who might be no more than an ordinary man after all. "Twisted how?"

"There are just so many things I don't know about anymore. They just feel wrong to me, or at least like they're not the whole story. I don't believe Mom's sickness has anything to do with her faith or unconfessed sins, and I don't believe ninety-nine percent of the world is going to hell. Laying on of hands, even the Book of Revelation, and you . . . I don't think you were sent to me by Satan as temptation."

"Oh," I said. My lungs felt squashed. He shook his head slightly and said, "I mean sent to all of us. I actually think maybe you and all your books were sent to us by God to show us how to think, because having your own thoughts is part of having a brain, they're not put there by the devil."

"I feel the same way about all of you too," I said.

We watched each other awkwardly for a minute, and then he stood. "I should go."

"No, don't. I mean wait a minute, I want to show you some-thing first. Can I show you something?" I jumped up and ran to my bedroom to retrieve my copy of *Catcher in the Rye,* brought it down to the kitchen and pressed it into Nate's hands. "You have to read this," I said. "Tonight."

From the outside, the book didn't look promising. No picture on the cover, pages worn and bent from teenagers' page-marking habits. But Nate opened it and read the first sentence, first to him-self and then aloud: "'If you really want to hear about it, the first thing you'll probably want to know is where I was born and what my lousy childhood was like, and how my parents were occupied and all before they had me, and all that David Copperfield kind of crap, but I don't feel like going into it, if you want to know the truth.'"

Nate looked up at me, met my eye, and then gave a slow smile.

"The boy in this story," I said eagerly, "he's just so *real.* He doesn't even understand who he is, what he needs. But when you read what he's thinking, you know exactly."

And then I told him about Holden's fantasy of catching chil-dren running through the rye, protecting them from adulthood. "That's kind of what I've been doing for all of you!" I said, and then I stopped. I hadn't meant to tell him that. It had been the thing that hit me hardest, reading the book, suddenly understand-ing myself. But telling him this would make him want to know what he'd been protected from, which would mean that protection would have to end. "I don't know why I just said that," I said.

Nate watched me, unblinking. "No, go on. What do you mean?"

"I don't know," I repeated, then shook my head. "It's just you're kind of like the kids he's protecting, there're all these things you don't have any idea about."

What could I tell him? About Son of Sam? Famine in Africa?

The neutron bomb? I didn't even think they had any sense where babies came from, just assumed God pointed a finger at married women, and bam, a baby. After my third session of sixth-grade sex ed I'd tried to feel them out to see how much they knew. But the Sinclairs didn't have a TV, didn't go to movies or read regular newspapers or magazines, weren't exposed to the crude jokes and jabs I saw everywhere and every day. They didn't seem to know and I hadn't wanted to tell them: the catcher in their rye.

And then I thought about Brett Harwood hooking a finger toward my American History exam, sliding it close enough to read. How I'd paused in writing till he was through, then finished the exam and slid the pages to him again. How passing him in the hall that afternoon I'd tried to catch his eye and smile, a co-conspiratorial grin. But the look on his face . . . well, it wasn't quite hostile, wasn't quite disgust, but it certainly held tones of disgusted hostility.

"It's just that the world's broken, Nate, people are broken. The things they do to other people, well, you wouldn't understand. Your life, I love how you guys live, but it isn't real."

Nate stretched his mouth lopsided into something that wasn't, but was maybe trying to be, a smile. "You think I don't know that?" he said. "I'm not an idiot, I know what we're being protected from; it's not like we never leave the house. We go to church and talk to the other kids. We've even been known to read newspaper headlines."

Well, of course. I'd somehow imagined them all living inside an opaque bubble, a womb. That I could look in on them, pretend I was one of them, but they couldn't ever really see my world or have lives and thoughts outside the frame of the story I'd created. Maybe that was the way their father saw them too. "Of course you have," I said.

Nate rose and walked to the door, stood facing it. "You don't have to protect me, I'm not innocent," he said, then turned back to look into my eyes, tucking the book under his arm. "Come by tomorrow and we'll talk." And then he left. The sound of the door closing behind him not quite a slam, but equally sudden and unexpected. Like an insult closing off the revelation of a secret only half shared.

It was drizzling the next afternoon when I biked back to the Sinclairs', the sort of drizzle that makes you feel like you're being continually sneezed on. And by the time I reached the house, I was drenched. I could see them all in the library, Mrs. Sinclair on the couch darning a man's shirt, the others gathered around her in much the same way they'd been the first day I met them. I stood there, watching as if they were one of the automated Macy's Christmas displays I'd seen on TV, feeling that same warm, pleasant ache of nostalgia in my chest. And then I knocked on the window. Their heads swiveled in unison; in unison they smiled. "Well, someone let the child in, before she drowns out there," Mrs. Sinclair said.

Grace rose to open the door, stood watching me a moment, and then patted my shoulder solicitously. "Come upstairs and I'll get you some dry clothes," she said. So I followed her up the stairs, my damp socks squeaking on the hardwood.

Unlike the rest of the house, Grace's room was barren and lifeless: ivory wallpaper with tiny yellow rosebuds and a matching oval rug, a bed with a blue corduroy spread and tall mahogany headboard, a matching wardrobe, a desk holding only a gold pen and pencil set, and a bookcase filled with coverless books, topped by a porcelain doll with a drooped head and flowered skirts, like a dollop of whipped cream.

Grace pulled a thick cotton blouse and skirt from her wardrobe, then turned her back as I changed. "We're studying the Tower of Babel," she said. "Did you know there's actual archaeological evidence it existed? Things called ziggurats, in Mesopotamia, and the Tower of Babel was a ziggurat called 'Etemanki,' which means the platform of heaven and earth. Isn't it the most amazing thing knowing you could just hop on a plane and actually touch one of the most famous stories of the Bible?"

Of all of us, Grace's faith was the strongest. The Bible could've said Moses climbed Mount Sinai to dance the hokeypokey and she would've believed it. She was obsessed with the Book of Revelation, was determined never to marry or have children since the world would end by the millennium, and it felt wrong to subject a child to the fear of it. Nate told me she'd calculated the number of days remaining, and every night slashed a mental line through the day, like life was an Advent calendar.

I wondered if Grace suspected I'd stopped believing in the Bible. This wasn't the first time she'd thrown real-life evidence at me, to try and prove the unprovable. Or maybe it was like the long-ago people who'd built the Babel tower, trying to reach God, layering towers of evidence to reach the truth; Grace was trying to settle any lingering doubts in her own mind. "That's so cool," I said, because I loved her.

There was a knock on the door as I was pulling up my stockings. She waited for me to finish before she answered it. "Nate," she said.

"I need to talk to Chloe," he said. "Just for a few minutes. Could you tell Mom we'll be down soon?"

Her mouth twitched, a flicker of a frown, and then she said, "Fine," and turned to the hall. Outside, thunder rolled, stones into a clay bucket. The room suddenly felt too dark and I reached for the bedside lamp, but Nate stopped me. "The book," he said.

"You read it?"

"Most of it, not all." He sat on the bed, hands clasped in front of him, elbows on his knees. "Does he kill himself at the end?"

"What? No! It's a happy ending, or at least happy-ish."

"I thought he was going to kill himself." He raised his chin and looked me in the eye. "So you're scared we'll go wild like Holden after his sister died, right? That's why you wanted me to read this."

In the encroaching dark, Nate's face looked gray and flat as cardboard. I suddenly wanted to escape back downstairs to the warm light of the library, where I could at least pretend not to know what he meant. Never before had any of them talked so bluntly about what was happening to their mother. Never had they even implied she might someday die. And now he thought I'd used the book to raise the topic first.

"That's not why," I said. "It's not even close to why. It's because I loved getting inside Holden's head, because he's so real and so messed up, but also so *good*. And I don't know, I guess I thought you'd want to meet him. I swear that's all it was."

"Okay," he said, then again, "okay." And then he lay back on the bed, looking up at the dark wooden crucifix on Grace's wall. "I think we should use it as our next dare."

Was there anything Holden had done that was outright dangerous? "Use it how?"

"Run away, Chloe. We could go to New York, do everything that he did, go to Central Park and the Museum of Natural History, ice-skate at Radio City, and see a Broadway play—"

"It's June. There's no ice in June."

"Right, okay, but that's not the point. Don't you ever want to, you know, escape? Like Holden tried to do, just pick up and leave without telling anybody where you're going? We could go and never come back if we wanted. Imagine us living in a little town in Tuscany, a two-room cottage with a flagstone path and flowers in all the windows; we'd spend all day writing novels, and then in the afternoon we'd take walks and go out to cheese shops for gorgonzola."

I wouldn't have been at all surprised if the dream of leaving had been brewing in Nate ever since I first met him. "You're turning us into a chapter of *A Room with a View*," I said, but when I thought of all the times I'd imagined visiting Hemingway's Spain or Austen's English countryside, Lewis's Narnia or Tolkien's Middle Earth, I could see the drive to leave for somewhere better had always been inside me too. All the best stories in the world were of escape.

In the end we didn't run away to New York, of course. No, our escape was much less dramatic and more about the act than the destination.

We were sprawled on our bellies on the lawn, Grace, Nate, and Cecilia studying from textbooks and me writing a final paper for my Earth Sciences class (mouthing the vicious poetry of the words: Igneous, Cretaceous, Mesozoic—they sounded like worms with sharp teeth). When suddenly Cecilia slapped her book shut and glared at it. "This sucks. Why do I have to know about Aborigine culture? It's not like I'm ever going to meet an Aborigine. Let's go swimming."

Nate reached for Cecilia's braid and lifted it over her shoulder to tickle her nose. "They haven't told you but their plan is to ship you off to Australia as soon as you turn sixteen. We all took a vote to let the other side of the world deal with you."

"Ha-ha, you're hysterically funny." She flopped back on the grass. "That'd actually be fine with me. Just get me out of here, it's so depressing all the time these days."

"We were just talking about that, me and Nate," I said. "I'd love to get shipwrecked like Robinson Crusoe, somewhere there weren't any other people except us." The picture in my head was half Crusoe but, to be honest, also half *Gilligan's Island*. I saw us making a phonograph out of coconuts.

Grace lifted her head, smiled dreamily. "We'd live in a little house we built out of palm leaves, and weave rugs out of dead ferns and hang seashells on the wall."

"Fish and build campfires at night to cook whatever we caught," I said.

Nate swiveled to look at me, then slowly smiled. "We should do it," he said. "Our next dare badges; we'll bike out to the beach, build a lean-to and catch fish, a seafood dinner every night, see how long we can make it. I dare you all to live on the beach for a week."

"Avonlea," Grace said.

"I forgot how obsessed you used to be with those books," I said, "like you asked me to look up how you might get adopted, so you could spend the rest of your life by the ocean."

"Oh right," Nate said, "let's all go visit an imaginary town."

"It's just as realistic as spending a week living on the beach," Grace said.

"The beach is like a half hour away. How would you even get to Nova Scotia?"

"You're serious? Don't you dare even *think* about it, Nate. What do you think Daddy would do?"

"Please, Grace, why do you always have to be so predictable?"

Grace popped the head off a dandelion, threw it at him. "*You're* predictable." More hurt than angry.

And that was the end of the conversation, other than some musing from Cecilia about how one might happen to find a ship one could get wrecked on. Nate throwing periodic disdainful glances at Grace, and Grace retaliating by throwing dandelion heads at his nose.

Until the next day, when Nate jumped up from the front porch as soon as he saw me enter the yard, like he'd been waiting, and grabbed my wrist to pull me into the woods. "I've been thinking about it," he said.

I pulled my wrist away and rubbed at it, watching him warily. "What?"

"All night I've been thinking, and I think we should do it, you and me."

"Do what? You don't mean the shipwreck thing."

"Don't you start getting all priggish too. You're the one I was counting on to show some guts."

Me? He thought I had guts? I felt a twinge of pride.

"I'm not saying that we should actually spend weeks out on the beach, just maybe one day and overnight, leave the next morning."

"Seriously? What would your dad say?"

"He won't ever even know." Something dark passed over his face, a quick flicker of shadow before he said, "Our youth group camping trip is next week, the bonding of boys praying and singing in God's great outdoors, hallelujah, pass the hot dogs. So I was thinking, what if I said I was going but I didn't?"

"Your dad *leads* the youth group," I said.

"But let's say I come down with a horrible migraine twenty miles into the trip. I'm holding my head and moaning, telling Daddy I'm going to be sick. And then Daddy asks if he should turn the van around, drop me home, and I say no. That it's a shame to interrupt everybody's good time, just give me some money and drop me at a phone booth, I'll call a cab and have them drive me. Which I do. I call a cab and have them drive me to your house, and then to the beach." He beamed at me, a triumphant, self-satisfied smile. "And then when I do actually get home, I'll tell Mom I needed to do a little soul-searching on my own, or something like that. She'll hate that I lied, but the way she is these days she'll do anything to keep Daddy from getting angry. I'm sure she wouldn't tell him anything."

I bit the inside of my cheek, watching Nate's face. Fear, excitement, they're cut from the same cloth, and I could feel them side by side, warring. But Nate didn't seem afraid at all, didn't seem to realize the massiveness of the lies he'd have to tell. Like soldiers hardened from boot camp before war, Nate had, apparently, successfully trained himself to become impervious to fear. "Your dad would kill you if he found out," I said softly.

"So you're saying okay? You're coming?" And then he must've seen the apprehension in my face because his expression changed, suddenly solemn. "Yes, he'd probably kill me," he said. "I realize that. Compare this to other things I've done that he's hated, this is on a whole n'other scale. And if you . . . extrapolate, if you extrapolate punishments for other things to the punishment for this level of lie, then I guess a fatal beating is a very real possibility." He looked into my eyes and smiled. "But at least I'll have lived a little before I died."

And so, a week later, a taxicab showed up at my door. I'd told my mother that Cecilia had invited me for a sleepover, and Momma had bought me a grown-up pair of silk pajamas, the prettiest clothes I'd ever owned. She'd also bought a pink oval hand mirror and a fake orchid in a terra-cotta pot for me to give as thank-you gifts to Cecilia and Mrs. Sinclair respectively, and I dutifully packed them in my book bag with the pajamas, a toothbrush, and shampoo.

Nate grinned at me when I opened the cab door. Immediately I could feel the electricity of excitement around him. A vibration like those I'd learned about in Earth Science, under the surface, an invisible force that set everything in the vicinity to vibrating in harmony.

During the drive, Nate told me about the research he'd done, how to build a fire without matches, the types of berries and roots that were safe to eat. And then he unzipped his backpack and pulled out a hammer and nails (to help build our shelter), a pocket-knife (for hunting), and ham sandwiches wrapped in wax paper and four cans of Coke, which he'd stolen from the youth group's coolers. "Yeah, it's cheating," he said, "but even Crusoe took a few days of food from the ship."

"Plus we'll need energy with all the work we have to do," I said. I took a can and clanked it against his. "Cheers."

The beach did not exactly match the description of a deserted island. If you squinted you could see a bed-and-breakfast up at the top of the bluffs, and foraging, I found four cigarette butts, a Cheetos wrapper, and the decapitated, amputated torso of a Barbie doll. They were shocking to me, felt like tumors, ugly and out of place. But if one looked only out over the ocean and deep into the woods flanking the sandbar, one could pretend one was hundreds of miles from salvation.

Nate, who had been squatting farther down the shoreline, started running toward me, calling, and as he got closer I could see he was holding a clam bigger than his hand. "Where's a container, do we have a container?" he said excitedly, then reached for his backpack, dumped its contents into the sand, and dropped the clam inside. "Now that the tide's out you can see the breathing holes everywhere. Did you see how huge that thing was? They're down pretty deep, but with the two of us, it shouldn't take all that long to dig them up." He shouldered the backpack, hesitated a second, and then took my hand. For a minute we both stood hand in hand looking out across the sand, and then he gripped my hand tighter and we walked back down the shore, feet bare, pants rolled mid-calf.

When Nate pointed wordlessly at a small hole in the sand, we both knelt beside it and started to dig, sleeves and knees wet, wind blowing cold from the ocean but sweat from the exertion still slicking my face. We both found the hard edge of the clam at once with a simultaneous, "There!" Nate dislodged it from the sand, brushed it off, and then we sat back on our heels, triumphant. "Find twenty more of these and we can have seafood dinners every night for a week!" he said. He threw it into the backpack and we started back down the shoreline. After a minute he took my hand again and we walked on.

In the end we only dug up five clams; our arms were getting sore, fingers raw. But we knew it would be enough for tonight, an appetizer to our sandwiches, and we'd dig again in the morning after a good night's rest.

Back at the campsite, Nate showed me how to start a fire with whittled sticks, and I worked at rubbing the sticks while he pried the clams open with his knife. When he was done he took over the fire building, but after a half hour's work bringing nothing but smoke, he said, "In the book they made it sound so easy. I probably should've practiced."

"Or, you know, brought matches."

"Ha-ha." He looked down at the sandy, slimy meat he'd loosened from the clam shell. "So."

"No way," I said.

He prodded it with the tip of his index finger, then wiped his hand off on his pants and set the shell down. "I guess we could look for berries."

"Or aren't there nuts inside of pinecones? We could dig out the nuts."

"With what, our chipmunk teeth? I also have these." He dug into his pocket and pulled out a handful of green. "Fiddleheads," he said. "There's a ton of them in the woods. You're supposed to be able to eat them."

I plucked one out of his hands and put it on my tongue, slowly chewed, then made a face and spat it out. "It tastes like earwax."

"Yeah, you kind of have to swallow them without chewing." He squashed one between his fingers, swallowed it like a pill, paused, and then said, "Well, that was filling."

I smiled. "Let's just eat the sandwiches, and then we can start building a shelter."

But in the end, after working for over an hour, all we were able to pull off were sore muscles and four branches carved to spears and driven into the ground. Fastening more branches to make walls was impossible; either the nails weren't sharp enough or the wood was too unyielding. Instead I set the fake orchid in between our four branches, and we lay back on the sand beside it with our hands behind our heads and eyes closed, absorbing the sun.

"Crusoe kept a journal," Nate said. "We should've brought a journal so we could write, 'We tried.'" He sounded tired, but not especially disappointed.

"Trying's the most important part." I completely didn't believe this, but said it because it seemed like a right thing to believe. "And besides, we're still alive. We survived for . . ." I checked my watch. ". . . six hours. We should mark it on a tree."

Nate smiled. "We resisted beak-attack by the deadly sandpipers."

"And we weren't mangled by the man-eating minnows. I'd call that a quasi-success." The word "quasi" made me happy so I said it again. "A semi-quasi-success." I lifted the fake orchid onto my chest and smiled, trying to ignore the growling in my stomach. "Only fourteen years old and we have semi-quasi-tamed the wild."

Beautiful sunsets, the type one sees in movie endings, were rare in Humboldt County. Even on nice days the fog usually descended onto the horizon by late afternoon. But on this day the sky was tempera-paint blue, and toward early evening when it began to bruise, Nate and I sat side by side, facing the ocean, and watched the show.

Funny how the mind can bend. I forgot completely where I was, the semiprecariousness of our situation, that we wouldn't have access to anything to eat or drink—besides the earwax ferns—until the cabdriver returned the next day at three. I might as well have been floating inside the vermilion sky, mindless, worriless; even my hunger seemed a component of the vacuous universe above us, both part of me and not.

Until Nate said, "Grace tried to kill herself."

It took a moment for my mind to return from the sky to puzzle out the meaning of the words. And even when I could decipher them individually, together they made no sense. "What?" I said.

"Last month. She was there, she was there with Mom's heart pills and the Bible, and it was late at night and I couldn't sleep, and I saw the light on under her door so I went in. The Bible, Mom's heart pills, and a glass of juice, and she turns to me—and the look on her face, I don't know how to describe it. Almost like a kid who lost something, a dog or a toy she wanted me to find."

Grace, I thought, Grace . . . repeating the name until it became nonsensical, trying to associate this image with the girl I knew, the girl who'd always seemed determined to teach us our failings, not to remind us of her own superiority but more because she felt it was her obligation to teach us right from wrong.

The previous summer Grace had seen me hobbling in sneakers that were a size too small. I'd been growth-spurting, it was already my second pair that year and I couldn't bring myself to tell my mother about the raw spots on my heels, knowing the pained, resigned look she'd get calculating what we'd have to do without.

Grace had sat me down, made me pry off the shoes, and studied my feet without saying a word. And then she rose and went into the house, returning a minute later with two twenty-dollar bills that she pressed into my hand. "For shoes," she'd said, "and whatever else you need. It's my mom's, but we don't need to tell her because I know she wouldn't mind."

At first I'd wondered why she hadn't just asked for the money, if she thought Mrs. Sinclair actually would have minded. But later

I'd realized she was trying to spare me the shame of it. Right and wrong, I learned that day, could not really be taught after all, only felt.

"I asked her what she was doing," Nate said. "She knew I'd seen the pills, and she jumped up, grabbed them with the juice, and told me she was bringing them to Mom. So she walked by me, but then she spun around and went back to the desk to tear something out of her notebook and stuff it into her pocket. She was writing something, I guess, that she didn't want me to see."

"A suicide note?"

Nate's eyes filled. I reached for his hand. "So what did you do?"

He pressed his lips together and shook his head quickly. I dropped his hand and put both arms around him, feeling lost. "I got into her bed," he said, his voice muffled against my shoulder. "I got in her bed, under the covers, and a few minutes later she came in and just stood there. My eyes were closed, I couldn't see how she looked, but after a while she crawled into bed with me and we lay together. I guess she eventually fell asleep, but I didn't; I was awake all night because I had to make sure."

I set a hand on the back of his head, as much to steady myself as to comfort him. "You don't think she'll try again," I said, "do you?"

"I don't know if she even would have then. I think maybe she wanted to be able to, or maybe even just wanted to try out the feel of it, like we do with our dares, coming close and imagining. But the next night when I was about to go check on her—I meant to stay awake all night again if I could manage it—but the next night she came into my room instead, got into my bed without asking. Every night since then she's come. Maybe to make me see she's done with it, she's okay, or maybe to keep herself from changing her mind."

I imagined this, Grace tortured by whatever it was that was torturing her but watching over herself now, telling her body what to do and where to go like it was something separate from her, a willful child. Getting dressed in—I imagined it must be this—a high-necked white cotton gown, perhaps even a bonnet, before crawling into her younger brother's bed.

A month ago, that's when Nate had started the game with the train. And suddenly I realized. "That's why you stopped telling Grace about all our dares. Not just because you thought she'd tell us off."

He didn't answer, just looked out over the horizon. The sun had already set; I seemed to have missed it. Gone but it still stained the sky, a bloodstain seeping through blue fabric.

I thought of Nate and Grace, how they acted during the day, Grace watching us with a mother's vague exasperation and resignation, and Nate's disdain for her, which now struck me as forced. Both acting out the roles they were expected to play, but at night showing the truth.

"The other day you told me you were trying to protect us from finding out about life," he said. "But we know, Chloe. We know much more than you do."

I sensed that there was something else he wanted to tell me. I knew there were parts of his life he kept from me; I had no idea the shape of their days after I went home. And I sensed there was something important he was finally going to reveal, a secret like a key that would unlock all the questions I had about their family. His shoulders tensed and I waited, but he only burrowed his head back against my neck.

"I'm sorry," I said softly, still holding him, feeling his chest rise and fall, rise and fall, as he breathed. In response he traced a finger slowly up my bare forearm and then back down.

I took his hand and he intertwined our fingers and brought my hand to his mouth. "Chloe," he whispered against it. There was fear in his voice; also tears. "I want," he said, "I want . . ."

I sat there frozen, a knot the size of a hard-boiled egg in the center of my chest. Alice floating down her rabbit hole, in limbo between the world she knew and a world more strange than anything she could have possibly imagined. But I pulled my hand away and rose onto my knees, between Nate's splayed legs. I brought both hands up to his hair and bent to kiss him.

Nate made a choked sound then and wrapped both arms around my waist, pulling me back onto the sand. And I kissed him again, harder, then lay there with my face just above his but not touching. His breath growing thicker, warm on my lips, the feel of him stirring under my belly, the exhilaration of that stirring and of the sound of the waves, of the moon rising above us and the sand between my bare toes, and of looking into his eyes.

PART V

BELLY *of the* WHALE

11

Kiss, that's all we did that night, although I probably would've let him do more—much more—if he'd just tried. Nate told me much later that at the time his only understanding of sex came from the way his body responded involuntarily during certain vivid dreams. I, of course, had seen soap operas and lived through junior high, which together had given me both an appreciation for what sex should be and a revulsion for what it probably actually was in real life. But that kiss, it was probably the sweetest moment of my life before and since.

Again so strange that I hadn't thought of that night more. Didn't most couples replay their beginnings, that planted seed, so they could laugh about how scared they'd been and how little they'd really known each other, and then marvel at how that seed had bloomed? Why didn't I ever think about our childhood? But Nate had remembered. For his encoding he'd chosen two books that symbolized our beginnings.

Now I brought *Robinson Crusoe* to the reading room, sat with my legs curled under me and began copying and crossing out letters from Nate's notebook. Just going through the motions, a task as monotonous and emotionless as picking out weeds from grass. Not letting myself read until I was finished.

Diwa soyobor niufenetheor geye ivaree me1632oríd oyonu heta tehecime fo tyrof wheyora tivek dofaneg?

Do you forgive me or do you hate me for what I've done?

I stared at this. What could he be talking about? And who was he writing to?

Gabriel. He was still writing to Gabriel.

Was I wrong? I was trying to control fate, which I guess is what this whole letter's about, the wrongness of trying to play God.

I want to believe you're there, and that you understand. My father tried to teach me pure, unquestioning faith, but I'm sure you sense how I've always struggled. Uncertainty or belief in an unjust God, I'm not sure which is worse.

And so I'm writing another letter, even knowing that if you actually can read it, as a spirit you already have far more wisdom than I do anyway. I realize—regardless of where you are or whether you are—that I'm mostly writing to my own self, but in the end the idea of not celebrating your birthday would feel like breaking a promise. And there's something strangely soothing in intertwining the words among the letters of this book that meant so much to your mother and me.

She's been sinking. That's the only way I can describe it. I'd thought over the past few months that she was coming back to me, but now I'm starting to realize that she probably never really will. Part of being a man means thinking you can fix everything, but, it turns out, nobody can fix grief.

I bought this house for her, thinking it might be a first step in healing, looking forward instead of back. Last month working on the spare room, with Joni Mitchell on the boom box and paint in our hair, she said, "All this work and we don't have anything to put in this room. What's it going to be?"

And I looked at the flush in her cheeks, listening to Joni croon about a woman waiting to hear from her man, and I said, "We could put in a crib."

Your mom, she froze, her whole body turned to ice. And then her face went red, she threw her wet paintbrush at me and left the room.

What was I thinking? I can't stomach the idea either, so what made me think she wouldn't hate me for suggesting it was a possibility?

This book, Robinson Crusoe, it was the adventure of it that excited us, but if you read a bit deeper it's a book about slavery, the fallacy of a man believing he's superior. Crusoe masters nature and bad circumstances, masters his own fate in the most inhospitable environment, but then he tries to master the people around him. This is a book about the right and wrong way to live one's life. Ironic, isn't it, how I planned to use Robinson Crusoe as the last step in making her love me. As if there are steps for such a thing as love.

Ever since I was little, your age, I thought I had that sort of power. So much like my own father really, and the thought of this disgusts me. Your aunts more or less did what I asked of them, even Grace, and they believed the lies I told. And your mom, she was so spirited and independent that "mastery" over her felt like the ultimate triumph. But of course I realize now that she was, forgive me, needy in many ways. So really it wasn't much of a triumph at all.

Losing my mother I learned that my control was limited in all the ways it really mattered. Losing you, I learned that I had no control at all. But still I try, I buy a house, I make it new again, I imply that we should try to bring you back in another form. And all it does is pull us further from what we once had, drilling the pain deeper into our bones, inescapable.

I put the pen down. Set my notepad upside down over top of it.

That day, the day he'd suggested we have another child . . . I'd hated Nate for that, part of me still did. It proved to me that he hadn't loved Gabriel anywhere close to enough. And reinforced the resentment of Nate I'd felt throughout Gabriel's life, for not being there.

I'd blamed him when Gabriel disappeared.

Do you forgive me or do you hate me for what I've done? So was that what he meant, that he blamed himself for abandoning us? But no, "what I've done" implied an actual event, a doing. *Trying to control fate,* he'd said.

And this was the theme of Nate's life. His father had tried to control every inch, down to his clothes, the books he'd read, the games he could play. And while he'd allowed the girls some freedom when he was home—even if it was only to help Sophia around the house—he'd been impossibly strict with Nate, making him attend church for hours, four to five days a week, even when he was sick, rise before dawn each morning to pray with him and spend entire mornings memorizing impossibly tedious Bible passages. He even tried to control Nate's emotions, telling him that any unhappiness was a sign of sin, impurity in his relationship with God. So Nate never cried in front of his father, even after Sophia's death, had learned to suppress everything, hide even from himself.

Over the years, he'd grown to see that level of control as part of manhood, but this had been tempered by his mother, who'd taught him rebellion, done what she could to bend Joel's rules, showing they weren't iron after all, maybe just a middleweight plastic. Rebellion and control, the two ingredients that brought us together that night on the beach.

My head was spinning, so I lowered myself to lie across two padded chairs and closed my eyes. Where was Nate now? What was it that he'd had to do that made him lie to me, pretend he was still helping Cecilia?

Who are you? I thought, but the question hurt so I stopped thinking it, curled my legs up off the floor and buried my face against the velvet chair cushion. Nate's jacket was still slung on the table where I'd thrown it after retrieving his cell phone, and as I pulled it from the table to wrap it around me, the key to the holding case fell from the table. I reached for it, then froze. Sat up.

He'd left the key here, flung on the table, and left the holding case cracked open. Had he been doing something with the case right before he left? Had there been something else hiding in the C. S. Lewis along with his notebook, Gabriel's hair, and the articles? Cecilia had called and he'd come here to the reading room, retrieved . . . *something*, so agitated that he forgot to relock the case and bring his jacket and phone. And he'd brought that something with him for Cecilia to see. Which, if that was true, meant Cecilia must know much more than she'd been willing to tell me.

The notebook, the articles, the hair, together with whatever he'd taken from the case to show Cecilia, all pieces to a puzzle.

Or maybe not. Maybe that was just my fondness for epic

novels—seemingly disparate subplots tying into neat conclusions—
and the only real association was that these were all things he
hadn't wanted me to know he was keeping.

I looked down at Nate's notebook, the next section of code,
then shoved it across the table and went out to my car.

My intention, hazy and half-formed, was to drive directly to
Cecilia's, get there by early morning, and unapologetically wake
her, confront her. But as I headed toward the main road, hands
gripping the steering wheel, the car seemed to slow all on its own,
then stop in the middle of the road. Then turn.

Away from town, into the fringes of the countryside where the
houses were smaller, flatter, more widely spaced. I pulled up in
front of a tiny white ranch, parked the car, and walked to the front
door.

Daniel was wearing blue pajama bottoms and no top, his hair
sleep mussed. He blinked three times, rapidly, and then his face
softened and he held a hand to me. I took it. "Hold me," I said,
"okay? Nothing else, just lie with me and hold me?"

He looked into my eyes, silently, then reached for my other
hand. Squeezed it wordlessly and then led me inside.

I woke late the next morning, blinded by stripes of sunlight an-
gling between the slats of vertical blinds, disoriented by the distant
clang of a pan lid and the crinkle of sheets, the color and stiffness
of a paper grocery bag, under my cheek. I lay there a moment,
dazed, and then at the sound of footsteps in the hall I jumped out
of bed to pull on my jeans, then dove back to throw the covers up
over my head.

I heard him place something on the nightstand, and then he
set a hand on my shoulder. I closed my eyes.

"Sweetie?" he said. "It's almost ten."

Sweetie. It seemed so proprietary. It felt too intimate, which, considering the current state of affairs, was an absurd way for me to feel. I pulled back the covers and blinked in a way I hoped looked like a person first waking, but that probably looked more like a nervous tic. "Daniel," I said.

He smiled. "I was going to say something corny about what deep sleep was a sign of, but I couldn't think how to phrase it in a way that didn't make me want to slap myself."

"Aren't you supposed to be at work?" I said.

His smile dropped. He watched me a moment before he said, "There aren't any rules when you're the boss. I wanted to be here when you woke up, because if I hadn't been, how rude? And to make you breakfast."

I glanced over at the nightstand, where he'd set a steaming cup of coffee and one pancake so large it overhung the edges of the plate. I wanted to tell him I had to go, that I'd planned to be on the road by now. But I didn't want to face his hurt feelings, didn't want to discuss what last night had meant. Especially since I had no idea what it meant. "That's a hell of a big pancake," I said.

"A lazy man's pancake. Enough batter for five, but you only have to flip once. Although that flipping, it takes real skill." He sat on the bed beside me and said stiffly, "You okay?"

How was I supposed to answer that? The question was weighted, an attempt to ascertain regret. I answered it as if I didn't understand this. "Just bleary from oversleeping," I said. "Plus I have to go somewhere today, and I'm not looking forward to it."

He raised his eyebrows but didn't ask, and I suddenly wished he *would* ask. I wanted to tell him, all of it, Nate's notebook, his disappearance, the words "what I've done"—they all lodged in my chest, too big for me.

"Right." He squeezed at the back of his neck. "You don't have to apologize, Chloe."

"Apologize?"

"For wishing last night hadn't happened, using me. I got something out of it too, obviously. But it's not going to happen again, you know that, right?"

"Daniel . . ." I wrapped an arm around his back, but his shoulders were so stiff and unyielding that my arm slid awkwardly down to the bed. "Stop it," I said. "Do you really think that's all this was?"

He hesitated, then took my hand, and I reached for him and buried my face in the crook of his neck. He smelled like Irish Spring, green and uncomplicated, and I swung my legs onto his lap and let him hold me.

I'd meant to pack and drive straight to Redbridge after leaving Daniel, but once I got home I found that I couldn't stomach the idea of seeing Cecilia, not that night, after what I'd just done. So instead I showered in scalding water, scrubbed at my face, my breasts, between my legs, then toweled off vigorously, dressed, and went down to the shop, where I unlocked the door and flipped the sign to OPEN.

I wanted distraction, customers who'd let me draw them into conversations about whatever they were buying, the baby they were carrying, even the weather, anything to keep me from real thought. But the few customers who came in walked through the shop distractedly, one never even pausing in her cell phone conversation. This was typical, of course; most people came inside just to look around, get out from the heat or cold, absorb the atmosphere and trace the book spines with their fingers and then walk out feeling cultured. And it always felt like a rejection.

In the late afternoon, I went upstairs and downed a bowl of Shredded Wheat, amazed in much the same way I'd been in the months after we'd lost Gabriel that my heart still insisted on beating, my stomach rumbling, and my throat calling for water. That one could be alive but so dead at the same time.

When I was done I retrieved Nate's notebook and *Robinson Crusoe* from the reading room. I brought the notebook to the register and spent the rest of the day working through the code, letter by letter, stopping only for bathroom breaks and to shake off my copying hand. I fell asleep at 10:00 P.M. and then woke hours later in the dark with no memory of having slept or dreamed, sleep like a cement block. I splashed my face with water, turned on bad eighties music, and jogged in place for twenty minutes, an attempt to clear my head, then returned to the register and continued deciphering.

Nate had written a letter for each year since Gabriel's birth, all of them beautiful, partly an ongoing, agonizing love song for our son but also what seemed to be a study of classic literature. They were letters from a father trying to convey the joy and significance of reading, which he'd always seen as one of life's most valuable tools to unlock wisdom and empathy and understanding of the world.

All the years of sitting with Nate in the woods, in the Sinclairs' house, in our living room, discussing whatever we were reading, trying to untangle and understand what it had taught us about ourselves. The words written in one mind in an attempt to understand the world, and inevitably remade differently in ours. All the characters different formations of our own selves, the settings re-created from permutations of places we'd already been, themes interpreted from our own experiences.

In the months after Gabriel's birth he must've imagined a future where he'd be able to share these thoughts. Must've dreamed of the day Gabriel would pick up books on his own, reading in that voracious way we ourselves had read as children.

He described books that had changed his life, as if providing recommendations:

> Fahrenheit 451 *taught me to question everything! Define my own values instead of letting others try to tell me how I should feel, and I'm telling you this because I only wish someone had pushed me to read it when I was younger.*

On *As I Lay Dying*:

> *Faulkner is a difficult read, but at first I'd suggest you sit with him and let his words flow through you, without even trying to understand the effect he's trying to convey. Let each character tell you his separate story and you'll feel their isolation, both from each other and from the outside world. More than anything else I've read, this book made me look at myself, the isolation I feel even surrounded by the people I love. It made me want to change.*

And then, in his discussion of *Slaughterhouse Five*:

> *Everything we've shared we are still sharing, unstuck in time. You're here sleeping in the crook of my arm, and also fitting shapes into a sorter, chasing geese by the lake, and batting at your mother's hair. Yes you're gone, but you are here with me as I turn twenty,*

thirty, forty. And knowing this, it's the only way I can make sense of it all.

Interspersed with these letters were reminiscences of childhood, as if he was trying to come to peace with all he'd been through. More anguish in these memories than he'd ever shown me, the gradual fraying of seams between him and his father. Nate had always seemed to be the stable one; Joel successfully taught him stoicism, and he'd rarely shown emotion through all the ups and downs. But in these letters, stories he'd never told me of those last months before his mother's death, his pain and fear were obvious.

Memories of my father, the tenderness with which he cleaned a scraped knee with Bactine and wiped off my tearstained face; cradling my mother's head after she'd been sick, smoothing back her hair, both their faces equally pained. Teaching Grace how to tie her shoes, sitting with her so patiently as her fingers fumbled with the laces, that's how I want to remember him.

But as Mom got sicker it was like that humanity was shadowed by The Other, the side of him we'd only seen before in smaller doses. Forcing us to sit with him in fervent prayer, frenzied hours of jumping, twirling, and strutting, falling to the ground and speaking in tongues, hours of this followed by hours of scripture until we were all too exhausted to see. We lost him under that darkness, and of course as time went on it only grew worse, but I kept looking for what I was sure must still be underneath. I think we all were trying so hard to find the father we thought had loved us, that's why we put up with so much. The soul is supposed to live on even after the man is gone.

How had nobody from the outside been aware of what went on behind their doors? I'd often wondered what the parishioners thought of their pastor's family, whether they believed his children, his marriage, and home were as perfect and poised as he worked so hard for them to seem. Or maybe their own lives were just as bizarre; most of their children were homeschooled too, all of them recognizable by their conservative dress and hairstyles and the bright, blank look in their eyes. Other people in town cast sideways glances when they passed and kids at school had called them the "Holy Cannolis," but other than that, nobody paid much attention to them at all. Maybe every small town has its oddball subgroups that no one wants to look at too closely because of discomfort, or perhaps for fear their strangeness might be catching in some way. What would have happened if people had been willing to ask questions? The ending to our story would have changed, Mr. Sinclair disgraced, removed from the parish, his children probably taken away.

But no, I wouldn't let myself go there.

After Sophia's death, Joel had spiraled even more inexorably out of control. There was blame and recrimination; the prayer hadn't worked because their faith wasn't strong enough. Joel blamed them for the escalating progression of Sophia's illness, and worst of all, he blamed Sophia herself.

I tried to defend her. Of course I knew how he'd react to that, but how could I not? It was the first time I'd ever really talked back to him, and after it things between us went from bad to worse. His first response, like he was trying to weaken my love for her, was to tell me about conversations they'd had over the years, how ashamed she was of me, disturbed at my behavior. And I know that must've been a lie, knew it even then, but part of me believed and felt it. I think part of me still does.

And then. *The next morning after I'd finished showering I tried to open the bathroom door but couldn't. He'd padlocked me inside. For almost a week I was in there alone, with nothing to do but lose my mind. Cecilia and Grace were forbidden from talking to me and he brought them with him to church each morning to make sure of it, although one of them—I don't know which—slid Saltines as well as torn-off pages of poetry under the door, a new page every few hours. As if they hoped the depth of the poems, supplying someone else's thoughts, would keep me from becoming lost in my own.*

The first day, I was determined not to scream, not even allow myself to cry silently. But when the next morning came and the door was still locked, that's when the panic set in. Rats circling in my brain, I could actually feel the little claws scrabbling as I sat there with my head vised between my knees, reciting the Lord's Prayer under my breath and then the hymn Grace would read to our mother, Everest's "Take Up Your Cross," over and over, a trillion times over as if they could possibly keep me sane. I can't really discuss those next days more than that except to say they changed me. I read later of a study done on monkeys bred in isolation, how in time they began rocking in place, circling their cage, self-mutilating. And yes, I did all of that. Being alone, without touch, with no one to confirm your existence, you stop feeling anything. Disconnected from yourself and the world.

After he finally let me out he started avoiding me completely at home, not looking at me, ignoring me the few times I approached him. Things were different in church of course; from the outside no one would've had any idea this was going on. But behind closed doors our family was falling apart.

Each of us reacted differently. Me, I just withdrew. I tried to stay away from home, with your mother as much as possible, partly because of him and partly because when I was away I could forget Mom wouldn't be there when I got back. I don't think I ever dealt with it really. Cecilia, she threw herself into her studies. She'd decided she wanted to be either an archaeologist or a paleontologist, something that involved travel to distant lands and the discovery of things that hadn't been seen for thousands, or hundreds of millions, of years. People enamored with ancient history say the past can teach you about the present but I say, at least in Cecilia's case, it was actually a way of avoiding the present entirely. So both of us were withdrawing in our own way, and Grace. Grace. I should've been there for them. That's one of the things I'll never forgive myself for.

I closed my eyes, tried to absorb what I'd just read. Decoding the words, revealing them one by one, they each stabbed at me, the horror escalating. At the time, he'd only told me he had spent a few days alone, I'd assumed to grieve. He eventually admitted what his father had done but never the intensity of the anguish it had caused him, and why not? Inexcusably, my main reaction to what I'd read wasn't pain over what he'd been through, but rather pain at the realization that this was yet another part of his life he'd kept from me.

And then there was Grace. Something had happened to her in the months after Sophia's death. She'd fallen in love, and sure, that was part of it. I'd schemed with Nate to make it happen, hoping it would help her heal. I'd been so naïve trying to twist emotions so soon after Sophia's death, like Grace was a magnet, flip her 180 and she'd be inexorably drawn along a straight path from grief to love. But in the next several months she'd become almost beatific, twirling; I think I remember her twirling barefoot across the lawn, laughing at random, sometimes inappropriate, moments, wearing flowers in her hair. But in retrospect there'd been something desperate about it, and after her relationship ended, suddenly and without forewarning, she'd sunk in on herself, closed up inside the shell of her faith. Where I'd thought she'd been stronger than any of us, I realized later that in fact the grief had completely drowned her.

Maybe she'd just finally understood the finality of her mother's death, although that seems like too facile an explanation. Toward the end I'd hardly seen her; she spent all her days in her room, or working in the church garden, and just weeks later she'd left to join the convent. And this is what I should've understood all along about Grace, that despite her flippancy, behind her patronizing and censoriousness, everything was harder for her because she *felt* more than the others. She put up a self-righteous, sometimes dictatorial front to hide how scared she was for us, for the world, to keep herself from thinking too deeply. I hadn't realized till now how much I missed her.

I blame myself for everything she went through. I knew Joel better than she did and I should have warned her. He'd never been cruel to her and she trusted him, believed in him and thought he believed in her, which must've made things just that much more devastating when they turned.

I reread this, wondering, then turned the page and copied down the next section of text, began attempting to cross out letters. It took five minutes of struggling before I realized it wasn't going to work.

I set down my pen, stared at it. I should stop now. I'd learned more than I wanted to know about all Nate, Grace, and Cecilia had been through; it was making me hate myself for not having seen it at the time, not having sensed what they were keeping from me. I wanted to run back in time to comfort these children, tell them everything would turn out okay, even knowing it had turned out anything but, for all of them in different ways. I knew there was much worse in the pages to come and I didn't want to see it, not now when there was nothing I could do.

So I should put the book back where I'd found it, open up the store, and let the work drain me of everything except sales and debt, black and red, future instead of past. But Nate was gone and the past was in shambles, and it felt like the future had no legs to stand on. All I had in me were questions that I needed Nate to answer. So I splayed my hands against the table and then pushed against it to rise, my face feeling numb as if coated in wax, and went upstairs to pack.

It took me over seven hours to get to Redbridge, and dusk was falling by the time I entered the town. Things had changed here, I could see that immediately, even since ten years ago when I'd come back for Mom's funeral: a new shopping center and movie theater, building facades either faded beyond recognition or painted in overly bright colors in an attempt to disguise that fading, and a collection of lumpy contemporary sculptures that sat on each corner looking vaguely pornographic.

Beyond the town I'd forgotten how rustic this part of the state was, the sunset colors of fall, the silent acres of land between houses. The run-down ranches in which people survived the understanding that their lives would never be more.

Here was the school that had tortured my childhood with its

baby-pink brick front, windows plastered with leaf rubbings and paper-plate pumpkins; the playground, its aluminum replaced with Day-Glo plastic, where I'd been either teased or ignored, not knowing which was worse. I never thought about this part of my childhood, had convinced myself it was all inconsequential back-story, but of course all parts of one's past live on in some way or another. The girl who'd stood alone in this playground was the same girl whose husband had abandoned her, the girl who'd gone to another man for comfort. Who'd let herself fall in love with that other man. For comfort.

A mile past the school I reached Bayard Lane. The driveway, once neatly topped with brown stones, was rutted now, tufted with crabgrass. I slowed the car, feeling a moment of panic. I'd biked down this road almost every day as a child, braving cold drizzle or the jam-thick heat of summer, expectant, hopeful, in love. Three children in pastels, their eggshell-pale faces framed by curls, Cecilia running to greet me, wrapping me in a hug, grabbing my arm to lead me toward a story, a project, a game. It was just a road, separated by a quarter of a century from that former destination, but this part of my past had brought me my husband and my son and my home, my sisters and my books, everything in the world I'd ever cared about. I turned down the drive, slid out from the car. And stared.

The house was almost unrecognizable. Several of the porch rails had buckled, the porch roof along with them. Grayish-white paint had chipped from the siding like a skin disease, and the inside of a broken window was patched with Tyvek sheeting. The garden—once tended so painstakingly—was in shambles, its beautiful rosebushes, flowering lavender, and bluebonnets now overrun by thistle, oxalis, and dandelions. The dust and clutter had spread like a cancer after Mrs. Sinclair got sick, and now I was witnessing the endpoint of that cancer's trajectory. It had taken over every-thing, as cancers do.

I looked up at Nate's bedroom window and then Joel and So-phia's, wondering if anyone was up there now, whether they'd see me if they happened to turn. I pictured Joel lying there on the bed where Sophia had spent her last days, under the same navy blue spread with his face as gaunt as hers had been. I pictured entering the house and climbing up the stairs, standing over him there and staring him in the eye, making him acknowledge me, forcing him to remember. Then grabbing the pillow from under his head, maybe the same pillow Sophia had died on, and pressing it over his mouth and nose.

My skin prickled, an electric shock, and I hurried toward the back of the house. Walking almost blindly toward the woods, the darkness so complete I could feel it rub against me, furry. Where once the fern and yellow asters had been trampled into an obvious path to the creek, now every direction looked like every other. The woods went on for miles; I should leave a trail, using scratch marks on tree trunks, torn clothes, torn hair, because if I got lost here, how long would it take for anybody to find me?

But then, in the distance, I heard a rustling that at first I thought must be wind through pine, or maybe the sort of rushing in the ears that might presage fainting. But the rustling continued and I started toward it. And there it was, the creek.

I remembered the stream as having been bigger. Maybe be-cause it actually had started to fade with age, the way people do, or maybe because one's perception fades; everything seems bigger when you're small. It was only five feet wide here, shallow but fast-flowing, and I followed it downstream trying to find the spot where we'd most often played. Half expecting to find Nate there, aged eight or twelve or seventeen, sitting cross-legged by the bank and waiting for me.

And now that I was here it all closed in on me, the memories like hawks with large wings blotting out my vision of anything else: moss and twig villages we'd built and decorated with the girls' hair ribbons, the tree we'd jumped from now leaning precariously to arch over the stream, the branches we'd climbed dragging in the water. Nate and I sitting here in the early morning dark on the day he'd left, terrified but oh so hopeful, this first morning of our new life.

And suddenly I knew.

Although of course subconsciously I must've known all along; it must be why my legs had carried me here to this spot rather than to the front door. In a daze I knelt by the large rock we'd long ago rolled beside the river and started clawing at the soil with my nails, then found a pointed rock and hammered with both hands at the earth, hair tangled in my face, eyes tearing with the effort and the dust I'd raised. Until, six inches down, the rock hit a clunk of metal.

I gouged wider, searching for edges, and when I found them I went back to using my fingers for leverage, nails tearing to the quick. Finding first a ragged piece of blue cloth that I stared at a moment, wondering, before I tossed it aside and continued to dig. Finally pulling up a gray plastic toolbox, the same box we'd hid for years under the holly bush with books and our encrypted notes.

I brushed it off carefully, reading it with my fingertips, the shape and sheen of the lid. Our past. And then I lifted the latch.

Inside, wrapped in a plastic bag, was a book.

Later I wouldn't remember anything of the walk back through the woods, my brain only kicking back into gear when I reached the

Sinclairs' yard with the book clutched in my hand. I'd packed Nate's notebook with my things, and was of half a mind to just sit in the car and work through the code right there, when an upstairs window opened. "I have a gun!" A man's voice. "Put up your hands!"

I looked up at the window, could only see a dark silhouette behind the screen and I stared at it, a weight on my chest too feral and many-legged to be simple rage. It was him, it was Joel, and I knew if I let myself get pulled through this black hole I'd never find my way out, so I clamped my teeth and forced down all thoughts but the most surface, all spiraling synapses in my brain except those necessary for the movement of my arms and tongue. I slowly put up my hands. "Please, I'm—" I'm what? Your daughter-in-law? "—a friend of Cecilia's," I said.

"Cecilia doesn't have friends. I'm calling the police. You stay right there, your hands up, and don't you try anything. I have a gun on you!"

"Chloe?" Cecilia's voice from the window. "Oh Chloe, you came. You shouldn't have come."

"You let your dad have a *gun*?"

"No of course not, don't worry. Daddy, please, let's sit down and I'm going to let Chloe in. Come to the door, Chloe."

I heard a shuffling sound from behind the window, Cecilia's voice in soothing tones. I looked down at the book Nate and I had long ago buried, then tucked it under my sweater, closed my eyes, and made myself breathe.

I hadn't seen Cecilia for ten years. We'd visited her after Mom's funeral, had dinner with her twice before leaving, and even back then I'd been shocked at how she looked: once so stunningly beautiful, her eyes were ringed with gray and she looked both bloated and muted, like her real self was hidden behind layers of batting.

ago, and when we were all dead they would still be here, still readable where all the books printed now would have long ago yellowed
and finally crumbled to dust.

I opened a bookcase and pulled out one of the volumes from
Galland's translation of Arabian Nights, *Les Mille et Une Nuits,* studied its pages, the French I didn't understand. I ran my finger over
the text, then held the book up to my face, closed my eyes, and
inhaled the sweet-sour scent of old paper and binding glue. Did
everyone who loved books do this when they encountered a new
one? I loved the physicality of books just as much as the stories inside, the feel of pages between my fingers, the intricacies of classic
fonts winding along the neatly lined rows of words. Patrons often
brought us used books in return for a discount off future purchases,
and seeing the state they were in with their cracked bindings, notes
in margins, page corners folded to mark a place, seeing this even in
contemporary paperbacks physically hurt me, almost as if they
were abused children.

I slid the book back onto the shelf and ran a finger across the
leather spines. There were tears in my eyes and I didn't know why,
maybe the beauty of all the embossed maroon, blue, and pine
green. Maybe the thought of these books that had endured all
these years, written and printed with so much care and dedication
but now sitting here on these shelves for so long unread. Soon passing on to other hands to sit on other shelves, I was projecting my
own loneliness onto them. Or maybe it was just that I was overwhelmed with all that had been lost; I wanted my old life back, not
life in the bookshop but the life I'd lived here, probably the last
time I'd felt fully loved and cared for.

Grace, Nate, Cecilia, and I on a winter afternoon, piled on
pillows by this fireplace, whispering so as not to wake Sophia who

was napping on the couch. "Everyone gets one wish," Nate had said. "If you knew nothing in your life would happen the way you want or expect except for that one thing, what would you choose?"

Nate had wished he'd grow up to be a writer, Cecilia had wished for psychic powers, and Grace had wished to be a wife and mother. I'd wished for money, to become rich and live in a home with a swimming pool, but in my mind I held one true and awesome wish, to never have to leave, to be able to stay here with the Sinclairs forever and ever and ever. Ironic that less than ten years later all I'd wanted was to get away and forget this house had ever existed.

I pulled the book out from under my sweater and sat with it by the unlit fireplace. I flipped through it looking for the lines Nate had marked for me decades ago, his secret message. But the pages were stained water, the faint pencil lines he'd made probably long gone. I opened the book to the last pages and remembered the early morning after I'd found the book, decrypted its message, and realized what it would mean. We'd been seventeen and eighteen years old, just days before Nate's suicide note, days before the decisions that would change everything that happened after. "They're us," I'd said, "aren't they. That's why you wanted me to read it."

"It's okay," he'd said, and taken my hand, his face grim but determined. "Just listen and I'll tell you exactly what we're going to do."

PART VI

I Defy You, Stars

12

STEREOTYPICALLY, it was raining the day of Sophia's funeral, a fuzzy sort of rain that shushed onto the canopy of umbrellas. Mr. Sinclair's whole congregation was at the cemetery, women and girls in long dark dresses, men and boys in poorly fitted suits. Mr. Sinclair stood at the head of the grave tonelessly reciting the benediction, and beside him, Grace, Nate, and Cecilia stood in a row, faces set in identical grim determination.

I couldn't hear Joel's words. I was hidden in the shadows behind a large oak, staring at the coffin and trying to imagine Sophia gazing up at its dark lid. Which of her dresses was she wearing? I should've asked Nate so I could picture her as she truly was. Her regular dresses didn't fit now; her arms and legs were too skinny, her breasts deflated and her belly too big, so one of the parishioners had made her a series of colorless, shapeless muumuus. But I didn't want her to be forced to spend eternity in an outfit that was basically a shroud, so instead, for now, I imagined her in the long cornflower-blue dress that she'd worn on the day I'd first met her.

She was lying there in that dress and her blue house slippers, hands folded at her chest.

Why was I even thinking about this?

Suddenly Grace dropped to her knees, then forward on all fours, her back heaving. Mr. Sinclair turned to her with his forehead knotted, then stopped speaking and sank beside her and pressed her head against his shoulder. My eyes filled, and I turned away and walked quickly back through the graveyard to my bike.

Wherever she was now (was she anywhere?), did Mrs. Sinclair know how much I'd wanted to be able to be with her in her last days? Hold her hand at the end? How I wanted now to climb down into the earth with her, slip into her coffin to keep her warm until . . . until judgment, I guess, that's what she'd believed, that she'd be waiting now under the ground to be judged. Which sounded horrible, but even if it was true it wasn't like she'd be waiting long. One-third of a second, that's how long it would take for God to decide where she belonged.

Give me a sign, I thought. Just something little, a rainbow, a cardinal. I need to know she's somewhere. Nate needs to see. I stood by my bike and closed my eyes, trying to feel Him, but feeling nothing. I wanted to believe, I always had, but how did people lean on something that had no weight? "You don't need proof, you just *know*," Grace had told me so many times. Everyone standing here over the grave had somehow found that weight inside them, but all I seemed to have inside me was loneliness.

"You're a smart girl." This was the last thing Mrs. Sinclair had said to me, the week before she'd gone to the hospital for the last time. "An astute girl, so you'll understand what I'm saying. That you shouldn't be sad because the truth is that I'm already gone. My body, it's been holding on to life much longer than it really wanted to. The parts of me you're mourning left a long time ago, and I'll only be my real self again after my body passes on."

Which was true, of course; she'd been eaten up by her sickness months ago, had holed up in her room watching us come and go without even acknowledging the coming and going, nothingness in her eyes. True but irrelevant, because part of me had always assumed she'd somehow come back again.

She'd closed her eyes after this and I'd sat with her, hollow and dry-eyed, until I was sure she'd fallen asleep. But as I got up to go, she grabbed for my wrist, held it with more strength than I'd realized she still had, and looked up into my face. "I know," she said softly. "I want you to know that I know, and that I'm happy." And that was all she'd said, never clarifying what she was referring to. Had she somehow found out about me and Nate?

Perhaps Cecilia sensed it too. Her personality had changed, her free-spiritedness had become a kind of frenetic energy, her mind clouded with unnamable terrors ("Where you going? What're you doing? Can I come?"), as if she sensed not only her mother but also Nate and me slipping away. But we hadn't done much, even in private, that would've given us away. The four of us still spent most of our afternoons together, sharing books and thoughts, caring for Mrs. Sinclair or completing the lessons that till a few months ago she'd still been finding the strength to prepare. When no one was looking, Nate and I would secretly touch fingers and exchange glances, and when we took walks we'd lag behind for brief, fevered kisses—better, I thought, because they were so risky. But that was all we did, really. The grasping and groping on the beach three years before was the furthest we'd ever gone.

Even recently—with Grace spending most of her time caring for her mother or in solitary prayer, Cecilia busy reading history texts and encyclopedia volumes she'd requested I bring from the library—still Nate and I spent much more time talking than touching. But maybe Mrs. Sinclair had somehow sensed how we felt, and loved me enough not to stop Nate from having a relationship outside the faith. Maybe she had a different sort of faith from Mr. Sinclair's, the sort that made accommodations for happiness.

Or, the other possibility, she could've been referring to our second, equally as epic secret. That Nate and I had applied for college next year.

Mrs. Sinclair had stopped homeschooling that spring; Cecilia was sixteen, Nate eighteen, and Grace almost twenty, after all, and Sophia was too exhausted to do much more than breathe. I'd given Nate my schoolbooks so he could learn about evolution and the Big Bang theory, and some of the cruelties of world history that Mrs. Sinclair had wanted to protect her children from. Nate devoured it all; there was so much of the universe he knew nothing about, and I think to him, gaining access was as monumental as stepping into the world of adult books had been for me. So much to read and so little time to read it; a realization of something we'd always suspected, how small our own world was and the nearly infinite expanse that lay beyond it.

We both filled out applications, early decision, to Berkeley. Nate, of course, didn't tell his family. And I hadn't told my mother because she'd always viewed college as something the other half did to avoid reality. So we applied in secret, obsessing over our essays, writing and rewriting. And on an early April morning we'd both snuck to a testing center and taken our SATs. We did well, Nate even scoring a perfect 800 on verbal. It had to be enough. College and then graduate school, in English, and then . . . well, we couldn't see beyond that. More school, maybe. All we really wanted was to learn. Certainly that was something Mrs. Sinclair would have approved of too.

I biked the long way home from the funeral, up hills so I could barrel down the other side, folded almost in half with my feet raised and legs parallel to the ground. Careening around corners, dodging potholes and fallen branches, splashing through puddles. The rain had stopped, my damp hair slapping into my face and drying in limp, ropy strands, my shirt clammy against my chest, and as I raced around the corner toward home I threw my head back and screamed.

I wanted Nate. I wanted to hold him, and I felt a sudden misplaced jealousy for all of them because they weren't alone with this. I wanted to be standing there with them at the grave site, driving home huddled against them in the backseat of a hearse and then sitting with them wordlessly, shoulder touching shoulder, hand squeezing hand, like that could mute the sharp angles careening inside me. As I reached home I stood a minute looking at the house as if it belonged to someone else, stared at the dark wood siding, the aluminum screen door too warped to close completely. I imagined my mother inside on the couch frenetically circling letters in her word find puzzles or leafing through magazines to study new hairstyles. Slapped with the sudden thought: *She shouldn't have been the one who died,* and I studied the thought, absorbed the fact that I'd had it. Then turned the bike around and pedaled slowly back down the road.

By the time I got to Bayard Lane the funeral procession had already started to arrive. I parked my bike behind a tree and made my way through the woods, ending up in the backyard.

Guests were trekking back and forth from their cars, setting plates of food on the tables that had been moved to the yard. I couldn't see Cecilia or Nate, but Grace was standing behind one of the tables with Cesar, the man the Sinclairs had hired on as a gardener when Mrs. Sinclair got too sick to tend the flowers herself. He had a hand on her back, his head bent to talk to her, and she was standing with her shoulders hunched, staring intently at a plate of assorted cheeses.

Joel Sinclair stood by the back door with his hands clasped at his waist, eyes closed, rocking from foot to foot. Nobody seemed to find this strange, although they did look like they were going out of their way to avoid looking at him, talking in small groups, fishing soda bottles from the large aluminum pail of ice by his side with their heads averted. Allowing him his private grieving.

And then I felt a tap on my shoulder. "I saw you in the cemetery," Cecilia said.

I spun to face her, my eyes wide.

"It's okay," she said. "Mom would've liked that you came. Actually, I'm sure she's up there smiling about it."

Without warning, I felt my eyes fill. "I wanted to visit her in the hospital," I said. "I wish I could've."

"She wouldn't even have known you were there. She wasn't awake in the hospital, they had her on morphine."

Cecilia seemed distracted more than sad, like she was half asleep, her mind somewhere else entirely. I reached to set a hand on her shoulder, but she shrugged it away. "So you're probably looking for Nate, but he went down to the river soon as we got back home. He hated all this." She glanced back at the gathering on the lawn, people talking animatedly. "Which I do too. I mean they're laughing. Can you believe they're laughing?" She watched them a moment, her eyes glazed and unfocused. "Let's go find him." She pulled me by the arm around the outskirts of the lawn, staying under cover until we reached the far corner where Grace stood with Cesar, his hand still on her back. Cecilia stood on her toes to whisper something in her ear, and Grace glanced at Cesar, then nodded and turned from him without speaking.

The three of us walked silently through the woods to the river. Grace and Cecilia seemed lost in thought. And me? I was doing my best not to think at all. Because it was sinking in slowly, the idea that somebody could, all at once, not exist anymore. Where had it all gone? The feel of her fingers French-braiding my hair, the velvety sound of her storytelling, the scent of the vanilla extract she dabbed on her neck in lieu of perfume. To let it in, the idea that all of it could just vanish into nothingness, made me feel like my insides had been beaten and clawed. It seemed as unlikely as a science fiction novel, as H. G. Wells's time machine.

Nate was sitting with his pants rolled to his knees, feet in the water, staring at the opposite shore. He didn't acknowledge our approach till Cecilia sat next to him and set her head on his shoulder. He pressed his cheek against her hair, and after a moment Grace sat on his other side and took his hand.

I watched them, feeling numb, knowing that this was *their* grief; they were the ones who owned it while I was just a bystander. I shouldn't be acting like I had any right to it; if I wasn't here they wouldn't be thinking of me at all.

But then Grace whispered something in Nate's ear and he turned and saw me, kissed the top of Cecilia's head, and rose. When he reached my side he asked softly, "You holding up okay?" And the fact that *he'd* asked *me*, as if I had permission to be not-okay, it broke me. I nodded, then shook my head, and when he reached to hold me I made a choked, squashed sound, so embarrassing that I pressed a hand over my mouth, biting hard on my fingers. He started to rub at my back but I swallowed quickly and pulled away, walked down to the river, and sat next to Cecilia with my arms wrapped around my knees. After a minute Nate sat back between her and Grace and we all stared down at the water, speaking without words.

Finally Grace said, "You guys know she's here, right?" She looked out across the river. "Can't you feel her?"

I followed her eyes. "You mean like a ghost?"

"Kind of like a ghost, her soul is with us." Grace closed her eyes and sat silently a minute before opening them. "She's glad we're all here together. Taking care of each other, she says that's good."

"That's spooky, Grace," Cecilia said. "You're trying to say you just talked to her?"

"Not *talking*, don't be stupid, it's not like she's a Ouija board. I just can feel her, what she wants to say. I felt it the whole time in the hospital too, she told me all kinds of stuff. I know you think she was completely out of it, but it was probably the best time I'd ever spent with her."

"What stuff?" Nate said.

Grace swept her hands across the ground, brushing fallen leaves and pine needles into a wall between her legs. "Like she's been telling me I have a calling. She says I'll find out soon what it is, and that I shouldn't hesitate, just accept it."

Nate raised one eyebrow, and Grace's face hardened. "Just forget it. I knew I shouldn't have told you."

"You know I really *don't* feel her," Cecilia said softly. "I mean, not at all. I didn't even feel her when she was here, not recently. And there's not much that's going to change now, is there? I mean we'll feel how she's gone, we'll know we can't go upstairs to hold her hand. We'll miss her more, but the truth is—" She glanced at Grace. "I know it sounds bad, but the day-to-day? It's mostly going to get easier."

"How can you say that?" There was ice in Grace's voice.

"No, I know what she means," Nate said. "Except for Joel. You see how he's been the past few days? She reined him in, and without her? Either I'm going to kill him or he's going to kill me."

"Stop calling him Joel," Grace said. "Why do you keep calling him Joel?"

"You don't think it's ludicrous to call him Daddy? I know the two of you idolize each other, so maybe it feels right to you. But 'Daddy' implies some kind of affection."

Out of the corner of my eye I watched Grace, who had started bunching and unbunching the fabric of her dress with both fists. "Grace?" I said.

She swung her head quickly to me, her face seeming blank, stunned, before she turned back again to the river and whispered, "What're we going to do?"

Of course Grace's life was going to change most now. She'd been the one to drive her mother to the hospital, help her bathe and dress, read to her from the Bible, and coax her to eat. It had taken up almost her entire life, and maybe everyone had thought this might go on forever, that there was no need to plan for some other future. But now that Mrs. Sinclair was gone, what else did she have in her life? She was nineteen years old and I'd never heard her mention college or the wish for a career. She'd had richly detailed fantasies of marriage and motherhood, but I'd always sensed she didn't really believe they might come true any more than she believed characters might jump out from the books she read and carry her into their romantic plots; they were entertainments to distract her from real life. I remembered the story Nate had told me about the night he found her with a bottle full of pills, and felt a sudden clutch of panic.

And then I thought suddenly of Cesar, the gardener, standing with his hand on her shoulder, the acute concern on his face. He was so good-looking with his dark skin, dark hair, and dark eyes, probably only a year or two older, and watching Grace now I thought, Hmmm.

Maybe something good could come out of Mrs. Sinclair's death, Grace's new freedom. Maybe I could do something good. *I know, and I'm happy,* Mrs. Sinclair had said to me, giving permission. And I couldn't help thinking she would've been happy for this too.

I brought the idea up to Nate several days later, after I had the chance to come up with an actual plan of attack. It had been a horrible week. I'd gone to the Sinclairs' every morning, needing to be with them, and I'd seen Grace and Cecilia once through the library window and once sitting on the front porch. But there was no sign of Nate, and because their father was home all I could do was stand in the woods looking up at the house, trying to see in the windows, waiting.

Until Saturday morning passing the holly bush at the periphery of the lawn, I saw behind it the old toolbox where we used to hide our coded notes. I crouched beside the bush and opened the box. Inside was *The French Lieutenant's Woman,* which I'd loaned to Nate the month before. I flipped through it, hoping for a note, and finally noticed the faint pencil marks on the title page. I squinted, studying the letters, then smiled. Our old code. I flipped to the first page of the story, used it to decode his message.

Woanent gasotert loychi surthech sumondstay dAMbe hisagere reate able 9.

I slipped the book under my shirt and pressed it against my skin. At least seven years since we'd last written these notes. And thinking back on it now, I found myself wanting to cry, because part of the mourning I'd felt that week wasn't just for Mrs. Sinclair herself but for those years, the relative simplicity of being eight, nine, ten. Much as I loved Nate, loved every second I now spent with him, I'd lost something in choosing him over the others. I'd lost the sense of being part of a family.

I was there the next morning in time to watch Grace and Cecilia climb stoically into the car, Mr. Sinclair driving them away. I waited an extra fifteen minutes to be safe before going to the door.

Nate pulled me inside without speaking. He closed the door behind me and kissed me so fiercely it hurt, and then he made a huffing sound and buried his face in my neck. I stroked a hand over the back of his head, staring at the wall behind him. This was the first time I'd seen him since the funeral, and it was all too much to process, his pain, the immensity of what had happened, and the fear of what might change because of it. And I had no idea what to say. "How's it been here?" is what I came up with finally, stupidly.

He pulled away without speaking, stretching a grimace. I couldn't tell if it was real or just a face made for effect.

"I'm sorry," I said softly.

"Yeah." He squared his shoulders. "Cecilia's all right, I think. She's been into her studies more than ever, taking notes and everything. Which is maybe okay, keeps her mind from going to bad places. But Grace? I haven't really seen her for a few days; I'd been, I guess you could say, taking time alone, to think. But from what I've seen, she's been spending most of her time in the bedroom, with her door closed. I knock, try and come in, and she snaps at me, so I've been . . . this is going to sound stupid, but I've been reading to her through the door. Just to let her know I'm there. I don't know if she's listening, she could be plugging her ears for all I know, but at least she doesn't stop me."

I studied his face, the dark hollows under his eyes. He seemed so thin, his pants loose on his legs; he must've lost ten pounds in just the past week. "And what about you?"

He turned away and shrugged, shrugged again. "I'm a hundred percent better since you're here," he said, which didn't really answer anything.

I touched a damp curl of hair at his temple. He swiped my finger away but then, like he regretted the move, raised my hand to his lips and kissed it. "I'm going to get us something to drink. You want to sit in the dining room and I'll bring it there?"

"Thanks." I squeezed his hand. "And listen, I had this idea, something we can do for Grace." Maybe the distraction, coming up with a plan and enacting it, would help him. Maybe distraction was the only way to deal with grief, like Cecilia was doing. And what Grace wasn't doing, yet. "I'll tell you when you come back," I said, walking into the dining room.

The table was cluttered with dirty dishes and three vases of wilting flowers. There was a basket of apples and pears swarming with fruit flies, another with rolls starting to spot. The ornate hutch on the far wall had been emptied of dishes and now held only Mr. and Mrs. Sinclair's wedding photo, the two of them standing solemnly side by side, not touching, Sophia in an old-fashioned, high-necked white satin gown. I stared at the photo a long while. She didn't look much older than me. Who had put it there?

I hadn't thought much until just then about how empty the house must feel for all of them without Sophia there, even though they had each other. Maybe that was the reason behind the hollowness in Nate's face, the weight he'd lost; he was collapsing against the space where she'd been.

A minute later he entered with two glasses, a bottle tucked under his arm. Ginger ale, I thought at first, until I saw the label. "Whiskey? Where'd you get whiskey? I thought your dad didn't believe in alcohol."

"He didn't," Nate said, filling both glasses halfway. "He used to say it's the way the devil blunts our testimony for Christ so he can squeeze us into his mold." He clinked his glass against mine. "Apparently he's changed his mind."

I lifted the glass, sniffed it, watched Nate swig from his glass, and then set mine down without tasting it. "Won't he know you stole some?"

"He does know, I'm sure he does."

I stared at him. This wasn't the first time? He'd been drinking?

"But he hasn't said anything because if he did he'd have to admit he's been getting drunk himself." Nate's expression was strange, I couldn't interpret it, maybe just disgust or maybe pain disguised as sarcasm. "And he knows I'd call him out in front of Grace and Cecilia, maybe even the rest of the congregation, for being a hypocrite. So we're both just looking the other way."

"How long has this been going on?"

"Just a couple days. Don't give me that look, Chloe, I'm not letting the devil blunt my testimony for Christ. I just like how it tastes. For a minute it makes you feel like you might maybe die, not be able to breathe, but then the heat goes away and you just feel stronger." He smiled again, rocking his glass back and forth against the table, *tap-tap-tap*, liquid sloshing against the sides. "So what's your idea?" he said.

"I don't think you should," I said. "Be drinking, I mean. My mom started drinking when she was our age, and she said it made her lose brain cells. It got to be really hard for her to stop, and the only reason she quit was finding out she was pregnant with me."

"Would you please stop acting like my mother, Chloe? I'm not looking for a replacement." He straightened in his chair, gripping his glass tighter. "Tell me your idea."

So I told him slowly, watching his face. Hoping to see the Nate I knew, the boy who loved schemes, would get a kick out of coercing Grace into something that seemed so against her nature, everything she believed. Something that might save her.

But his face showed nothing until I was done, when he swigged the last of the whiskey from his glass and held it in his mouth, watching me contemplatively a moment before he swallowed. "Joel would totally have a stroke," he said. And smiled.

Nate started with Grace, telling her how a month before their mother's death he'd found her sitting among the roses, looking mournful. "She said it was one of the things she felt saddest about," he told her, "leaving the roses. They felt like they were part of the family to her, and knowing the person taking care of them from now on wasn't part of the family, it made her feel like she was betraying them."

Grace looked stricken. "Why didn't she tell me any of that? I would've learned how to garden."

Nate glanced at her cagily. "I'm sure Cesar could teach you. You know he really likes you."

She'd stared at him, looking almost horrified. "What do you mean?"

"I mean he *likes* you. He's always asking about you, what you like to do, your plans for the next few years, that kind of thing."

He'd shrugged one shoulder nonchalantly as he turned from the room. "You should ask him to help you with the roses," he said. "For Mom's sake."

And that was it. A seed planted. Next it was my turn, and my part was easy. After telling Cesar that Grace wanted to take over care of Sophia's roses, when he agreed to help I cast him a sideways glance. "She's awfully pretty, don't you think?" I said. "I mean, I'd say she's beautiful even."

He looked startled, then red-faced, watched me with a quick smile that looked like it had been slapped on. "Yes, yes, you could say she is," he said.

I gave him a wink that I hoped looked much less fake than it felt. "She might've told me she likes how you look too," I said. After which, my job was done.

Now we just waited and watched, pleased with ourselves, as Grace developed a new interest in gardening. Of course we didn't see any proof that they were doing or talking about anything other than flower care. Grace knew how her father would react if he got even a hint that anything was going on. She was his favorite, the one he counted on to do right, and she seemed to need that, to define herself by it. So we didn't see anything overt between them, but there was an unmistakable change in their relationship. Cesar's countenance changed when they were together; he looked at the same time taller and softer, almost like a father with a child. And Grace started singing under her breath as she did chores; she tied ribbons in her hair and stopped wearing the clunky brown shoes they all had worn as firmly attached as calluses for as long as I'd known them, instead walking barefoot through the house and garden.

And she smiled. Grace, who had always seemed to feel that

smiling was beneath her, or maybe that it was just inappropriate; now she smiled all the time at things as trivial as fireflies or oldies on the radio.

But as heartening as that seemed on the surface, I could sense something unhealthy behind it. It all happened too fast, like she was trying to mask the intensity of one emotion by pasting on another. I just hoped that underneath in her subconscious the distraction was helping her heal, in the way a break heals under a cast when no weight is placed on the broken bone.

It was about five months after the beginning of whatever had begun that something seemed to change in Grace. She grew quiet, sitting with us but not joining in conversations, staring out at the lawn with her eyes fierce and hands clasped in her lap. When we talked directly to her there was a strange delay before each response, like one sees in interviews with reporters across the world, our voices traveling thousands of miles before reaching her ears.

And then on an unseasonably warm afternoon I was sitting on the lawn with her and Cecilia, Nate napping beside us with an arm flung over his eyes—hungover, I was almost sure of it—when she said, "Do you ever think about how little in life you actually control? Things happen without you making a conscious decision, and suddenly everything spins backwards and you're heading in a completely different direction than before, and there's no way to spin forward again."

"You mean losing Mom," Cecilia said.

"Well, yeah, sure, and other things." She splayed her fingers on the grass. "I just wish you could get hints of how things would turn out before you were slapped over the head with them."

I looked down at her splayed hands, the nails usually so clean now ragged and ridged with dirt, one scabbed and torn past the quick. I wished more than anything that I could tell her it was okay, that Nate and I knew and were happy for her, and more than that, that we understood perfectly what it was like to hide feelings for someone forbidden. We'd kept our relationship a secret but never actually discussed the secrecy; it just had happened, probably at first because it was too new and slightly embarrassing, and then because it felt so awkward that we *hadn't* told them. But of course they'd have to find out eventually. Could I tell her about us now without discussing it with Nate first?

But then Grace said, "What if something happens that there's no good way out of? You're not thinking right, Satan takes you over momentarily. And you think you know the extent of the sin at the time, but suddenly you're walking hand in hand with Satan with no way of letting go."

"What are you talking about?" Cecilia said.

"Everything," she said, then closed her eyes, her face perfectly still. "I don't know, everything and nothing. Don't worry about it, it was really only a hypothetical." And then she rose without saying more and walked into the house. We both watched after her, Cecilia's jaw set, and then she reopened the book beside her and began to read.

"Cecilia?" I said.

"It's her business. She'll tell us when she's ready."

Did Cecilia know about Cesar? Or was there something else going on that none of us knew about? Walking hand in hand with Satan, no way to let go; was she talking about something as simple as falling in love? I wanted to run after Grace, try and talk the fear out of her even though I had no idea what I could say. The mile markers their father had laid on the path to eternity were so deeply set that I was pretty sure only God's voice could displace them, but

I had to say something, even if only to make sure she knew she wasn't alone.

How could Cecilia have gone back to reading so quickly? Why didn't she seem to care? "Are you okay?" I said.

She held a finger against the page as she looked up at me, blankly, then smiled and bent to kiss my cheek. "Of course," she said. "But I love you for worrying so much about us." And then she went back to her reading.

But she wasn't even close to okay, I knew that. It wasn't just Grace who had transformed into someone unrecognizable; Cecilia had become a different person too. I think she must've stopped showering, always seeming to wear the same long green dress, her hair stringy and slick against her head. Where she'd always been the first to approach me when I entered the yard, pull me close and fill my ear with stories and ideas, now when I talked to her she'd listen with her head cocked and eyes focused somewhere above my head, as if to suggest that she was trying her best to hear but unable to understand over the ruckus around us.

Something about all of them scared me now. I sensed a sort of disintegration beginning to happen to the family without Sophia as a centering force and with Joel now staying at the church long into the night. Grace lost in another world, Cecilia lost in her own head, Nate drinking almost every day, obviously hurting but refusing to talk about any of it. But I pretended to myself that none of it mattered, that it would all be temporary. One of these days when I entered their yard Cecilia would run from behind to hug me, Grace pulling me close to straighten my collar and tell me whatever they'd been doing before I arrived, after which we'd all traipse off together into the woods to play. The rest of the world disappearing behind discussions on who might win a Frankenstein versus Sandworm fight, our own private timeless time. I pretended to myself that healing was possible.

And then one day, as I entered the Sinclairs' yard, Grace jumped up from the porch and pulled me into the woods. There was something strange, frantic in her eyes, that scared me.

She stretched a wide, fake smile and leaned one hand nonchalantly against a tree. "I'm here because I have a question," she said, "and I thought I'd ask you since you know more than any of us about how things are done out there." She nodded over my shoulder, gesturing, I guess, to the rest of the world. "Let's just say a person wasn't part of a church but had it in her mind to get married, how exactly would that person do it? I mean without a pastor? There's a judge or something, right? Do you just show up and say vows and he signs a paper and bam you're married?"

I felt my brain zip-zipping back and forth against my skull and tried to tamp it back into place, responding like she'd just asked me how one might go about getting a fishing license. "Well, I'm not sure about the details exactly, but I know *a person*"—I raised my eyebrows—"could do it with a justice of the peace. I read this book that came out a few years ago; you know *Watership Down*? It's by the same author, and the wife in the book didn't want to get married in a church. I don't remember the details of what they actually did, but I can find out."

Grace must've heard something in my voice because her face flushed pink. "Whatever, don't bother, I was just curious." The arrangement of her expression was all wrong. She should've practiced this in the mirror. "I didn't know he had a new book out."

"You wouldn't like it." I said this partly because it was true, the book had been awful, but also partly because the marriage had ended very, very badly. "Some authors only have enough inside them for one book, and anything else they write is just the dregs of what's left."

"Interesting," she said, not sounding interested. She tilted her head back and peered up a minute at the tree branches against the sky before saying, "It's that way with relationships too, you know. That's what happened with my dad; he used up all the love he had in him on my mother, and on God I guess, and all he has left for anyone else are the dregs. But I don't blame him for that any-more."

I watched her a moment, considering, then said, "I know about Cesar."

She took a step back.

"It's a good thing, Grace," I said softly, wanting more than anything to hug her, but she seemed on the verge of either running or hitting me. "I'm sure you think it's a sin or whatever, I'm not up on what your father thinks constitutes sin. But it's not, it's not even close to being wrong."

"Please don't, Chloe. You have no idea what you're talking about."

"You're old enough to leave here, and you're old enough to make your own choices. You shouldn't ever feel bad for doing what's best for yourself, it's not like it's going to hurt anybody."

"Stop, okay? Do you know how cliché you sound? Seriously, you and Nate are just like my dad in a way. You think of every-thing as being black and white, right or wrong."

"I'm sorry, I didn't mean to make this sound easy, I know it's not."

"Oh don't apologize." A lock of hair had come loose from her braid and she swiped it back, then rested her hand at the side of her head, face covered by her forearm. "I want it to be easy, you know? All my life what I've wanted is for the Lord to guide me so I'd know I was traveling to the right place. Immediately I'd know, it would feel settled that way like slotting in puzzle pieces. But how can you know whether what you're feeling is a sign from God or just an inevitable part of being close to someone? And whether what comes from that closeness is fate, or your mind being so swamped by everything that's happened that the only way you can sort through it is by pretending there's such a thing?"

I didn't know what to say, the only possible responses more clichés and meaningless platitudes, and besides, she wasn't looking for answers, was talking more to herself than to me. But I wanted to find some way to steady her, so I reached for her hand with both of mine. Immediately she flinched like I'd stung her. "Don't tell anybody any of this, Chloe, promise you won't." And with that she turned and started back to the house.

I watched her climb the porch steps, my mind racing. Was she seriously planning to marry Cesar? The idea of one of us getting married seemed so bizarre to me. In my mind we were still eight, nine, and eleven, marriage as far away as death. But of course Grace was twenty now, an adult. Three years older than my mom had been when she gave birth to me. The only real curiosity was that she was able to accept the idea of marrying outside the church.

I remembered one summer when I was nine or ten, Grace showing up at my front door disheveled and flushed with sweat, carrying a bedsheet slung over one shoulder like a hobo bag. The bottom of her dress was gray from road dust and her hair was loose, wild wisps framing her face. I'd never seen Grace looking anything other than perfect, so I was momentarily terrified.

"What's wrong?" I said. "What happened?"

Grace dropped the sheet on the floor, and with her eyes on me she spread it to reveal its contents. There inside were the miniature mice and dollhouse furniture we'd played with many times in the attic, and the blond-haired baby doll Grace had been holding on the day I first met her. I stared at them, then back up at Grace.

"There's more," she said, "more dolls and their dress-up clothes and the dollhouse, it's so big I'll have to find some way to bring it. And some of our books . . ." She sank onto the sofa, stared mournfully at the toys. "There's so much."

I picked up the doll, bewildered. "But why?"

"Cecilia's been spending too much time with them. If my dad knew he'd burn them, maybe even make us burn them. So I'm basically rescuing these by giving them to you."

I cupped a hand against the doll's cheek, horrified. "*Burn* them?"

She watched me for a moment, unblinking, then recited, "Genesis 6:5: 'Every imagination of the thoughts of his heart was only evil continually.' And Genesis 8:20 says the imagination of man's heart is evil from his youth." She raised her chin. "Imagination distracts from the truth and leads to sin and deception. There's no fantasy in God and His Word."

"Your dad said that?"

"He didn't have to say it, the warnings are all over the Bible." Her eyes were suddenly fierce, fervent, and for the first time I saw her father in them. "If he had any idea how much time Cecilia spends on her toys, he might just destroy *her*. You want them, don't you?"

I thought of the first time I'd seen the baby doll in her christening gown, the dollhouse with its elegant carved wood furnishings, upholstered sofas, tiny books, and cooking utensils all so beautifully formed one could imagine shrinking and living comfortably inside its rooms. The hunger I'd felt each time I played with them. "But what about Cecilia?" I said.

"I'll tell her Daddy took them. And not to tell Mom because we don't want to upset her. She'll be sad, but she'll get past it and it'll be better for all of us."

And so the toys I'd coveted for so long were finally mine. But the next week, just two days after Grace brought over a number of their books, including the Narnia collection, she returned asking for the books back, saying her father had noticed the empty spaces in the library.

Now, thinking of this ten years later, I realized how little I understood about Grace. Would her father really have thought playing with dolls could be a sin, or was her fear of him unwarranted? Hadn't he approved of the Narnia books? Was it all just something she herself believed?

The truth, I think, was that Grace had more of an internal fantasy life than all of us put together. She used to talk about books for days, even weeks, after she finished reading them, as if she had a hard time removing herself from the worlds they'd carried her into. She'd talked endlessly about the future, her dreams of a husband and four children she'd already named (Thomas, Sarah, Eli, and Katherine), a small house on Prince Edward Island—Anne of Green Gables' home—with an ocean view and a garden to grow vegetables, which she and the kids would collect in baskets each afternoon for dinner. That vivid imagination probably spread to her religious convictions themselves, her belief God was speaking to her in actual words, through prayer.

And now this, the speed with which she'd fallen in love with Cesar and was imagining a future, showed how easily she slipped into fantasy. Maybe this was the type of "sin and deception" she'd been afraid of; maybe she'd been fighting against her own imaginative tendencies all her life and now was working to find a way to accept them.

I felt a sudden trilling inside me, like I'd just swallowed something with wings. If Grace could marry someone outside the church, Grace who acted like she had a direct phone line to God and His endless list of shalt-nots, then why couldn't Nate? Nate refused to talk about his father, but I could see the conflicted emotions in his eyes whenever Grace or Cecilia mentioned him, anger, but also—much as he pretended he didn't care—something close to longing. The idea of how his father would react if he found out about our relationship probably terrified Nate, but if Grace did it *first,* well maybe he'd be all out of fury by the time he got to us.

I wished I could tell Nate about the conversation. First because he'd helped carry out my plan, so of course he'd want to know it had been a success. But mostly because for the past few years he'd felt responsible for Grace, for keeping her safe, so I knew what a huge weight it would be off his shoulders knowing somebody else might be taking that on.

But Grace had asked me not to tell, and of course he'd find out soon enough if she really did leave home. So instead I gathered information on civil weddings, looked up the name of a justice of the peace and the address of the local courthouse. And then I wrote it all on a sheet of paper and waited for the chance to slip it to Grace.

But I never had that chance. Because it was only two weeks later that things exploded.

13

I never found out exactly what had happened, but overnight things changed; I was cut off from their lives. I continued going to the Sinclairs' every day after school, but no one ever came to the door. Why hadn't Nate come to find me? He must have known I'd been looking, had to realize I was scared, so how could he not find some way to tell me what was going on? Were they not home or just not answering? Impossible to tell; the only signs of life were of past life—books propped open in the library, new arrangements of crumbs on the dining table—but the house itself was silent.

Finally, on a chilly April morning, I cut school and biked to the Sinclairs' early to find out whether they were actually leaving each morning or spending their days at home, pretending not to hear the doorbell. I huddled in the woods with my hands tucked inside my sleeves, watching lights switch on and off, silhouettes in the windows. Finally at eight-thirty they all left the house and filed silently into the car. First I focused on Nate, willing him to look my way. But then I saw Grace following behind Mr. Sinclair. And I stared.

Grace was almost unrecognizable, looked like a distant, terminally ill cousin of her former self, her skirt too long and stained at the knees and butt, her hair unwashed and tangled, her skin grayish without the glow she'd gotten from her days spent in the garden. I watched them drive away, fear lying heavy like cold, wet clay in my lungs.

What had happened? Where were they all going? I climbed on my bike and sped down the driveway in time to see the car disappear down the street in the direction of downtown.

I continued down the road till I got to the church, looked at Mr. Sinclair's car in the driveway and then up at the church doors. I stood there a moment, trying to figure out what to do, and finally set my bike down and walked around the periphery of the church grounds to peer in a back window.

The window looked in on Mr. Sinclair's office, books piled on unfinished pine shelves, his vestments hanging from a hook on the wall, and a large white desk where both Mr. Sinclair and Nate sat with notepads and pens. Mr. Sinclair was talking, a hand pressed over his eyes, and Nate was scribbling furiously, his face grim and set.

I pressed my fingertips to the glass, feeling a burrowing loneliness. It had been two weeks since I'd last seen him, and without him I felt hollow, like one of those blow-up dolls weighted at the base, the type children punch to the floor, let bob back up, and then punch down again.

I stood there willing him to look up at the window, see me, but he was so focused on whatever he was writing that he didn't even glance up from the page. I finally turned away and started looking for Grace and Cecilia.

Cecilia was in the sanctuary carrying a broom and dustpan, sweeping the floor between the pews. What was she doing cleaning the church? Was Mr. Sinclair suddenly putting them all to work? Maybe it made sense now that they didn't have to take care of their mother during the day and were no longer being schooled. Really, I was surprised it hadn't happened sooner, that he'd allowed them time to grieve. But did this mean they'd be here every day of the week? When would I be able to see them? Was working at church supposed to be a permanent thing, and if so what would happen to Cecilia's dream of studying history and Grace's dream of marrying Cesar? And why wouldn't they have tried to find some way to tell me what was going on and when I could see them again?

I tapped on the window, trying to get Cecilia's attention, but the windows were too thick for her to hear me. She bent to sweep dirt into the dustpan, glanced surreptitiously over her shoulder, and then dumped the dustpan into the pew rack. I smiled.

"Chloe? What're you doing here?"

I spun around, and there was Grace with a hoe and shovel and bag of flower bulbs. "You came to find us," she said, then stretched her lips into the sort of smile one uses when pretending amusement at a bad joke. And then she glanced at the church and gestured with her elbow to a Dumpster.

I followed her behind the Dumpster and stood beside her, resisting the urge to pull her into a hug. I was taller, I realized for the first time. When had that happened? She seemed so small and broken, the way the elderly are small and broken. "What's going on?" I said. "Where've you all been?"

She shrugged. "Here. Just here."

"Your dad found out about you and Cesar, that's it, isn't it. Or is it about Nate's drinking?"

"Oh Chloe . . ." Her face suddenly squinched up like the face of a toddler who's on the verge of explosion, and she fell back against the Dumpster's wall and slid down it onto the dirt.

"Grace!" I knelt beside her, set a hand on her shoulder, but she scuttled away from me, her face red.

"Don't act like you understand, like you have any idea what's going on, because you don't, Chloe, you don't! It's a trillion times worse than anything you're thinking." She pressed a fist against her forehead, then swung the other at the ground in front of her. "Fuck!"

I stared at her. Grace using that word, even knowing the word existed, was startling all in itself. And she seemed equally shocked with herself, clamped a hand over her mouth and started to cry.

"Grace?" How should I react to this? I had absolutely no idea what to do. I touched her leg, pulled away, then touched her leg again. She looked down at my hand and then back up at me.

"I need to find a way out," she said. "I can't stand it anymore, I can't live with him, you have to help me out of here."

"To go to Cesar? I got some information on a justice of the peace and the paperwork you'll need to fill out. It'll take a little while but it's not all that hard."

She splayed her fingers against the ground. "The sisterhood," she said. "I'm going to join the sisterhood." This confused me for a minute. I imagined a neighborhood of black women. But then she said, "There's a convent in Santa Barbara, the Poor Clares."

I stared at her, something numb and on hold inside of me. "Convent? You mean for Catholics?"

"I'm going to convert, you can do that. My dad's crazy, I've probably always known it, and now I realize everybody in our congregation is crazy too. I mean, speaking in tongues? I always faked it, Chloe, I never told anybody that, but the spirit never really took me over. And I thought that meant there was something wrong with *me,* that I didn't have enough faith or God didn't love me enough. But now I realize it's all crap, it's not God's language. *Al-laya mushumbi alacha malissti, baba-mama-dada,* it's baby talk!"

How hard must this be for her to admit? Religion, the church, had been the most important part of her life. Like water, or maybe more like books were to me, something to grab onto and hide inside. Or, like Mrs. Sinclair had been to all of us when she was still healthy enough to mother: something steady, loving, but also slightly disengaged and therefore fully trustworthy. And now Grace was saying she'd been faking it?

"I still love God, I just can't stand what they've done to Him. Right before Mom died her spirit was trying to tell me I have a calling, and now I finally know exactly what she means. In the convent, all you're there for is to serve God and atone for your sins and the sins of the rest of the world. That's what I want, Chloe."

"What happened between you and Cesar?" I said.

A lightning flash of something more like horror than agony tore open her face, but it closed just as suddenly. And she pretended not to have heard me. "I need you to send them a letter," she said. "I can't risk putting it in our mailbox and I don't know their address, so I'll need you to find it. Give them your contact information so they can tell you whether it's okay to just show up there. When they write back you can leave their letter behind the bush where we used to leave our notes, and then . . . I need you to help me escape."

I imagined Grace dressed in a habit, silently kneeling in a candlelit chapel hundreds of miles away. Picturing it, there was a twist in my belly, a homesickness, and a realization. That much as I loved Nate, he wasn't enough. I needed the Sinclair family even more, and losing Mrs. Sinclair, and now Grace, meant there'd be no family left. With just me, Nate, and Cecilia, all we'd feel is the holes left from where they'd been. "I want to talk to Nate," I said. "Can you tell Nate I have to talk to him?"

Her face went blank a moment, and then she said, "I'll have him bring you the letter."

"What? You mean he knows you're leaving?"

"Of course he knows, it was his idea. He was the one who realized what Mom must've meant, what she wants for me."

I felt a cold flush of sweat. Nate *wanted* her to leave?

"Tomorrow night," she said, "after Dad's asleep. I'll ask Nate to meet you by the bush, okay?" She rose, glanced back at the church, pulled me into a quick hug, and then strode back to the garden.

I watched her begin to work, struggling to turn the soil. Her eyes seemed unfocused and strange, like something nebulous was moving under their surface. And watching her, I suddenly thought I understood. That Nate was doing the only thing he could think of to protect her.

Grace hadn't told me what time to come the next night, so I left my house at seven, right after it got dark. My mother didn't ask where I was going; we were living separate lives these days. I was already older than she'd been when she left home, and somehow forgetting the mistakes she'd made at my age, she saw me as capable of directing my own life. On top of that, for the past few months she'd been dating a logger named Brad, ten years younger. She'd only mentioned me in passing as her "young daughter," without adding any qualifiers around the word "young."

"He thinks I'm twenty-five!" she'd told me. "I didn't lie to him, that was just his guess and I didn't correct him. But telling him I have a seventeen-year-old daughter, well that obviously would present technical difficulties." After which she'd smiled brightly, like she expected me to be equally amused at this predicament.

So it seemed she was happier when I wasn't around, having a chance to pretend she actually *was* twenty-five. And when I told her over dinner that I was going out and wasn't sure when I'd be back, all she did was distractedly wave a fork of beef at me and tell me she wanted to take me to Planned Parenthood for a diaphragm.

By seven-thirty I was behind the bush, looking up at the house. The garden, which Cesar had cared for like it was a cherished pet, had become overgrown with clover and crab weed, wild roses and wisteria strangling all the delicate perennials that Sophia had worked so hard to cultivate. And when I looked closely I could see the house itself seemed to have faded, the paint on the shingles worn and peeling, several of the terra-cotta tiles missing from the roof. When had that happened? How had I never noticed it before?

I could see the Sinclairs in the dining room, just from the shoulders up from my angle, Mr. Sinclair at the head of the table and the others around him, all eating silently and solemnly. Rather, I thought, like cloistered nuns.

And then they all rose at once, Grace and Cecilia started gathering dishes, and Nate followed his father from the room. Within fifteen minutes Grace and Cecilia joined them, and Mr. Sinclair opened a large book and began to read aloud, every now and again looking up, his brow furrowed as if he was trying to ascertain whether he was being understood.

It reminded me so much of the afternoons with Mrs. Sinclair, all of us gathered around her, pulled in by her words. And I was almost tempted to walk in unannounced like I had in those days, nestle against Grace's arm, be a part of what they had. Thinking of this, of what I'd lost, hit with a shock the same way divorce must feel, that sudden amputation of some vital body part. I'd sometimes thought of my loneliness almost as a form of indigestion that flared up on occasion. But standing there I realized it was probably more like skin, sometimes covered, always there.

I stayed watching from behind the bush until, an hour later, the Sinclairs rose and left the room. I watched the bedroom lights go on upstairs, then off again, one by one. And I waited.

Ten minutes later Nate emerged from behind the house, walking quickly with his face set, grim. When he darted behind the bush he almost ran straight into me, and he startled back before he smiled. "Chloe."

And just like that something broke inside me; I was crying, without even knowing exactly what I was crying for. He pulled me into his arms and made shushing sounds against my hair, which only made things worse, grief falling like a spike through me.

I slumped against Nate and he lowered me gently to the ground, sat with his legs straddling me, arms around my waist and cheek on my shoulder, rocking me from side to side.

After a minute I wiped the heels of both palms against my eyes, then pulled away. "Sorry." I swallowed sharply. "Sorry, I'm being stupid, it's just I missed you. I was looking for you, that's how I found you all in the church."

"Joel has us working. Idle minds are Satan's plaything, and now that he's understanding more what our life's been like ever since Mom got sick, he thinks Satan's been kneading us like Play-Doh." His voice was singsong, frightening. "So now he's doing what he can to slap us into his own image, or more likely into something completely shapeless."

"I saw you in his office."

He gave an amused half smile. "You were spying on me?" And then his smile dropped. "He's trying to turn me into a deacon, can you believe? My job would be to try and hold the church together, and to brainwash anyone who's wavering in his faith. Which is so ironic; I'm sure he doesn't trust me to do it so I think he just likes the idea of making me into his servant, that's basically all a deacon is."

"I wish you'd found a way to come and tell me all this. Why didn't you even try before now?"

"I'm sorry, I know . . ." His gaze shifted over my head. "It's just there's been a lot going on and I didn't want to get you involved."

"A lot like what?"

"I can't talk about it, Chloe. I'm sorry, it's just not my story to tell. Plus these have been like the worst days of our lives, so it's not just that I can't talk about it, I can't *think* about it."

I watched him, tried to read something from his expression, but it was like his face had completely closed off, a shell. Even his eyes seemed glassy cold. "You want Grace to leave," I said. "You gave her the idea."

He glanced fleetingly into my eyes, then back away. "She has to. She can't stay here."

"You want her to become a nun? Aren't there rules about that kind of thing? You can't turn into a nun just because your brother says you should; aren't you supposed to be invited by God or whatever?"

"If God was going to call anyone to serve, don't you think He'd call Grace? And even if He doesn't approve, what's He going to do about it?"

"But why a *convent*? You know, I looked up the Poor Clares and they're worse than other kinds of nuns, I mean it's scarier and harder. They can't ever leave the convent, they have to wake up at twelve-thirty every night to pray for like an hour, and then they get up again before dawn to work. They eat pretty much nothing, just bread and soup, and they can't hardly ever talk except for an hour a day when they talk to each other about the lives of the saints. It's like they're in a cult!"

"I know." All at once something sank inward on Nate's face; he looked lost. "I pictured, I don't know what. The kinds of convents you read about that're out in the countryside, overlooking the mountains, where they'd plant flowers and paint prayer cards and sing hymns, and gossip about . . . I don't know, the priests, I guess. And not have to worry about anything except trying to understand God, which is exactly what Grace used to love. But this, it's like she's punishing herself." He pulled an envelope from his back pocket, stared at it, then handed it to me. "I guess you heard she wants you to mail this. When you get a response from them, just leave it here under the bush, okay?"

I pulled out the letter and read it, her assertion that she'd heard God's call ever since she was a little girl, that her love for Him overpowered everything else in her life. That she was drawn to the Poor Clares' vows of enclosure so she could "fully reside in the Lord." They didn't sound like Grace's words. They sounded like the explanation Grace would think a nun was supposed to give. "Do you think any of this is true?" I said.

He gave a dismissive shrug. "I think she wants it to be true. But I don't know if she even knows what she believes in anymore, which is probably part of the reason she's punishing herself. Maybe when she figures it out she'll come back."

Nate looked suddenly so lost. I smoothed back a lock of hair that had fallen over his eyes. "She'll come back," I said.

"She has to." His eyes filled and he swiped at them. "I'm sorry."

I touched at his cheek and he leaned to kiss me, softly, just a brushing of his lips in a way that seemed almost regretful. I pulled away to look into his eyes, but before I could see his face he leaned it against mine, slid his cheek against my cheek and whispered, "I miss you."

"Me too," I said, resting my hands tentatively against his back, trying to work out what his use of the present tense could possibly mean. And then, a branch snapped behind him. We both startled back, looked up to see Mr. Sinclair standing there by the bush, staring down at us not with shock or anger but with pure horror.

I scrambled backward on my butt and Nate swiped at the ground, sweeping Grace's letter under his leg. "Dad," he said quickly.

But Mr. Sinclair's eyes were latched onto mine, and I felt that same strange sense I'd felt the first time I'd met him years ago, of elasticity in my body, of being stretched taller. "You," he said. "The girl with the bike."

Amazing to think he remembered me. But also amazing to think he only knew me from the one time he'd seen me almost a decade ago, the day we'd put on the Narnia play. We'd been careful, meeting only when he wasn't home, staying under cover of the woods whenever possible. The only sign I left behind of my presence were the books I brought, so maybe there was no way for Joel to have known I'd been there without somebody telling him. But I couldn't believe he wouldn't have somehow sensed my presence, since I felt like part of me was always here even when I was at school or at home in bed. And now I felt a sudden discombobulation, as if the years in between hadn't happened, as if the part I'd played in all their lives was as simple as an eight-year-old summer.

"I'm Chloe," I said, standing. When he'd learned I had a bike he'd called me "industrious," a word I'd had to look up later. And over the years I'd thought of that many times, maybe just a flippant comment but now somehow it made me feel like everything might be okay. "I'm Nate and Cecilia and Grace's friend."

"Frie-eee-end," he said, drawing the word out into more syllables than I'd known it could possibly contain, his brow knitted like he was trying to translate and understand it. "How long exactly has this *friendship* with Nate been going on?"

Nate stood, Grace's letter behind his back. "Nothing's going on! Chloe was all upset, she was actually crying." He glanced at me. "About a girl she knows who's leaving home. And I heard noises outside, so I came to check them out and I found her. I was just trying to help her feel better, that's all."

"Enough. Stop talking Nathaniel, it's not helping. You might not believe this, but I understand how it is to be a teenage boy. But I also know that Satan comes in many forms, even in the form of lovely young girls."

He'd just called me lovely. But he'd also just called me Satan, which pretty much negated the compliment. And I felt like I should respond to this, but I didn't have any idea what to say. I shoved my hands into my pockets, confused, fingered pocket lint and a Wrigley wrapper of chewed gum. "I'm not Satan," I said.

"Miss Chloe, it's time for you to leave now. And you won't be coming back."

His voice shook slightly on the last word, and it suddenly occurred to me that he was afraid. What could he be afraid of? Of me? "It's okay," I said.

"I mean this. You come back one more time, and Nate will be gone." He turned to Nate. "You understand what I'm saying?"

For my part, I had no idea what he was saying. My first thought was that he meant Nate would be dead. But Nate nodded, backing toward me. "She won't. She doesn't have any reason to come again." He was waving Grace's letter behind his back, holding it between two fingers. And when I reached forward he pressed it against my palm. I slipped it inside my sleeve, and Nate stood for just a moment blocking Mr. Sinclair's view before he walked past him, toward the house, without looking back.

Mr. Sinclair watched him enter the house, then exhaled deeply, eyes still on the door.

"I'm a good person," I said softly.

He stayed silent for a long while, then finally turned to me. "Maybe you are. But that doesn't give you a right to be here, or to be part of our lives. I know you don't understand but I'm protecting my son, and there'll be consequences if I see you here again." And with that he turned and left me standing there.

I wrote my address and phone number on the spaces Grace had left for them in her letter, then went out to set it in the mailbox. But as it turned out the mail had already come, and lying in the box were two envelopes from Berkeley, one thick and one thin. I set the envelope with my name on it in my lap, turned it over and then back over before opening it. I glanced inside, then opened Nate's and read.

It maybe would've been a solution. If Nate was at college, what could his father do to keep us apart? But the truth was, I wasn't even sure what Nate would've done if he *had* been admitted. I'd been thinking about Nate since our strange conversation the night before, for the first time realizing that his personality had changed since his mother's death. It was partly the drinking; although I'd only actually seen him drink a handful of times, I knew he was getting drunk several times a week, and it made him quieter, more brooding, and the mood seemed to carry over for days. But even on days he was completely sober he seemed more intense, fiercer, swinging from emotion to emotion within seconds.

I'd talked with him about school several times over the past few months, wanting to help him look forward instead of back, see that things might not be so hard once we got away from his house, this town, the memories. But now I couldn't remember how he'd responded, if he'd even said anything at all or just smiled wistfully, or indulgently, or changed the subject.

What would I do now? Go to school without him? Live hundreds of miles away, come back for holidays when I might or might not be able to see him, somehow concentrate on classes when all I could think about was what he might be doing at home?

I raised the envelopes to my face and held them against my forehead. Our future. Then rose and stuffed them both into the trash.

I didn't go back to the Sinclairs' until I'd gotten a response from the nuns. A Sister Marguerite had written, inviting Grace to visit, stay a week, and learn more about convent life. Over the past two weeks I'd been stealing money from my mother's purse, just a little at a time, and now I had almost enough for a round-trip bus ticket. And after school that afternoon, I went to the Sinclairs'.

The car was gone from the driveway, I assumed they were all at church, but still I kept the Poor Clares' letter under my shirt as I skirted the edge of the woods toward the holly bush. There, lying half buried in the tall grass, was the toolbox where we used to hide our coded notes. I crouched beside the box to open it and tuck the letter and money inside. And found a book.

It was a leather-bound edition of *Romeo and Juliet* and I leafed through it hurriedly, looking for a note. But there was nothing between the pages, and nothing written on them that I could find other than a handful of faint pencil marks in the margins. I studied some of the marked lines, looking for meaning, but they seemed completely arbitrary: *Drawn with a team of little atomies; Virtue itself turns vice, being misapplied; He made you for a highway to my bed.* Had someone just been using the lines to mark their place?

I knew the Romeo and Juliet story only vaguely, a love affair, a balcony scene, and a tragic ending. So was the story itself his message? Was it just that their relationship had been forbidden too?

I stared at it, fingering the cover as if the grooves in the leather might give me some kind of guidance. And then I went back home to read.

14

I read the musty copy of *Romeo and Juliet,* falling in love first with the phrases, the rhythms of each line, and then with the story. The language was hard at first, but after a few pages it was like my mind bent to fit around its shapes. I let the story carry me, the all-consuming love and all-consuming despair, the hope and the death, so that by the end I was half in tears.

Nate was associating the story with ours, that was obvious, but how much of the story? I reread the ending two times, three, and then in desperation I went back through the pages, trying to find some kind of meaning in the lines he'd marked. I wrote them out on a notepad and studied them, trying to figure out if there was anything that might tie them together. But they all seemed completely random, scattered throughout the book, some of the most inconsequential lines.

It was when I set the notepad down and started to rise from my desk that I saw it. I reached for a pen and slowly circled the letters.

Nay, as they dare. I will bite my thumb at them
Ere he can spread his sweet leaves to the air
Earth-treading stars that make dark heaven light.
Drawn with a team of little atomies
Too great oppression for a tender thing.
Of this sir-reverence love, wherein thou stick'st
Like a rich jewel in an Ethiop's ear
Else would a maiden blush bepaint my cheek
And I'll believe thee.
Virtue itself turns vice, being misapplied,
Either withdraw unto some private place
Come, sir, your passado!
A plague o' both your houses! I am sped.
No, 'tis not so deep as a well, nor so wide as a
     church door;
Citizen. Which way ran he that kill'd Mercutio?
Some twenty of them fought in this black strife,
That you shall all repent the loss of mine.
And bring in cloudy night immediately.
Your tributary drops belong to woe,
Was woe enough, if it had ended there;
In that word's death; no words can that woe sound.
Take up those cords. Poor ropes, you are beguil'd,
He made you for a highway to my bed;
Your lady mother is coming to your chamber.
O, by this count I shall be much in years
Unworthy as she is, that we have wrought

So this was what Nate had been trying to say, encoded because he didn't even want Grace and Cecilia to know. That he was leaving me.

I didn't sleep at all that night. Why was Nate leaving? And when? How long had the book been sitting under the bush? Could it be that he was already gone?

I'd go to the Sinclairs' first thing tomorrow, watch until they left for church. And if Nate was still there—oh God please let him still be there!—I'd spend all day at the church if I had to, sneak into the men's room, hide in a stall, and wait for him to come in.

This had to have something to do with his father; Nate wouldn't have left Cecilia on his own. Had Mr. Sinclair threatened him with something that made him think he had to run away? It had to be something like that; the more I thought about it the more sure I became, and soon I was on the verge of panic, imagining all kinds of wild scenarios, Nate sent on missionary work in Kenya, or imprisoned under false charges, or locked in the attic with duct tape over his mouth. And as the night slipped into early morning, half dream, half deliberation, I imagined holding a knife to Mr. Sinclair's throat, demanding he tell me, and if he refused, cutting off fingers and then toes one by one. "Where is he!"—an index finger—"What did you do with him!"—a thumb. Picturing it in gory detail, the sharp blade, the gristle and bone, his tears, my tears, when suddenly—

Thunk.

I sat up in bed, stared blindly around the dim room until again, *thunk.* I stood and walked to the window.

And there was Nate, hair wet from the misting rain, a pinecone raised in his hand. I pulled up the window, my whole body feeling swollen with the urge to scream, more anguish in it than joy.

He dropped the pinecone and smiled, beckoning with his arm, and I ran down the stairs and outside.

"I thought," I said, "I don't know what I thought! I was going to cut off your dad's fingers!" I buried my face against the clamminess of his damp sweater, then pulled him into the living room, took the afghan off the sofa and wrapped it around him, tucking it behind his back. Then sat with him, my arms around him, legs on his lap, head resting against his shoulder. "I thought you were running away from home. That's what you were trying to tell me, right?"

Nate sat motionless, not hugging me back. "Next week," he said. "I haven't even told Cecilia yet, don't want her to know until I figure out what I can do to make sure she's safe. Joel wants me to go to Central Bible College in Missouri, he signed me up for summer classes and got me a job in their library to keep me out of trouble till then."

"Missouri? Like Missouri the state?"

"It's okay, I'm not going." He seemed pleased by whatever my face was showing. "I have plans."

"What do you mean?"

He took my hand, cradled it between both of his. "Did you read *Romeo and Juliet?*" he said. "All of it?"

I twisted my legs off his lap feeling a chill, cold metal down my spine. "They're us, aren't they. That's why you wanted me to read it."

"It's okay," he said again, his eyes on mine. "Just listen and I'll tell you exactly what we're going to do."

If he'd asked me at that moment to guess what he was about to suggest, I would've guessed he'd planned a dramatic, passionate double suicide, something that would serve to both destroy his father and ensure we'd never be apart. And, at that moment, I think

I actually might have agreed to it. Lying in the dark before he'd come, imagining the very worst, there'd been even darker shadows in the corners of my mind.

So when he told me his actual plan, it was such a relief and so much *less* crazy that it felt both rational and inevitable. Not that it wasn't somewhat ludicrous to think his plan would work, the type of strategy only fictional characters would attempt, overcoming all odds to reach their happy ending. Crazy not to think about the possible repercussions, but I was carried away by the romanticism of the idea, a residue from the romanticism of the story I'd just read. And repercussions seemed somehow beside the point.

"I just can't stand the thought of Cecilia being on her own with Joel, which is why I asked you whether she might be able to stay here. I never would've convinced Grace to leave if I'd known Joel would try and send me away."

"Could you take her with you?"

"That's my plan eventually, soon as I'm settled. But it's going to be precarious enough in the beginning just trying to get by on my own, I don't even know if I'll have food, or a place to sleep. I was trying to convince Grace to take her to the convent, but in the end I knew Cecilia wouldn't be able to stand the confinement, and Grace probably feels like Cecilia living there would diminish what she's really started to think of as a calling. So that's why I need your help, till I can send for both of you. The things that've been happening . . . it's been worse than you know."

A dark twist in my stomach. "Happening to Cecilia? What do you mean?"

"It's to both of them. I talk back to him or refuse to go to work, anything he considers a sign of the devil, and he punishes *them* because he knows it'll hurt me worse to see it. Like last week he found Thoreau hidden inside the Bible on my lap, and because of it he made Grace sit in the basement for six hours even knowing there are mice down there, and spiders, what that would do to her. She'd never really been punished before, he let her get away with almost anything. It seemed like he almost revered her, thought of her as saintly, or at least thought her faith was so strong she didn't need discipline. But this isn't about her, it's about me. Like he thinks seeing her suffer could make me repent, drive out my unclean spirit, I don't know. All I know is I could hear her down there screaming—" His voice broke and he pressed his lips together and swallowed, then raised his chin. "—screaming, and I tried to break down the door, finally broke a basement window instead but I couldn't get to her, the window's too narrow. Stupid of me because in exchange for the broken window, Cecilia was locked down there too."

I shook my head blankly. "How long has this been going on? That kind of punishment?"

"Forever, at least for me. I mean never like this, he wasn't cruel. But one of my first memories, I was four or five, was of him waking me up in the middle of the night and forcing me onto my knees to pray for forgiveness, I don't even know what for. I grew up thinking I must be the most wicked kid in the world, but I think I understand it now. He had this vision when I was born of who his son would grow up to be, and he's been pushing me to live up to that vision. So fine, I'm used to it on some level, but he's never been like this to Grace and Cecilia."

"I wish you'd told me some of this. You all hardly talk about him, it's like he's this huge secret you keep between each other, and why? Is it because you're embarrassed about how he treats you? Or scared of him?"

"No, Chloe, it's complicated. Let's just say we understand him in a way nobody else would. We know who he used to be and we've seen him change, and there's no way we could talk about who he is in a way that would make sense to anybody who hasn't lived through it. All I know is that with who he's become, I'm scared of what he'll do in retaliation if I stand up to him face-to-face. He's losing control, more every day. I just have to think if we all disappear he'll finally see what he did to me and to his family." A salt wave of grief washed over his face. "I don't know when I'll see Grace again. I didn't even think about that till just now."

I huddled up against his arm. "What about me, Nate? How long till Cecilia and I can see you?"

He stared straight ahead, wearing that same pained expression, and at first I wondered if he'd even heard me. But finally he turned to me. "I don't know. A month maybe, it shouldn't be much longer. I'll tell you when I get settled, let you know as soon as I've saved up enough to support us."

"So Cecilia would stay with me and Mom till then."

"Please, Chloe . . . it's the only thing I can think of to keep her safe."

"Do you think your dad would come after us?"

"What could he possibly do? Threaten you with kidnapping? Since it won't be for long, he might not ever even find out where she went. I realize your mom would have to agree to it."

"I'll ask tonight, tell her what he's done to you. Really the timing's going to be perfect, Cecilia and I can leave right after I finish school." Already I was coming to terms with this. It felt like something already done. "I could actually go to Berkeley! I was thinking I'd just get a job here, save up enough money that I could rescue you and we could run off somewhere together. But if you can find some kind of work in the Bay area, then I could go to school, the three of us could live in an apartment."

"Berkeley?" His voice was almost awed. "Do you know if we got in?"

I hesitated, then said, "I got in."

He watched me, waiting, then said, "Right. Well, I knew it was a long shot anyway. Not having any grades to show them." He wrapped the afghan tighter around his shoulders, staring into the distance. "You'll teach me whatever you're learning, right? I can read your notes and your books."

I took his hand. "You could probably even slip into the bigger classes when you weren't working. Sit in back and nobody would ever know you didn't belong."

"And over dinner we'd talk about our days and what we learned—"

"And we'd study together! All-nighters; you could help me with essays or theses or take-home tests."

He brought my hand to his mouth, kissed it, and then held it there. "Escaping together, all of this, it's like a fairy tale," he said, which seemed like a strange comparison, overstating the enchantment and understating the direness of all we were facing. Until I thought of the book of original *Grimm's Fairy Tales* my mom had well-meaningly but completely misguidedly bought for my tenth birthday. A prince blinded by thorns after climbing into Rapunzel's tower, a woman killing her own sister to marry a count who later devoured her; good and evil, nightmare and heartbreak, lessons taught the hard way. But evil vanished in the end, retribution, and happy endings usually coming to those who deserved them.

Although, thinking of the impossible lies we'd have to tell, I didn't really know what we deserved anymore.

"I have to ask you a favor." It was the next night and I was sitting across from my mother at dinner trying to think of the right words, how to say enough without saying too much. "Because you know my friend Cecilia, she's been going through a really hard time."

Momma managed to construct a suitably concerned face. "You mean because of what happened to her mom."

"Well, that and her dad, he's not treating her right. The thing is, if she doesn't get away I don't know what he might do to her."

"You mean he *abuses* her?"

"I don't think he's actually hit her or anything, he wouldn't want to do anything that would get him arrested. But he's hurt her, really hurt all of them in other ways. And now . . ." I raked my fork across the rice on my plate, right and then left. "Grace is leaving, I don't know where she's going to but she said things have gotten so bad at home she can't stay there anymore. And Nate, he's going too, his dad's sending him to Bible college in Missouri, so Cecilia's going to be alone with him and she's scared."

"Really. And here I thought they were so perfect."

"Mom!"

"I'm sorry, I just always looked at them and looked at us and thought . . . well they're just so flawless, aren't they? But things can be pretty on the outside and nasty on the inside, like rotting fruit. It's just interesting hearing the Sinclairs are rotting." She set down her fork and shoved her plate away. "And now I'm sorry again, I know they're your friends and I do feel awful for the kids. Okay go on, what's the favor?"

I sat back in my chair and met her eye. "Could Cecilia come to stay here? Just for a little while?"

"What? What would her dad say?"

"She's almost my age, she's old enough to decide where she wants to live. Really he doesn't even have to know where she is."

"But she's still a minor. If you bring her here without her dad's permission, he could cause a lot of problems if he wanted to. Why doesn't Nate tell the cops what's going on there? Or even tell their parish; I bet he wouldn't even have to actually tell them, just threaten to so he could keep using it as leverage."

"Their dad's not whipping them, so I doubt the police will care that he makes them pray in the middle of the night. And the parish, well some of them might not approve, but most of them probably do the same things to their own kids, or at least they would if he told them it was the best way to raise a godly child. So there's a chance Nate turning him in wouldn't do anything except make things worse for Cecilia. Please, Mom, Nate's going to send for her as soon as he gets settled, she can live in Missouri with him, but just for the next few weeks this'll help make sure she stays safe."

Momma stared down at her plate, expressionless, then looked back up at me. "Well, okay."

I studied her face, looking for signs of amusement or sarcasm. "What do you mean, okay?"

"There are multiple meanings of the word?" She crossed her arms and sat back in her chair. "Look, you know I ran away from home when I was your age, younger than you actually."

"That's when you met my dad," I said. She'd been raised in poverty, her mother a drunk, and he was the first rich person she'd ever met. A businessman named Gary Groves, whose table she'd waited on when she was working at a four-star restaurant. He'd taken pity on her and let her live in a guesthouse on the outside fringes of his property, paying for groceries in exchange for light housekeeping, inviting her to stay for games of chess or dinners prepared by his cook. Slowly over a period of months they'd begun to fall in love, until they slept together at a weak moment and I was conceived. After the initial shock he was thrilled, having always wanted children, and he'd been at the hospital when I was born, was the first to hold me. That week they spent together as part of a family was the happiest in my mother's life. But sometimes too much happiness can break your heart. My father died in his sleep eight days after I was born.

"I don't know who your dad was," she said now.

I felt everything in my body still. "What?"

"I'm sorry, I know I should've told you this before, I just couldn't think of the right way. Not like there's any good way. Christ, I feel like I want to take you onto my lap and stroke your hair while I'm talking."

"My dad was Gary Groves," I said slowly, as if she needed a reminder.

She folded her hands against her chin, fingers interlaced like she was praying or pleading, and I felt a tangle of fear behind my ribs. "I'm going to tell you about this guy I met," she said, "Big G."

Big G. I pictured him as the giant from my old "Jack and the Beanstalk" board book with his stubbly square chin and ham-hock feet, and the tangle behind my ribs became a knot.

"The story's just one big cliché really, it's more embarrassing than tragic. I was working at a diner, clearing plates and filling water glasses, and this man kept staring at me. I was about to dump ice water in his lap when he asked me if I wanted a more profitable job. Said I could make hundreds in one night, so of course I was intrigued, followed him out of the diner and down the street. I was just a kid and he kept telling me how beautiful I was, how he never approached girls unless they had that special kind of one-in-a-million beauty. And there I am all excited, sure he wants to make me into the next Veruschka, until he leads me inside a place called Dangerous Curves."

"Dangerous Curves," I repeated. "It sounds like a roller coaster."

She smiled distractedly. "A strip club, Chloe. I was a stripper."

I looked at my mother, her hair frizzy, eyes heavy with fatigue. But I knew what happened when she put on her face and the skirts she wore for dates, the transformation. "No," I said.

"And there was more than that, favors some of us did for the men, including Big G, for more money. I had dreams, and big dreams require cash . . ."

I watched her blankly, wanting to believe she only meant that she'd shined these men's shoes or cleaned their floors, something with a similar flavor of humiliation but nowhere near the intensity. "So." I met her eye. "So one of them is my father."

"I consider you an immaculate birth, actually. In my mind none of them were real; they might have provided the mechanism to bring you to me but you don't have a father. You're all mine."

I should've guessed this, of course, because why hadn't she asked for money from my father's estate? Why had she deflected all my questions about him, the times I'd asked for a physical description or begged for a chance to visit the home where they used to live? Maybe subconsciously I'd guessed some of this all along, because after the initial shock I felt all the loose pieces sliding into place, and the truth of it seemed inevitable. "I'm sorry," I said. "That you went through all that, I'm sorry."

She reached for both my hands, squeezed them. "So what I'm saying is I know what it's like out there, and what it did to me. I felt like garbage, like a tissue the men were blowing their noses into over and over until it was tattered. I don't ever want anyone to feel like that again, and I think it'll be therapeutic helping another girl who needs it."

And so there it was, for me the circle complete. Our lies saving

Nate, saving Cecilia, and now maybe my mom. It is easy to convince yourself, especially when scared and unsure, that things are meant to be, providence, and so beyond control.

Two days after Grace left for Santa Barbara, Nate and I wrote the letter. He planned it this way, the double whammy, Grace vanishing into the night without explanation, followed closely by his suicide and Cecilia's disappearance. Mr. Sinclair had flown into a rage when he found out Grace was gone, tearing apart the house, demanding answers, and Nate showed up at my door late Friday, unshaved, his face bloated with anguish, and told me we couldn't wait. "He could kill Cesar," he said, "literally kill him. I kept telling him Grace broke things off with Cesar and hasn't seen him for weeks. But he won't believe me, he thinks Grace is hiding there."

I watched Nate, wide-eyed and silent.

"It'll stop when we're gone, he'll realize he's completely failed in everything he was trying to do to us. But right now he's completely out of control, so Cecilia and I have to be gone before he wakes up tomorrow."

And so we wrote the letter that night.

> *By the time you get this note it will already be too late, because tonight I'm taking a taxi to Harris Beach. I won't be coming back.*
>
> *Virginia Woolf weighted her pockets with stones to keep her body, already heavy with grief, from rising. I'll be doing the same, Father, even though my body is already weighted by you, fear of you, horror of you, disgust, it's like sludge in all of our bodies. Was worst of all in Mom because she loved you and yet hated you at the same time. It smothered her, that sludge, and in the end it destroyed her.*

How can you possibly give guidance in the church after what you've done? I sometimes wonder if you really even believe in God. I know He doesn't believe in you, not anymore. And now you have yet another death on your hands.

Nate

The letter was almost a melodramatic parody. Nate had always been one for melodrama—hence the faked suicide when disappearing without a note would've had virtually the same effect—and he probably would've written the note in blood if the idea had occurred to him. But at the same time all of it felt right, the note on the same scale of heart-wrenching momentousness as our plan to leave, and after sealing the envelope we each held one end as we kissed each other for luck. Nate was shivering, I could feel that when his lips touched mine, so I wrapped my arms around him, buried my face in his neck, and whispered, "This is the hard part, Nate. You'll be able to push it down in a few hours, as soon as you ride away."

He nodded against me, paused and then nodded again, then pulled away. "Let's go," he said.

Nate rode my bike back to his home, standing on the pedals, me crouched on the seat behind him with my legs tucked back. He brought the note inside and returned a half hour later with a shopping bag holding two ham sandwiches in the toolbox we'd used to hide our books and coded notes, a bottle of whiskey, three changes of underthings, a handful of books, and eighty dollars stolen from the church's collection plate. I'd emptied our kitchen cabinets into a knapsack: Fritos and Mini-Wheats, American cheese and three kinds of crackers. It wasn't much, but it would last him for at least a few days.

He looked jittery, overly tense. Like someone trapped but determined, Houdini in handcuffs being lowered into water. "Cab's coming in three hours and Cecilia's going to be out waiting for you in three and a half," he said, then looked up at the house, face opening to reveal a brief second of anguish. I took his hand and he turned away. "We'll wait by the stream," he said.

We walked hand in hand through the woods, our path lit only by the dim patches of moonlight freckling through tree branches. And as we approached the stream in the dark, with no distractions, I felt the momentousness of what we'd just done.

Both of us had lived in this town our entire lives. All the other towns I'd read about, imagined living in, were just two-dimensional compared to it, scrapbook pictures behind the characters who lived there. With Nate, Cecilia, Grace, and Sophia gone there'd be nothing tying me here, only my mother and my house. But the town itself was still part of me, in the same way my too-big ears were a part of me; I might wish they were different but that didn't stop them from feeling essential. "This feels like jumping off a cliff," I said softly. "Once it's done, even if it turns out to be a mistake, there's no going back."

"Don't . . ." Nate stared blankly at the dark water. "Don't—" I reached for him and he pressed his face against my neck. "I love you," he said, or maybe it was *I need you*, his words muffled against my shoulder.

I held him close, synchronizing my breathing to his so it felt like we were connected at the chest, both of us rising and falling together like we were on water or air. This was probably the last time I'd see him for weeks, maybe months, which was incomprehensible, and I didn't want to let go. So without really thinking what I was doing, I unbuckled his belt and undid his fly, the feeling inside me a mix of fear, loss, and a desire that was centered only in my heart and stomach. "I love you too," I said hoarsely, and reached under his waistband.

He gave a quick, high-pitched moan and ground against me, blindly, until I pulled away and stripped off my sweater and jeans. He stared at me, his cheeks flushed, then touched my thigh, ran his hand up to my hip, his face questioning. So I reached again for him, put him between my legs, felt for the right spot, and then squeezed my eyes shut and arched quickly against him.

It didn't hurt. Or at least didn't hurt anywhere near as much as I'd expected, these expectations coming primarily from books about first love. As he pushed against me, the sounds he made more like sobs of pain than anything else, I felt a glimmer of pleasure, a bass-string thrum between my legs and a sense of holding all of him inside me, surrounding him and keeping him safe, muffling his thoughts of anything else as he moved faster, his expression fierce. I pressed my palms against his back, the cords of his muscles shifting against my fingers until everything stilled in him and he cried out, shuddered, and then fell against me.

When he was done he buried his face in my chest, his breathing a rushed whisper against my skin. "Chloe," he said hoarsely, and then his voice broke and he started to cry.

I smoothed my hand over the back of his head, over and over, feeling his wetness on my legs. All I wanted was to stay there, just like this, here in the woods in the dark with Nate, stay there until . . . until we died of starvation, I guess. Romeo and Juliet.

But he rolled off me and lay on his back, looking up at the sky. After a minute he whispered, "I'm sorry, Chloe."

I spread my palms flat on the ground, silently rubbed them back and forth, back and forth, pebbles and pine needles grating at my skin. "Why?"

"I shouldn't have done that. We shouldn't have."

"Because we're not married yet?"

"That's part of it, I mean obviously it's a sin, but there's more than that." I turned to face him, saw only the curve of his forehead and long eyelashes. "Because you can't marry me, Chloe, ever. I'm too messed up, there's too much been going on, and I don't even understand myself anymore."

I wrapped my arms around my chest, tried to focus on the rhythm of my breath. "I don't show you the worst of it, but I'm really messed up too, Nate, just as much as you. We'll help each other get un-messed." I tried to force a smile into my voice. "We're each other's only hope."

He sat up slowly and looked down at me, touched my cheek and ran his hand down to cup my breast. "You're so beautiful, Chloe. You could go to college and meet somebody amazing, somebody who'll get a degree and a real job. I'm probably going to end up in a field or a factory, I'll be exhausted at the end of the day, and if I was with you, I'd pick fights because you got to live the life I wanted. And in the end you'd be making ten times more than me, so you'd think about getting a divorce but feel guilty about it because you were the one who convinced me it could work."

"Stop it! That's one of the reasons I love you, Nate, you have this crazy-ass imagination, but this is out of control." I pulled on my sweater and jeans, and then reached into the bag of food I'd brought and took out the copy of *Romeo and Juliet,* held it up so he could see. "Here's what we're going to do," I said. "We're going to put this book somewhere safe, somewhere nobody could find it. And in fifty years when we're old, we've had kids and maybe grandkids and we own the world's most successful bookstore, and we've figured out the meaning of life, we'll both come back, dig it up, and read it again and think how awful things were, and how great they turned out in the end. And we'll wish we could go back and tell our today selves not to worry."

He took the book from me, held it tightly in both hands. He stared down at it, then gave a quick nod. "Here," he said. "We'll hide it here." He emptied his shopping bag onto the ground, wrapped it around the book, and then took his sandwiches out from the toolbox and set the book inside. He crawled closer to the stream, searching, finally found a wide stick, and began to dig. "Help me," he said. "I'm running out of time."

I found another stick and helped him shovel, remembering the first day I'd met him digging his way to London, to another world. And now we were digging our way to the future and it felt poetic, destined.

When the hole was a foot deep, Nate dropped the toolbox in and the two of us refilled it, rolled a large rock to mark its place, then covered the bare patch with pine needles until there was no other sign of where the hole had been. We sat looking down at it a moment, and then Nate reached for both my hands. "Pray with me, Chloe? I know you don't believe, and I know it seems pretty obvious that God's abandoned us."

"I'll pray," I said, then kissed his hands and folded mine into my lap. "Let's pray."

Nate closed his eyes for a long, silent moment, then raised his chin. "Lord, please be our guide and our protector on the journey we are about to take. Watch over us and keep us free from harm to body and soul. And support us with Your grace when we're tired so that when our voyage is over, we'll remain secure in the knowledge that You will always be there to guide us safely. Amen."

Keep us free from harm to body and soul. Did he sense the irony in what he was asking? Faith in God, like faith in their father, groundless but unrelenting. "Amen," I said.

Nate checked his watch and turned to me. "I have to go."

The fear hit suddenly, cold mud in my stomach. I looked up at him, my face feeling swollen with tears, but I didn't cry, just wrapped my arms around my waist. "Okay," I said, "okay."

He rested a palm against my cheek, held it there a moment with his eyes locked on mine, and then he stood and started back through the woods, turning only once to raise his hand goodbye.

15

THE whole plan, of course, was insane. Joel never even called the police, never showed anyone Nate's note, telling his parishioners that Grace and Cecilia had started short-term missionary work overseas, and Nate was studying at the Bible college in Missouri with the intent of later getting a graduate degree and taking over for him when he retired. He didn't tell anyone about the "suicide," partly, I'm sure, to conceal what his perfect family had done, and because the note was so condemnatory it shamed him. But also, as Cecilia told us years later, he never actually believed it. The note was too overwrought, the pain in it forced, the type of romanticized drivel one would imagine one *should* write, rather than the stilted sort of note one actually would.

Why didn't the parishioners question Joel when he'd never before mentioned impending missionary work? Didn't they think it was strange he hadn't used his children as examples of faith and servitude when he'd *always* used them as examples? But maybe evangelicalism was like totalitarianism. You couldn't question your leader or soon you'd start questioning everything, the immensity of which was too terrifying to bear.

Cecilia came to stay with us, sleeping first on the sofa and then, after I found her crying in the middle of the night, in my bed, where we'd hold hands and try to sleep. Both of us in limbo, waiting for word of the future as I finished my last days of high school and Cecilia read through books on the Bay area, circling coffee shops and museums, libraries and bookstores she wanted to visit.

Four days after she arrived we got a note from Nate that said almost nothing.

> *Just writing to let you know I'm okay, and not to worry about me. I've been traveling looking for work, and although I did find one job, unfortunately it didn't stick. It's a bit harder out here than I expected so this all might take longer than I thought, two or three months before I can send for you. But get this. Today I was sitting on the Greyhound and this little girl across the aisle was watching me in that totally uninhibited, questioning way kids do. I smiled at her and asked her name, and she told me her name was Cecilia Grace. Which was a sign, don't you think? Just when I was starting to feel unsure. I love how God took this opportunity when I was most scared to show He's on our side.*
>
> *Love,*
>
> *Nate*

The next night my mother came home with a large bag holding jeans, tee-shirts, and a pair of sneakers. "Since you'll be here awhile," she said, "you can't be dressing like a prairie girl." She nodded at the bag. "If I had your figure I'd go for something flashier, but I was scared you'd be paralyzed from the shock of it."

Later I walked into my bedroom to find Cecilia dressed in her new clothes, standing in front of the full-length mirror with her legs spread awkwardly, arms raised stiffly at her sides. "Scissors," she said. "Do you have scissors?"

I brought her a pair, and without even undoing her braid she snipped it at her shoulders. She fingered the resulting loose waves, smiled, and said, "Take that." I saw then that her hand was shaking.

"It looks beautiful," I said, and it did, framing her face and curling under her chin, emphasizing her wide eyes.

She flashed a fake, nervous smile. "I look like a normal person. Like you."

"Totally," I said, but the truth was that her face was too luminous to ever look "normal," eyes lit from behind, and I had the sudden thought that if circumstances were different and she wasn't a Sinclair, she'd be one of those girls in my school that everyone tried to emulate, not just because of her looks, but her easy smiles and vivacity. She probably wouldn't want anything to do with me.

The plan was for her to stay hidden in the house for the few weeks it took Nate to find a job and a place for us to live. But the night after cutting her hair, as she lay beside me in the dark, she said, "I'm going to visit my father tomorrow."

"What?" I said. "Why?"

"I know it'll be hard for you to understand, but I'm worried about him. When Mom died it broke him, I could see it, and now that we've all left him . . ." Her voice trailed off and I turned to her, trying to make out her face in the dark, seeing only one arm she'd slung across her eyes. "Well, I didn't think I was going to feel this way, but I'm scared for him and sad for him. He's all alone and I'm sure he's hurting."

There was a frailty in her voice I didn't recognize, a little girl, or maybe an old woman weakened by regrets. I spoke softly. "Seriously? How can you have any compassion for him after what he's done to your family?"

She pulled her arm from her eyes. "He *is* my family, Chloe, the only family I have left here. I'm just going to see how he's doing and then I'll be back."

It was true that Cecilia never seemed to feel the hatred Nate did or the fear that Grace had. But she'd also always seemed the most blithe and detached, and I'd thought leaving would be easiest for her. Maybe this was associated with the haircut and new clothes and not knowing how long it would be before she was with Nate again. With everything else, it had become too much.

I lay there feeling the tenseness of her body next to mine, this girl who used to cartwheel in a blur across the yard, set up impossible obstacle courses only she'd been brave enough to complete with tree swings and log balance beams five feet above the ground, who'd laugh so loud I'd often hear her as I approached their driveway on my bike, making me race toward the house to join her. She'd changed over the past year, of course, but part of me had thought taking her away from her father, sheltering her here, would bring her back.

I took her hand, held it a minute before speaking. "Okay," I said, "but I'm coming with you."

I was relieved at first when she didn't argue. Until I realized it must be because she was scared too.

Going with Cecilia would change everything, showing Joel where she'd been staying, and I knew Momma wouldn't approve. So we didn't tell her, left after she'd gone to work. Cecilia used my mother's bicycle, biking in front of me to the church. She was wearing one of her old dresses and had pinned her braid back onto her head where it hung awkwardly; seen from behind, obviously not a part of her.

Mr. Sinclair was in his office, we could see him through the small window on his knees, surrounded by papers. The papers were everywhere, scattered on the desk and floor, even hanging like limp flags from each row of his bookshelf. As we watched he raised two pages, one to his left and one directly in front of him, and switched their places. At first I thought all the pages were blank and I felt a sinking horror until I looked closer and saw each was covered in tiny, penciled script. Silently, Cecilia took my hand, then knocked on the window.

Mr. Sinclair looked up, held her eyes for a long, blank minute, and then rose to open the back door. He peered over her shoulder, looking perhaps for Grace, and when he saw me his eyes hardened. I looked back at him, noticing the new lines on his forehead and bracketing his mouth, a wilting. And where I'd expected to feel a profound hatred over what he'd done, instead I found myself recognizing for the first time the humanness in his eyes, wondering how he'd become the person he was now. Had he been raised the way he raised his own children? The same certainty that there was only one narrow, rocky path to heaven, and adamant insistence that his children follow it? What values had been drilled into him? What kind of upbringing produced this, the vibrant magnetism I also saw in Cecilia, the intensity I saw in Nate, and Grace's fervent faith?

But as I watched, his face seemed to change, to still like he'd slipped something sheer and lifeless overtop. "Whatever you have to say, I don't want to hear it. You've all built yourself a nest beside Satan, pretty-looking, foul-smelling. And now it's your home, so I hope you enjoy it, but I don't want any part of that."

"Daddy." Cecilia's voice shook. I reached for her hand but she brushed me away. "Please, just for a minute. I want to explain."

He studied her face silently, then stepped away from the door and gestured inside with an overdone flourish. I started to follow Cecilia but he set his hand on my chest and held it there. "Nate told me about you, you know. Maybe he was trying to shock me by revealing what had been happening behind my back all these years, make me feel stupid, but instead it just confirmed every decision I'd made for him. You managed to weasel your way into my children's lives, to take advantage of my wife's soft heart. So I should've known you were behind all this, but no more." And with that he pulled away and closed the door behind them.

I stood a minute staring at the closed door, half expecting Cecilia to open it again and run out or beckon me in. When she didn't, I jammed my hands into my pockets, a knot in my belly, waited another minute, and then walked back to the window.

Cecilia was standing with her head down, hands behind her back, brow furrowed. Mr. Sinclair's hands were also behind his back as he paced through the room, walking across his strewn papers as he talked. Suddenly he froze, then reached toward Cecilia, grabbed at her braid, and yanked it from her head. I slapped a hand over my mouth to keep from crying out.

He held it limply in one hand, then let it fall. And as I watched, shocked, he followed it onto the floor, hunched over his knees, and started to cry. Cecilia hesitated and then set a hand on his shoulder. *I'm sorry, I'm sorry,* I saw her say, and he looked back up at her, tears glossing his cheeks. She knelt beside him, took his hand, and together they bowed their heads to pray. And with that I knew Cecilia would not be coming back to me.

It terrified me, thinking of Cecilia alone in that house with a man who'd so obviously lost control. Momma wanted to call the police but I begged her to wait; there'd be no proof of abuse other than Cecilia's word, and I didn't even know at this point whether Cecilia would be willing to talk against him. Not knowing how to reach Nate, in desperation I wrote to Grace, and she showed up at our door two days later. "I stopped off at home already," she said, "and I'll be staying with her."

"Is she okay?"

Grace kept her eyes focused over my shoulder. She'd lost weight, or at least seemed more fragile, her face sunken like it had been molded from tissue paper over pipe cleaners. "She will be. It's good I'm here."

"I'm sorry, Grace. If you can convince Cecilia she has to leave, either now or in another couple months when Nate's settled, then you can go back to the convent."

"Right." She still wouldn't look at me. "Or maybe I'll just stay. The Poor Clares . . . well, the convent was perfect for me in some ways, I've never felt more at peace than when I was praying with the nuns, chanting, working . . . it felt like where I'm meant to be. But at night, at night I was thinking of day after day of this, the rest of my life. It should've felt full and complete, and it did, in a way. But behind that it also felt empty. How could I feel lonely when I was surrounded by the Lord?"

"You were just homesick. I bet everyone goes through that at first."

"Maybe." She gripped onto the door frame. "Or maybe your letter about Cecilia was a sign from God that I'm meant to be here instead. Or at least this was His way of helping me make a rational decision as to which is best." She finally looked down at my face, her eyes seeming haunted and bruised. "Thank you for writing to me," she said, then turned and disappeared into the night.

The last words she would say to me in almost three years.

16

I later learned that in those next months, life at home for Cecilia and Grace became unbearable. Although Joel expected them to keep up appearances at the church, smile and sing and hold intelligent conversation, they were kept from sleeping more than two hours at a time, their father waking them and making them traipse behind him to the back patio so they could kneel on the cold flagstone and pray for forgiveness. Cecilia told me she'd started hallucinating, believing she saw her mother hanging from the trees, laughing at them and throwing rocks. Grace was often already praying when their father entered her room to wake her, and Cecilia started to wonder if she ever slept. Her nose began to bleed spontaneously.

They were kept so secluded I only saw them twice in those months. The first time was just a fluke, running into them downtown in front of me and across the street, the three of them walking in a silent row. My heart seized, standing frozen with my arms limp at my sides as they disappeared down the street.

The next day I went to the church in the early morning so I could watch them climb out from Joel's car. Cecilia seemed to have gained a good deal of weight, her cheeks plump and belly swollen under her loose dress, and at first I was reassured by this until I saw the way she was walking with her eyes on her feet, a quick shuffling step like the ground beneath her was unsteady. Grace walked behind her, arms around her own waist, hands gripping her sides tightly enough to whiten the knuckles.

What kind of hold did Joel have over them that they'd stay with him? Was it some sort of cultlike brainwashing after a childhood of subjugation? Did their faith make them believe deserting their father was a sin? Or was it just that they loved and respected him simply because he was their father and it was inescapable? Their relationship with him seemed so complex, the mix of fear and longing I'd seen from all of them, that I couldn't even begin to understand it.

I had no idea what was happening behind the doors of their home, but seeing Grace and Cecilia, I had some sense of it and realized Nate needed to know. I needed to tell him his plan had somehow backfired, but I still had no idea how to get in touch with him.

He only wrote me two more letters while he was away, the first upbeat, talking about the job he'd found in a strawberry field, the joy of working in the sun to harvest heart-shaped jewels. His next letter was more strained, although he continued to keep the hardest things from me. I found out later that he'd spent those months living in barracks with the other workers, cement floors and cots with scratchy beige blankets and no pillows. Half his salary was deducted for rent, much of the rest for meals at the canteen, and for drinks; he was drinking even more now, cheap sour beers and a sickening concoction the laborers called "wine," which they were making from fermented strawberries.

I knew none of this, continued to imagine us in a sweet cottage with three bedrooms and a front porch we'd sit on every night to read and study and talk about the future. How had Nate ever thought he'd be able to find a house and support all of us on the only types of jobs one could get without a degree? The thing is, he'd never had to worry about material objects, his next meal; everything had always been provided for him, so the possibility of worry never even crossed his mind. And like Nate, I had no idea about money, whether rent cost twenty dollars or two thousand.

I sent an acceptance letter to Berkeley and registered to begin in the fall, poring over the catalogue with its pictures of white stone buildings and terra-cotta roofs, sweeping lawns and students reading cross-legged on stone benches. Of course I added Grace and Cecilia to my fantasy, imagined rescuing them from their father and bringing them to live in our cottage. I'd play the part Sophia had played, gathering them around me to teach them everything I was learning, their anchor.

And I was so enamored with that dream, the idea of being their savior, that it took me almost a month to realize my period hadn't come.

PART VII

CRIME *and* PUNISHMENT

17

Cecilia entered the library slowly, almost ceremoniously, carrying a teapot and matching chipped cups I recognized. She set them on the coffee table then sank onto the couch next to me, focusing her attention on pouring the tea before she turned to hand me a cup. "It's oolong, do you like oolong? The packet says it's infused with the aroma of rose petals, but that's obviously just marketing hype. It's good, though."

I took the cup and thanked her, and we both sat staring down at our tea for a silent minute, then started to talk at once, then stopped again. Cecilia gave a strangled laugh, then said, "I was just going to say how heartbreaking it is sitting here with you. I feel so old these days, like my life's over and I'm just waiting for it to end. Obviously there's a lot of the past I wouldn't ever want to relive, but I have to say that despite all that I'd do it again if I could. I want to remember what it's like to be young."

"I've missed our old life," I said. "It's just been the past few days I'm realizing how much."

"Yeah," Cecilia said. "Me too." Her face looked distant, weighted.

"It's got to be excruciating, all this. You're a saint for taking care of Joel. After everything he did, you don't owe him."

"He's my dad." Her voice was suddenly sharp. "Corinthians says that love bears all things, believes all things, hopes all things, and endures all things. I owe him my life, Chloe, you have to understand that."

"He destroyed your life when he made you get married; you were so smart, you could've really *become* something. He destroyed all our lives in different ways, and I don't get how you can possibly feel any kind of loyalty."

"Look, Chloe, all I can say is regardless of everything he did he always loved us. I realize you've never understood, I realize you'll never really get it, but if your father hadn't deserted *you*, you might have some idea why I'm not about to desert him."

This sounded so cruel, so unlike Cecilia. I wanted to lash out at her, or at least to correct her since whoever my father was, he'd never even known of my existence. But of course that was completely beside the point. Instead I said, "I know a lot of what went on now, and it was such a twisted love I don't see how it counts. I don't know that I understand any of this, really. Was Nate just here for you, or did he actually want to be here for your dad? Or was it something completely else? Actually, I'm *sure* I don't understand anything. How could he even stand to be here after what must've happened in this house?"

Cecilia stared out the window, her face slack, then turned to me. "We talked about Gabriel when Nate was here. A lot. It was so agonizing for him, the guilt of not having been a real father, hating that he'd never really gotten the chance to know him and blaming himself for not being able to protect him. You sound so angry when you talk about Nate, like you don't think he cared enough. But it killed him inside, Chloe."

"I know that." I followed her gaze out across the lawn. "I didn't really even realize how much he was hurting until just recently. I mean obviously I knew he was sad, but he never talked about it. And I guess I used to think it was just that kind of a surface sadness you feel after famous people die, like a news anchor you used to watch every night. You miss seeing them, you might even cry, you feel sad about all the great things they might've done, but then a year later you'll see a retrospective and realize you'd completely forgotten they weren't around anymore. I thought the death wasn't really part of him."

"How could you not realize? That's all he's been all these years, is the guilt and the hurt."

"It's because he never talked to me about it. I don't know if he was protecting me, or just trying to deal with it privately. But it always made me assume that since he'd never gotten to spend much time with Gabriel, he hadn't ever actually felt the kind of love a father's supposed to feel."

If I'd had some sense of his pain, would the little annoyances and spats and disappointments have permeated as deeply? If our life had been fiction, with the realization that Nate had loved and mourned as acutely—had blamed himself for everything I'd blamed him for—I'd now be looking back over the years of our marriage, seeing that all the rough edges, most of the places we'd fragmented, had been a result of my misunderstanding. Layer by layer those fissures would heal and we'd be rebuilt, like those films where just for kicks they show you a building's demolition in reverse. I'd remember how much I loved and needed him, he'd ask me to forgive him and I'd say no, I'm the one who should ask for forgiveness. And we'd rebuild on the foundation we'd realize was still strong after all.

But our life together had so much history that I didn't even know where all the fissures were.

"He hides things from me," I said. "He has from the beginning, and even more after Gabriel died, like he's trying to protect me, or protect himself." I hesitated, then set my cup down and stood. "Hold on, I'll show you something."

I walked out to the car, retrieved the hollowed-out book and brought it back to the house, where I opened it to show Cecilia what was inside. "Articles about your dad's arrest and release," I said. "And a lock of Gabriel's hair, and this." I handed her the notebook. "He was writing letters to Gabriel."

Cecilia opened the notebook, stared at the pages blankly. "To Gabriel?"

"It started before he died. I guess he wanted to keep some record of Gabriel's childhood; they spent so little time together he was probably trying to hold on to as much of it as he could, and also he was trying to teach a little about his philosophy of life, things for Gabriel to read later. But even after he died Nate kept writing, first the letters and then it became more a way to work through everything that happened. All of it in the code you guys made up, using books from our childhood and talking about the time in our lives when we'd read them; all these pages he went through the trouble of encrypting. Hidden inside this book he'd made into a shell, and that's so symbolic of the way he's always been with me, hidden and pretending to be something else."

She flipped slowly through the pages, then pressed her hand flat on the text like she was trying to comfort it. Her face was drawn when she looked up at me. "And Gabriel's hair. He saved his hair."

"He must've taken it from my drawer after Gabriel died, before we left Redbridge. I was heartbroken about losing it, he knew that, so why didn't he tell me he'd taken it?"

"He must've had reasons. Like maybe the hair was more than just hair."

"What the hell's that supposed to mean?"

"Nothing. Nothing, I was just musing out loud."

I kept my eyes on hers, unspeaking, waiting. She turned away, but I reached for her chin, made her face me. "I don't believe you, Cecilia. You know things you're not telling me. And there was something else along with the hair and articles, something else he was hiding in the book. I know there was, and he brought it here to show you."

"No he didn't. He didn't bring anything, and I don't know anything more than I told you, Chloe. He came here to support me and make sure I could manage Dad on my own, and then it all got to be too much for him so he left. I'm sure he'll be home soon, and then he can tell you whatever there is to tell. But you can't expect me to give you any answers."

"Because you don't know them or because you don't want to tell me?"

She didn't respond, just flipped slowly through the notebook. "Have you read all of it?"

"Not all. It seems like it's written in sections, and each section he uses a different book to encode it. So I was stuck until I remembered this." I reached for the copy of *Romeo and Juliet* I'd set on a side table, and told her how we'd buried the book in the woods meaning to dig it up when we were old. "I haven't checked yet, but I'm guessing he used the text to encode the next section."

"Nate with his games," she said, her eyes distant. And then,

"Could it be that part of him actually wanted you to find the notebook at some point?"

"What do you mean?"

"Maybe just subconsciously, but he could've encoded this with completely obscure texts you never would've figured out, or used some other sort of code, or even hidden the book in a safe-deposit box. Isn't it always the way with secrets? You're not going to let yourself share them openly but in the end they're too big for just you, so subconsciously you're wishing they'd be discovered. You have to admit he could've done a better job of hiding this."

"What are his secrets, Cecilia?" I said slowly. "If they're in here I'll find out eventually, so you might as well tell me."

"I'm being honest, I'm as curious as you are what's in the notebook." She paused, then leaned back against the couch and closed her eyes. "God I'm tired, I'm pretty much always tired these days, so I don't think straight. Dad wakes up at five every morning, sometimes even earlier. It's like taking care of a newborn."

"Cecilia."

"And you must be exhausted! You have to stay the night, okay? You could sleep in Nate's room, and if you're careful, I promise you won't see Dad at all. He's always with me except when he's sleeping, and you can stay in the bedroom and only come down when we're out. It'll be a lot more comfortable than a motel, you can work on Nate's notebook or just sleep if you want. We'll be out most of the day tomorrow actually, so you'll have free run of the house till mid-afternoon." She stood and raised her arm to me. When I didn't take her hand she dropped it again. "Daddy takes a nap at four like clockwork. We can talk more tomorrow afternoon, okay?"

She obviously knew something, but what could I do? Strangle it out of her? And plus I *was* exhausted, too exhausted to fight for something she wasn't willing to share. "Okay," I said. "Okay, we'll talk tomorrow."

I brought my bag from the car and followed Cecilia up to Nate's old bedroom. At the doorway she reached for both my shoulders, then kissed my cheeks right and left, European style. "I wish you hadn't come, but I'm glad you're here," she said, then turned away toward her bedroom.

Nate's room hadn't changed at all, his cherrywood four-poster bed with its green-striped spread, matching green curtains, and oval area rug. His clothes were still in the cherry wardrobe, the cotton pants, crew-neck sweaters, and plaid cotton shirts I remembered from his childhood.

I pulled one of his shirts from its hanger, fingered the stained collar, then pulled it against my face. It smelled old, dusty, and slightly sour, like something dying.

I set it back and opened his dresser drawer by drawer, his tee-shirts, underwear and socks, a Bible and a blank notepad, both badly yellowed, an old razor and shaving lotion and two framed photos of Sophia. She looked so much younger than I remembered, had been at least a decade younger than me when she died, so pretty, so delicate and obviously frail. Both pictures had been laid upside down in the drawer like he'd wanted to keep the pictures but couldn't bear to look at them.

I picked up the Bible, glancing through the pages he'd marked with small slips of paper in the way he still marked novel pages he wanted to reread. All his life Nate had been searching for answers here, trying to interpret the Word in a way that felt true to him while at the same time feeling guilty for daring to question. How had his faith made him feel about me? About premarital sex and an out-of-wedlock baby? I'd always wondered whether the immensity of his guilt about Gabriel's existence had dwarfed whatever guilt he felt about not being there after his birth. Whether that guilt had been the real reason he'd done what Joel asked of him without protest, leaving us to go to Bible college. Joel, after all, had once been his direct line from God. It might have felt to him like atonement.

How did he still have faith after everything done by the man who'd constructed the foundations of that faith? How had it not crumbled? Maybe it was the need for a replacement father, to know that at least somebody was in charge of this world that had fallen around him. Maybe it was just that he'd wanted to find a purpose behind all the pain.

I set the Bible back beside Sophia's pictures and opened the last drawer. There, under stacks of old school notebooks, was a large manila envelope, stuffed full, and I knew immediately what was inside it. This was where Nate had kept the badges he'd earned from our dares, saving them like medals won in battle. Had Joel looked through his drawers after he left? If he had, what would he have thought these were? I unlatched the envelope and dumped them on the bed, shuffling through them.

How naïvely reckless we'd been! Did we really think we were invincible? Or no, maybe we just didn't care if we weren't. When you're fourteen, death is so romantic, like Beth in *Little Women*, adored and deeply mourned, wept over for centuries by millions of girls. When one is fourteen one imagines one's own funeral in order to feel loved.

I suddenly noticed there were words on the back of some of the badges. In fact, when I flipped the others over I saw there were words on almost all of them: *sensible, time, dying, escape*. Were the words somehow associated with the dares the badges represented?

And then I saw *Chloe* written on one of the badges. I held it flat in my palm, and started trying to arrange the others. It was when

I saw the word *madness* on two of the badges that I understood what to do.

I started plucking out words, a quote from Françoise Sagan that Nate had sent me in one of the letters he'd written from college, the deeply romantic quote he'd recited years later as part of his wedding vow.

> *I have loved to the point of madness; that which is called madness,*
> *that which to me is the only sensible way to love.*

I set those words aside, remembering the intensity of his eyes as he quoted them at our wedding, how even then I'd sensed there must be something rabid and impermanent in that kind of love. And almost despising him for claiming it when all I really felt in those days after Gabriel's death, all I sensed I'd ever be able to feel, was loss.

With those words removed, there were still tens of badges left over, so I started fiddling with them absently. Placing and replacing and switching until I'd constructed the message he'd meant for me to read.

> *I can't do this anymore, Chloe. I'm dying inside every night*
> *without you both, literally going mad. Which means the time has*
> *come. We'll be poor but happy. Marry me and we'll leave this*
> *place tonight, we won't tell anyone, just escape, one madness to*
> *another.*
> > *I love you.*
> > *Nate*

When had he written this?

Oh Christ, I knew, I knew when he'd written it. Everything he did and said had angered me in those last days, exhausted from long hours at the factory and life with a toddler and dreams that got farther away every day. But if I'd taken the badges from him, figured out his little ridiculous, heartbreaking puzzle, our story would probably have had a very different ending.

I pressed my hands flat against the badges, a clawing in my stomach. And then I grabbed for them, closed my fists around the words and threw handful after handful across the room.

I hadn't thought I'd be able to sleep that night, in a bed that still smelled like Nate, on a pillow where I knew he'd laid his head just a few nights before while he figured out the best, least hurtful way to lie to me. For ten minutes I burrowed and twisted, trying to root out the cascading fireworks of disjointed thoughts and memories. But then what seemed like seconds later my eyes opened and the room was bright with morning sun. If I'd dreamt, I didn't remember any of it, and the sleep seemed to have made me even more exhausted, like my brain was now muffled under a down quilt.

I rose slowly, testing out my joints, listening for sounds in the rest of the house. When I didn't hear any, I walked to the bathroom to shower and brush my teeth, dressed in sweats, then went cautiously downstairs. And found on the dining room table a covered dish, with a note.

> *Took Daddy to church, then doctor, back by 3. Help yourself to anything.*
>> *Love,*
>> *C*

I lifted the cover on the plate, congealed eggs and white toast, and brought them up to the bedroom where I gnawed on them distractedly while I started to work, the notebook on one side, *Romeo and Juliet* on the other.

~~Grimego nusyominy gawtorrageddy towedill snoguticaseth rerry eealtor agaledsy, grasifeth gatorcoyomy wulord midwetill ganotte earits rugylieo aness~~

I'm using a tragedy to disguise the real tragedy, as if that could mitigate its ugliness. It's haunted me for years what he did to Grace, echoing against what he did to you. And my hatred, my rage, they're the iron mallets I use to try and sublimate the horror and disgust and ludicrous need to understand the un-understandable.

I've tried to get inside his mind. Of course I have, he's my father. I wanted to blame the church, because if I couldn't it meant I'd have to accept that it was all him, that he was evil. So I try to believe he thought he was saving us all. When he found out about Grace, he was scared her sins would give Satan a foothold not only into our family, but also into the whole church. This is my attempt to understand something incomprehensible, explain why he reacted so strongly when he first saw me with your mother, and then when he found out you were coming, Gabriel.

I want to believe this, but in the end it makes no sense because did he really think he was reversing the sin? Removing Satan from our family? I'm sure not, so the only reason that makes sense is that what he did to Grace, to you, were both only to protect his name in the church.

For Grace, his perfect child, to have had relations outside of a marriage, outside the faith! He worked so hard at making us appear flawless to the outside world, and this would've destroyed that illusion, any hopes he might've had for the furthering of his career, a bigger following. All our lives we must've disappointed him; Grace was the only one of us he'd ever approved of, and now he was desperate to remove all traces of what she'd done . . .

I only saw the aftermath, the blood. It soaked through the socks she'd stuffed between her legs, through her skirt and onto the mattress where she was huddled. She didn't make any sound and that's what haunts me now, her face pale with pain but her eyes blank and staring through the contractions, as her body fought to get rid of the last of it. I don't know if she saw it, what size or form it might've had because I'm not sure how far along she was. I do know she tried to save everything she could, including the knitting needle, in a shoebox. I don't know what she did with the box when it was over.

Maybe I should've told the authorities, but I knew if Grace had been willing to come forward to anyone with her pain, her shame, she would have first shared it with me. It destroyed her, Gabriel, it destroyed her belief in my father, which destroyed

her faith, which was really all she had in life.
Maybe it destroyed me too.

I try to fill this book with lessons, teach you
things I've learned, but my stories are seeping over
the edges because they're the biggest part of who I
am. I'm writing them down, finally letting myself
remember as if years later I might have a new
perspective. But age doesn't help it make sense;
nothing can be learned from the stories, they have
no meaning and maybe that's been the hardest
part of it all. Fiction has morals and consistent
themes and conclusions, written in an attempt to
teach us about life and make us feel less alone. But
in the end the most important moral you learn is
that real life is often meaningless.

I closed the notebook, stared at it, then shoved it away and
curled up on the bed.

I should've guessed, seeing the hollowness in Grace's face, the
urgency with which she'd needed to get away, to join the Poor Clares,
wanting their stark simplicity. Nate had told me she was punishing
herself, and I'd never been able to understand what for. No wonder
she hadn't been there for us when we lost Gabriel. No wonder.

And suddenly I thought, for the first time in years, of the bond
Nate shared with his sisters, something that excluded me. All this
time Nate had kept this from me, and yes it wasn't his story to tell
but it explained so much of our past. This must be why he suggested she join a convent, and it explained the children's loss of
freedom, why Joel forced them to work in the church. But also it
put context behind the changes in Nate's personality, and the sort
of deadness I'd seen in all of them. The fact that I hadn't known

any of this, it hurt, which was a completely wrong emotion. But it must mean that on some level he hadn't trusted me.

I was still hunched in bed when the phone rang. And hearing it I felt a little hiccup of hope that wherever he was, he'd somehow sensed that I needed him. I wanted Nate, needed reassurance that despite the fact he'd kept this from me, and despite the fact he'd been so secretive about his visit here and run off Lord knew where without explanation, I was still the most important person in his world.

I dug into my pocket and pulled out the phone. It was Daniel. I considered not answering. Then answered anyway. "Daniel."

"Hey, how are you? *Where* are you? I stopped by last night and again this morning. Your newspapers are piling up."

Hadn't I told him where I was going? No, of course I hadn't. It was part of keeping that life as separate as possible from this one, and I knew I'd already shared too much. Ridiculous as it seemed, I'd been trying to make the time I spent with Daniel feel like the time I spent consumed by a movie, or a book, a simple, tightly constructed story, a romance with no subplots, little suspense, and a pat ending. "I told you I had to go somewhere," I said.

"I thought you meant somewhere like a doctor's appointment. I didn't ask because when I saw your face I assumed it was something embarrassing, like . . . a proctologist. You could've at least given me some idea how long you'd be away."

Nothing was ever as simple as a romance novel. Even romance novels weren't as simple. "I'm in Redbridge," I said. "Looking for Nate."

"Aaah, right." Daniel paused, then, "Is he there?"

"No. He was but he left before I got here. I'm here with Cecilia, and their dad."

"Their *dad*?"

"Daniel, don't . . . I can't talk about this now. There's too much going on, I'm too full up with it now and I'm trying to work through it."

"Right, I guess you would've told me where you were going if you had any intention of talking about it."

"You sound angry."

"I'm not, I realize this is another of the myriad of things just between you and Nate."

"Please don't be like this. Hell, Daniel, I wish you were here, actually, it'd make things feel more steady." I imagined him helping me work through the rest of the notebook, holding me close whenever Joel passed in the hallway. I imagined telling him about the baby Grace had gathered inside a shoebox, feeling his lips in my hair as I spoke, as if that could absorb some of the horror of it. "I just have to talk to Cecilia, I'm pretty sure she knows more than she's telling me about where he went and why, and as soon as I know I can come back home."

"And then what? When you find him?"

I looked down at the notepad where I'd penciled Nate's words, began drawing X's in the margins. "I don't know, I just need to talk to him about everything, all of this."

"Good. That's really good, Chloe. It's time."

He sounded relieved. And I realized he'd misunderstood. I curled my legs up on the bed, trying to figure out how to respond, having no idea. It was *past* time, of course; I should've told Nate months ago, made a decision as soon as I started having feelings for Daniel on whether to move forward or back. Instead I'd waited to see whether the feelings were real, and even after knowing they were I tried weighing one love against the other, one foot on each side to see where I'd land.

And the truth was that I still didn't know. The other night with Daniel had felt good, his arms and his words and eating breakfast beside him, and the fact he'd stayed home from work so he could be there when I woke, all felt *good,* but I couldn't say it felt right. And I didn't know if the not-rightness came from guilt or if I still would've felt it if there'd been no Nate, an intrinsic unrightness. The question millions had weighed since the phrase "in love" was coined: I loved Daniel but I didn't know if it was more, there were no check boxes to differentiate one sort of love from another, like those magazine quizzes: *If you scored 18 or higher, then congratulations, you're IN LOVE!* Whereas with Nate, it had never been a question. I knew I'd been in love with him. Reading his notebook I knew I was still in love, but also knew that sometimes "in love" wasn't enough.

"I'm not exactly looking forward to this," he said, "but whatever happens after, at least you'll know you did the right thing. It'll help you figure things out once it's all out in the open."

Was that the reason everything was so snarled inside my mind? The deception was a crushing fist without which everything would unfurl and become clear? It sounded too simple, but I suspected it might almost be true.

"Listen, I have something for you. When are you coming home? I've been waiting for the right time and . . . this seems like as good a time as any."

I felt a sudden clutch in my stomach. But no, he couldn't be talking about a ring; Daniel was a romantic, but he was also a pragmatist.

"I've had it since high school, it's one of my most cherished possessions, an autographed copy of *Lonesome Dove.* It was my favorite book, probably still is. You know how some men will keep, I don't know, a pearl necklace that's been handed down for generations, waiting for the right woman to give it to? This was my ancestral pearl necklace."

"Wow," I said. I had a sense what this meant to him; Daniel felt the same way about books as Nate and I did, and giving me the most important book from his childhood probably meant almost as much to him as an engagement ring. "Wow," I said again.

"The day I went to hear Larry McMurtry talk I was all nervous. He was signing copies of *Texasville,* and here I was handing him a book I'd already bought a year ago and read three times, and I blathered out something that meant 'I love you.' Not exactly those words, but that was the gist of it. So he's watching me with this strange smile on his face, and I'm blushing and trying to find the most discreet way of slithering under the table when he takes my hand, thanks me and tells me to keep reading." He paused. "In retrospect that felt much more profound than it sounds when I say it out loud."

"No," I said softly, "I get it."

"Of course you do. That's why you're the first person I've ever even considered giving the book to."

I nodded without speaking. Because what could I say? I'd slogged through *Lonesome Dove,* it took me months. And I knew it was a good book, a great book even, but it just wasn't me. Instead of the "In Love" questionnaire, could one do a compatibility test based on favorite books? Could an Anaïs Nin fan love a Dean Koontz fan? An Alice Munro woman love a James Joyce man?

"Thank you," I said finally, knowing I couldn't take the book from him, also knowing I couldn't tell him that over the phone. It was stupid of me, and I was probably injecting symbolism where there shouldn't be any, but the conversation scared me. Not least because the idea that he'd give me a cherished book as a token of his love was irresistible. "Sorry, Cecilia's car just pulled up," I lied. "I better go."

"So you'll be back . . . ?"

"I'll call from the road. In not too long, a day or two. As soon as I can."

"Soon," he said. "Come see me first thing, okay? I miss you every minute."

I hung up and sat back on the bed, cell phone cupped between both palms. Wondering if maybe in the end that was all I wanted, what every woman really wanted. A man who would think to say the words *I miss you every minute,* without irony.

I continued with Nate's notebook, his brief summary of the weeks between Grace losing her baby and leaving for the convent, writing about how he'd find her in the mornings with her knees bruised and skinned from hours of prayer. In these sections he'd given up any pretense of writing to Gabriel, or maybe was writing to Gabriel-as-healing-angel rather than Gabriel-as-son. This was a diary, a confession, words raw like they'd been torn from somewhere deep.

> *I started sleeping with Grace again every night, and she let me maybe because she needed comfort or protection from Joel, maybe because she knew she needed protection from herself. She started having nightmares, I'd wake up and she'd be writhing against the bed, so I'd hold her without waking her, try to make her dreaming self realize she was safe. And then one night, she was still asleep, she rolled onto me sobbing, moaning, burrowing against me. Then pressed her face against my neck and called me Cesar.*
>
> *And there was more.*

I didn't try to wake her, but the next day I brought up the idea of the convent. I knew she needed peace.

All they'd been through that year, and they'd been so young, just eighteen and twenty. We'd all thought we were adults; Nate and I had planned out the rest of our lives without guidance from anyone. But now when I saw kids that age coming into the store, usually looking for cheap copies of the Twilight saga, it was so obvious they were still just children. I couldn't imagine them going off on their own, getting a job, finding a place to live. Losing a parent. Falling in love. Having sex or aborting a baby. Being able to make any sort of rational decision on how to handle any of it.

I continued reading, now not bothering to copy down his words, crossing out letters straight from his notebook. At some point this morning I'd realized I couldn't hide this from Nate, that I'd need to confront him with all I'd learned. That pretending I hadn't found the notebook would be a worse betrayal than having read through it.

How could a marriage go through all ours had and still survive? I'd let Daniel believe I was going to confess to everything, and it was true in the end I knew I'd have to. So maybe I'd lump it all into one confession, as if each might dilute the impact of the other. As if both Nate and me coming clean with all our secrets could minimize the weight of our having had secrets in the first place. Although really, really I wasn't that naïve. When he came home (if he came home) I'd have to confront the fact that we might not survive.

On the next page Nate talked about the nights he'd spent awake trying to find a solution to save all of them, and then about his suicide note. Angry, so angry at his father and at himself for having let fear paralyze him for so long.

About his last night, the night we'd first made love, he wrote only:

> *Samuel R. Delany said, "The common problem, I suppose, is to have more to say than vocabulary and syntax can bear." Which is the case for almost every major emotion one tries to solidify in writing, loss and joy, anger and envy. And love, so much has been written about it that there's no way to come close without molding your words around clichés, but I'll just say this. That being with the right woman feels as pure and as innate and as vital as choral music. All at once I understood everything that had been written, from the sketched outlines in classics to headlong poems and intricate rhapsodies of women's fiction, and for the first time realized they'd only touched the surface. I'd thought I understood before, but it's like thinking you understand what it is to have a child. There are no words.*

I read this, and then again, trying not to feel it. Observing my thoughts from a distance, my bizarre longing to go back to that night, the ridiculous notion that everything had been so much simpler then. When of course, although we'd had fewer years and so fewer threads in our lives, the knots and tangles in those threads had been pulled just as tight. And as he began to write about work in the fields, and the horror of the labor camp where he'd spent his nights, I let myself remember.

PART VIII

The PIT *and the* PENDULUM

18

You wouldn't recognize me, Chloe, my skin's gone so dark and my hair so light. I'm not burning anymore, and I think I must've built up a lifetime supply of vitamin D. And I'm learning so much about life, that's the best part. I think more even than you'll learn at university in some ways. Please give Cecilia a hug from me. I miss you all more than words can say.

I folded the letter back into the envelope. Then set it into my desk drawer beside the white stick. The line on the stick, so faint last week I hadn't been sure it wasn't my fear playing tricks, was on this morning's test a stubborn, definitive blue.

I set my hand on my belly, pressed my fingers against it. Remembering sophomore Biology, a cluster of cells, the beginnings of a spinal cord, a heartbeat the size of a gnat. I thought I could feel a new firmness, lower down than I'd thought my uterus could possibly be, and I imagined it was a foot. A fist. And felt a twist in my chest, the ache of tears behind my nose, because I already knew what I needed to do.

Mom was in the bathroom putting on her face before a night out with Brad, the logger. I stood in the doorway watching her oval her lips as she applied mascara. "Ma?" I said.

She startled, a freckle of mascara on her right cheekbone, and I focused on it as I pulled the stick out from behind my back, with an unintended flourish like I was performing a magic trick. I set it on the counter beside her makeup bag.

She licked a finger to wipe off the smudge as she glanced down, then dropped the mascara wand, leaving a black worm trail in the sink. She turned slowly to face me, and we stared at each other a minute before she said, "Whose is it?"

"It's . . . mine," I said, flustered, then understood. "And Nate's. Well, of course it's Nate's."

"Christ." She sat on the toilet lid and stared down at her knees. Then said, "I'll help you."

I sank onto the edge of the tub, my eyes filling. "I looked it up, there's a clinic in downtown Eureka, I called them. But it'll cost almost six hundred bucks."

"What? What the hell are you saying?" She reached for the stick. "Look at this, Chloe, it's your baby waving at you. I was younger than you when I got pregnant, and I didn't have a mother for support. Where would you be if I'd paid six hundred bucks? You'd be nowhere!"

I felt a swirl of nausea and set a hand on my stomach, wondering if it was morning sickness or terror, or something as simple as relief. "I'm going to school," I said. "To Berkeley, and I didn't tell you because I didn't know how you'd react. But I got a scholarship, and I'll pay for the rest through work-study. Me and Nate are going to find a house, he's working and I'll go to classes—"

"Would you listen to yourself, Chloe? Haven't I taught you this in all these years, that when you make your bed, no matter how badly it's made, you have no choice but to find a way to slide under the covers? I'm not going to stand by and let you go to some fancy-ass hotel just because your sheets stink."

"It's not just that, Ma, this is really complicated. His dad can't ever find out about this."

"Of course he can, he has to. If you're scared of how he'll react, I'll go with you to tell him." She sat beside me on the edge of the tub, took my hands and squeezed. "Either Nate can come home to help support you, or if his dad wants him to stay in Bible college he can damn well pay to support you himself in Missouri. I'll tell him that, okay? Let me call Brad and cancel, and I'll go over with you right now if you want." She seemed strangely giddy, words conspiratorially excited. Why?

But as she wrapped her arms around me and patted awkwardly at my back, I suddenly understood. She was seeing this opportunity to help me and the baby as an unexpected chance to finally do it right.

I told her the rest of it then, as she listened wide-eyed. It seemed so strange to me now that she didn't know. I hadn't said anything because I'd had no idea how to tell her the truth. But now as I watched her pale face, I wished that I'd told her back when Nate first left. This had been too big for just me, crowded every crevice of my mind and stretched my insides so that every part of me felt sore and bruised with it. And now as I started to talk, it was like a stopper was loosening and then violently springing free, the story pouring from me, words tumbling as fast as my tongue could get around them.

Mortifying.

Because suddenly I could see the story from my mother's perspective, a ridiculous game played by petulant children, like those fantasies I'd had years ago of writing angry notes and then taking off on foot with a hobo bag. It was naïve and ridiculous, childish impulsiveness with adult consequences, and when I was done, a sharp claw of regret in my stomach, I buried my head against my mother's shoulder with the only word I had left. "Please . . ."

"You need to find Nate," she said softly. "He needs to know."

With my ear on her chest her voice sounded deep and sure, like this was the first step of a puzzle that actually had a defined correct solution. I closed my eyes, focused on the softness of her breast against my cheek. "But then what? What can we do? We'll have to find a house, but how can we afford it? Nate, he's picking strawberries now, that's his job, but I don't know how close he is to the university or what happens when the strawberries stop growing. And how can I take care of a baby and go to school and work at the same time?"

"Well, you can't, obviously. But I can help if you stay here, and I can find you both a job at the factory, or help you look for something downtown. And when the baby's born we can all work in shifts and watch it in shifts, you, me, and Nate."

"You'd do that?" I felt a little blip of hope. "But not Nate; he could work wherever else until he saved up enough money to take care of us, or got a better job. But he can't come back, not after pretending to be dead. His dad's crazy, Ma, you know that. The way he treats them, he pounds on them and pounds on them like he wants them flat enough that he can stand on them to lift himself up. It was bad before, but if Nate came back, I know it'd be ten times worse for all of them."

"You told me Joel doesn't hit them, right? And I have to say that in my mind it seems like Nate could use a little nonviolent pounding. He's going to have to face up to what he's done, lying in his own badly made bed. Going off without even thinking about the people he left behind, he needs to face up to that. And to this." She touched my belly. "What if you told him about the baby and he decided to just disappear inside the strawberry fields because it's easier than acting like a grown man?"

"He wouldn't do that," I said. "He's not like that."

"Or even if he came back eventually, imagine if this baby grows up and finds out its dad wasn't around for the first however many months or years? The one thing I regret most in my life is that you didn't have a father growing up. Partly because it would've been easier for me not being the only one responsible, but also for you. It would've made you stronger."

I pulled away from her. "I am strong."

"Oh Chloe." She brushed a strand of hair behind my ear. "You're like me, Chloe, you're hard but not strong, and this all is evidence. Strong is on the inside, a root that keeps you standing whatever might hit you. But hard is only on the outside, this shield you put up to keep all the pain on the inside from showing. The soft inside is still there even when you don't let yourself see it. And the shell keeps you safe, but it also keeps the good things from penetrating; love and trust and joy. It can keep you from liking yourself much too. If you had self-worth you would've told him how you really felt about this craziness, faking a suicide, you following where he leads. You wouldn't be letting him get away with it now."

I knew my mother had always held animosity toward men, only dating those who were weaker than her and could—like her boyfriend Brad, a decade younger—be controlled. So I shouldn't trust her judgment on any of this, but if I really let myself think about it, I could see how I'd let Nate lead me around all these years without questioning, from the days he left me notes in code direct-ing me on when and where to meet him, Cecilia, and Grace, to the games we played and the stories we acted out, to the afternoons on the train tracks, to the night we spent on the beach. To this.

And now when I thought of the baby growing inside me, the despair I'd seen the two times I'd run into Grace and Cecilia, and Nate who was now standing in the sun somewhere with nothing to worry about except the picking of fruit off bushy stalks, part of me hated him for not loving us enough.

"I'll find him," I said. "I have letters with a return postmark, so I know he's on a farm somewhere in Dixon. I'll find him and tell him he has to come home."

"Okay, then. I'll drive you out there."

I studied her face. Was there anger there? Empathy? It shocked me how fierce she sounded. Like a mother. She was a woman I'd put inside a strangely shaped box made up of love and flippancy, attachment and disengagement and misguided attempts at friend-ship: the maker of dinners and distracted queries about my day; a worn face at the breakfast table shielded by the paper, emerging only to tell me not to drink from the juice container. But also there were the brief moments her guard was down: her haunted eyes when she'd talked about her own childhood, wanting to teach me something I didn't know if she even really understood; at night after I returned home when she'd sit on my bed and ask where I'd been, rising to bring me another blanket which she tucked tightly around me. Trying. And now sitting with her and the beginnings of a baby I'd just minutes ago thought I might not keep, I knew that in a way, she was me.

"I'd like that," I said, feeling an inexplicable sense of loss. "Re-ally, I need you to be there."

We drove down to Dixon the next day, six hours without stopping. The town seemed dusty and colorless; utterly flat with a distant view of hills—gray with distance—on the horizon, small brick and stucco houses joined by sidewalks and overly manicured lawns, and a featureless downtown, with scrappy trees and rows of beige diners, gas stations, and banks.

We spent the night at an equally dingy motel and set off the next morning to the biggest farm in the region, driving by slowly as we stared in dismay at the strawberry fields. They were nothing at all like I'd pictured, plants sprouting through plastic sheeting, the furrows between them muddy from rain or irrigation. Mom pulled off to the side of the road. "Wait here," she said, "I'm going to exercise my high school Spanish." She got out of the car and jogged into the field, toward the closest group of stooped pickers.

I leaned back in my seat, watching her, hugging my waist. And as I sat there, something, maybe fate or physics, some law of attraction, made me turn to look across the road. There, in the distance, I saw a familiar hunch of the shoulders, thick hair bleached light from the sun. I jumped out of the car and without even closing the door behind me, I ran to him.

He didn't see me until I was less than ten feet away, and I didn't call to him because I felt strangely awkward. He'd changed in the past two months, I could tell that just by the way he walked between the rows, his posture strained, burdened, he seemed almost elderly. And when he finally looked up at me, his skin dark from the sun and flushed with exertion, mosquito bites pocking his cheeks and arms, I didn't recognize his eyes. They'd lost something, a spark, a fierceness, like the hope had been drained from him.

He stared at me, then pressed a finger and thumb against his eyes, held them there a moment before pulling them away. I tried to smile. "Yes, I'm real," I said.

"How—" he started, and then his face flushed suddenly pink and he strode forward to reach for me, crushing me against his chest and burying his face in my hair.

I pressed a hand against the back of his head, noticing that he even smelled different, like sweat and the cloying sweetness of fermenting strawberries and something darker, earthier, like the inside of a cave. He gripped my shoulders tightly, too tightly, his nails long and digging into my skin. I pulled away.

"You have to come home now," is all I said, and he stared at me, his mouth a firm line. At first I was sure it meant he was going to protest, but when I held out my hand he looked down at it, then took it. And passive as a child dazed by a too-long, napless day, he let me lead him to the car.

He didn't speak except to direct my mother to the labor camp, sitting in the backseat staring out the window with his hands folded between his knees. When we pulled up to the low-slung gray wooden barracks, he told us to wait in the car, but he looked so small walking toward it, dwarfed by the surrounding chain-link fences. *This* was where he'd been living all this time? It was like a prison, like the photos I'd seen of Japanese internment camps, and watching him walk inside I felt a burrowing sense of horror. I got out of the car and stood squinting up at the building, the sun reflecting off the pavement stinging my skin like teeth. I jogged to catch up, took his hand. He startled in surprise, but he let me follow him inside.

The hallway we walked down was dark, flanked by numbered doors, echoing with our footsteps and the smell of damp. Halfway down he opened a door on the right marked 43, and stepped back so I could enter. The room was about twelve-feet square, windowless with cement floors and a gray metal cot at each corner, each with a flat pillow and scratchy beige blanket. By one of the cots was a tin cup holding roadside daisies and asters, like the inhabitant was trying to make the room feel like home.

"Welcome," Nate said. "Wish I could offer you a drink."

"You should've told me this was where you were living."

"Why? What would you have done about it?" He pushed the mattress off the cot, revealing several Saltine boxes, which he up-ended on the springs, revealing books. "You know they stole six books? Six! And most of them don't speak English; most of them don't even *read*, so what exactly were they planning to do with them? They even stole the cheap paperback Bible I'd bought. Who the hell steals a Bible?" He threw the books into a garbage bag along with two damp tee-shirts that had been draped across the cot's posts, replaced the mattress, tied the bag into a knot, and then stared at it. Let it fall onto the ground. "What the hell am I doing?" he said.

"What?"

"What the hell are *you* doing? You can't actually expect me to go home, and why'd you bring your mother? How could you let her know I was still alive?"

"She didn't even know you were supposed to be *not* alive, I never told her. And your dad must not've believed your note because he never even reported you missing, just told people you were off studying in Missouri."

Nate's face seemed to go pale under his tan, from a ruddy brown to dried clay. "That's why I wasn't in the papers. Hell, maybe he does believe it and he just covered it up because suicide is embarrassing and he didn't want anybody to know. I could see him just pretending to himself that I'd never even existed. He'd never mourn me, I realize that, even if he saw me with his own eyes lying in a cooler on a slide-in gurney."

He leaned back against the wall, then slid slowly down it until his butt hit the floor. "I don't know what I'm doing, Chloe. I don't even know why I'm here anymore; it stopped having any meaning after the first week, and all I'm doing is getting through the minutes and days without letting myself think. But what's going to happen if I go back? If he doesn't kill me, which is definitely a possibility, he'll try and send me away. I'll be right back where I started before I left." He leaned his head back against the wall, stared up at the ceiling. "I don't have anything except Grace and Cecilia, and being this far away is like having my arms chopped off."

"You have Grace and Cecilia and *me*," I said, then sat beside him. "And *me*," I said again, sharply, and then I took his hand and set it on my belly. "And . . . and . . ."

He turned to study my face. Pulled his hand away like I'd burned him and said, "Why're you here, Chloe?"

I didn't answer, just pressed my lips between my teeth, and he stared at me, his face blank. Until slowly his eyes reddened and filled with tears.

We walked back to the car silently, side by side. When I slid into the passenger seat Mom glanced at Nate behind her, then turned to me. Mouthed the words, *He knows?*

I gave a short nod. She looked into my eyes a moment, then said loudly, "I think we could all use a cheeseburger!" and started the engine.

We didn't speak during the drive or when we first sat down in the Denny's booth, avoiding one another's eyes, Nate's face blank, shell-shocked. Nobody spoke until the waiter brought our sodas, when Mom swept off her straw wrapper with a flourish and said, "So, we're going to figure this out."

We turned to look at her. Nate reached for his Coke, wrapped both hands around it.

"Nate, I'll tell you what I'm thinking, and I'm counting on you to agree with me. Because you got my daughter into this, and I'm not going to let you walk away from it."

"I wouldn't do that," he said.

"Well, good, then we're on the same page. So I'll tell you what I'm thinking and you can debate it all you like, but it won't change the facts. Because the two of you can't do this on your own. You can't, but you're lucky that I'm willing to help. I'll give you a roof over your heads, I'll even help take care of the baby, but I'm expecting you both to work to help support it moneywise. And of course, Nate, I'm expecting you to marry Chloe."

Nate looked like he was going to cry, not the reaction one wants to see in response to the suggestion of marriage. I reached for his hand under the table and he let me hold it for a moment, his fingers limp, then pulled away. "But then I'd have to tell my dad. And if the congregation finds out—" He stopped, then blinked. Blinked again. Then said, "I know exactly what we're going to do." And for the first time since I'd told him about our child, he smiled.

Our conversation was stilted through the first half hour of the drive back, our heads too swamped by thoughts of what was coming to string together thoughts about anything else. But when Nate started musing about the future, me in school and him at our home in Berkeley taking care of the baby, and then about the baby itself—imagining whose hair it would have, whose eyes, whose talents—it was like a drug for me, swept a haze over all the fears with hallucinatory brushstrokes of what might come in ten months, two years, ten; another, better life.

Gabriel, we'd name it if he was a boy, Gabriella if she was a girl, to symbolize the change the baby would herald in our lives. And by the time we reached home we'd synthesized an entire future for Gabriel/la, imagined the baby as a college professor, a physician, a Nobel Peace Prize winner and philanthropist, all the p-words that to us epitomized success.

Throughout the ride I kept my hands on my belly, imagining our child fully formed, the size of a grape, warm and content and smiling at the sound of my voice. This grape-sized baby with my blue eyes and Nate's thick hair, my energy and Nate's passion, and my love for it was a spear through my chest and a wrench in my stomach. I adored this baby, and I couldn't wait to see who he'd turn out to be.

Nate spent the night with us on our living room couch, and the next morning, early, Mom drove us to the Sinclairs'. Nate had a strange, sardonically amused look on his face as he stared up at the house, as if he was somehow looking forward to the confrontation. He got out of the car and stood there a moment, then started slowly toward the door, his eyes on the upstairs window that led to Grace's bedroom. He lifted a rock by the front porch steps, retrieved a key, unlocked the front door, and entered.

Mom and I both looked over at the house without speaking, my hand again on my belly, using the baby's presence to calm my nerves. I imagined I could feel it kicking, a burbling sensation like gas bubbles, and I pressed my hand against it, hoping it could feel me.

Ten minutes passed, fifteen. I expected to hear yelling, sense some kind of rumbling of fury behind the walls, but all was silent and still. I reached over and took my mother's hand.

And then the front door opened and Nate emerged from the house alone. I pulled away from my mother as he slid into the backseat. "He's going to meet us at your house," he said. "He wants to talk to you but you need to drive home now, before Grace and Cecilia see the car."

"To me?" Mom peered at him in the rearview mirror, her face set, then started the engine. "What happened?"

"I don't know." Nate's voice was hoarse. "Before we got here I thought he was going to kill me, I mean literally I was all ready to defend myself, I knew how I was going to grab him, pull his arm up behind his back. But he . . . started to cry. That's how he re-acted, he started to cry, and I don't even know what that meant. Because he didn't even break down when Mom died; the only place I ever see him cry is at the pulpit when the spirit takes him."

"Is he going to give us the money?" I said.

"I don't know." Nate looked at me, his face blank and eyes dull. "I mean I think so, I think that's what he wants to talk to you about, but I'm guessing there'll be more strings attached."

"What do you mean, strings?" Mom said tightly. "What kind of strings? Attach too many and the whole thing's going to be grounded."

"He didn't tell me anything. He didn't . . ." His voice trailed off and he stared out the window, didn't speak again till we reached home, when he said, "That wine in the fridge, could I have a lit-tle?"

"Are you of age?" Momma said. Then, "You know what? I don't even care. I think we could all use some wine."

And so we went inside and poured three glasses from the gallon jug. Nate drained his and poured another, and then another. By the time Mr. Sinclair arrived I was buzzed, but Nate, who'd drunk at least twice what I had, didn't show any sign of it except a certain stillness, becoming, if anything, even more solemn.

I was the one who answered the door. Joel was standing right against it, as if peering in the window, and it was the closest I'd ever been to him; I could see the lines in his forehead and bracketing his mouth, the dark flecks in his blue eyes, but what struck me was his tallness. I had to throw back my head to see him, an angle that made him seem unreal, like a portrait against a sky-colored ceiling.

I saw his eyes flicker down to my stomach, then back up. "So," he said, "you win."

"I wasn't playing," I said. "I love Nate." If I was sober I would've left it like that, but in my semi-drunkenness the statement seemed to need embellishment. So I added, "More than you do."

His lips twitched. "Let me in," he said.

I stepped back from the door and he walked past me, into the kitchen, where his eyes took in the wine jug and three glasses before fixing on my mother and narrowing. "You must be so proud," he said.

I thought he was referring to the wine, a sarcastic dig at her having served children, but she understood what he meant. "I'm very proud of her. Not for this, maybe, but there's a lot to be proud of."

I felt a little gallop in my chest. She'd never told me she was proud, never even hinted it. I found myself wishing she would elaborate.

But Mr. Sinclair said, "Right, you're condoning blackmail, extortion, so I can see that you would be."

"I'm only asking your son to give my daughter what she and their baby deserve. She didn't do this on her own, and it's obviously not the baby's fault, so they deserve a husband and dad, and support so they can have a decent life. I'm doing my part, I'm taking care of Chloe throughout the pregnancy till she leaves for school. And I'll protect *you* by keeping the whole thing a secret, so it's only fair of you to do your part too. If it takes blackmail to make you see that, then I don't have a problem with it."

He spread his fingers, stared at them, then slowly lowered his splayed hand onto the table. "I'm a reasonable man, Ms. Tyler. Despite what Nathaniel might've told you. And even though in my mind it was an act of Satan that brought this child, I have no intention of letting a baby starve. But, I have conditions."

He turned to me, held my gaze as he said, "I'm not giving up on you, Nathaniel. I know you like pretending that I don't exist, that I don't have any stake in what you become. But the fact is all you can really do is pull on your leashes. Grace thought she could leave too, and look how far she got. I'm still holding the ends; you can pull but you'll always bounce back."

He finally turned to Nate, facing him without focusing his eyes. "I've told people that you're going to Bible college, and that's what I'm expecting you to do before you make decisions that'll change your life forever. Chloe can stay here or go to school, whichever she chooses, and you can visit your child as often as you'd like. I wouldn't stop you, and if you still haven't learned anything after four years of school, then you can get married instead of continuing on to seminary. I'll let go of the leash, all of your leashes, and walk away."

Nate glanced at me. "School where?"

"Missouri, Nate, I never unenrolled you. It's one of the top Bible colleges in the country, and you were lucky to get in. And in exchange, I'll keep you in my will and release the trust fund money Sophia left you, two thousand dollars that can go to the baby every month for the rest of your life."

I waited for Nate to protest or laugh in his father's face, but he just looked into Joel's eyes, his face still.

"Are you serious?" I said. "How is that a compromise? How's he supposed to see the baby if he's in Missouri?"

"I'll pay for flights; he can even fly monthly if you want, as long as he doesn't miss school. We can make that part of the deal. And you can see Grace and Cecilia too, Nate, as long as you don't tell them about the baby."

"I don't trust you to be alone with Grace and Cecilia," Nate said. "That you won't hurt them."

Something in Joel's face shifted, a crack in the ice. "They're my girls. You don't realize I love them?"

"What I realize is that you don't understand love."

"Don't be ridiculous. You happen to fertilize an egg and think that gives you a right to lecture me on parental love?"

Nate held his father's eyes a minute before he said, "I'll be calling them every day I can. And I swear, if they tell me you've done anything to them, even looked at them funny, I'll come back here and kill you."

"No," I said. "You're not considering this, Nate!"

Nate reached for my forearm, gave two soft squeezes like he was milking it. "I have to talk," he said, then turned to his father and added, "To her." And then he pulled me to the living room and through the front door. Closed the door behind us and leaned back against it without speaking.

"What?" I said. "What! You're not going to let him make rules that don't even make sense. You can't go to Bible college when you aren't even sure you believe in God, and you can't be a dad for the baby when you live in freaking Missouri!"

"Right." He shoved his hands in his pockets, looking lost. "You're totally right, but he . . . he almost forgives me. I thought he was going to kill me, but he's trying to find a way to get me back."

I stared at him. "Are you *kidding* me? After everything he's done, you care more about him than me? It doesn't make sense!"

"Of course I care more about you. I'm not letting him lead me on his leash, whatever he seems to think, but he made a compromise. I'll come see you as often as I possibly can, every single weekend if you want. Since Grace and Cecilia are so adamant about staying in the house, this is the best way for me to make sure they stay safe, which I couldn't do if we both went off to Berkeley. And in four years I'll come back for good and we'll get married. That'll be the best revenge really, he'll pay for my education and get nothing out of it. The money's really going to help, Chloe; in the long run it's the best thing we can do for the baby."

"The best thing we can do for the baby is give it a father! Oh whatever, Nate, I don't care, go become a pastor and marry some nice, saintly Pentecostal girl. I don't care!" I felt a bizarre, inappropriate hilarity in my chest, something raw and scratchy threatening to shatter into laughter. I'd learned something today, and much as it tore at me it was so much better that I knew it.

There was a sordid imagination game I'd played, trying to quantify love. If my mother and Nate were drowning and I could only save one, which of them would I choose? My mother and Cecilia? My mother and Grace? Grace and Cecilia? Coming up with an awful but unquestionable ranking:

- Nate
- Cecilia, then
- Mom, and then
- Grace

Nate would choose his sisters first, I'd always known it, and accepted it. But where on that list would his father be?

I strode down the driveway and Nate ran after me, grabbed at my arm. "Chloe, stop! I don't know what to do, just tell me what to do. You want me going back to Dixon so I can try and save money? The camp cost almost all of what I made, but I'll sleep in the streets if you want. Just tell me!"

He didn't mean it, I knew he didn't mean it, and I wanted to call him on it but my heart hurt and my head hurt and I didn't have the energy. It was possible to be so full of rage that it caught inside your throat and twisted around itself, strangling any words. I couldn't find the strength to do anything but run, so I wrenched my arm away, and ran.

I didn't need him. I didn't! If Mr. Sinclair gave me money, I could use it to hire a babysitter while I went to school, come home and study with the baby on my lap, read to it from my textbooks (it would become the most well-rounded baby ever!), carry it through the streets of Berkeley and San Francisco on my back, introducing it to culture and good food.

Really it didn't matter if we never saw Nate again, because in the past few hours my love rankings had shifted. Our baby, *my* baby, was my first and last, and only.

19

It turned out I never got to Berkeley. Maybe it was just psychosomatic, my body rebelling, but a week after Nate left for Missouri, I was hit with morning sickness so severe that I spent half my time in bed forcing down electrolyte drinks, the other half in the bathroom watching them come up again in a festive spray of red. I was admitted to the hospital where I was diagnosed with hyperemesis and put on IV parenteral nutrition. There was never any question of me being able to leave home.

Through this Nate called me every day from school, the conversation stilted because I didn't have the energy to either hide my bitterness or to express it and confront the attempt I knew he'd make at defending his decisions. Several times he asked if he could fly out to see me, and I told him no. Expecting he'd understand what I really meant.

Days and nights blurred. Over the next few months I learned every crack on the ceiling above my bed, every scab of rust on the inside of the toilet bowl. I talked to the baby, the boy whose image

I'd now seen on the ultrasound, a blue-gray ghost floating silently inside me unaware of everything he'd already lost.

I told him about my life and my dreams for the future, the bookstore I'd run, imagining Gabriel toddling beside me as I shelved new inventory, summarized stories, and described authors' voices and visions. With the checks Nate sent each month, the money not spent on medical bills all went into the bank and I spent the interest on books I knew Gabriel would love, *Make Way for Ducklings* and *Madeline*, *The Berenstain Bears* and *Yertle the Turtle*. I read the stories over and over, then began fabricating elaborate spin-offs: the adventures of Horton and his hatched elephant-bird, the escapades of the very hungry butterfly that the Very Hungry Caterpillar had become. I imagined him already absorbing love of story and of the cadence of language. Mom, when she passed my room, would stop to listen at the doorway, her brow furrowed, maybe scared I was going insane. But then she'd enter silently and fluff my pillows, check my IV line, and then kiss my cheek. "At least teach him something practical," she said once. "The times tables, or macroeconomics." A joke, but I knew she must be questioning what kind of mom I'd be, maybe even the type of person I had become.

My belly grew, my breasts and ankles grew, and my brain shrank to the size of my baby. Nate nothing but a voice on the phone, someone I'd become pretty sure I never actually knew.

And then, when my labor pains started, my mother made a phone call. Eight hours later, just as the clamping vise inside me was becoming unbearable—*"He's killing me!"* I screamed—Nate appeared at the door of my hospital room.

He looked different, his hair slicked to one side; he seemed taller, his spine straighter. "Scholarly" was the word that came to mind, and I hated him for it, for the hours he'd spent in classrooms while I'd been writhing with nausea. Living the life I'd thought would be mine.

"Chloe!" He approached the bed and set a hand on my swollen belly, gently like he thought I might shatter. "What do I do? Is there something I can do?"

He seemed half in tears, and even though I wanted him to take my hand, hold me, part of me also hated him for appropriating this fear, showing any ownership of this pregnancy and labor that was all mine. "You can get the hell out of my room," I said.

He searched my face a moment, looking helpless, then apparently chose to ignore what I'd said. "I came as fast as I could. You should've seen me, I almost punched a ticket agent. But you're okay, the baby's okay, and everything's going like it should? It's so unfathomable seeing your—your . . ." He gestured at my belly. "Knowing Gabriel's in there and now we're going to meet him, it's just overwhelming." He bent to set his cheek on my forehead, whispered, "I've missed you so damn much."

I pushed him away fiercely. "Cut it out!"

"Oh . . . !" He stepped back. "Is there something I can get you that'll make this any easier? You look so worn-out, like you've been beat up."

"I'm in labor. This is how women look when they're in labor. What the hell are you doing here?"

"How can you even ask that? I'm sorry, I know how hard this all has been on you, it's been impossibly hard being away from you while you went through it. I wish I could've been here the past few months; every night I'd lie in bed and weigh options and wonder if I was doing the right thing—"

"Stop it, Nate, you don't have any idea how it was! You weren't alone kneeling over a toilet ten times a day, retching so hard you were scared your baby was going to come out through your throat. I would've killed myself if I could've done it without hurting Gabriel, *that's* how I felt. And you show up now so you can think you were here for the important part and feel better about yourself? Well, screw that! You don't have any right to be here, pretending like you've been part of this. Get the hell out, go back to your little classroom. Get out!"

He stared at me, his jaw slack, then turned and walked back down the hall as I watched after him, in tears. "Nate!" I called, but then was seized by another contraction so fierce that the word caught in my throat.

I found out later that he'd stayed in the waiting room until after Gabriel was born, that he stood with my mother outside the nursery window, hand on the glass, watching our son sleep. But at the time I knew only that getting him to leave me had been too easy. And as the fists wringing my insides began to claw and tear, I imagined Nate going home to his family, hugging Grace and Cecilia tightly for comfort, but keeping his promise to Joel by telling them nothing about how my body, my life, was twisting inside out. Joining in their dinner conversation while I screamed, relaxing in the library while Gabriel screamed, and while I held this new world in my arms, talking about life at college, his world, nothing to do with me. Allowing himself to forget.

And picturing it, the seed that had been planted when Nate left for school, a seed that had set down roots over the months I'd writhed in bed, now sprouted and grew thorns. And even after I learned he'd actually slept in his rental car on the top floor of the hospital parking lot, returning the next day to stand again at the nursery window, it was too late to stop that bitterness from growing.

In the months after Gabriel was born, as I wrestled with nights of interrupted sleep followed by days in front of hot ovens at my mother's factory, I felt the thorns inside me every single time I thought of Nate. To be honest they were there throughout our marriage behind everything, just hidden, stabbing through in the trying times whenever we were weakened by disagreement or disappointment.

And it was ridiculous and unfair but the subconscious isn't reasonable; it lurks and flares and, when you aren't bracing against it, inexorably draws you closer. Consumes you.

PART IX

The ROAD NOT TAKEN

20

~~Donthe efair ardaga bugh trielewhar tofrieca~~
~~h nicaw prite abule tasoum tineo thon shemonters~~
~~shosher siniss sceth onomoli?~~ ~~Ine wasran edadaly~~
~~toicha tome bitind, dandis navem whanayt twah~~
~~yosumi dust icombidne.~~

Dear Gabriel,

*What can I write about those months in school? I was ready
to hate it, and in many ways I did. The students both annoyed me
and scared me, the vacant look in their eyes, alternating between
zombie blankness and—when praising God or extolling the
brilliance of the Pauline Epistles—like zombies on a feeding
frenzy. So I didn't even try to make friends. At first they must've
thought I was shy because they tried to coax me into joining them
for study groups or Chinese takeout, but pretty soon they stopped
trying. I'd stand at the window and watch them traveling in packs,
playing Frisbee on the lawn, shouting greetings, and I'd think of*

you and your mom, of your aunts, trying to imagine what you all were doing now, and now, and now, and I'd feel the most immense homesickness, like my insides had been gouged.

But the classes were actually fascinating. Sure, some of them drove me crazy, the intensive study of the Gospels as if every issue an individual or a community (or a country!) might face in the present day had been foreseen, addressed by words written millenniums earlier. What Would Jesus Do if forced to sit through these classes? Roll His holy eyes, I think, and ditch class in favor of a jazz concert, or a good movie where at least nobody was pretending to provide more than just a resemblance to truth.

The classes that interested me were the studies of other writers (we even studied C. S. Lewis!) and the exegetical studies, analyzing the Bible through interpretation from the original languages. Change "of" to "for" and the entire meaning of a message can flip sideways, to something completely different. Fascinating not just because it makes so much of what churches and temples have seen as laws seem almost arbitrary, but also because it proves how powerful each word a writer chooses can be. This was when I started dreaming of becoming an author, and began writing what would later become the Prince Gabriel book. I had fun with it, couldn't wait to share it with you, but I also dreamed of creating something bigger, the grandiose dreams one only has at twenty.

On top of all that, the study of words made me start reading everything differently, especially fiction. And, more importantly, reading my life differently.

Every conversation, every turn of phrase, and every question and answer can be flipped sideways, interpreted in ways you never intended while speaking. As I sat there dissecting my life moment by moment, what I wished more than anything was to be able to make different choices and say different words. But, one can never go

backward. And once the choices are made and the words said, the
people you've hurt won't be willing to let you explain.

I'd just gotten home from the early morning shift at the factory
when Nate came to the house and showed me the envelope, exhausted but hoping to get a few minutes with Gabriel before his
nap. I opened the envelope and peered inside. "Your badges? You
seriously saved them?"

"You didn't?" He looked hurt, which I thought was ridiculous.

"I was keeping them in a baby doll," I said. "I forgot about
them, and when I threw the doll away, they got thrown away too.
They were stupid, Nate, a game, and it could've killed us."

"That was the year we fell in love. That's why I saved them."

"And look how well *that's* turning out," I said.

His face seemed to solidify, ice. I could see a wrinkle, the first
I'd ever noticed on him, at the corner of one eye. "I'm trying,
Chloe. I'm sorry if I'm not trying in the way you think is right, but
I was thinking about tomorrow as well as today. Somebody had
to."

"I'm going inside, I have a baby to take care of. Today."

"Please just . . . take the envelope, okay? I want you to take it,
look at the badges and try and remember what it was like. We have
history and history never goes away, and as soon as we get out of
here we'll have it again. I'll come back tonight, after you get a
chance to look at them, and we'll figure out how to rebuild it, okay?
Because under everything we still have what we had then, even
more now with Gabriel."

"You don't even understand, do you. You see Gabriel once or
twice a month, you hear him say 'Daddy' and you get all happy,
but don't you realize he has no idea what that even means? Your

name is Daddy just like the butcher at Oakville Grocery's name is Scott. It doesn't have any meaning to him."

Nate stood there watching me, looking lost, both hands gripping the envelope. Then leaned it against the mailbox and walked away. When he reached the road he turned back to look at me and I squared my shoulders and walked back to the house. Later that afternoon, when I came back outside, the envelope was gone.

Twice more that weekend he'd returned to try and talk to me, but I didn't even open the door for him. After that, he finally gave up.

Misinterpretation of words, of choices; what I'd really been saying was, *Please. Please, we need you, don't leave us; I'm hurting more than angry so just tell me you need us too, say those words through this closed door and I'll forgive.* If he'd understood what I meant, or if I'd found the message on his badges, then everything would've changed. If, if, if; we'd been given chances and chances and chances, untaken branches in the path that led to here. But, like Nate had written, one can never go backward.

Now I read through Nate's next few pages as he described his few trips home, the strain of having to keep the existence of both Gabriel and our relationship from his sisters, when it was all he could think about. *I sold out to the devil for two thousand dollars a month,* he wrote. *Sold my firstborn son, how biblical. I knew what I'd done, of course, but somehow I didn't actually comprehend the sacrifice. Until Grace finally made me look at what I was doing to Chloe, which made me look deeper inside myself and realize how miserable I'd been. And that's when I finally confronted my father, the biggest mistake of my life. Knowing what he was capable of, but not really deep down believing it. Even after Gabriel was gone, before I understood the reasons behind what he'd done, I didn't really believe it.*

Fingers were squeezing inside me as I turned the page. There were only three pages left, and much as I didn't want to read what came next, I knew it was what I needed to see. What had happened after Gabriel's disappearance, on the night Nate had gone to his father's church? What had he seen? And why hadn't he been willing to talk about any of it with me? There was something very off in the little bits he'd been willing to share about that night, even the testimony he gave at Joel's trial. And he'd come home after confronting Joel with scratches on his arms and dirt under his nails, neither of which he'd been willing to explain. Had something horrific happened that night? Something he thought I wasn't strong enough to hear?

It was true that things had changed between us, and he might've thought he couldn't trust me. After the shock had sunk into bottomless grief, I'd walked side by side with him but not together. I'd stopped trying to see him, maybe because it seemed like remembering the headiness of our first years would feel like mocking the intensity of our grief. Like answering the question of whether we could survive this with the answer, *Of course! Because we have each other!*

The times he'd made love to me, part of me had hated him for it, because I was sure in those moments he was forgetting. When the truth was, he'd only found a way to forage a path between the pain and the necessity of moving past it, everything he'd become touched by both of them. When I talked to Nate, I'd tell him I understood this, that he'd only been doing his best in a situation where there was no best. But first I needed to know everything.

I held my finger to the first line of text, began to cross out letters. Only struggling for a minute before I stopped.

Of course. Once again he'd used a different book for encoding. Like each of the three previous sections when he'd switched books, the following text had changed and informed what came before. Maybe he'd actually paused between writing each section because he needed to steel himself before writing the next, then came back with a new book as a way of taking a deep breath. Or maybe it was like Cecilia had said, that subconsciously part of him had hoped that I'd find the notebook, and he wanted to give me the opportunity to stop between sections without reading more. And I was terrified by the thought of what these last three pages might contain. If he talked about holding Gabriel's body, unearthing and lifting him into his arms, well, some secrets were better left in the past.

I closed the notebook over the top of my pen, sat a minute, my mind blank, then slowly emptied the badges, the message I'd never read, into a pile on the bed. I lifted a handful of the colorful disks and let them sift through my fingers, then lifted them again. Lifted and let fall, lifted and let fall, like I was panning for gold.

I was on the library sofa when Cecilia returned with Joel, and when I heard the key in the lock I ducked behind a bookshelf so he wouldn't see me. But Cecilia brought him to the library and walked him to the sofa saying, "Sit here, okay? And I'll bring your tea." And then she walked out, leaving me trapped, staring at the back of his bird-wing-frail shoulders.

I leaned closer, watching his fingers pick fretfully at the leg of his pants. He seemed so distracted by the picking that I was sure I'd be able to sidestep against the wall and make it to the door without being noticed. But before I even took a first step, Joel swiveled suddenly to face me. He cried out and jumped to his feet, raising his arm threateningly.

Something rough and heavy as concrete lodged in my chest. "Mr. Sinclair."

He slowly lowered his arm, his eyes round and flat as ceramic dinner plates, then shook his head quickly and gave a self-deprecating laugh. "Why yes, yes of course, hello. I'm sorry, my memory's declining a bit with age. What was your name again?"

I stepped toward him, hands curled like claws, the heat in me pure animal, no human thought behind it, only instinct. I could kill him; I could pummel him to the ground, stomp on his face and crush his skull. Unthinkingly I surged toward him, but the sofa was between us, too far, and my mind was too paralyzed to figure out how to get around it. Instead, I grabbed a book off the shelf and hurled it at him with all my strength, smacking him in the face. "What's my name?" I said. "What's my name!"

Footsteps racing down the hall, Cecilia's voice, "Chloe!"

For the past twenty-five years Joel Sinclair had haunted me, every piece of who I was, even my feelings for Nate, all circling around and warped by my hatred of him. The only thing that had kept me remotely sane was imagining that it must've haunted him a hundred times more. But he had no idea who I was?

He raised a hand to his cheek where the book had hit, pulled it back to study his fingers like he was expecting blood. And seeing the bewildered look in his eyes, the rage drained from me, my knees came unbraced and I had to hold on to a shelf to keep from falling.

Cecilia stood in the doorway watching me, her eyebrows tented in a plea, or maybe an apology. "You're okay, it's okay," she said. I didn't know which of us she was talking to, only that I wasn't even close to okay. Because I wanted to destroy Joel Sinclair, wanted him writhing in physical and emotional anguish, but Joel Sinclair didn't exist anymore, and whatever revenge fantasies I'd had were now ludicrous.

Cecilia reached for his arm. "Your tea's getting cold, Daddy. It's steeping in the dining room, so you better come quick and pour before it gets too dark."

Joel wrenched his arm away, peering at me, and for a second I thought I saw a glimmer of shocked recognition before his face closed again. "I don't like my tea too dark," he said, then turned and followed Cecilia out into the hall.

I leaned against the bookshelf and slowly slid down it, my shirt lifting, book spines scraping against my back. Listening to their sounds from the dining room—china clinking, Cecilia's voice so much like Sophia's, a mother to a child.

I was still on the library floor when Cecilia came in an hour later. She eyed me a moment before stepping closer, her arm outstretched. I took her hand and she pulled me to my feet, set the other hand at the small of my back. "He's napping," she said. "I'm sorry, Chloe. I wouldn't have brought him into the library if I knew you were here."

I stared at her blankly. "What am I doing here, Cecilia? Why did I agree to stay in the same house with him? Part of me must've known we'd run into each other, how could we not? So did part of me actually want to see him? All these years I've imagined jamming a knife into his guts and twisting, getting him to scream and cry and beg for mercy I wouldn't give, I've imagined it every day of the past two decades and now . . . what do I do with that?"

Her expression darkened, an undercurrent of grief, but all she said was, "I know how it is. You feel like all the rage needs somewhere to go."

"But it was so stupid, as if anything I could do to him could make him feel even remotely like what I've been through. I might as well just punch a pillow."

She smoothed a hand against my back, a slow clockwise circle.

"The rage," she said, "in the end it's a way of trying to deal with your own pain. You have to deal somehow, so you end up externalizing. I obviously can't pretend to imagine how you feel, but I've spent years hating him too."

I studied her face, all the prints age had left. "I guess at least this showed me something I need to come to terms with."

"That he's not actually the person who destroyed our lives, right? I wouldn't have taken him back if he was that same person. But now . . . I guess this has been healing for me in a way. I've accepted him, if that makes any sense." She pulled away. "Yeah, that probably doesn't make sense."

"Things've always been different for you," I said. "I mean you never seemed to hate him. I used to think it was because you seem to skate on the surface instead of getting pulled down, you can separate yourself, and the things that should faze you don't. But you went back to him after Nate left, and then you let him manipulate you into marrying a man who turned out to be cruel. I always thought you'd . . . I don't know, run off to Paris or Madrid and live in a tiny studio, fall in love with a poet till you got sick of him, then an acrobat and then maybe you'd go off to the jungle and study chimpanzee society. But you were the one who ended up doing exactly what he wanted from you."

She smiled. "You've made my imaginary life into a Choose Your Own Adventure book. I choose a poet in Paris, is he cute? Does he have a short, dark beard and John Lennon glasses?"

I forced myself to smile back, but she wasn't watching me; she wrapped her arms around her waist. "That's not who I am anymore. Maybe it never was and it was just my way of trying to get attention, I don't know. I just wanted . . ." Still hugging herself, she shrugged. "My dad, I guess. Grace was his perfect daughter, the one he was proud of, and Nate was his son, the one who was supposed to inherit the throne. But I was just kind of an afterthought. It meant he left me alone, so maybe I was lucky. But I wondered sometimes if someone had asked how many kids he had, and he'd answered without really thinking it through, whether he would've said three or two."

Was that why she was here now, taking care of him? So he'd finally have to acknowledge and appreciate her? We'd all lived the same story from different angles, and like any story, what one took from it reflected the perspective of one's past. But how could she possibly see this particular story any differently?

"I hardly even remember those years after Nate left, the months before I married Samuel. Those were the years you were raising Gabriel, so every day probably had meaning, but for me it's a complete blur. All I remember is little snatches, watching brown maple leaves blow past the front window, shivering under the covers for a week because Dad had forgotten to pay the oil bill. Fainting in church one morning because I hadn't eaten since the morning before, and being sure losing consciousness was a sign I'd finally been baptized by the Holy Spirit. I'd gone a little crazy by then."

"I knew Joel was keeping you and Grace mostly sequestered from the rest of the town; maybe he was scared you'd run into me and Gabriel. And I'm sure that kind of isolation can mess with you."

"It wasn't all him, I didn't especially want to go anywhere either, and I guess that's when I really started sinking. Plus making Daddy happy made me feel a little less worthless, and I didn't have the energy to deal with disapproval. So yeah, I married Samuel because that's what Daddy wanted. There weren't really any other eligible men in the parish, and all along he'd been envisioning pairing him with Grace, he'd been talking to her about Samuel since she was twelve or thirteen. But with all that happened with Cesar, Daddy's relationship with her changed, and I guess part of me saw this as a way to be the one he was proud of. It wasn't a conscious decision and it's not something I feel good about, but yeah I guess I'm not the person you thought I was."

"You'd lost your mom," I said slowly, "you were young and he was the only parent you had."

She wandered to the couch and sat, gazing out the window. "I do wonder if Grace would've stayed with him. The whole time I was married I was grateful it was me instead of her, because I think she probably would have stayed. She hated herself for having slept with Cesar; to her it was the worst kind of sin and she probably would've seen Samuel as divine retribution."

"It was more than just sleeping with him." I sat beside her and tucked my legs up under me. "Nate wrote about it in his notebook, did you know?"

"You mean about the baby? Let's just say I knew some of it and guessed the rest. I thought at first Dad must've done something physical to her, but now I think it was probably just that he put the idea of abortion into her head, intentionally or not. She needed his approval as much as she needed God's; maybe to her they were the same thing. That's where she got her sense of worth, but his approval of all of us was so sporadic. Maybe that's why it was so powerful, and maybe the abortion was an attempt to get it back; I don't know. But losing that baby destroyed her. The person she turned into, I didn't know her."

I thought of the few times I'd seen Grace that winter and spring, the empty, deflated look in her eyes. The last time I'd seen her had been in the days after Cecilia's wedding, when she found out about Gabriel, the emptiness replaced by bitterness. Which was, I'd thought, better. Not healthy maybe, but healthier, at least proof of life behind her eyes. But just a few days later she was gone, and I'd never seen her again.

"I wish we could've all gone to live with Nate in Berkeley like we'd planned," Cecilia said. "Everything would've been so much better. When I think about it that feels like the life we *should've* been living."

"Gabriel would still be alive," I said. I tried to imagine Cecilia and Grace sharing our spare bedroom in Truckee, Gabriel on a toddler bed in our room. Of course Gabriel would be in his twenties now, but still . . . Oh, it was stupid to think about it, the What If games I'd tortured myself with for years, if I'd just done *this* or *this* or *this*. If I'd just seen the future. "I always wonder if Grace ever got past losing her baby," I said. "I've imagined her having some kind of normal life, you know? I mean, a non-nun life."

Cecilia's whole body seemed to slacken. "I imagined it too."

I tried to read her expression, something underneath the sadness. "What?" I said.

"What?"

"You heard from her? Or something; there's something about Grace you're not saying. You look like you're about torn in two."

"Chloe, stop."

"I haven't been part of her life in a long time, I realize that. But don't you realize I still love her too?"

She closed her eyes, her face and body still; she hardly seemed to be breathing. When she finally spoke again her voice had changed, sounding almost robotic. "Okay. Okay, look. The truth is I got a letter from her, about four months ago. She begged me not to tell anybody, but of course I had to tell Nate."

I thought of the call history I'd seen on Nate's cell, the calls between him and Cecilia. "He never said anything to me."

"I know, I told him not to. Not just because she asked me not to tell, but also because she wouldn't have wanted you to see the letter. She cared more about your opinion than you probably realize; she wanted you to respect her, think of her as an older sister who could guide you. And in her letter she sounded, I don't know, a little crazy. Talking about rivers of tears and quoting Bible verses about the end of days."

I felt a prickle of grief. So not a normal life after all, but of course how could it be? That punishing routine of the Poor Clares, the nights of no sleep, the mundanity, it would drive anyone insane over time. I tried to imagine Grace, almost fifty now with no makeup or hair dye to hide it, maybe grown heavy from no exercise or skinny from the Clares' meager diet. Legless, the way nuns seem to be, gliding from room to room as if on wheels, face vacant and pale. "Did she say anything about how she's doing? The fact she finally wrote to you after all these years and years, does it maybe mean she's looking for some kind of connection again?"

Cecilia stayed motionless a minute, her eyes trained somewhere over my shoulder, and then said, "Listen. She's dying, Chloe, that's why she wrote me, she might even already be gone. That's where Nate's been, he traveled down to spend time with her before it's too late."

ALS, that's what Cecilia told me. Autoimmune diseases ran in the family: Sophia's lupus, an aunt's rheumatoid arthritis, a nephew's juvenile diabetes. Nate and Cecilia had so far been spared, but Grace had the worst possible diagnosis. On a breathing tube when she'd written Cecilia, still at the convent being cared for by the nuns, writing with an eye-activated computer but unable to swallow or speak, and it was only a matter of time.

It was unthinkable that Nate hadn't told me what was happening. Even if Cecilia had asked him not to, he knew I'd once thought of Grace as a sister, that I'd want to know before she was gone. It must be that he was trying to protect me from mourning one more person, and I hated that he thought I was that weak. I held Cecilia when she started to cry, feeling a sort of despair. Not just at the loss of Grace but something more, the loss of a fantasy I still must've held somewhere deep inside even after all these years, that we'd all be together again someday.

Now up in the bedroom I squeezed my eyes shut, filled with a wordless prayer that Nate would find her, that she was still alive. I'd hop on a plane and stand by her side and . . . what? Did I even mean anything to her anymore? Seeing her would be more for me, an attempt to add last words to this story that in reality had ended decades ago.

Two days before she'd left, the morning after Cecilia's wedding, Grace had been so angry. Mostly at Nate, but also at me and probably even at Cecilia because the three of us had moved on. She must have pictured us all living the life she'd always dreamed of. She'd always been so guarded, wearing the veneer of the person she thought she should be, but in those moments she yelled at me she'd shown her true self, finally vulnerable. I should've realized it. How hadn't I realized it? This was another reason I so wished I could see her, because I wanted to make sure she understood, in these last days, that she'd deserved so much better.

She'd gone off on Nate, asking how he could possibly treat me and Gabriel like an inconvenience, and I hadn't been able to answer because of course I'd agreed, and part of me had hated her for digging the frustration from my gut to throw it in my face. But what I should've done is tell her that her time had come, that I'd seen Cesar waiting tables at the Fish Fry where I took Gabriel for

Friday dinners; I should've made up some story about the loneliness in his eyes.

Had learning about Gabriel that day reflected against her own loss? Had seeing what she perceived as Nate's desertion reflected against her father's condemnation of her own child? I'd thought it was the wedding, the sense Cecilia wouldn't need her anymore, that had made her go back to the convent so soon after. But maybe it was actually the pain of seeing Gabriel, her attempt to muffle that pain with prayer.

I tried to remember how she'd looked at the wedding but could only remember her prim, shapeless blue dress, and the redness in her eyes as she listened to Joel behind the podium. He'd seemed so melancholy talking about his love for his wife, how he only hoped Cecilia and Samuel would, over time, come to understand what marriage was supposed to mean. And maybe in the end this was really why she'd left, to find that love by creating her own marriage in Christ.

It had touched me too, that little speech, made me understand the momentousness of the day, made me reluctant to ruin that for Cecilia. So in the end I'd rushed Gabriel out of the church instead of finally revealing him to the world as I'd planned. Another opportunity to twist the plot of our story onto a completely different path, another Schrödinger's cat universe, where Nate stepped forward from the receiving line and stood with me to tell the parishioners what Joel had done to hide the truth. A path where Nate and I were maybe now already dreaming of grandkids, dropping pointed hints that Gabriel would laugh off. "You married way too young," he'd say. "Nobody gets married that young anymore."

To which we'd say, "You're arguing this to the wrong people, Gabe. Because just look at how happy we have been."

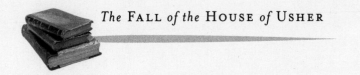

PART X

The *Fall* *of the* HOUSE *of* USHER

21

CECILIA was on her knees at the altar, dressed in a high-necked, corseted satin gown with a crocheted yoke and lace-trimmed sleeves. Her hair was up in a loose chignon, her eyes downcast, her hands folded at her waist, and she looked both impossibly old-fashioned and impossibly beautiful. The tuxedoed man kneeling beside her was tall and bony, with skin and hair so equally pale it was impossible to tell where his face ended and his hair began, making his head seem blurry and misshapen. Throughout the ceremony they hadn't once looked into each other's eyes.

I'd been shocked to get the wedding invitation the week before, with a note scrawled on three Post-its.

I realize you haven't seen any of us in so long but we all miss you so much, talk about you all the time, and I'm hoping now I'll be away from Dad, we'll be able to see each other again. Nate's home from college and I know he'd love to see you too, he misses you so.

Please come to the wedding? I don't know Samuel well but I know he's a Godly man and that marriage will be good for me, that I'll grow to love him as much as my mother grew to love my father. Someday, Chloe, I hope we'll be able to continue where we left off, looking back

on these past few years as just a regrettable memory brought about by an unfortunate mix of fear and unchecked youth.
Much Love,
C

Cecilia, Grace, and I had written back and forth a number of times over the past three years, letters we'd hide by the bush along with library books I loaned them. In the letters, we talked mostly about the books, which they read lying together in bed late into the night, about our love for one another and sadness over the years we were missing. They'd only revealed bits and pieces of their lives, the mundanity of their days, work at the church cleaning and helping Joel prepare his sermons, nightly Bible study, and then home to make and eat dinner with their father. And I'd also told them only bits and pieces of my own days, sweating over the stoves in my mother's factory. All of us focusing more on life themes than plot points, like we had as children, avoiding all that didn't fit into the image we wanted to portray. In none of the letters had they ever mentioned Samuel. And in mine, I never mentioned my son.

It amazed me that Cecilia didn't seem to know any of what had gone on between me and Nate, that she didn't realize how her father would react at seeing me in his church. I knew how sequestered she and Grace were now, hardly leaving home except for church service and work. So many times I'd thought of going to see them, stopping myself because how could I stand in front of them and not tell them about Gabriel?

But Nate, who had seen them several times a year since Gabriel's birth, must not have talked about us at all even though he was visiting us at the same time. It made me feel so irrelevant, like we were something he'd forgotten to mention. Who cared that this was a condition Joel had tried to impose? Nate must have realized they'd never reveal to their father that they knew, so the only conceivable explanation for the continued secrecy was that he was ashamed.

The more I thought about it, the more I felt consumed with a hollow, desperate anger. Gabriel was my life; I was so proud of everything about him, his sense of humor, the easy laughs and wide smiles he directed at everyone he met, the way he concentrated so hard whenever he tried to figure something out—how to skip, how to spin a top or pronounce his R's—his eyes narrowed, a furrow in his brow. He was such a good boy, I could already see the beginnings of kindness in the way he treated stuffed animals or cuddled silently against me when he saw me cry. But Nate had somehow been able to pretend that Gabriel didn't even exist, treating him like a venereal disease or an alcoholic uncle, something with flaws that he wished would either heal or disappear. And the gall of this was what drove me to do what I'd been longing to do since the day Gabriel was born. I brought him to the church.

I sat in the back with him in my lap, sweat heavy on my forehead and upper lip. More than two years I'd been waiting. Two years I'd been hiding my son from his own aunts, telling anyone who'd asked me that his father was a college boy from San Francisco I'd had a fling with. But I'd been trying to shove Gabriel under a misshapen blanket with too many loose threads to hold him. I knew it couldn't last much longer.

So. I had a plan.

When the ceremony was over I was going to bring Gabriel up to the receiving line, stand beside Nate and let everyone see Nate's bluish-green eyes in Gabriel's face. I wouldn't say anything, just stand there waiting for conclusions to be drawn. I could picture the gasps, Christian wives turning wide-eyed to Christian husbands, *Could it be?!* And I'd just take Gabriel's hand and walk away.

Defying Joel, I knew everything was going to change. He'd stop sending us money until Nate turned twenty-five, when mandated by Sophia's trust, and I wouldn't be able to keep putting money away for our future. But what kind of future was I building for Gabriel here anyway? I didn't need Joel's money. So far I'd saved over twenty thousand dollars in the bank, enough to support us for years if I was careful, in time build us the kind of life I'd imagined.

And what would Nate do? I wanted to believe he'd realize I'd done the right thing, would leave school, get a job too so we could use the savings to buy a home. Three years ago this wouldn't even have been a question, but Nate had changed so much since starting school. I didn't know him anymore and had no idea how he'd react.

Each time he visited he talked about the courses he was taking, things as diverse as astronomy and philosophy and American Lit. About his creative writing instructor who'd told him he'd been "blessed with the voice of a poet," squeezing both my hands as he told me, face expectant like he thought I might congratulate him on his brilliance.

He asked me to sit beside him while he studied, read his texts with him, help him with papers—not because he needed help, I was pretty sure of this, but because he somehow thought I could live vicariously through him, all the dreams I'd had of school, of listening to great minds sharing all they knew about the world. Of course I'd planned to do the same thing if I'd gone to Berkeley, teaching him secondhand. But this was different; in the end school had been *my* dream first, and how could he not understand his words just felt to me like flaunting? Why hadn't he once said he wished I could be there with him too?

That was the thing about Nate, and in retrospect it had always been true; he thought of himself first. He'd *needed* to think of himself growing up, all of them did, and it wasn't that he was selfish; he'd give the world to anyone he felt was in pain. It was just that he sometimes seemed to have a strange mental block, an inability to really put himself in other people's shoes and see how his actions might affect them.

So what would happen now that I was finally backing him into a corner? I didn't know, but at the moment I didn't even care. All I knew was that taking money in exchange for lies had started to feel like I was selling Gabriel, almost as if the sole purpose of having him had been this bribery. From the beginning this had been wrong, and the older Gabriel got, less formless baby and more perceptive child, the more I'd seen I couldn't do this anymore.

Now at the podium Samuel turned to Cecilia, gave her a distant smile, and closed his eyes. "Dear Lord Jesus, thank you for this beautiful day. You have fulfilled the desire of our hearts to be together in this life, and we pray that your blessing will always rest upon our home. That joy, peace, and contentment will dwell within us as we live together in unity, and that all who enter our home may experience the strength of your love."

There was a sort of overexuberance about his speech, like he was a performer in a second-rate musical act. And watching him I felt a chill.

On my lap, Gabriel was sleepily playing with one of the buttons on my cardigan. I rested my cheek against his head, breathed in his sweet apple juice scent, and he leaned his head back to gaze at me drowsily. "Let's go," he said.

I held a finger to my lips. The couple in the pew ahead of us turned, and I ducked my head and nestled Gabriel against me whispering, "Soon . . ."

"Eternal Father," Joel said, "may this couple always turn to You for guidance, for provision and direction. May they glorify You in the choices they make, and in all that they do. Use them to draw others to Yourself, and let them stand as a testimony to the world of Your faithfulness. We ask this in Jesus' name. Amen." He lowered his head. "Let us pray."

I took Gabriel's hand in mine, willing him to stay silent, rubbed a thumb across his chubby knuckles, and he grabbed onto my finger and shook it lazily up and down, as if expecting it to rattle.

When Joel raised his head again there were tears in his eyes. "Cecilia, I see you here in your mother's dress, and you're the spitting image of Sophia on the day I stood beside her, scared out of my mind, and told her I'd honor and remain faithful to her forever. We were so young, we had no idea what forever meant, and I was scared that I had no idea what marital love meant. But what I told myself, standing there, was that I'd do my best to love Sophia the way Christ loved the church, give myself up for her to make her holy."

I saw Cecilia look up at him, then glance shyly at Samuel. What was she thinking? Did she love this man, or was she just using him to get away? Or worse, was her father pressuring her into marriage to keep her from making the same mistakes his other two children had? The Cecilia I knew would never have let herself be pressured into a marriage she didn't want, but this woman at the altar—her body heavier, every movement seeming slow and studied, something missing from her eyes—she wasn't the Cecilia I knew.

Joel raised his head to look out at the parish. "My Sophia, she was so easy to love. I actually have to say, that word 'love' doesn't even come close to the depths of what I still feel. So Samuel and Cecilia, I pray that you'll come to this same place in your lives, the place that I've shared with my wife, a depth of feeling that reaches down into my soul. It's a love that's still growing even now that she's gone."

This speech was genuine, I could tell that. And for the first time it occurred to me that maybe that was the thing that made Joel so powerful, that he *did* care. He could be cruel, but there was a real person behind the ranting. He'd loved his wife, and I could see love in his eyes when he looked at Cecilia. And maybe this explained the devotion Nate still seemed to have for him, the love mixed in with the hate. My thought, as I sat there cradling Gabriel and listening to him talk about his wife: that it was his convictions that were cruel, but perhaps not Joel himself; that maybe ending Grace's relationship with Cesar, and attempting to end Nate's relationship with me, were to protect *them* rather than himself.

"In the Septuagint, the Greek translation of the Old Testa-

ment, the Greek word for this love is *agape,* a wide-open, all-encompassing sort of love. And then there's the Hebrew word *rayah,* the
kind of love you find with a close friend, sharing interests and sharing life together. It implies that you've seen both the good and the
bad in each other and you're still choosing to walk together, hand
in hand."

I looked over at Nate, standing beside Cecilia. I hadn't told
him I was coming and he hadn't seen me, although I'd tried to
catch his eye as he walked Cecilia down the aisle, hoping to . . .
what? Shake him up, I guess, make him think. Didn't he see how it
should be us up there?

I imagined Gabriel in a tiny bow tie, carrying our rings on a
white satin pillow, how carefully he'd walk, sensing the enormity of
the occasion. And Nate would smile down at him, beaming with
the recognition that things were finally as they should be.

"Me and Sophia, we found that love in each other, and when
we—" Joel's voice broke and he swallowed, gave a little shake to his
shoulders and continued. "As we saw the depth of the love Jesus
shares with us and the world, our love also grew deeper. So that's
what I'm wishing for the two of you, that you share the depth of
agape and the tenderness of *rayah* with each other, ordained by God
and brought to completeness by His love." He smiled at Samuel,
his flushed cheeks making him seem almost shy, then lowered his
head, turned to a bookmarked section of his Bible, and began to
read.

All-encompassing love and unconditional love, we'd had both
of those, hadn't we? Was the problem that the love I felt for him
wasn't truly unconditional, or that sometimes all-encompassing
love wasn't enough?

I brushed a hand over Gabriel's hair, hardly listening to the
exchange of vows and rings, a chaste kiss, closing prayers, my

mind too focused on what I was about to do. The procession started up the aisle, the congregants gathering jackets, purses. I held Gabriel tight, let him touch my nose, cheek, jaw, as he liked to do in strange situations, as if he was reassuring himself that I was still there. And then I stood to leave the pew, join the line to the vestibule.

They stood in the receiving line, Samuel and Cecilia followed by Mr. Sinclair, Grace, and Nate. As I got closer I saw that Cecilia was finally smiling now, allowing her hands to be clasped, her cheeks to be kissed. Mr. Sinclair's glances at her were approving, even proud. And remembering how he'd spoken about his love for his wife, and seeing Cecilia surrounded by these people so happy for her, so much love, I suddenly knew I couldn't do this today.

Maybe I'd come to morning mass tomorrow after work or later in the week, but this was Cecilia's day, a day she should be able to tell future kids about, hold in her memory as a small piece of perfect. To take that away would be so selfish, especially since I knew that somewhere amid the mire of motivations—the anger and hurt and desire for revenge against Joel and Nate—was jealousy. I was jealous of Cecilia for her uncomplicated marriage, for all the mornings ahead where she'd be able to wake up next to someone she loved, travel, play, talk late into the night about stupid everyday affairs, plan for a future. I might not have any of that, in the end might not ever find it with Nate, but that certainly wasn't Cecilia's fault, and she deserved every bit of happiness she could find.

I squeezed Gabriel's hand. "C'mon, Boo, it's time to go home."

"Want to see the princess!" Gabriel said, the beginnings of a whine.

"I know, but not today, okay? Not today, but I promise you'll meet her sometime soon."

"I want, I want—" he said, then gave up and rested his head against me. "Juice," he said.

"Okay, we'll go home and get you some juice." I sidestepped around the line and started to the door, glancing back only after I was outside. To find Grace staring at me.

I stood, frozen, watching her as she studied Gabriel's profile, her face slowly slackening. She took a step toward me, but a small, gray-haired woman grabbed for both her elbows, grinning and talking animatedly. Grace's eyes were still on me as she acknowledged the woman with one- or two-word responses so I gave my head a quick shake, willing her to stay where she was, then hurried down the church steps toward my car.

So that was it. She knew. She understood, and all I wanted to feel in that moment was a sense of victory. But I didn't have any idea what would happen next, and as I strapped Gabriel into his car seat I tried to replay the moments she'd stared at us, interpret the look in her eyes. A hauntedness, a longing sadness, which seemed to exactly echo my feelings about the wedding. But also, something sharper crackling at the edges. Something that looked a lot like rage.

22

It was before dawn the next morning when I returned home from work to find Grace huddled beside the front steps, hugging her skirted knees. She jumped up when she saw my car approach and stood there with her arms limp at her sides. I stayed behind the wheel a moment, steeling myself, then got out of the car.

"Your mom told me you were working," she said. "You work Saturday nights?"

"I have night shift three days a week, yeah. And afternoon shift for two."

"Must be hard, especially with . . ." She reached for the iron stair railing, curled her fingers around it. ". . . the boy."

We held each other's eyes a minute before I said, "Did you talk to my mom about him?"

"No. I didn't, I just wanted to talk to you. You're not married to Nate, are you?"

Was that really the most important piece of this? "No," I said.

"How old is the boy?"

"His name's Gabriel, and he's two."

"So . . . born after Nate left for school?" She thought a moment. "And conceived after he ran away three years ago. Does he know?"

"Conceived right before he ran away, actually, and yes, he knows. I actually drove down to the labor camp after I found out I was pregnant, brought him back here. And he's been visiting us for a weekend every month or two."

"Every month?" She watched me blankly. "There are times he travels home but doesn't come to see us? How does he even *afford* to come out here, is he not actually in school? How many lies is he telling us?"

"Your dad's been flying him out here, Grace, and giving us money from your mom's trust."

"So Dad knows?" There was something jagged and raw in her eyes. "He knows and he's supporting you?"

"Well, 'supporting' is too strong a word, but yes, monetarily he's been helping to support us." I sank onto the steps, looking up at her through the slatted rail. "I'm so sorry, I know I should've told you, and it's why I brought Gabriel to the wedding, because I wanted you to meet him." And why hadn't I told them sooner? Yes, Joel had made our silence a condition of continuing to support us, but Grace and Cecilia wouldn't have let on that they knew if I'd asked them not to. I could've tried to find them at church or tucked a note against Grace's windowsill; I could've tried harder, I knew that but . . . wasn't the truth that, with all the secrets between Nate and his sisters, part of me had cherished this one momentous secret that was just between him and me?

"Don't apologize, this is all on Nate, *he's* the one who should've told us. Look what he's doing to you now, going off to school when that was your idea first, abandoning you and his kid. Nate could have everything, a perfect life, a marriage and a baby. It's the only thing that matters in the world, so how can he treat it like it's an inconvenience? How can you let him?"

There was no right way to respond to this. Not when I agreed with her completely. For a minute I stared numbly into the darkness, then said, "Do you want to meet Gabriel? Or you could come back tomorrow, when he's awake?"

She followed my gaze, silent for a full minute. And then everything in her loosened. "I'm leaving tomorrow, going back to the convent. Now that Cecilia's gone there's no point in me being here, and I don't want to be alone with my father."

"I was wondering what you'd do," I said softly. "But you could go anywhere, why the convent?"

"Because they'll take me." She shrugged back her shoulders. "Because they're a family like the family I used to have; I mean not really but kind of, in the important ways. It feels like the right thing to do, I just have to stop imagining how I would've reacted ten years ago if I'd seen myself now. I always thought when it was time for me to leave home that I'd do something big with the opportunity, go to Prince Edward Island like I dreamed when we were little, even eventually have a child and raise it by the ocean, build us the American dream. The way this is actually playing out would be hysterical if it wasn't my real life."

"You could go there," I said. "Why not?" I thought of the house I'd imagined when I'd read *Anne of Green Gables,* its green pitched roof and shutters, acres of land that smelled of salt. "We could come up there, me and Gabriel, get away from this place. Seriously, we should do it! I have money saved up and we could get jobs. We could each of us take care of Gabriel while the other was working, and Nate could join us when he got out of school."

"Stop, okay?" Her voice was tight, but singsong with sarcasm.

"This is real life, Chloe, good things don't necessarily happen to good people and pipe dreams don't come true. I'm going to the convent, I already wrote last night to tell them. It's the only place I belong anymore." Grace's face hardened, like she was trying to fight back tears with brute force. And then she raised her chin and said, "But I would like to see Gabriel. I realize he's probably sleeping, but I want to look at him because I don't know when I'll be back, if I ever will."

I stood and extended my arm to her. "Come on."

She approached and took my hand, then unexpectedly wrapped her other arm around my shoulders. "I've missed you," she said softly. "I miss everything, what we all had when Mom was alive, even when she was sick, how we'd all sit with her, talking about ancient history or playing Scrabble or making up stories. That life felt like those padded boxes for different-shaped Christmas ornaments, a candy cane, an angel, a snowflake, a bell, all nestled together perfectly where they belong."

"Who was the candy cane?" I said. She pulled away, and I said, "Sorry. Sorry, Grace, I know exactly what you mean." I took her hand again and squeezed it, walked with her inside and up the stairs.

When we reached Gabriel's room I walked to the toddler bed and stood with Grace, looking down.

After a minute Grace whispered, "He's so beautiful."

"I know," I said.

"He looks . . . like me. He looks like me."

"There are times I can't even see myself in him. He's definitely a Sinclair."

Grace reached toward him, hovered her hand above his face.

"Do you want to hold him?" I said.

She quickly dropped her hand.

"It's okay, he's a deep sleeper, probably won't wake up. And I don't even care if he does wake up, he should get to meet you before you leave. He deserves to know his family."

Grace's eyes in the dim light from the hallway seemed huge. She gave her head a slight shake. "Please, I can't, I can't."

"What do you mean? Why not?"

"I have to go." She looked down at Gabriel, whispered, "I'm sorry," then backed away, her eyes on him till she reached the door.

I listened to her footsteps across the hall and down the stairs, the front door opening and closing. I watched out the window as she strode down the street, arms wrapped around her waist against the cold.

I should follow her, offer her a ride home in my car, but all I wanted to do was hold Gabriel, burrow against him. I lifted the deadweight of his sleeping body and sat with his head cradled against my shoulder, thinking how it was possible to feel both lucky and lost at the same time. All these months part of me had been just waiting for the day we'd all be together again, as interwoven as in childhood, whether here, in Berkeley, or somewhere else altogether. And now I had no idea how long that wait might be.

Nate came by the next afternoon while I was outside watching Gabriel cruise up and down the driveway on his Big Wheel. He stood by the side of the road a moment, smiling, before Gabriel noticed him.

"Daddy!" He jumped up, let Nate hug him, and then said, "You ride this."

"I don't know, Gabe, I'm too big. I'll probably break it."

Gabriel grinned at me impishly. "I'm big too, it won't break."

"Ah, good reasoning. Fine, I'll try but I don't think I'll be much good at it so don't make fun of me." He knelt beside the Big Wheel, then straddled it. So far he hadn't looked at me once.

I watched him ride, bent-legged, knees pushing against the ground, Gabe all-out laughing now. "Daddy, you're slooooow!" And I felt a wrenching sadness.

"How much longer are you staying?" I said.

He stopped riding, sat a moment with his eyes on the handle-bars, and then pulled to his feet, still not looking at me. Gabriel was now bouncing on his toes. "Ride it! Ride it!" And Nate lifted him, nuzzled his face in his neck, and growled, making Gabriel squeal. "Yeah," he said without turning to me, "I want to talk with you about that."

"Okay," I said slowly. "Talk."

"I think . . ." he started, then, "I've decided I'm not going back. Ever."

I watched him wordlessly, waiting.

"Grace told me she knows about Gabriel, that she came here to meet him last night. She finally knows, and I have to say my first reaction was relief; you have no idea how hard it's been to keep this from them. But when I talked to her, she was so angry at me, I'd never seen her like that. And the thing is I knew she was right, everything she told me was right. I spent all these years trying to get away from Joel, so why am I letting him rule my life now, sac-rificing this most important thing?"

He finally looked up at me, hesitated, and then reached into his pocket. "I bought this two years ago, right before Gabriel was born. I wanted to give it to you then, I almost did but you were so angry I had no idea how you'd react. But I've been carrying it with me everywhere, waiting, I even sleep with it under my pillow be-cause it feels like I'm carrying around our future."

I stared at the ring box he'd handed me, and he finally reached to close my fingers around it. "Please open it," he said. "I want to marry you, Chloe. We can stay here awhile if your mom's okay with putting us up for a few months, I'll get a job, I'll save up money, and you can stop working and take care of Gabriel, that's how things are supposed to be."

I slowly opened the box and stared at the small diamond, my mind too busy whizzing in circles, processing, to find anything other than sarcasm. "Well, that's an antiquated view," I said.

"I'm sorry," Nate said quickly. "I mean you can work, or even go to school, and I can watch Gabriel. I'd love that, really."

"I was kidding," I said, then pulled the ring from the box and slowly slipped it over my finger.

Nate's face broke into a boyish grin. "I think I was supposed to do that!"

I bit back a smile and pulled the ring off again, and he reached for my hand. "I love you, Chloe, I think I've loved you since the first day you showed up on our lawn. Our lives are coiled together, it started that day, and everything that happened since then just made the coils tighter and more intricate and extraordinary. I was stupid to focus so much on what I wanted for us instead of actually focusing on *us,* the extraordinariness."

The words were so unlike Nate, probably rehearsed, maybe refined over years, but heartfelt and so perfect because I knew how difficult they must've been for him to say. Dimly I realized that I was crying as he slid the ring over my finger and kissed it. And I tried to hold on to the moment, his words, so I could replay them whenever I needed the memories. Decades from now when Gabriel's face lit up as he told me he'd proposed to a future bride, I'd be able to close my eyes and remember. "What about Gabriel?" I said. "If you stay here, if we get married—"

"Everybody's going to know what I did, and for me that's an

added bonus. I'm going to tell Joel tonight, Chloe. Grace was planning on leaving this morning, I guess she must've told you that, but she said she'd stay till tomorrow so she can be there when I talk to Joel, maybe keep him a little calmer. You could be there too, if you want. I don't have any idea how he'll react, but I'm sure it'll be entertaining."

So many times I'd imagined Mr. Sinclair's face, finding out Nate had chosen me and Gabriel. He didn't think I was good enough to be part of his family, had almost succeeded in ending my relationship with Nate, but in the end our love was more powerful than his God. I reached for Nate, buried my head in his neck and slipped both arms around his shoulders, Gabriel between us. "I wouldn't miss this for the world," I said.

23

LATE that afternoon we stood on the Sinclairs' front lawn, Gabriel in my arms, looking up at the house. Before we'd left, I guess trying to lighten the mood, Mom asked Nate if he thought we should bring a gun. I laughed but Nate said, "I won't let him touch Chloe or Gabriel," then must've seen something in my face because he gave a disjointed *heh-heh-heh* sort of laugh. "Maybe a wooden stake instead," he'd said.

Now, I was shivering. Nate gently squeezed my arm. "Just don't say anything, let me talk. I know you'll want to yell at him, but he's not going to ever understand how wrong and hurtful he's been. You'll just make things worse."

I nodded silently and he kissed Gabriel's forehead and led us to the house.

They were in the library, Joel working at the rolltop desk and Grace curled on the couch with a piece of embroidery on her lap, not sewing, just running her fingers across the stitched flowers. She saw us first, frowned slightly, and then gave a short nod.

"Dad." Nate's voice was low, strained.

Joel turned his head and saw Gabriel in my arms, and in the sudden slackness of his face I could tell he knew why we were there. He pulled to his feet. "Grace, go upstairs."

"No, I think I'm going to stay for this." Her voice shook a bit, but she shut her mouth in a firm line, watching us.

Joel's face reddened. *"Grace."*

"I know who he is, Dad. I know who the baby is, so making me leave is kind of pointless."

"Don't you want to meet your grandson?" Nate nodded at me and I squared my shoulders, then set Gabriel on his feet, took his hand, and walked toward Joel.

"Say hi to your grandpa!" The tone of my voice was completely wrong. I cleared my throat as if trying to suggest the chipperness had been the result of phlegm, then said, "This is Gabriel."

Gabriel stared at Joel, gave a tentative smile, then burrowed against my leg.

Joel looked momentarily stunned, but within seconds his face had hardened, his eyes fierce. "We have an agreement, Nathaniel. What're you trying to do?"

"The thing is, I don't think I fully understood the terms of the agreement, what I'd be giving up." He turned to me. "I was trying to build something, but over the past few months I've realized I was actually destroying it. I made the worst mistake of my life, and now I'm just trying to set things right. So I'm marrying Chloe, that's what we're here to tell you. Her mom's letting us stay in her home, and I'll try and find a job in town."

I waited for Joel to respond, but he just stood there with his eyes on Nate, a response that was somehow far scarier than outrage.

"Did you really think three years of religion classes would make me forget I was in love with Chloe? That I have a son? And yeah, I realize this might get uncomfortable for you, but look at him! Do you really think he's less worthy of loyalty than you are?"

"You think this has to do with me?" Joel said slowly. "I'm trying to save you, Nathaniel. You're still a child, and part of that's my fault; I realize I should've guided you all to make the right decisions instead of forcing them. But while you're still a child you shouldn't be allowed to do things that'll destroy your life, and ruin whatever chance you have left for salvation when your life is done."

"Shouldn't be 'allowed'? Do you think I'm a toddler? I know what the right decisions are, and the times I refused to let you rule my life were the best decisions I've ever made. You really expect me to believe the past two years have been for my own good? What about what you did to Grace when she was my age, was that for *her* good?"

Grace's eyes widened, her skin washing pale.

I watched Joel's face. Nate must mean ending Grace's relationship with Cesar, and now I wondered what exactly had happened. Grace had completely changed since then; I didn't recognize the person she'd become. And Joel seemed to understand exactly what Nate meant because he strode to Nate and slapped him in the face.

Nate stared at him, mouth hanging open in shock.

"Mommy?" Gabriel's voice was high, scared.

I pulled Gabriel against me. "Damn you! How dare you? How dare you think I'm bad for Nate, that the existence of my son is a bad thing? You've done whatever you could to ruin your own kids' lives, but you're sure as hell not going to ruin my son's!"

He turned slowly, his eyes on Gabriel, the look on his face like he was being asked to swallow decaying meat. "He shouldn't have been born," he said. "Think about it, and tell me the truth. When you found out you were carrying him, didn't you consider ending your pregnancy? You don't seem like the type who'd think twice about the sin of it, so tell me the truth. Didn't the thought of not having to worry about a child make you feel a sense of relief?"

"Stop!" Grace strode to Gabriel, scooped him into her arms and tucked his head against her neck. "Shut up, shut up! How can you say that in front of him? You're not a human being, you're like a . . . a rattlesnake!"

Gabriel struggled to be let down but she only held him tighter, and I watched them, a crackling static inside me, remembering the hours I'd sat staring blankly at the pregnancy stick in my hands.

"You wish for other people to die just to protect yourself, and how can you live with that? Babies!" She was in tears now. In her arms Gabriel started shrieking, and she rubbed his back fitfully in an ill-advised attempt to soothe him. "I hope you rot!" she said, then spun away, began to stride out of the room with Gabriel still in her arms. Nate and I both ran after her to stop her, and she let Nate take her into his arms.

Nate stroked at her back, looking lost, and I took Gabriel from her and set my head on her shoulder making shushing noises, trying to calm both of them.

"I'm not staying here tonight," Nate said softly. "You come with us, Grace, I'm staying at Chloe's. We'll get a good night's sleep, come back tomorrow when he's at church to get your things, and you can figure out what to do from there. But come with us now."

I watched Joel over Grace's shoulder. His face was full of a twisted emotion I wasn't sure how to read, anger or agony. But then he met my eye and his face broke. He started to chuckle dryly, and then to outright laugh, and I widened my eyes, grabbed onto Nate's arm, and pulled him and Grace to the door.

We walked onto the lawn and stood there beside my car, silent except for Gabriel, who was in tears and trying to bury himself under my shirt. Being in the outside air, the light, the space, was stunning. Like waking suddenly from one of those dreams where you've been someone else entirely in a place you don't recognize, caught up in a drama you only dimly understand.

"We're okay," I said, the statement directed at nobody, at all of us, myself. "It's over."

"I shouldn't have had either of you here when I confronted him." Nate's voice cracked and he brought a hand to the top of his head, grabbed a fistful of hair, and then slid his hand to cover his face. "I probably shouldn't have confronted him at all, just, I don't know, sent a marriage announcement. Doing this, having Gabriel here, it was all for me, so I could see the look on his face."

Grace was shivering. I could only imagine how this must've been for her, finally standing up to Joel. And suddenly, amazingly, maybe sensing her distress or maybe because she looked so similar to his father, Gabriel reached his arms toward her.

It was a perfect gesture. If Grace still decided to leave tomorrow, they'd have this brief chance to become close. At the very least, he would be a comfort. "He wants you to hold him," I said, and Grace's eyes instantly filled. I handed Gabriel over and watched Grace nestle him against her bosom, jiggling him and rocking from foot to foot as if he was a much, much younger child.

Back home, after I'd put Gabriel to bed, we all sat with my mother in the living room, Grace and I cupping mugs of cocoa, Nate and

Momma with glasses of warm brandy. "I should go over there," Momma said. "I really should go over there and knock his ugly mouth off his ugly face."

She was gearing herself up to actually do it, I knew, so I said, "He's not worth it, Ma, and it wouldn't do any good. It's over now and we won, so let's just forget everything he said and move on."

"It's not over." Grace's voice was flat, nothing moving except her mouth. She seemed to be somewhere else, her words not connected to her body but coming séance-like from over her head. "You don't know him, Chloe, he's dangerous. He's more dangerous than any of you have any idea."

"He can't do anything to us now," Nate said. "Chloe's right, we won and we don't even have to ever see him again."

"You really think he'll allow that?" Grace seemed to all at once snap back into her body, tensed like she was ready to punch or flee. "You're not safe if you stay here, none of us is! There are things about him you don't know. Like I said when we were there, he'd do *anything* to protect himself!"

"Like what, Grace?" Nate's voice was calm but firm. "In a few days, regardless of what he might try to do, everybody in town is going to know Gabriel's mine and that me and Chloe are together."

"And you don't think he's capable of revenge? Look how he's treated us all his life!" She was in tears now as she huddled back against the couch, spilling her cocoa in the process, not even seeming to notice the brown stain spreading across the top of her dress. "I should've told you everything before you went there today, I should've told you it wasn't safe. You have to get out of here, you and Chloe and the baby, don't you realize that? He's crazy!"

Nate took the cocoa from her and set a hand on her knee. "Let's go up to bed, okay? You're exhausted, tonight's been crazy, but we can talk about this all tomorrow."

"Exhausted," Grace repeated, then pressed the heels of her hands against her eyes. "I am, I've been exhausted all my life . . . I don't know anything anymore."

My upper lip prickled with sweat. I'd never seen her like this, but of course I'd hardly seen her at all over the past three years. "Here," I said, standing and holding my hand to her. "You can stay in my room. I'll show you where you can wash up, and I'll bring you pajamas and clean sheets. Nate, you want to bring the sofa pillows to sleep on?"

Grace stared at my hand and then looked up into my face, her eyes pleading. Finally she stood and, without taking my hand, walked upstairs.

After getting ready for bed, I sat in the nursery watching Gabriel sleep beside me, listening to the frantic pitch of the conversation from the next room. And despite it, despite Grace's fears and whatever she was going through, I felt a muted excitement. Yes, tonight had been awful but we were here together, me, Nate, Gabriel, and Grace. I'd be able to convince Grace not to leave us, I knew I would. Eventually she'd meet someone, have her own child, and find her own happiness. Maybe we'd find a new town to live in, somewhere miles away, rent neighboring houses and get together for dinner on weekend nights. It wasn't far-fetched really, not anymore.

Over an hour later I was lying beside Gabriel, running my fingers through his hair, when Nate knocked softly at the door, peeked his head in, and then entered. "Good, you're not sleeping," he whispered.

"Yeah, too much to think about, I'm still absorbing all this." I shifted over and Nate lowered himself to the bed and sat with his arms wrapped around his knees.

"What's wrong?" I said.

"I don't know, I'm just worried about Grace. She told me some things . . . things I kind of knew about but that we'd never talked about, and tonight, with all Joel said, it just made her relive them."

"You mean what happened with Cesar? I know he did something that ended the relationship."

"There's more than that. She's scared, Chloe, she's scared for Gabriel and there isn't anything I can tell her to change that. And who knows, maybe she's right to be scared."

I raised my eyebrows, but he just shrugged back his shoulders and said, "I realize I'm not thinking straight. This has been the longest day of my life and that was probably one of the most disturbing conversations. Could I stay here tonight? I could sleep on the floor."

"Of course," I said, wishing so much that he'd reach for me. If he'd pulled me onto the floor just then, wanting to make love, I would've done it even with Gabriel in the room. I'd worked all these months to push him away, hold my feelings for him at a distance, inside a cage so I couldn't see them, hoping I'd forget, sure they'd start to atrophy from disuse. But I'd missed him, missed him so much, I wanted to swallow him and hold him inside me, the same fervent love I felt when Gabriel spontaneously threw his arms around me or exploded into a belly laugh. "You could almost fit here on the bed if you wanted," I said. "Look." I lifted Gabriel's sleeping body, laid him on my chest, and then shifted against the wall. "There's room."

He watched us, the look on his face both sad and hungry. Then slipped off his shoes and slid under the covers, took my hand and interlaced his fingers. I lay there feeling Gabriel's weight on my chest, Nate's body pressed against my side, like being swallowed in a warm cocoon. I squeezed my eyes shut and bit hard on my tongue, then pressed my lips between my teeth so they wouldn't hear me cry.

The next morning I woke to feel Gabriel stirring against me. The bed beside me was empty.

I kissed the top of Gabriel's head. "You've squashed me! I knew you were big, but man, you've officially squashed my ribs."

He laughed, squirmed away, and stood on the mattress, probably intending to jump on me to finish the deed, so I sat up and grabbed him around the waist. "Tackle!" I said. "Let's hurry up and get dressed, okay? Your dad's here, he spent the night."

As we dressed I listened for sounds in the rest of the house, finally heard Grace's voice in the kitchen directly below us. I felt a wash of relief. Yesterday had been real.

Downstairs, Nate and Grace were sitting across from each other, Grace with a glass of water and Nate with what looked to be another glass of brandy. Grace's eyes seemed bruised, her dress still stained with last night's cocoa. I lifted Gabriel onto his booster seat. "I'll get you guys some breakfast," I said. "Eggs, maybe? Or I could do something fancier, like French toast."

"Toast!" Gabriel said.

Grace shoved away her water glass. "Not for me, thanks. I have to leave soon and get on the road."

"On the road?" I said.

"I was already home this morning." Her voice caught and she swallowed, then folded her hands in her lap and squared her shoulders. "I packed up a few things, all I'll need. The bus leaves at eleven, and if I catch it I can be there in time for Compline."

I sank into a chair. "I thought maybe—"

"I can't stay here, I can't be in the same town as him. I've been thinking about it all night, I didn't sleep, and talking to him this morning just confirmed what I already knew. He's dangerous,

Chloe. You all don't get that, but he's not like other people. All that time he spends talking about saving our souls, when I'm almost positive he doesn't even have one."

"French toast?" Gabriel said.

Grace smiled at him. "I'll make it, can I make it for him, Chloe? And Gabriel, you can help me. You look like you'd be a good bread-dunker."

I rose silently, retrieved eggs, milk, and bread, and watched Grace help Gabriel spastically, messily, beat the eggs, dip the bread, watched her hold him up to the sink so they could wash their hands together, Gabriel laughing as they splashed against the stream of water.

It couldn't be forever. Didn't Grace see what she'd be missing? I couldn't understand what would make her sacrifice everything, sacrifice *life*, especially now that she had the opportunity for freedom. Was it that after all these years of imprisonment the idea of freedom scared her? Yes she was drawn to the routine, the quiet simplicity, but how could she listen to Gabriel's laugh, feel the squirminess of his little limbs, without asking herself whether simplicity was really the better choice?

Across the table Nate was also watching, his mouth set in a grim line. He shifted his eyes to meet mine. "She'll be safe," he said softly. "At least she'll be safe."

I watched Grace kneel beside Gabriel, using a dish towel to dry his hands, then took my purse from its hook by the door, pulled out my checkbook, and wrote a check for twenty thousand dollars. It had come from Joel, what was left of the money he'd given us in exchange for keeping Gabriel's existence secret, and I didn't want it. I had never wanted it.

I folded the check in half, then walked to the sink and handed it to Grace. "Don't ask questions," I said. "Just know this money isn't mine, doesn't belong to me, and I don't need it. It disgusts me, so either you take it or I'll throw it all in the river. It's for just in case, in case you ever want to leave the convent and start a new life, maybe even come back here someday and start new. And if you decide you really are going to stay, just give the money to the convent so they can—I don't know—buy you better mattresses and healthier food, anything to make life a little easier."

She slowly took the check, looked into my eyes questioningly, and then whispered, "Thank you," and slid it into the pocket of her dress.

I put my arms around both Grace and Gabriel and she flinched, then allowed herself to briefly rest against me. "I'll miss you," I said.

She gave a stifled laugh. "You haven't seen me for months."

"But I always knew you were there. Everything's different now."

"I know. I'll miss you too." She hesitated and then kissed my cheek, held her face against mine as she spoke into my ear. "You be good to each other, take care of each other through whatever happens and whatever God chooses for you next. Just lean on each other and you'll get through."

"We will," I said. "You take care of yourself too."

She stretched a smile and turned toward Nate, who stood to reach for her, wrapped his arms around her shoulders. They held each other, unspeaking, Grace's face buried against his neck. It seemed so intimate, that embrace, so I turned away and bent to retrieve a griddle from under the stove, began to fry the bread. By the time I turned back to reach for plates, Grace was already gone.

24

THE next weeks passed in a blur of plan making, future building, fantasizing and, for the first time since Gabriel was conceived, making love. There were times Nate seemed distant and I knew he must be thinking about Grace, worrying and wondering when we'd get to see her again. She'd sent a postcard from Santa Barbara the day after she arrived, saying only that she loved us and that she was safe. Nate had held the postcard for a long while, forearms resting on his knees. Late that night I'd seen the corner of the card peeking from under the front of his pajama top, probably the only way he knew to hold her close.

But overall he seemed happy, soaking up time with Gabriel, all the simple pleasures of life with a toddler: ball throwing and belly tickling, *Goodnight Moon* and *Itsy Bitsy Spider*. At dinner every night, when Gabriel started to fuss from boredom, he improvised another thread to an ongoing story about Prince Gabriel and his triumphant slaying of dragons and vanquishing of villains. Gabriel would gaze at him in awe, amazed at either the conquests of the boy with his name or at his dad's ability to fabricate such elaborate adventures. And I'd watch them together, father and son, thinking of all the years I'd longed for a center, a real family, feeling a twist of joy.

Nate found a job bussing tables at a café four towns over, and I sent for information on Humboldt State University. We set a date for our wedding in the town hall; I filled out all the paperwork and bought a simple white dress and veil. We hadn't seen Cecilia since she and Samuel had left for their honeymoon, had tried to contact her but she hadn't answered our calls. So we still hadn't told her about Gabriel or our engagement and we assumed Joel hadn't said anything either, trying to delay public humiliation for as long as possible, letting her believe Nate had returned to Missouri. The truth is we didn't try especially hard to talk with her; over the past three years she'd become increasingly more devout, and Nate was worried how she'd react. We'd tell her everything the week before the wedding, hoping our sins might be easier for her to accept if she knew our marriage was only days away. We hoped she might even be happy for us. She and Samuel, Gabriel, and my mother would be our only guests. I couldn't wait.

And then, March 15.

I'd been working night shift, returned at 4:00 A.M., and as always I stopped in Gabriel's bedroom to check on him, touch his hair or kiss his cheek. Sometimes he'd burrow his face against me, more often he'd just smile without opening his eyes, waking just enough to sense my presence, and it was enough to push back the guilt I felt at having had to leave him. Even if he stayed mired under the weight of sleep, I needed the reassurance, the little clang of joy I felt whenever I saw him after time away.

I could smell his honey apple scent when I entered the room, saw his tousled sheets and Mulligan, the rabbit he slept with every night. But stepping closer I saw his bed was empty. Gabriel was gone.

At first I didn't think anything of it. He'd had a nightmare, I assumed, padded to my room for comfort and, finding me gone, had either settled into bed with Nate or gone to my mother. Even after checking our rooms I felt only a twinge of fear, sure he must've wandered somewhere downstairs to sneak a treat, or maybe watch TV, then gotten too tired to climb back to his room before falling asleep. So downstairs I called at first softly so as not to wake anyone, and then louder, checking behind and under the sofa and tables as if he was a missing puzzle piece. "Gabriel!"

There were footsteps on the stairs and I spun around in relief. But it was only Nate traipsing down, his hair sleep-rumpled, eyes questioning, and then, when he saw my face, alarmed. "What is it? What's going on?"

"Where's Gabriel!"

Nate stared at me.

"He's not in his bed, so where the hell could he be? What if he was climbing somewhere and he hurt himself? His closet, I didn't check his closet." I raced past Nate, up the stairs.

Not in the closet, and I stood a minute staring at his little sweaters, OshKosh overalls, white-toed Keds, a fireball of terror in my stomach. Then dropped to the floor and searched under the dresser, crawled under his bed till I could see the back wall. "Gabriel!"

"Chloe?" Nate's voice was stiff, frightened. He was standing by the window, looking down. My body feeling suddenly numb, weightless, I rose and floated to his side. Inside me nothing but the word *No*.

There, on the ground, twenty feet below, was a tiny white sock.

The weight dropped all at once back into my body, so sudden that I actually stumbled on my way to the door. I scrambled back to my feet and raced down the stairs and outside, calling Gabriel's name, searching the front bushes and the weeds between bushes, praying that I wouldn't find him. I was screaming, not even hearing the sound, just feeling the airlessness of it. I started to drop to my knees to search under the brambles when Nate grabbed me, wrapped his arms around me, his eyes at the kitchen window.

The window was closed, but there was a large, ragged tear across the screen. I felt my knees begin to buckle, felt a fireball rise from my stomach up into my throat, a gray shade dropping quickly and noiselessly over my eyes. Then, nothing.

I woke to a cool hand stroking back my hair, another cupping my cheek. In the distance, Nate's voice. "I don't know, I don't know!" he said. "I went to bed at eleven and he was fast asleep, I went in and pulled his blanket to cover his feet, I pulled down his blanket and—" His voice broke. "What's with all the questions? Just stop with the questions, this isn't helping!"

I opened my eyes. I was on the sofa in the living room, my head in my mother's lap. Nate was in the kitchen doorway on the phone, his face red and hair rumpled, and all at once I remembered the screen and felt my mind start to fog and swim.

"You okay?" Mom said, then, "No, why the hell did I ask that?" A sob in her voice. She stroked again at my hair. "It'll be okay, it'll all be okay."

"She was out working; her mom was here but she was asleep. Chloe got home and I guess went into his room to check on him and he was gone. Didn't I say that already? I said it already, damn it! When are they going to be here?"

With those words I heard the sound of an engine at the front of the house, and sat up to look through the window at the car pulling off the road. The doors opened and two cops emerged. Nate hung up without speaking and went to let them in.

Later I wouldn't remember the questions asked, only the look of the policewoman, Jessica Yarrow, stricken like she already sensed there was no hope. At one point I started screaming, repetitive, high-pitched Janet Leigh shower screams. My mother wrapped both arms around me, squeezing tight, and Nate took both my hands. But I couldn't feel them, I was there inside the screams, twirling like an insane top alone.

A doctor was called, I was injected with something that spiraled me out from and over the screams, and Nate carried me up to bed and sat with me, a hand on my chest. From a distance I heard the sound of tears, maybe my mother's, maybe my own, and when I closed my eyes I saw Gabriel above me looking down, wearing that puzzled look he got when he was trying to understand new toys or adult conversation. And as I watched he raised a hand to me, and then disappeared.

I don't remember much of the next week. The days were a medicated blur from which I'd periodically emerge in a panic, screaming, held by someone I couldn't see or hear or feel. I knew our home was being searched, the kitchen and whole upstairs temporarily cordoned off, bags collected, bloodhounds brought to trace Gabriel's scent. I knew people had come from as far as Sausalito to help comb the woods, our home filled for days with strange voices. But as soon as I was allowed back into Gabriel's bedroom I stayed huddled there, first straightening the aftermath of the search, folding clothes back in drawers, scrubbing fingerprint dust off doorknobs, headboard, and sheets, then curling on his bed with my eyes closed. Activity everywhere, voices from the floor below threatening to break through. I don't remember feeling anything.

There was questioning and more questioning; Nate and my mother were brought in day after day, interviewed by the local police and then the FBI. Nate told me our story was on the news and that he'd spoken to reporters; my mother told me that within the first minute he'd broken down on film. And hearing this I momentarily hated him for acting like he knew my son, pretending he had a right to cry. I wanted to scream at him, for the first time letting in the fury because it was easier than letting in anything else and because I blamed him, blamed him for letting Gabriel be taken. If he'd just been vigilant enough, just loved Gabriel enough, wouldn't he have sensed what was going on in the next room?

Cecilia came as soon as she heard. She never asked me questions about Gabriel, or even showed me any sense of the shock she must have felt at hearing about a nephew she'd never even known existed. When she first arrived, looking white-faced and grim, she only reached for me wordlessly and held me, rocking side to side. For an hour she held me, and leaning against the soft warmth of her chest, for the first time I let myself sob.

After this she came early every morning; I don't think she said anything to me at all, just sat with me silently, maybe knowing there really was nothing to be said. Until, five days after she'd first arrived, I found her in my bedroom holding a photo of Gabriel, studying it. The picture had been taken over a year ago, Gabriel on a playground swing, the laugh on his face so wide you could see his first molar. For ten minutes she held it before replacing it on my nightstand, then turned and saw me standing there in the hall. She stepped back, her face reddening. "I'm sorry. Chloe, I'm sorry, I just . . . I wanted to get to know him."

I nodded silently.

"He's beautiful, and he looks so much like Mom. He has your nose and cheekbones, your cleft chin, but he has Mom's eyes and her same smile, he even has the same one-sided dimple!" She brushed a finger against her right cheek, then said, "Some people are just too good for this world."

I felt those words like something solid, clay thudding into my stomach, and seeing my face she widened her eyes. "Oh gosh, I totally didn't mean that like it sounded. I know he's okay, Chloe, you'll find him and he'll be just fine."

"You should go," I said tonelessly, and then I turned back toward Gabriel's bedroom.

I slid under his sheets and stared a minute at the ceiling, then slowly reached to his nightstand for the book we'd been reading, the *Just So Stories*. We'd been on the story of the elephant's child with his "satiable curiosity," and the night before Gabriel disappeared I'd flipped through the pictures as I told him the story first in my own, simple words, hoping he'd understand when I later read Kipling's version. I remembered how his eyes had widened, how he brought a hand to his nose as I described the crocodile pulling on the elephant's trunk. "He'll be okay," I'd whispered, "I promise there's a happy ending, because bad things don't happen to either elephant or people children." I'd said this knowing it was a lesson that would need to be amended in time. But that his childhood would be so different from Nate's and mine that by the time he was forced to learn it, he'd be old enough to understand that whatever cruelty and hardships he'd face weren't in any way a reflection of his own worth.

Before leaving that night I'd cuddled him on my lap as I did every day before naps and every night before bed, singing the words to "Summertime" from *Porgy and Bess* as he looked up into my face, playing lazily with my fingers. I think I must have told him before leaving that I loved him. I wished I could remember it.

Now I opened to the story we'd never gotten to read, then hugged the open book against me, rocking back and forth, back and forth. Five minutes later I reached into my pocket for two of the Valiums I'd been given, dissolved them on my tongue. And let myself sleep.

I was in Gabriel's room the next day when I heard Nate and Cecilia talking softly in my bedroom. I stepped out into the hall to hear.

"Should've heard him in church," Cecilia was saying. "He was ranting and raving about Gabriel, actually sobbing, but he never once mentioned he was his grandson. Does he seriously think they don't know?"

"He's assuming they're so taken by the power of his oration that they'll overlook it." Nate's voice was too lyrical. I could tell he was drunk. He'd been drinking pretty continuously since Gabriel's disappearance; not in front of me, but there'd been too many times I smelled it on his breath.

"What do you bet he'll be able to twist things around so he looks like a victim? Poor man with the lost grandson; hell, in the end it could be good for his career."

"Oh, the irony," Nate said bitterly, then paused before he added, "Listen, Cecilia, Grace thinks . . . that it was him. She sent me a letter yesterday, said how she wishes she could be here for us, that she's crying for us and praying for us, everything you'd expect from her. But then she threw the possibility in at the end. Said she was sure the idea had crossed our minds even if we hadn't let it stick, and that I should say something to the police."

I stared at the wall, then pressed my palm flat against it.

"So what do you think?" Cecilia's voice was hushed.

A beat of silence before Nate said, "Okay, so the truth is, I did already tell the police it could be him. I told them all about our conversation last month, the things Joel said to us, and I don't know. They said they'd question him, maybe they actually already have, but in the end I think it made them more suspicious of *me* than of him. They'd already looked into our relationship, apparently, and they were trying to get me to admit I wanted revenge. He's such an upstanding citizen, right? Automatically above suspicion. And they were asking me, 'Why would you turn on your own father?' So I told them exactly why."

"You really think he could've done something." Her voice was dark. "I mean I know he's capable of awful things, but this? He's cruel, but he's not evil."

"Can you really say that? Tolkien said that you shouldn't leave a dragon out of your calculations if you live near him. Since Mom died, do you even know who he is anymore?"

"But why would he want to make this into the biggest story the town's ever seen if he didn't want anybody to know you had a son?"

"Joel knew it was too late to keep this a secret, that the whole town was going to know soon enough anyway. Maybe he saw this as a way to show me and his little flock how sins don't go unpunished. Maybe he even saw that as a greater good."

"It might even be revenge." Cecilia was quiet a moment, then said, "The things he's said about you over the past couple years, it's disgusting. I'm not going to tell you details, but just know that sending you off to Missouri was as much about revenge for your faked suicide as about any hopes he had for your future. He was sure you'd be miserable there, and this . . ." Her voice trailed off, and she continued in a hoarse whisper. "He wouldn't actually hurt a baby, would he? Take him from you maybe, but not hurt him."

"I don't know. That was my first thought too, that he just took him somewhere, he's having somebody watch over him. But who would he have found to take Gabriel that wouldn't notify the police? Is there some black-market baby trafficker?"

"Or somebody in the parish?"

"Would they lock a baby up and not let anybody see him? Everybody from miles around knows he's missing so I'm pretty sure at least he isn't here. I was thinking he might've taken him to one of the more secluded churches, like Life Tabernacle, people who don't read the news. He could've told them Gabriel's parents had died and no one else in the parish was capable of taking him, so he wanted to find another UPC family to raise him. But I don't know, I don't know, Cecilia, really he's capable of anything." His voice shook. "I'm going to talk to him. I'll be able to tell by looking at him."

"You'd ask him directly?"

"Why not? You think he'll beat me up or something? Wouldn't *that* be an interesting piece for the cops to add to the puzzle."

Cecilia didn't respond for such a long time that I peeked into the bedroom. Her cheeks were glazed with tears and Nate was holding both her hands. I slipped back into the hallway, closed my eyes, and leaned back against the wall.

"I can't stand this," she said finally, her voice glottal. "I think Grace could be right. I don't know if he'd actually hurt Gabriel, I want to believe he wouldn't, but the truth is I think he's capable of anything. At the wedding, with everything he said about Mom, I started to feel so bad for him, I almost forgave him for everything.

You know how much he loved Mom, and it really seemed like he genuinely wanted me to be happy, that maybe that's why he pushed so hard for us to get married. But I should've realized nothing about him is genuine, it's all show."

"I'm going over there." I heard a shuffling as Nate stood, and all at once there he was in the hall. He froze when he saw me, his eyes wide.

"Your dad?" I said. "Your *dad*?"

Cecilia appeared at the door, staring at me with red-rimmed eyes.

"I don't know, Chloe," Nate said, "I have to talk to him."

"But he wouldn't hurt Gabriel. He wouldn't *hurt* him, right? Maybe take him, maybe bring him to another church like you were saying. If he was the one who took him I'm sure he wouldn't do anything really awful to him, so it would be a good thing!"

"I don't know! Just let me figure this out. I just . . ." He pressed the heel of one hand against his forehead, held it there, and then said, "I just have to see him, Chloe. I'll talk to you after I do." He wrapped his arms briefly around my shoulders before striding down the stairs.

Nate returned late that night. I didn't hear him; after hours pacing fitfully, I'd gone to bed early in Gabriel's room, a dead, dreamless tranquilizer sleep. I woke late the next morning, and before even opening my eyes the panic seized me, claws in my belly. I hunched forward with my eyes squeezed shut, hands over my face, digging my nails into my cheeks. Sat there fighting for breath, red behind my eyelids, then grabbed Gabriel's pillow and rocked it forward and back, forward and back, my face buried inside it.

After a minute I rose, still hugging the pillow, and went to the bedroom to find Nate.

He was sprawled on the bed, a nearly empty bottle of Smirnoff on the floor beside him. What did it mean? Had he learned anything? For sure he would've told me if he'd found out anything that might lead us to our son. Or if he'd found out the worst. So the fact he'd gotten drunk and passed out, did that mean he still didn't know?

I stood a moment in the doorway, watching, then crawled into bed with him. And stared. All up and down his forearms were scratches, some of them deep gouges that had stained the front of his shirt with blood. And, most horrifying of all, there was dirt under his nails. Had he been burying something? Or . . . digging something up? I couldn't think about it. I couldn't, so I crawled onto the bed beside him and buried my head into the pillow. He shifted slightly away from me, and as he did I heard a crinkle of paper. I sat up and looked over his shoulder.

There was a thick, lined notepad on the bed beside him, its pages filled with careful handwriting. I slowly reached for the pad so I could read.

Once upon a time, in a kingdom far, far away, there was a valiant prince by the name of Gabriel Milford McPimple. He was still a young prince but already braver than an army of ten thousand soldiers, and as wise as a storyteller. Prince Gabriel was raised by his mother, the enchanting Queen Chloe McPimple, and his father the bumbling King Nathaniel, about whom there is not much I can say, except that he tried his best.

I traced my fingers over the letters. How long had he been writing this? There were so many pages, at least a couple hundred, that he must have started writing these stories well before he returned home, just waiting for the opportunity to tell them.

I began reading, these tales of a boy who, with the questionable help of his ungainly father, saved his friends from wandering goblins, skulking sea dragons, and various other nasties. Each adventure ended with father and son cuddling together before bed, talking about their day. Prince Gabriel biting back a smirk as King Nathaniel attempted to hide his cowardice and missteps and vowed to keep the prince safe for another day.

Had Nate slept with the story last night in an attempt to convince himself Gabriel was strong enough to be safe? Or maybe he'd reread the words just to relive the time in his life when he'd written them, when there was more hope than fear. My chest hurt, a dull hammer throb of pain like my ribs were too tight. I set the notepad back beside him.

Nate woke at the movement and turned to me, his eyes wide. He held my eyes a moment and then rolled back to stare at the ceiling.

"What?" I turned to face him, waiting, then finally whispered, "What happened? You have to tell me."

His mouth twisted into a smile, which horrified me until I saw the tears glazing his eyes.

I sat up and pulled the covers off of him, my entire body swollen and numb. "Tell me!"

"I don't know," he said. "Chloe, I'm . . ." His voice was shaking. Why was it shaking? "I'm going to the police."

"What do you mean? What happened to your arm? What did he say? Where's Gabriel!"

"I don't know. He told me . . . things, but not details. I can't tell you, Chloe, I just know he did something and I don't even think he meant to, maybe he just wanted to scare me."

"Did what! Where'd Joel take him! You have to tell me what he said, all of it, and don't look at me like that. Just say it!"

"I can't, Chloe, just trust me on this, okay? It's better that you don't know. I'm calling Cecilia, I'm going to have her and your mom stay with you today, and I'm going to the police."

I felt the blood drain from my cheeks, clammy sweat under my eyes, all the nightmares from the past few days of Gabriel alone and crying for me, stumbling barefoot through the cold, dark woods. "He—" My voice broke. I couldn't say the words. "He—"

Nate set a hand on my knee and I swiped at his arm, pushed him with both hands, and then swung my fists at him. "You let him in here! You let him take our baby! I can't do this, Nate, I can't do this!"

Nate grabbed onto my arms, then wrapped me in a bear hug. I cried out and squirmed against him but he held me tighter, hand clutching at the back of my pajama top. "You'll be okay, we'll be okay, we'll be okay," saying it over and over, the syllables slurred and completely meaningless.

25

I never learned what Joel had told Nate. But apparently it was enough to spur the police to bring him in for a second round of questioning, and while he was at the station they obtained a search warrant. Searched the house and found it, the soiled diaper in his trash. Traces of Gabriel's hair on his rugs and clothes. A tiny white sock under the sofa. And a letter in Joel's handwriting, tucked into his rolltop desk, never sent.

I'm writing this because I know your mother would have wanted me to. She'd want us both to find peace with what happened, what we both have done. I just pray that you understand this was beyond both of us, that neither of us can be blamed, and I know how hard things must be for you at this moment but in the end I'm sure it was God's will. Your child was born from sin and his existence would have soiled all of us, you and me,

*the family, the church. I can only hope that, gone
so young, he himself won't have to suffer for
eternity. I'm sorry for your pain, but can't be fully
sorry for the reason behind it.*

Joel was arrested immediately. Held without bail, awaiting trial. I learned later that he didn't give more than the most curt answers during questioning, claiming innocence and then lapsing into histrionic prayer. Seeming to believe prayer would absolve him from whatever he'd done, that was the final nail in his coffin.

I was subpoenaed for the trial, and sat in the witness box with my eyes on the prosecuting attorney as Nate had directed, away from the defense table. Until when the questioning was over I stood, and my eyes turned of their own volition to see Joel Sinclair sitting calmly with his hands folded in his lap. I surged toward him with a hoarse scream scraped from the darkest depths of my rage and terror. "Where is he!"

Nate grabbed for me but I wrenched away. "You son of a bitch, what did you do with him? Where did you take my baby, you *tell* me!"

From the jury pit I heard a woman start to sob; I felt arms circle me from behind and gently lead me from the courtroom while I flailed against them, shrieking, "He's somewhere, I know he's somewhere, make him *tell* me!" Straining to jump on him, strangle and claw and tear, Nate and my mother following me into the hallway, surrounding me, all of us sinking together onto the tile floor.

For months I focused all my longing on the sock they'd found under Joel's sofa. If I could just bring it home, this last thing he'd worn, I'd be able to feel him, hold him, understand. But they carried it away in an evidence bag and no matter how much I pleaded with Nate, with the police, they wouldn't let me see it. And of course it didn't matter. Nothing mattered, not the sock nor the length of Joel's sentence, nor the fact he'd still be young enough after release to live for years as a free man. For twenty-five years, nothing in my life had mattered.

PART XI

The TELL-TALE HEART

26

THE aftermath must have been horrifying for Nate and Cecilia in even more complex ways than it was for me, knowing what their own father had done, knowing they shared blood with a monster. It must've changed even the way they thought about themselves. But I'd hardly thought about them in the next few months; I was buried too deep inside the bottomless pit of my own pain.

A year after his conviction, Joel told authorities God had finally commanded him to proclaim guilt in his grandson's murder. I remember finding Nate late that night huddled in the backyard, his body wracked with sobs, and I'd felt stunned at the seeming depth of his emotions. Before then all I'd seen was his support of me, his tenderness, fixing me tea and bubble baths, listening to my endless stories about Gabriel, holding me while I cried. And now I wondered if he'd been angry at me for not having supported him too.

He'd had nobody, especially since Cecilia soon stopped calling or visiting. I'd felt hurt by her silence at the time, then angry, but I learned later some of what she'd been going through with Samuel, the verbal abuse and, within a few months of their wedding, the bruises and sprained wrist, the broken nose. Her own private hell.

And Grace, after the one letter she'd sent offering sympathy and suspicions, also didn't even try to contact us. Had she been able to follow the story after that? Did she know Joel had been arrested? I couldn't blame her for not feeling brave enough to outright face the fact those suspicions had been true, and I knew Nate hadn't told her about the trial and conviction, wanting to spare her the pain of it. But I'd always felt like it was wrong for her not to know, and now—understanding exactly why she'd been so scared of her father and so sure he was capable of hurting a child—I couldn't help but feel like she would've felt a sense of closure, like he was finally paying for what he'd done to her baby as well.

If Nate had found her, was he telling her any of what had happened? Were they talking about her own loss? Trying to reach some kind of peace? The silence hadn't been good for any of us, I knew that. The only way to come to terms with the pain was to sift through it, separate it layer by layer, and spread it in the light to dry.

Nate had known this; it must be why he'd written it all out in his notebook. Peace and connection with what had been buried, it was probably what novelists and poets looked for when writing, laying out their own fears and pain and lost love on paper word by word, examining. Maybe that was also why Nate had written the stories to Gabriel while he'd been hundreds of miles away, to forge a connection with him but also to finally look at and come to terms with—in the form of King Nathaniel—his own inadequacies as a father.

Now I sat on the bed and reached for my phone, dialed the number to Nate's cell even knowing the phone would ring in our empty bedroom, our empty home. When voice mail picked up I closed my eyes, listening to his voice and imagining he was there. A beep and I sat inside the following silence, my thoughts stilling.

And suddenly, I knew.

Of course.

I walked to the desk where I'd left Nate's notebook, and opened it to where I'd left off.

At one time I'd had the first paragraph of Nate's book memorized, I'd read it so often. But it had been years since I'd opened the book, so it took a few minutes of searching and stumbling before I found the right letters to cross out.

Ivonecew ~~upoondna~~ tered himoweini ~~wasaksing~~ trodomfang renofa ~~raught~~ ~~waogoyt~~ bacherek towaJoes lavandaskal thianteprin ceright quebys tionthes whennami kenofew thegaban sweri relmsilm fighort dedstromye mepim.

I've wondered how I was strong enough to go back to Joel and ask the right questions when I knew the answers might destroy me. But in the end it had nothing to do with strength, it was disbelief. I fully expected to be guided to a different truth. Because these things don't happen to real people, only on the news, Lindbergh, JonBenet, Elizabeth, and in nightmares you wake from in stunned relief. For weeks I waited to wake up. Maybe part of me is still waiting.

So this was it, I was finally going to learn what had happened that night. Part of me hadn't wanted to know. I assumed he hadn't told me because whatever he'd seen was either too painful for him to remember or too horrifying for me to hear. But all these years it had haunted me, one of the biggest missing pieces to this puzzle with too many missing pieces. How had Gabriel died? Had he felt fear? Pain? Had he called for me?

I didn't know if I could stand the answers, but all these years not knowing had felt almost like I was betraying my son, being so separated from these last moments of his life.

I stood and walked downstairs to look for Cecilia. She was in the kitchen, standing at the sink and staring at the running water, her hands braced on the counter.

"Cecilia?"

She spun to face me, a look of panic on her face.

"You okay?" I said softly.

"What? Oh!" She nodded quickly, shallowly. "Yeah, sure, I'm fine, I just was cleaning." She turned the faucet off.

I studied her face and she waved a hand at me, then turned back around. "I should tell you that Nate called a few minutes ago. He's on his way back."

My eyes widened. "And Grace? Has he been with Grace?"

"He didn't say, he refused to tell me anything. But . . . I'm guessing no. Because if she was still alive, wouldn't he have said so? The plan was for him to come back and stay here for a few days, watch Joel so I could go down and spend some time with her myself."

"Maybe that's what he's planning. But he must've known you'd ask about her, and he just might not've wanted to talk about it over the phone."

"You mean he didn't want to tell me how sick she is." She swallowed, her eyes looking briefly stunned, then continued with her words rushed like she was trying to erase the thought. "Well, he's on the road now, says he's driving straight through so he should be here by the middle of the night."

So, I thought. Here we go.

"I told him you were here and he said he wasn't surprised, that he was actually glad about it."

"I guess he knows we have to talk things out, that we should've talked a long time ago."

"How far have you gotten in his notebook?"

"Almost done, I still have a few pages more but he switched to a different book for his encoding."

Was I wrong or did I sense a change in her expression? A loosening of her shoulders? "You don't want me to read the rest," I said.

"What? No, I don't know, I wouldn't say that. I guess maybe it's just my first instinct to feel like some things are better left in the past."

"Sometimes you have to understand the past to move on from it," I said slowly.

"Right. You're right, Chloe, that's true."

"I was actually hoping you could help me, because it turns out the last book is *his* book, and I was wondering if you had a copy."

Cecilia's face stilled. "The Prince of Poppington book?" Her eyes drifted sideways. "I have a few copies, sure." She started toward the door. Then turned. "Are you going to tell Nate you found the notebook?"

"I feel like I need to tell him at this point. There's too much I learned that he's been keeping from me, and if I didn't confess I knew it? I don't know if our marriage could survive. Maybe he'll be glad of it, not having to keep secrets."

"I told you my guess was he was subconsciously hoping you'd find the notebook all along so he wouldn't have to keep hiding.

So . . . let's do this." She tilted her chin in the direction of the hall-way. "Come on."

She led me to the library, the corner by the rolltop desk, and pulled out one of several copies. She gripped it in both hands without giving it to me. "You know Dad had a copy of this in jail," she said. "I should've told Nate that. Looked like it had been read over and over too."

I felt my stomach twist. "That's disgusting."

"Yeah, I guess. I guess I can see how you'd think that." She handed me the book. "Okay, then. I'll be either here or in the kitchen if you want to talk."

Did she have some sense of what he'd written? I watched her face wordlessly a moment before saying, "Thanks. It'll probably take a couple hours, but I'll come find you then."

I brought the book upstairs and sat a moment fingering the cover before opening to the acknowledgments. *For my little prince,* it said simply, *who is standing somewhere beyond my reach, still with his sword raised in victory.*

I'd cried the first time I read it, of course, although when I thought about it later it just felt overdone and insincere to me, Nate's attempt to seem poetic. But now, as I began to work through the rest of the code, my heart hurt not just for Gabriel but also for Nate, who'd spent months with these stories after Gabriel disappeared, preparing them to be submitted for publication. How had he been able to stand it? Maybe it was his way of connecting with his son, just like it had been when he was first writing it. Or maybe he'd wanted the pain, penance for having missed so much of Gabriel's life.

I still imagine you like I did on the nights I spent at school, alone in the dark scribbling stories

I knew I'd tell you later. Invincible Prince Gabriel
with the wisdom to save himself from the most evil
beasts. So many stories in my mind, so many plot
twists, but in each of them—as in most children's
stories—death was only approached, never reached.
So how can I accept that you aren't still fighting?

I don't know how to write about that
afternoon. After all these years I still don't know
how to process it. His words sit frozen inside of me,
I'm picturing the neurons that hold them quivering
in the jelly of my brain refusing to let go. I can still
see his face.

He was in the church office when I found him,
sitting at his desk with the Bible, murmuring to
himself, maybe reading aloud. And there on the
desk tucked beside a stack of books was a pair of
folded pajamas. Pajamas with blue teddy bears.

I stared at them. I stared at them and my legs
gave way. I don't remember what I said, although
I guess I must've cried out. But I remember the
pain of hitting the floor and the look of pure terror
on his face.

He startled to his feet, then followed my eyes
and his face flushed nearly purple. He quickly
pushed one of his books on top of the pajamas and
then sat back in his chair and looked down into
my face as I stared at him, my entire body numb.

"I don't know why they're here," he said.

I was trembling, my vision blurred, a ringing
in my ears. I could taste blood on my tongue.

"Is this supposed to be a lesson?" he said. "I

can't stop looking at them, I don't know what the Lord wants from me, that's the thing! Maybe He was just trying to tell me the boy's in His arms now, I hope that's it. But it might also be what I've been so scared of since the beginning. Because much as I've tried to convince myself otherwise, there's no hiding from the fact that children who are born unclean, to unsaved parents, they're born anti-Christs." His fist closed around the pajamas; there were actual tears in his eyes. "I'm sorry, Nate, but what I'm scared of is that maybe this is God's way of reassuring me that His will was done."

That's the word he used, "unclean," and then he told me he'd found the pajamas the day after you disappeared, folded on the altar. He'd gone in to pray for you, he said, but when he saw the pajamas he'd realized your fate was already decided.

All these words I remember but I don't remember my reaction, remember only the sound of a roar and know only that I must've attacked him, because an hour later I found myself roaming the streets downtown, scratches on my arms, blood under my nails. The pajamas clutched in my hands. And in the midst of that blankness, there on the dark street, decisions.

I dug my nails into my palms thinking of that night, the pure horror of those days, all that Nate had known. He'd told me none of this, I guess thinking Joel's words would be too much for me. Maybe even wanting me to hold out hope for as long as possible.

*I couldn't bring the pajamas to the police, I
knew that. They already suspected me, and if I'd
showed up there with this evidence, especially after
having attacked my father, who would they believe?*

*So instead I went back home, I walked into the
woods and knelt in the same spot by the stream
where you'd been conceived. And I buried the
pajamas there, digging with my hands, my nails
tearing, the wounds on my arms reopening, your
endings in the place of your beginnings.*

*When it was done I sat there for what must've
been three hours, hands splayed over the ground,
my eyes closed. Forcing myself to breathe because
I'm pretty sure if I'd stopped pushing my lungs, they
would have forgotten to push themselves. And then
finally I stood, knowing I'd never be back, and
went to your mother's house to sleep.*

The piece of blue cloth I'd found when I was digging up the
book? I should've recognized it, the color, how could I not have?
And it was all I could do now to stop myself from running back
into the woods, finding the cloth and holding it to my face, inhaling it, swallowing it, this last thing Gabriel had worn.

*It wasn't until late the next morning that I
went to the police. Because I'd realized as I was
falling asleep that it had been a mistake to bury
that one piece of evidence, that I should've
pretended I didn't know it existed, let the police
find it in a search.*

And so. An idea and I don't know, maybe a

mistake. I don't know what to believe anymore, only that at the time it felt like the only right answer.

Guilt, it's been the pervading force in my life. Maybe even a protective mechanism in a way, because if all of what happened is my fault, then I wasn't completely powerless, at the mercy of fate. Of course I've been writing these letters all these months in an attempt to sort through and get past the guilt of not having been there for you. The letters started as an attempt to connect with you and I guess ended as an attempt to connect with myself, find some kind of peace with the life I've lived. All the bigger fragments are here but I'm still only skimming the surface. Everyone's story is a trillion times more complex than words can describe.

I imagine all authors feel that way when they type the words THE END, that what they've created only touches the outlines of what they'd imagined when they first sat down to write, and even what they imagined only touches the outlines of truth.

I thought I knew the truth, most of this was written from that place of certainty. But it turns out that truth moves, even after having been set in stone it flips and slides sideways. And now after getting Grace's letter, I'm wondering if her certainty that Joel was responsible had more to do with her rage at what he'd done to us, to her, than with the truth. I'm wondering whether I knew anything.

Forgive me.

Forgive me. And that was it. The end of the notebook, and I reread the last page feeling a growing panic, wings flapping in my stomach. He'd gotten a letter from Grace? Saying something about Gabriel? How could he not have told me!

I strode downstairs meaning to talk to Cecilia, but hearing her with Joel in the dining room, instead I walked to the library and dialed Santa Barbara information and asked for the number of the Poor Clares convent.

The woman who answered sounded ancient, her voice worn, perhaps from disuse, and harsher than I would've expected for a woman who spent her days praising God. "I'm sorry," I said, "I'm sorry but I have a kind of unusual request. Because I'm looking for someone . . . my sister, she's my sister, she's served there for many years and I'm hoping I can talk to her because this is kind of a family emergency."

"I'm sorry," the woman said. "The women here, they're in seclusion. I'm sure you know this, they're not allowed to talk to anyone from the outside."

"But you don't understand . . ." My voice shook. "It's my son, I have to ask her about my son. Because he was only a baby, Sister, two years old and something awful's happened to him and I need her. I need her!"

"Oh goodness . . ." Her voice trailed to silence; she paused for so long I was sure she was going to refuse, but then finally she said, "What's your sister's name?"

"Thank you." My eyes filled. "It's Grace, Grace Sinclair."

"Oh . . . I'm so sorry, dear."

I felt a fist close over my stomach. "She's gone," I said.

"What? No, no I don't know, it's just someone else called a week or two ago asking after her. But you both must have the wrong convent, because she's not here."

Someone else had called to talk with Grace? Well, of course, it was Nate trying to let her know he was coming. "Right, that was probably my husband. And yes she is there, or at least she was. She might be in the hospital now, but I know she was at the Santa Barbara Poor Clares for twenty-five years. Did she maybe change her name? Nuns do that, right? You'll know who I'm talking about, she has ALS, she's been sick for a while now and she's reaching the end. She has dark curly hair, really pretty—"

"I'm so sorry, dear, I'm so sorry about your son and sorry that your sister isn't doing well, but I'm very certain she's not here. I've been here for over thirty years myself, we're a small community and I have no idea who you might be talking about. Could she be at a different monastery?"

She wasn't there? I stared blankly at the bookshelf in front of me and said, "Thank you." And hung up.

Grace wasn't there. But hadn't she told Cecilia in her note that she was? I covered my eyes, trying to think, then feeling a feverish panic I strode out to the entryway.

Joel was sitting at the head of the dining table with his hands on his knees and the remains of dinner in front of him, and Cecilia was in the chair beside him with a pill case, doling out multicolored capsules from several bottles. I stood in the doorway waiting till she looked up, then gestured wildly at her.

She glanced at her dad and stood. "Be right back," she said, then followed me into the library. "You okay?" she said softly. "You look like you're about to be sick."

"I don't know, I don't know." I shoved my fists under my arms, looked up at the ceiling and said, "Grace isn't at the convent, Cecilia, did you know that? I just called, talked to a nun, and I don't know that she's ever been there."

Cecilia's face washed pale. "What?"

"She told you she was in the note she sent, right? Specifically Santa Barbara? And somebody, it must've been Nate, called the convent a week or two ago to ask about her. Which I'm sure was why he decided to come here, to try and figure out where she might actually be and how to find her. He didn't tell you any of this? And a letter, he got a letter from her that said something about your dad and Gabriel, so did he show it to you? I'm pretty sure he took something out of our glass holding case before he left."

"Chloe . . . No, Chloe. I mean you're right, he did bring the letter, I saw it. But I was the one who called the convent."

"So you *knew?* Then where is she!"

"I'm not sure." She leaned back against the rolltop desk, arms hugging her waist. "I wanted to talk to her. I knew she didn't want us to see her before she died but it was haunting me, I couldn't sleep or think for weeks on end and I knew I had to find a way to see her regardless. But when I found out she wasn't there last week, I called Nate to tell him."

"Which is when he came here? Why didn't you tell me? Why didn't he!"

"Because . . . It's complicated, Chloe, there's a lot behind this, there are things he thought would be upsetting for you to hear, and he'd never forgive me if I said anything. Look, I'm going to get Dad to bed early, Nate should be here in an hour or two and then we'll talk."

"Cecilia—"

"Just an hour or two, okay? You have to understand I can't talk about this without Nate here." She set a hand gently on my arm. "I made up a dinner plate for you to microwave, it's in the kitchen, so why don't you eat and then go up to the bedroom and rest." She kissed her hand and touched it to my cheek. "Try to relax because it might be a long night." And then she turned back to the hall.

I listened to her talk with Joel, the sound of their feet on the stairs. Then went to the kitchen and looked at the plate of food she'd left, a thick slice of meat loaf, peas, and a hill of potatoes crowned with a square of butter. I set it in the fridge and then returned to the library, walked to the window and stared out at the dark sky, listening to the noises upstairs, not letting myself think.

All of me felt so empty, so alone, the thoughts like gnats flying in endless spirals too fast to see more than the blurry outlines from where they'd been. And I wanted Nate. I wanted him here so I could have something to focus on, someone to ground me.

I rested my forehead against the windowpane and closed my eyes, the way I had as a kid on rainy days filled with a longing I couldn't have put into words. Opening my eyes to look at the breath cloud on the window, draw my name or a heart or a tic-tac-toe game and watch as it melted away. Now I set my index finger in the middle of the cloud, pulled it away to look through the clear spot it left, then obliterated the cloud with my sleeve and walked to the front door.

It was a clear night, cold, the moon blue and huge and low in the sky. I pulled a flashlight from my glove compartment and walked back through the woods, the damp ferns I walked through soaking my sneakers and the ankles of my jeans.

When I reached the stream I knelt by the hill of dirt I'd dug up the night before, and raked through it until I found the frayed swatch of blue fabric a little bigger than my hand, one side elasticized. The waistband. I brushed it off as best I could and studied it, running a finger across what little was left of the faded teddy bear pattern, then held it against my chest, tucked up my knees, and curled around it. Rocking side to side as I had when Gabriel was still an infant, crooning the words to "Summertime," which I'd sung him every night since he'd been born, this song about endings and loss, as well as beginnings.

>   *One of these mornings, you're going to rise up singing,*
>   *Then you'll spread your wings . . .*

When he was ten months old Gabriel had started humming along with me, the soft *hmms* and *ehhhs* mingling with my voice in a strange, haunting dissonance. Often I'd repeat the verses again and again, standing over him in the dark as his voice began to drift and fade, his eyes closed and his breathing slowed and deepened. And even after he was asleep I'd still sing on, so soft the words became indistinct and ethereal. Wishing our song, our bedtime rituals, these last vestiges of babyhood, would go on and on forever.

27

It was almost ten when I returned to find Nate's car in the driveway. I stood a minute looking at it, then walked into the house.

Nate and Cecilia were sitting in the library, Cecilia in the armchair with her hands folded between her knees, Nate on the sofa looking drawn, his eyes heavy and face worn. As I entered he jumped to his feet, stepped toward me but then stopped, questioning.

"You should've told me," I said. "You should've told me where you were going and why."

Nate raised an arm, then dropped it. "I know."

I could feel the remains of the pajama bottoms against my chest, smell the dank decay of them. Standing here with Nate, the first time since having read his secrets, seeing the twists of gray in his hair and the lines in his forehead I hardly recognized, it felt like it had been years since we'd last been together. And maybe it actually had been. Each wrinkle and gray strand had happened without me; he hadn't been missing a week, he'd been missing since those afternoons in the woods when we talked about the world, insights we gleaned from other people's words rather than from our own experiences. Those had been our best years, and the first time he'd run away, the night Gabriel was conceived, he'd never really come home.

"Why don't you trust me! That's been the problem all along, you think I'm too weak or that you need to keep parts of your life out of our marriage, but that's not what marriage is about, Nate. Those parts you didn't tell me explain everything, so it's like you crippled our marriage, you took away legs! I'm supposed to be the most important person in your life, but you've never let me be!"

"Chloe," he said, sounding lost, and all at once the grief hit like a sodden blanket. I pulled the blue cloth out from under my shirt and held it forward with a sob. Nate looked blankly at the fabric, then at my face, and the understanding seized him all at once, a drawstring tightening and pulling. He strode forward and enveloped me in his arms and I fell against him, let him surround me, the soft warmth of his rugby shirt, arms firm against my back.

When was the last time he'd held me? I couldn't remember the last time we'd made love, the last time we'd cried together or showed each other anything deeper than conventional, everyday fears. But here was the thing, maybe the thing about every long-term marriage. Even if I'd lost Nate years ago, everything we'd lived through, it had its own life, something that was part of us but also wholly separate, like stories are separate from their tellers. Even over the past year, even through the hours I'd spent with Daniel and all the anger and the betrayal and hurt and whatever might come next, the story was still there. And at least in those minutes he held me, the story we'd lived through together was more essential by far than what we hadn't shared.

———

I sat on the sofa with Nate, my eyes still swollen with tears, cradling a cup of lukewarm tea. Nate's face was haggard as he spoke, his voice cracking at the end of each phrase, like bits of it were being chipped away.

"I didn't find her," he said. "I don't have any idea where she is now, or if she's still alive or if she was even telling the truth about being sick. All I know is what you found out, that she hasn't been at the convent all these years. I don't know if she ever planned on going back or if she just told us that's where she'd be because she didn't want us worrying about her. Maybe she only realized after she got to Santa Barbara that she actually wanted the freedom she'd never had growing up. Whatever it was, I looked everywhere, even hired one of the best PI's in the state when Cecilia first told me she wasn't at the convent. He's former FBI, has contacts in multiple states, but he hasn't found any trace of her anywhere in the country, it's like she never existed. Part of me kept expecting to pass her on the street, or for somebody who saw me to do a double take and say, 'Oh my gosh, you look exactly like this woman I know!' But there's no sign she was ever there at all."

"Did you check hospitals?"

"After the convent that was the first place I checked. All the hospitals in the area, I must've called twenty of them. But there weren't any records of a Grace Sinclair, and no death records, which means either she changed her name or she was never actually sick."

"She cashed the check I gave her when she left," I said. "I thought she must've given it to the convent like I suggested, wanted to imagine her in a nicer living environment, maybe not having to work as hard. But if she was never there, she could've used the money to start a new life anywhere."

"The letters she sent us were postmarked from Santa Barbara, and she wrote that she was living by the ocean, so I don't know where else she can be."

"What else did she say? Something about Gabriel, right?"

"Seriously, Chloe, there wasn't anything else you need to know. Trust me, it was mostly just rambling."

"Trust you? Goddammit, Nate, if it has anything to do with my son, then you better tell me. I don't care if you think it'll hurt to hear, there's a limit after which a person's already been so hurt that nothing even touches them anymore, and I reached that limit a long time ago. Just tell me!"

He glanced at Cecilia, then pressed his palms together. "Here's the thing. Grace started to second-guess whether Joel actually was the one who'd taken Gabriel."

I stared at him blankly, then said, "Okay, I mean I guess I'm not altogether surprised at that. She was the one who was always trying to defend him. I was actually more surprised that she accused him in the first place."

"Just listen, okay? She said that as she'd gotten more distance from him over the years, and especially now that all she could do was lie in bed and try to sort through and reorder the past, she'd started to rethink some of the stuff that happened while we were growing up. She told me she'd sent Joel a letter last year, and that he wrote back to her and told her things that made her question whether she'd made a huge mistake. We all thought of him as abusive, but with a little perspective you start to understand it was mostly just strictness and fear. Like his insistence on us memorizing huge chunks of the Bible."

"Whenever he thought we were out of line he'd make us memorize the begats!" Cecilia said.

"But Grace wrote that she finally understood he'd really thought everything he'd done to us was for our own good. She thinks that must've been why Mom pretended to go along with it even though she let us break his rules. It wasn't because she was scared of him, it was because she knew it was his way of loving us, of being a father, doing what he could to make us good people. I think at the time Grace accused him she thought he might be, I don't know, demonically possessed or something. But in the letter she said even though he'd changed after Mom died, she thought it was only because in his mind saving us had become even more urgent."

"The strictness was mostly from his own upbringing," Cecilia said. "His father was a pastor too, and he actually whipped Daddy. Now that I have to help him change I've seen the scars, and they're awful and everywhere, crisscrossing his arms and legs and back like a barbed-wire fence, so with all he's been through, really it's kind of amazing he wasn't worse, that he didn't cross from strict and demanding to cruel. He never intentionally hurt us."

My stomach wrenched. "Are you kidding? How can you say that? How could Grace even think it! He made her abort her baby!"

"But that's the thing, Chloe," Nate said, "one of the things she realized. He'd overheard her praying for guidance, that's how he found out and he exploded, calling the baby the devil's spawn, saying it and she were cursed for eternity, the same things he told me about Gabriel. And there were other things; he said if the child was born it would corrupt not just her but the family by association, even give Satan a foothold in the church. Imagine feeling that kind of responsibility."

"So what're you saying, that he didn't force her? She decided to do it on her own to protect the family?"

"I wouldn't say that exactly, just that she misinterpreted what he meant. He did actually say it would be best for everybody if the baby was stillborn, the only chance for its soul to be saved. And it was probably just the heat of the moment, his own fear; he was trying to terrify her because he was probably terrified himself. Remember this was pretty soon after Mom died, in those days he was half insane. And yeah, it worked, she was scared for all of us. She was sure he meant she only had one choice, so . . ." He brought his fists together. "So."

I remembered the anticipation in Grace's eyes when she'd asked me about marriage outside the church, and then the hollowness in her face when I'd next seen her. "Poor Grace," I said. "Jesus, Nate."

"I'm sure when he found out she'd aborted the baby he was horrified. But he saw how it was affecting her, he did what he could to make Grace think the baby was never meant to live, that its death wasn't really her fault. And in the next few weeks, all the hours he made us work in the church, he was probably trying to keep her busy so she wouldn't think about what she'd done. But Grace was sure it was exactly what he'd wanted, that if she hadn't done it herself he would've done it for her."

"And that's why she was so scared when she found out about Gabriel," Cecilia said, "and why she was so sure, when he went missing, that Daddy had been the one who hurt him. What she wrote to tell us was that after all these years she wasn't sure anymore."

"But it *was* him! Whatever she's second-guessing now, it turns out she was right. He wrote about it! There was a goddamned diaper in his trash!" I stopped, stared at Nate. "Wait, are you saying she thinks he actually didn't hurt him? Just maybe brought him somewhere and he's still alive?"

"Chloe." Nate's eyes filled. He shook his head quickly. "There's another side of this. It was why I didn't tell Cecilia about the letter until I absolutely had to, I knew it would kill her in the same way it was killing me. Because the evidence in the house, the only evidence they found, we were the ones who put it there. Me and Cecilia."

A chill enveloped me, clammy hands squeezing. "What?" I tried to say, the word catching, coming out in a simian bleat. I turned to Cecilia and her gaze shifted quickly over my shoulder, her face flat and empty like she'd been distracted by some other conversation playing in the far distance.

"Chloe . . . Chloe, I'm so sorry. I didn't want you to find out about any of this because I knew you needed to feel like the whole thing was completely over and justice was done. But the note in his desk wasn't meant for me and wasn't about Gabriel; he'd written it to Grace after her baby died. She sent it to me with her letter accusing him, as evidence of what he was capable of. So I brought that to the house and I took a diaper from the bottom of our trash, a sock from Gabriel's drawer, strands of hair you'd saved from his first cut, enough to make sure the evidence would be incontrovertible. And Cecilia and I brought them to the house while Joel was at church."

"No . . ." I felt a cold weight rolling in my stomach, lead ball bearings. "Nate, what?"

"It was awful trying to find things from Gabriel that I could bring." His voice was hollow, pitched too low. "It was like they had life, like a song he was singing to me about how sweet and ordinary his life used to be. Finding them, leaving them here, it was probably the hardest thing I've ever done."

"It doesn't make sense!" I said, trying to find a foothold in this conversation that had shifted everything I knew out from under me. "How could you plant false evidence? Why would you?"

"Because I was sure he was guilty, of that and of Grace's ba-

by's death, and I was going to do whatever I had to in order to
make sure he was arrested."

"But—" I started, then inhaled quickly and cupped my hands
over my nose and mouth. "But okay, it's okay, it's done. It's done
and he went to jail, and it doesn't really matter if he was convicted
with false evidence, all that matters was that he was convicted."

"But what if he shouldn't have been?" Cecilia said.

"What the hell are you talking about? He admitted he'd done
it! You found him with Gabriel's pajamas!"

"That afternoon in the church," Nate said, "he told me he'd
found the pajamas on the altar the day after Gabriel disappeared.
The truth is really anybody could've put them there; everybody
knew by that point that Gabriel was his grandson, so maybe whoever took Gabriel set them there because he wanted Joel to be
blamed for it."

"In the beginning Daddy told authorities he was innocent,"
Cecilia said, "and then he said it again when he was released.
Grace wrote in her letter to Nate that she'd always wondered if he
only started acting resigned because he thought prison was God's
will. He'd been questioning since Mom died whether his faith was
strong enough, so maybe he saw it as a further test, or even retribution. And if you think about it, he never actually admitted he was
guilty, just said he was proclaiming guilt because God told him to.
He used to imagine God's voice all the time, he considered himself
a prophet, so when he already felt guilty about one baby's death, I
can see why that voice might have turned on him. Accepting prison
time was his penance."

There was a roaring in my head so loud I could hardly think
through the noise of it. "I can't stand this, what does it even mean?
What if you're right that it wasn't him, and what if they would've
been able to find Gabriel if they hadn't stopped looking when they

arrested your father? What if he'd still been alive then? Or what if . . . Nate, could he still be alive now?"

Nate reached for my hand, held it between both of his and squeezed, a movement that seemed so patronizing that I snatched my hand away. "Don't give me that look. It's possible, right?"

"This is what I was scared of. God, I wish you didn't have to find any of this out. There were other leads being followed before I told the police to search Joel's home, a pedophile in Klamath, a nanny in Trinidad the police suspected had drowned the girl she was caring for, it could've been them or it could've been somebody else entirely, we just don't know."

"Regardless of who took him," Cecilia said softly, "the disappearance was so widely televised that I'm sure if anybody had suddenly inexplicably shown up somewhere with a two-year-old boy, people would've immediately realized who he was."

"This is what I've been living through ever since I got Grace's last letter. It's harder thinking we'll never know the whole truth for sure, who took him and where he was taken. So this is going to torture you forever now, I know that, almost like right after it happened. You'll be wondering if he's hurting, if he's missing you . . . so isn't it better to just feel like he's at peace?"

"At peace! How can you know he's at peace? You don't know anything!" I pressed the heels of my hands against my eyes, nails digging into my scalp. All those days I'd been so sure I could feel him, feel his presence somewhere out there in the world; if he was actually gone, wouldn't some primitive part of me have felt his death in the way amputees feel phantom pain? All this time I'd been trying to convince myself of the irrationality of this, but what if I hadn't felt anything because he really was alive?

"The letter your dad wrote to Grace," I said, hands still covering my face, "I'm not ever going to believe Joel had nothing to do with this, but what did his letter say that made her change her mind?"

"I guess he still claimed he wasn't involved in Gabriel's disappearance, but I think it was mostly that he apologized for the way he'd treated us, and he said it in such a way that it felt genuine, and she started looking at our whole childhood differently. I can show you what she wrote, but she didn't say much more than that." He walked to a knapsack in the corner of the room, rifled through the front pocket, and pulled out a worn envelope. "I guess that's another reason I wanted to find Grace, to see exactly what Joel said to her so I could interpret it myself."

He handed me Grace's letter. The envelope was typewritten, addressed to Nate, no return address and a Santa Barbara postmark, the kind of letter I would've handed to Nate without thought, thinking it was either some kind of bookstore correspondence or junk mail. I pulled out the three printed sheets of paper and unfolded them, skimming until she began to talk about her father's letter.

> *I wrote to him last year, and I talked to him about some of my anger. He wrote back almost immediately to say that his mistakes had haunted him throughout the years, and I know this sounds bad, but for the first time I saw him as a human being. I wish so much that I'd seen this side of him when we were teenagers and started to hate him, the side Mom must've known. I think it would've changed so much about how we all interacted with him, maybe we could've found a way to show him who we were. Maybe it was this spiral of our reactions and his reactions to our reactions that ended up sinking us all deeper and deeper. I keep thinking without that, I might have been able to love him in the right way.*
>
> *So I guess that's why I'm writing this, because I want you to*

look harder at what you believed. I made a lot of mistakes because I was scared of him, but now I know it's time to mend whatever pieces of our family can still be mended, and as part of that I need to tell you that I believe everything Daddy told me in his letter. That he wasn't the one who took your son.

I'm sure of it, actually, he just wasn't ever capable of it. It's true he could've told the police the letter they found had actually been written to me, but I think he might have been trying to protect me by keeping the loss of my baby from becoming the story of the week. He accepted his imprisonment as penance for the way he'd treated us, for the things he said to you about Gabriel and the things he said and wrote to me about my child. He told me he knew if he'd acted differently, accepted both my and Chloe's pregnancies as a blessing, there's a good chance both our children would still be alive. And that because of the mistakes he'd made he'd never believed anything he'd been through was unfair.

But I think he's suffered enough, Nate. I want you to try and forgive him, look underneath the person you remember and try to find the person he really was. Which comes with its own repercussions, all the guilt for not having seen it sooner and made different choices. But in the end it's so worth it, I hope you'll see that and make the effort to get to know him before there's nothing left of him to know. Please go to Daddy now, listen to what he has to say. It's more important than you realize.

I wish things had been different. I wish we'd lived the life we were supposed to live, and that we'd all been together all these years. I imagine that sometimes, my child and yours becoming friends, cousins as close as brothers. Here I am living the life I thought I wanted when I was a girl, by the ocean, near people I love who also love me. But it turns out it's not the right life after all.

I love you, Nate. I'm so sorry for the way things turned out. I
miss you more than you'll ever understand.
                    Grace

I refolded the letter slowly, slipped it back into the envelope,
and then held the envelope between both hands, staring down at
the seal. Something was niggling at the corner of my mind, something I couldn't quite put my finger on with all the words and images writhing around it. I held onto the letter a minute longer
without speaking before handing it back to Nate.

"It's funny," Cecilia said, "because her letter to me wasn't anywhere near as lucid. All her Bible quotes and worries about the lake
of fire, I thought she must've at least partly lost her mind as well as
her body. It's like she knew there was something important she
needed to get across in Nate's letter, and she summoned up every
last bit of her strength to silence whatever else was going on in her
mind. After that, when she wrote to me, all she had left was the
fear."

I felt dizzy, my mind spinning in the same vicious spirals it had
in the days after we'd lost Gabriel, the bottomless horror of not
knowing. Nate rested his cheek against my shoulder and just the
feel of that weight settled me, tamping the spinning. This, maybe,
was the difference between then and now, knowing that I wasn't
completely alone. "I think we should all go up to bed," Nate said
softly. "This was a lot to take in, and I know we'll be able to sort
through it better tomorrow."

I nodded silently and he took my hand, interlaced his fingers.
"I'll see you guys in the morning," Cecilia said, and Nate squeezed
my hand and rose. Together we walked upstairs.

After getting ready for bed I lay with Nate on the small twin mattress, nestled against him as he smoothed a hand up and down my back. I tried to center myself against that, the weight of everything we'd had together before it started to fall apart, trying to imagine that leaning on the past could steady us through the future.

"I missed you," he said softly. "I was there, walking up and down the streets alone, and I felt so lost. There were so many times I almost looked for a pay phone to call you, but I didn't want you knowing about Grace until I found out whether she was alive. I didn't want you hoping like I'd been hoping." He pinched the bridge of his nose and held his hand there. "I'm so sorry, Chloe, I should've just told you everything a long time ago, I don't know. I wanted to, except that felt so selfish because I knew it would've been for myself and not for you. But this was worse for you than it would've been. Reading the notebook without me there to explain and finding out after all these years what I'd done, I should've realized."

"It's okay," I said, "I loved so much of what you wrote. It helped me remember so many things I'd forgotten, and now I don't know why I worked so hard to forget them."

"Because remembering forces you to think about what you've lost. And I'm not just talking about Gabriel."

I turned to look at him, a dark knot in my stomach.

"I think that's what I was doing while I was writing, forcing myself to remember. But I also think it's why I kept hiding the words in code even after I knew Gabriel wouldn't ever be decoding them. Because I wanted the words out there, out of me and in the world, but I couldn't stand to have them visible, a continuous echo of everything we used to have together. Which was stupid really, since it's not like everything disappears just because you're not looking directly at it."

"I slept with Daniel," I said. No forethought, no chance to lead up gradually, temper the words. Maybe they'd been pressing too long in my throat, grown too big to swallow back; all I knew was that in this minute they felt essential.

Nate didn't respond at first, I didn't even feel his body tense, so I slowly sat up to see if he'd heard me, knowing that if he hadn't, I wouldn't be able to tell him again. His face was still and blank. I pulled the blanket up around me. "Nate, God I'm sorry." So inadequate, the only words I could find.

He sat up suddenly, threw off the covers and stood, walking unsteadily to the far wall before he turned back to face me. "So? So what does this mean?"

My eyes filled and I bit my tongue.

"We never talk about what's happened to us," he said, "to the marriage, like that'll keep it from solidifying. But look at this; I guess this is as solid as marriage issues get." His hair was rumpled and in his eyes; he suddenly looked so young, and I felt a wave of nostalgia, an almost maternal wish to protect him. So the anger that came next was startling. "Jesus Christ, with *Daniel*? Oh I know how he feels about you, that was always obvious, but you, I seriously thought you were better than that. How long ago was this?"

I didn't answer, and of course the silence was louder than any words I might've said. "So this is an ongoing thing. You've slept next to me, eaten dinner with me, looked me in the eye and smiled and every minute of it was a lie."

"Not a lie, Nate, not how you mean it. I didn't think about Daniel when I was with you."

"Did you think about *me* when you were with *him*?"

"Nate."

"It hardly matters, does it. So was it just for the sex? Or as revenge? Or . . . do you love him?"

Why hadn't I anticipated this conversation so I could formulate answers to these questions? Maybe because I'd seen enough movies and read enough books about these types of confessions to know there were no good answers, nothing that would make this easier to stomach or to understand. Should I say I'd never loved Daniel because it would be kinder? "I was lonely," I said so weakly I could barely hear my own voice, then, "That's not an excuse, but that's how it started. And however I feel about Daniel, it's nowhere close to how I feel about you. I've known you almost my whole life, Nate. I've *loved* you almost my whole life, and there's no way I could ever feel even remotely the same with anybody else."

"Except that you've also hated me for the past twenty-five years."

I felt everything in me still as I watched him, his face slack, shadowed and bruised by the dark. "Do you really think that?"

"You've been sleeping with my best friend, Chloe. If that's not hate, then what is? I thought . . . I don't know, that maybe tonight was the start of some kind of change. But obviously the past, the distant past, isn't enough to keep us together, and I have no idea how you feel anymore."

I rose and approached him, hesitated, and then reached for his hand and lifted it, buried my face inside. "I'm sorry," I whispered, "I'm so sorry. And I don't know if we can get past this; all I know is that I wish we could find some way to."

He stared off into the middle distance, his hand still on my cheek, then turned away and walked to the doorway, stood there without looking at me. "I've lost so many people," he said. "I could stand losing my mother because I had you, Grace, and Cecilia. And now I can barely, just barely stand losing Grace. But losing Gabriel was impossible, and now how can I stand losing you too?"

We didn't talk much more that night, just got ready for bed and then lay side by side in the dark, listening to each other breathe. And then just as I was drifting into sleep Nate said, "I can't forgive you, I know that much, but I'll have to figure out whether I can see around it."

I took his hand, brought it up to my chest. And he stiffened, but he didn't pull away.

28

I didn't sleep well, kept waking to be sure Nate was still lying beside me, replaying our conversation as if that would help me understand whether there'd been a conclusion. And then, sometime in the early morning, I woke at the sound of Joel crying out. I sat up, swimming blankly through the haze of sleep, then rose and pulled on my robe, walking into the hallway. The hall was dark, silent. I stood a moment waiting, then started toward Joel's bedroom just as he called out again. The noise was coming from outside.

I walked downstairs to find the front door open wide, the porch light on. "Mr. Sinclair?" I called, stepping outside. The air was heavy, damp and cold, and I wrapped my arms around my chest as I strode across the yard. "Mr. Sinclair!"

Around to the back of the house and then, "Sophia?" His voice was coming from the woods and I followed it, calling to him, squinting in the dim predawn light. And there he was, huddled on the ground in his undershirt, his face streaked with tears. He looked up at me. "I seem to have lost my shoes," he said.

His feet were bare, the soles caked with mud and dried pine needles. His right foot was dark with blood. "I'm going to help you up," I said, "okay? I'll help you back inside."

I reached under his arms and pulled him to his feet, his body so thin and frail it was like lifting a tree branch. I swung an arm around him and let him lean on me, making tight mewling sounds as he limped with me slowly back to the house and up the stairs.

I walked him up to the bathroom and cleaned his foot as best I could, searching through the cupboards for hydrogen peroxide and then bandaging his foot with a hand towel. I worked without letting myself think or feel anything, the motions mechanical as if I was fixing a broken chair. Until I'd helped him to bed, tucked the covers around him, and stood in the doorway watching to make sure he fell asleep.

He looked like something that had been stripped of an outer shell, soft and too pink. Almost indecent. But I could see in his face the outlines of the man he'd been, his cheekbones and full lips, the set to his jaw. And watching him I'd like to say all I felt was pity, but it was so much more complex than that. There was too much history, and like Nate had said, the past didn't just disappear when you weren't looking directly at it. But at least, amidst the muddle of emotions, hate was no longer overshadowing the rest.

I suddenly remembered a conversation I'd had with Grace years ago, soon after Sophia died. "Nate only thinks he hates Daddy," she'd said. "In reality I think it comes from being angry at God, and since he can't hate *God* he redirects it." Of course, Nate had legitimate reasons to hate his father, more and more so as time went on, but had the chicken or egg come first? He'd acted out as a child because of Sophia's illness, the resultant anger at the man who represented God to him, which made his father more strict in an attempt to bring him in line, which made Nate angrier, which made Joel harsher, and on and on. How much of who Nate was, and the way he'd reacted to the events in our lives, had come from his struggles with faith?

I stood by the open doorway of Nate's bedroom for a long while watching him sleep, the only time he was ever truly at peace. Then lay back on the bed, trying to warm myself, stop myself from thinking. But when it became clear I wasn't going to be able to sleep, I rose and quietly pulled on my clothes and went downstairs to start a pot of coffee. Opening the fridge for milk I saw my dinner plate was still there, now covered in foil, so I pulled it out and brought it to the dining room where I ate it cold, filling myself without tasting.

After washing my plate I brought my mug of coffee into the library and sat on the sofa. Hesitated, then pulled out my cell phone to call Daniel and said the words right away. I hunched forward over my knees as I talked, eyes squeezed shut, and after the conversation was over I covered my face, rocking back and forth, back and forth frantically like I could shake it from memory. It hadn't even been as harrowing as I'd dreaded, Daniel just seemed stilted and resigned, words sharpened at times by the hard edge of anger, hiding whatever else he might be feeling. And I had a sense that part of him had just been waiting for this from the day we first made love, had at least subconsciously seen it as inevitable. Speaking, I'd almost felt relief, a loosening in my chest, until he said, "In all of this what hurts the most is losing what we had, the three of us. Our friendship." And then he hung up. The finality, that was what felt hardest, more even than the idea I might never see Daniel again. And maybe that in itself was proof that I'd only been in love with the romance.

Now I wiped the tears off my face with the back of my arm and stood. Walked to the window, watching as the sky faded from pale pink to pale blue. It was so beautiful here, so different from Truckee. There was a difference between loneliness and solitude, and this was the kind of place one could be alone without feeling lonely. Thomas Wolfe had said that loneliness was the central and inevitable fact of human existence, so maybe it didn't even make sense to try and find ways to mend it, just to accept and find the beauty in it. Maybe one could be lonely and whole at the same time, and maybe the wholeness I'd felt as a child around the Sinclairs, and in the years Gabriel had been alive, had less to do with their part in my life than with myself when I was with them.

I'd thought that was what Grace was looking for in the convent, the peace of solitude. Had she found that kind of wholeness in herself wherever she was now? Or maybe she had found friends after all, maybe leaving home had given her the freedom she needed to find them. Hadn't she said she was near people she loved? Of course, it was very possible she wasn't telling the truth about any of it, that she just wanted to reassure us that she wasn't dying alone. But I'd pretend it was true. Really, I could imagine anything for her life, try to convince myself I was imagining right—that she'd found happiness, friendship and family, a career that fulfilled her—because probably I'd never know either way.

Could I live with not knowing? Could any of us? It was the same as not knowing where Gabriel's body had been buried, the knowledge so pointless but the lack of it so unsettling. Not knowing how Grace had spent the last twenty-five years was like ending a piece of music on a dissonant note; one waited and waited for the resolving chord that never came. Searching for it now because I was still sure there was something written between the lines of her letter that I sensed but hadn't been able to see clearly.

The letter was still lying on the coffee table where we'd dropped it last night, so I pulled it from the envelope and sat back to study it. This time I read it slowly, from the beginning, both to reassure myself that Grace was finding at least some peace in her last days, and trying to work out what it might have been tickling at the edges of my consciousness. Until I reached the end.

Here I am living the life I thought I wanted when I was a
girl, by the ocean, near people I love who also love me.

I stared at this.

"I was thinking," she'd said the morning before she left home for good, "when it was time for me to leave, that I'd do something big with the opportunity. Go to Avonlea like I dreamed when we were little, even eventually have a child and raise it by the ocean, build us a perfect life."

I stood and walked to the phone to dial information. "I need the area code for Nova Scotia, Canada," I said. "Prince Edward Island."

For Grace, the *Anne of Green Gables* books had been more than just a phase, they were an obsession, her wish to be adopted into an island family surrounded by friends, to fall in love. Avonlea, with its steepled churches, red cobbled streets and white picket fences, girls in petticoats and ribboned hats running barefoot along the beach, as close to heaven as one could get while alive. And Anne, full of spirit and spunk and wild adventure, the kind of girl Grace wished she had the courage to be, the girl she had been briefly with Cesar.

My voice was unsteady as I asked whether there was a listing for Grace Sinclair, closing my eyes, filled with a wish. There was a click and a recorded voice listed a number, which I echoed in my head again and again, the weight of everything from the past few days dropping through my chest into my stomach. I took a deep breath, then clamped my lips between my teeth and dialed the number.

It was a man who answered, and I took a deep breath and said, "I'm sorry, I hope I have the right number. I'm looking for Grace Sinclair?"

"Oh," he said, then, "I'm sorry, this is Thomas."

"Are you taking care of her? Is she there? I realize she can't talk anymore, but if I could just do the talking, I have all these things I've been wanting to say to her and also questions she might be able to answer. I know she has some way of typing, so maybe you could read the answers?" My voice sounded breathless, too anxious. "But mostly I want to make sure she knows we're here for her, we always have been, and how much we all love her."

"Who *is* this?" He sounded reprimanding.

"Oh right, sorry, this is Grace's sister Chloe Sinclair. Or Tyler, she'd know me as Chloe Tyler."

"What do you mean her sister? She didn't have a sister."

"Yes she did. I mean I'm her sister-in-law, but she also had a sister and I'm married to her brother Nate. We—" I stopped suddenly, closed my eyes. "You said *didn't*."

"Chloe and Nate," he said.

"I'm too late, aren't I. It's already too late?"

"I'm sorry . . . You knew she was sick?" His voice had changed; now he only sounded bewildered, like he was trying to work something out in his head. "Two weeks ago she got pneumonia. It was quick after that."

"Two weeks? We missed her by two weeks?" I said, then bit my tongue, willing back the tears. How was I going to tell Nate and Cecilia?

"I had stuffed animals named Chloe and Nate," Thomas said slowly, "a cat and a bear."

"What?"

"We used to put on plays with them, or I guess you'd call them puppet shows, the cat and bear, a stuffed monkey and a lion. Up until I was twelve or thirteen, way too old to play with stuffed animals but I did it to make Mom happy. It really did make her happy."

"Mom?" I said blankly.

"You're telling me you really are her sister-in-law? She had a brother?" His voice trailed to a whisper, then, "She told me about her father, she was estranged from him, he was in jail. And that her mother died when she was pretty young, but she never told me she had anybody else. I always thought there had to be some kind of family somewhere, I mean nobody has *nobody*, but she never told me, acted like she was completely alone in the world. Why wouldn't she tell me?"

I shook my head. She'd had a child. She'd had a child?

"Cecilia and Sophia?" he said. "My monkey and lion . . ."

"Her sister," I said. "And her mom."

"Oh hell . . ." He didn't speak for a long while; I could hear his breath ragged on the other end. Then, "I always wanted to have more family, you know? I mean maybe I should've found her father, but she'd told me so many stories about him and I guess I was scared to meet him. When the only family you know about is a murderer, and you're only looking so you can find parts of yourself you can relate to, you kind of figure you're better off not touching those parts."

"I'm so glad she had a child," I said softly. "Was she married? Or . . ."

"I never knew my dad, he died when I was just a baby. She told me a little about him, but I always got the feeling it was too hard for her to talk about him so I didn't ask much."

So she had found a new life after all. A life touched by more tragedy, and how much tragedy could a person take before breaking? But maybe happiness too. At least she'd been able to move on.

"I'm sorry," Thomas said, "this is crazy. I'm just trying to absorb it. Is her mother actually dead? And was her father actually in jail? She had me help her mail a letter about a month ago, addressed to Pelican Bay State Prison, but it was returned after a few days with 'Return to Sender, Address Unknown' handwritten on the front."

"He was in jail but he was released a few months ago. And yes, her mom passed away almost thirty years ago." I paused, then said, "You said she sent it last month? Did you read it?"

"I didn't want to read it. She was crying when she wrote it so I was pretty sure it was a goodbye, and I didn't really want to see that. I never even told her the letter was returned because I knew the important part was writing it, so I'm hoping she did feel like she got to say goodbye."

"She sent letters to Nate and Cecilia too a few months ago, also a kind of goodbye. But the letters were postmarked from Santa Barbara, California. Did she actually go to Santa Barbara?"

"She wanted to," he said slowly. "She talked about wanting to go to California before she died, see the house where she grew up, and she wanted to see Santa Barbara where she lived with me till I was around two, before we came up here. But she was already too sick, this was right before she went on the C-Pap." He paused. "So okay, this is what must've happened. She had me send a thick envelope to Santa Barbara, and I know if you send mail with postage to the post office they'll stamp and mail letters from that location. She used to do it for me when I was little, letters at Christmastime from Bethlehem, Indiana. But that's so bizarre. Why would she go to all that trouble?"

"Because," I said, "she was doing whatever she could to keep us from finding her. I wish she'd let us be with her, I have no idea why she worked so hard to keep us away; maybe because she didn't want us seeing how sick she was. But she wanted us to believe she'd been living at a convent in Santa Barbara; that's where we thought she was going when she first left home. We only just found out she wasn't there."

"I wish you'd been able to find her," he said softly. "I know she didn't want anyone seeing her the way she was at the end, but I think it would've helped her find some peace. Writing to you helped maybe, but it wasn't enough."

So . . . she'd moved on but she hadn't found peace, which was really the most important measure of a good life. I closed my eyes, tried to feel her. *Are you there?* After all these years I still didn't know for sure what I believed, just that it was a fluctuating mix of agnosticism and hope. *I love you,* I tried, to Grace, to my mother, my son. *I love you and I wish I could've done more.*

Would Nate and Cecilia find comfort from this? Sending love up to somewhere invisible, nothing reflected back except the emptiness of everything you could no longer give? Yes they'd find some, and this was one of the magical things about faith. One of the reasons I still had that hope.

So many times I'd asked Nate how he continued to believe, and he'd answered only that it was a part of him, all he knew. Until finally he'd told me that it felt to him like life was insistently feeding that faith: a book he was reading would coincidentally speak to an issue he'd been facing, or he'd score a huge sale within a week of our mortgage being due. He considered it a miracle that I'd found the Sinclairs in the first place, an even bigger miracle that we'd fallen in love.

"It's all in how you choose to look at things," he'd said, "whether you let life tear you away from God or lead you to Him." And inevitably he'd see this, Grace being strong enough to contact him, her letter leading to this discovery of her son and forgiveness of his father before it was too late, as a sign that God was leading us all by the hand. Maybe not a perfect resolution with ends tied in a beautiful bow, but that wasn't the way the world had been designed. And this was another magical thing, being able to grab onto these everyday, imperfect miracles and let them carry you through the heartache, on the way to something bigger.

"I still have the last letter she wrote to her father," Thomas said now. "I can send it to him if you have the address or . . . I could bring it to him. I thought I'd never want to meet him, but with Mom gone it feels different, knowing there's a part of her out there. And the others, I have an aunt and uncle." His voice trailed off and then he said, "This is just so hard to wrap my mind around."

"Would you want to visit? That'd be wonderful, Thomas, so wonderful. We're all together now, at least for the next few days, staying in Cecilia's home. Maybe it's too short notice but I know we'd all just love it if you came before we have to leave. Like you were saying, thinking that part of her we didn't know about is out there and going on even though she's gone, it makes things feel less final and absolute. Part of the reason people have kids, I guess."

"I'll come," he said, "yes, definitely. I've just been sitting around Mom's home, trying to get her papers in order, and it's been the hardest few weeks of my life. I've been so alone with this . . . And maybe they could tell me more about her; there was so much of her life she wouldn't talk about. I just want to know what turned her into the person she became."

"And you can tell us who that person was," I said softly, the grief lodging like a bullet in my chest. The story of a life, broken and loosely mended, perhaps breaking again along the seams because the scars were always there. If this were a book, we would have found Grace in time, maybe worked to fade some of the scars before she left us. But since she was already gone, maybe those broken parts had stopped mattering. Maybe all that mattered now was healing our own.

We spent the next day and night cleaning the house, Cecilia in the kitchen planning elaborate meals, eyes red as she chopped vegetables and prepared sauces, maybe mourning Grace, maybe mourning everything, maybe also overwhelmed at the idea of Thomas's visit. This nephew we should've gotten to know years ago, symbolic of everything we'd lost, but maybe also everything we still had.

He arrived late the next afternoon, after three connecting flights. We were sitting in the library, me, Nate, and Cecilia, when we heard the car pull up the drive. Silently we all rose and walked to the window.

I rested my head against Nate's shoulder, my eyes filling as I saw his Sinclair hair, more reddish than the others but just as thick and wavy, his Sinclair heavy-lidded eyes and wide mouth. We watched him reach into the backseat for a bag and approach the door, then ducked away so he wouldn't see that we'd been spying.

Nate and Cecilia answered the door and I stood at the entrance to the library as they both reached for Thomas. He made a sobbing sound and brought a hand to his mouth and they silently wrapped their arms around his shoulders, held him.

When he pulled away he looked shell-shocked, his face pale and eyes glazed as he turned from Nate to Cecilia and back, and then he glanced at me and gave a shy smile. And I saw it.

The dimple in his right cheek and the cleft in his chin, my ski-slope nose and high cheekbones, and I stared at him blankly, an anesthetic numbness rising from my toes up to my scalp, a hushing inside me like static. I felt the blood rush from my face, my knees buckling, and my head swimming; I heard a crash. And then, everything dark.

29

Dear Daddy,

This is probably the last letter I'll write to you, because I can sense I don't have much time left. I've just been so haunted, even more so after getting your reply to my last letter. I've made so many mistakes and I just want to do whatever I can to, if not make things right, at least make things better.

You told me you'll wait till after I'm gone to tell them, that a year or two won't make a difference to them now in the way it does for me, but I'm telling you I know that's not true. I understand the pain of losing a child, that it's every day and always. A constant twisting and wringing of your insides and then the waves, a bludgeoning at the times you least expect it, driving alone down a highway or stirring dinner, listening to music and suddenly there it is and you can't breathe. Every day your baby dies again and again, the horror chipping away at your soul, and so yes, every day makes a difference.

I've told Nate to go to you, without telling him why. I'm

hoping that he does go, that he understands it's important to see you and try to reach peace with you, but if not, I'm pleading with you to be the one to go to him, show him this letter because I'm not strong enough to do it myself. He's the person who loved me best in the world, and seeing him find out, hearing his confusion and then rage, well I . . . can't do it. I just can't be there.

I've pictured in my mind so many times what I'd say, for years I've engineered and reengineered words and ways I might tell him. I've written countless letters and summarily destroyed them, knowing much as I want to believe carefully crafted words have heart and spirit this is something that needs to be spoken face-to-face. First Nate needs to know, and he and Chloe need to be the ones to tell Thomas.

You told me I'd been used by Satan, and maybe that's the truth. But of course Nate and Chloe are going to need more explanation. I can tell myself I was insane and just a child, and really that wouldn't be altogether untrue, at least at the time I left. But I also know I wasn't insane enough or child enough to believe what I did was right.

Of course it's true I was scared of you. I'm sure you know that, regardless of whether the fear was warranted. I tried to convince Nate and Chloe to leave, get them to see the danger, but they wouldn't listen, they thought I was overreacting. For hours I talked to Nate about this, well into the night, I was trying my best to talk rationally, but I'm sure instead it sounded like ranting and raving. And then that morning when I went back to the house to pack, I made one last attempt to reassure myself. Do you remember what you told me about Gabriel? It was the same thing you told me about my own baby, that you'd rather he die before he reached the age of accountability, that there'd still be a chance his soul might be saved. I don't know if you meant it, if that was just spoken in the heat of rage and frustration and fear, but that's what put me over the edge. I was terrified for this boy who already almost felt like my own.

That's my excuse for taking him, for putting his pajamas in the church and writing to Nate accusing you, doing what I could to make sure you were blamed. I did it because I was afraid but, deep down I know, also for retribution. You'd taken away the life I should have had, so now I was taking yours. At the time I was sure it was only going to be temporary. I'd send him back to Nate, disappear somewhere, a convent in the backwoods where I could do penance for the rest of my life. But then, I fell in love with him.

And that is where my ability to justify myself ends. Because I could've told Nate, could've given him back. You'd been arrested for his murder so you wouldn't have dared to hurt him after you were released. I knew this but . . . he'd already become mine, fully my son. The knowledge he'd been born to someone else became somehow beside the point, especially because I made myself believe I'd be a better parent. Nate and Chloe wouldn't baptize him, I knew they wouldn't raise him in the faith, and I told myself I was sacrificing my own soul to save his. Mom talked to me after she was gone, I truly believe that, told me I had a calling, and Nate tried to convince me she'd meant the convent. But I came to believe she'd meant my calling was to raise this boy to serve God.

And now I have to admit that in time, part of me actually started believing he was the baby I'd lost, not a reincarnation even but the actual baby I'd seen leave me. And my anger at you, for what I thought was your wish that I abort him, became tied up in anger at Nate and Chloe when I imagined them taking him from me again.

So there it is, my unreasonable reasoning. Take it for what you will. Tell Nate as much of this as you think is needed, choose

whichever of these words you think will help him understand
because I know the whys must have been haunting them all this
time.

All my life I've hated myself, and maybe that's why the
revulsion I've felt about what I've done has felt almost natural. I
was able to accept it. I've told you already and I'll tell you again,
even knowing the words are as worthless as the ink on this paper.
I'm so sorry, Daddy. I'm so sorry for not being the person you
thought I was, and I'm so very sorry for hurting you.

Grace

"I thought it was a dream," Thomas said. We were sitting in the library, my brain, my body wrapped in vibrating barbed wire, no thoughts, only a wordless, sizzling panic. I knew I'd been crying, perhaps still was, but all I could feel was Nate's hand gripping mine. So I tried to center myself on that, a weight I could orbit around, the press of each finger and the dampness of his palm.

"I'm sorry," Thomas said, "I just don't know how to think about all this. I wish my mom was here; I can't even start figuring out how to feel without having her here to explain. This isn't even close to enough." He flung the letter across the table. "It's like my whole life was a lie."

My mom. All those years I'd seen Gabriel in every young boy I passed, knowing it was impossible but still staring after him, longing to run after him, stop him because what if? In my mind this boy would know me as soon as he saw my face. His whole body would still, his face filled with wistfulness, then yearning as he burst into tears and grabbed onto me, a child lost in a department store despairing of ever finding home. Never in my mind was Gabriel older than three.

"These distant pictures in my head," Thomas said, "riding on someone's back through a forest with trees so tall they made me dizzy, a bed in a beige room with a green corduroy bedspread. A . . . stuffed bunny?"

My voice, it must've been my voice, saying, "Mulligan."

"Mulligan," he repeated, staring fixedly into the distance. "Mulligan?"

"He was actually Peter Rabbit but you gave him your own name, after *Mike Mulligan and His Steam Shovel*."

"Was that my favorite book?"

"You had lots of favorites."

"Right, I bet I did."

I bit against my tongue until I tasted blood, and then tried to focus on the meaty salt of it, something visceral and familiar. Under the barbed wire was fury, along with terror and a raging hunger and two years of memory collapsed into seconds, the little boy who'd spontaneously wrap his arms around my leg and crow the word "Love!" Who'd do what I called his "snack dance" when I handed him a treat, who'd play endless games of hide-and-seek by bending forward to mash his face against a bookcase or curtain, then turning to crow, "A boo!" All the years we'd lost, tree climbing and bike riding, the expectant days leading up to Christmases and birthdays, they'd disappeared when Gabriel disappeared, but now that he'd returned to us, where were they? Where were they!

I looked at the man on the chair across from me, a man I didn't know at all, squeezed Nate's hand so hard he pulled away, and then tensed my shoulders and screamed.

I woke the next morning still dressed in jeans and a sweater, my mouth gummy with the taste of the brandy Nate had coaxed me to drink. I lay without moving, eyes closed, the thoughts entering one by one, slicing like ice picks. Then slowly opened my eyes.

The room around me was grayed with dawn, Nate in bed beside me, sitting with his back against the wall, watching me. "Have you been sitting there all night?" I said.

"I wanted to be awake when you woke up." He reached for my hand.

"Thank you." I lay there with my hand in his, staring up at the ceiling, then finally said, "Joy and agony are like different sides of the same knife blade."

Nate brought my hand to his cheek. "Our son is home."

My eyes filled and, maybe to distract me, Nate said, "We talked to Dad last night after you were asleep and I think he understood, at least on some level. We'll ask Pastor William to tell the parish Sunday; that'll make things easier for him too. I just wish . . ." He gave a flat smile. "I guess my knife has three blades. I can say it was Grace who took away his life, but I did it too."

"You called him Dad," I said.

"Did I?" He leaned back against the wall. "I guess I did. And that's the thing, I'm making peace with him before it's too late, and trying to make peace with the past. We can't go back, so you just have to focus on finding peace; it's the only thing that'll keep you sane. We've been given this incredible blessing."

"I don't," I started. "I think . . ." and then I shook my head and stood, walked into the hall. Grace's bedroom door was half open and I stood outside it and looked in at the man sprawled across the bed. Just like Gabriel doing his best to take up every inch of mattress space.

In this dim lighting he looked younger than he'd seemed last night, his hair sleep-mussed, and for the first time since he arrived I felt the fierce stomach-clenching fist I'd felt the night they first put a swaddled Gabriel into my arms. All of me wanted to grab onto this man I didn't know, squeeze him against me, squash him into a shape I recognized. Because he was there still, somewhere inside, formless as a ghost. Spend time with him, dig and search and maybe I'd find him, the fingerprints I'd left behind. We wouldn't get back the bike riding, the lost Christmases. Thomas would probably never think of me as his mom, not in the ways that mattered. Gabriel was never coming home, but I'd already mourned that, already felt the anguish of *if only*. All I could do now was start from today, these cracked foundations and walls, patch them imperfectly and then keep building.

Nate walked up behind me, and silently I took his hand, together looking down on our son. And studying his sleeping face, all at once the buzzing in my head quieted and I saw it, not just the shape of his features but the pure Gabrielness inside him. The soul.

It was as if time hadn't just moved forward in a straight arrow, leaving only memories and regrets, the present was folding and intertwining with the past like the ripples from a skipped rock. The water itself not moving, always there, above it the ripple of my life touching the ripple of Gabriel as a child, spreading to Thomas the man and back, widening and joining. If I tried I might be able to find not only the boy who'd been my heart but also the years of him I'd missed, just under the surface. Waiting.

And in just the same way, if I stilled my thoughts and looked, maybe I'd see the marriage I'd been sure I'd already lost, always there in the depths of that water, just as whole.

Epilogue

"She told me we'd lived in Santa Barbara until I was two," Thomas said, "but then when my dad died he left us some money, enough to move up to PEI." Cecilia had taken Joel to church, and Thomas, Nate, and I were sitting in the library with tea and a plate holding some of the approximately two trillion cookies Cecilia had baked the day before Thomas arrived. "That's how she explained not having pictures of me from before I was two, she said she couldn't afford a camera. Why didn't I question it?"

"And she told you your dad had passed away," Nate said.

Thomas studied his face. "I'm sorry, I know this has to be almost as hard for you to work through. You were sure your son was dead." He made a strange, tight face, then said, "She didn't even tell me how he'd died, which I guess should've been another red flag. When I was little I'd ask about my dad all the time, but I stopped when I was old enough to see how upset it made her to talk about him. So I really didn't get any details, she just said he was a writer and that he was a good man, kind, always protective of both of us, and that she loved him with all her heart."

"A writer?" Nate said.

"Probably because she knew I loved to read, and she thought it would make me proud. We had this one children's book, pretty well known, the author's last name was Sinclair, so she told me he was my dad. I guess she wanted me to feel special thinking I had a famous author father; she used to read me a chapter almost every night. When she got to the end we'd start over again; I had the whole thing memorized. Probably still do."

Nate turned to me, looking bewildered, and Thomas stared at him. "Oh hell, it's your book? Nathaniel Sinclair, that's you obviously, and Prince Gabriel was your son." He stopped short, then shook his head quickly. "Was me. God, I'm so stupid."

Nate's eyes filled. He rose quickly to hide it, strode to the corner of the library, and pulled out a copy of his book, which he handed to Thomas. "Did you read the acknowledgments?"

Thomas turned to the front of the book and read aloud. "'For my little prince, who is standing somewhere beyond my reach, still with his sword raised in victory.'" He smiled shyly at Nate and turned the pages slowly, running his finger across the text. "All of it, it's almost like you were talking to me every night without either of us knowing. Maybe that's why Mom read it to me."

I smoothed my hand up and down Nate's back and said, "Nate used to tell you the stories every night, it was your after dinner ritual. You'd stop fussing and listen, all entranced by everything Prince Gabriel had been able to pull off that day. He was so proud of you and he wanted to make sure you knew it."

Nate smiled, but his eyes seemed muddy, so much behind them. "After you disappeared I wrote you letters too, since I couldn't spend anywhere near enough time with you. I started when you were a baby while I was at school, and I kept writing even after you were gone, all the things I wanted to tell you and I guess also things I needed to work through myself. Part of me believed you knew what I was writing, that you were reading it from heaven, I guess."

I hesitated, then said, "You should show him your notebook. He should see it."

Nate turned to me, his face blank. "I wrote everything in there."

"Right, and you wrote it for him. It'll help him learn more about us, especially about you, and he deserves to know everything we can tell him about the past. Maybe it'll help him understand Grace better, what happened and how it could've happened, if he sees what her childhood was like."

"We were so embarrassed about our life," Nate said slowly, then looked up at Thomas. "Or at least I was. I knew we were brought up so different from the rest of the world. I never wanted anybody else to know." He pressed his palms together, looked down at them, and then gave a quick nod and stood. "I'll get it." He rose and walked from the room.

Thomas followed him with his eyes, then turned to me and studied my face, gaze roaming from my hairline down to my nose and chin. "You look like me," he said, his voice hesitant. "I mean, I look like you."

"I always used to think you looked like a Sinclair," I said. "But yeah, even the way you smile with just one side of your mouth, that's exactly like my mom. I remember that smile from when you were a baby."

He shook his head slightly. "I'm sorry, I don't know what to call you."

"Just Chloe," I said softly. "Chloe and Nate, I'm sure nothing else feels right."

"Right," he said. Then, "I remember, you know. I remember lying in a bed with side rails, looking up. I can't see a face but there was singing, I remember begging for one more song, and then one more. 'Hush Little Baby' and 'White Coral Bells' . . ."

"And 'Summertime'?" I said. "From *Porgy and Bess*?"

"I think I remember that!" he said, jubilantly, like he'd just answered a game show question.

Nate walked into the room, holding the notebook against his chest. He sat on the arm of Thomas's chair and handed it to him. "So," he said, "do you like puzzles and codes, by any chance? Or would you rather look at the translation Chloe already wrote out? It'll be easier, much quicker, but there's something about working through the words, I think, that makes them mean more . . . and less at the same time, if that makes any sense, easier to accept. There's time for them to penetrate without them slapping you in the face."

Thomas took the notebook from him. "I love puzzles," he said.

"Oh good!" Nate smiled at him and set a hand on his shoulder, then quickly pulled it off and the two of them bent over the notebook. "Okay," he said. "You'll see how it works, I used words from some of the books that changed my life. There's a story behind each book I chose, and the first was from the day I met Chloe. Grace and Cecilia and I were digging a hole in the backyard, trying to reach London, because Cecilia wanted to meet C. S. Lewis. We all dug while Grace told Chloe the story of *The Lion, the Witch and the Wardrobe*, and through the whole thing Chloe was enraptured." He glanced at me. "She was the prettiest girl I'd ever seen, and I think that was the beginning of my lifetime crush."

I smiled back at him, watching as he pointed out the letters, struck by the sudden memory of Gabriel tucked under Nate's arm as he read bedtime stories. From Thomas's perspective, Nate's notebook would probably seem like not just a tragedy but also a love story, love of Gabriel and of Grace, and of me. Maybe from a distance most lives seem more love story than tragedy and the key is finding enough perspective to see that, to be able to manipulate emphasis and rearrange. Because all memories are a form of story-telling, rewritten with that distance because of new wisdom, or maybe based on what we wish had been. We're all authors continually editing in an attempt to make sense out of our lives.

I've probably stretched truth in telling this story, made myself seem more victim and hero than I can legitimately claim, something I think we always do in remastering our lives. I won't point out the future struggles Nate and I will probably always face in trying to rebuild our marriage, since as long as there's success, the struggles seem beside the point. Maybe I've made the villain of this story more villainous than Joel deserved, since after all this time it's hard of me to think of him as anything else. And I know I haven't shown the goodness of Grace anywhere near as much as I should have, leaving out subplots that might have emphasized it, while also leaving out stories that might have emphasized her periodic thoughtlessness, because both make her harder to understand.

This is the only way my story makes sense to me, using this artistic license. I look back and simplify characters and themes in an attempt to tie loose threads as any good storyteller should. Every satisfying epilogue contains sadness mixed with happiness, and in accepting that sadness I'll be able to move forward, maybe even to forgive myself for many mistakes. To be a good wife. To find a way to be a mother to a boy who is already a man. And to accept everything about where I'm going, and where I've been.

ACKNOWLEDGMENTS

I want to first of all thank Kim Lionetti at BookEnds, for her support throughout my career. A special thanks to Caitlin Alexander, the first person to read this manuscript, for helping me shape and strengthen the plot, and for her wisdom and insight over the last six years. Thanks also to Kelli Fillingim and Ratna Kamath for taking over so seamlessly and enthusiastically to champion this novel, and help me shape it into its final form.

I want to thank the dear and clear friends who've helped keep me sane through the stresses of writing, motherhood, and life in general: Kristen, Maria, Ashley, Ellen, Maura, Megan D., Lisa, Destiny, Melanie, Steph, Andrea K., Kathi, Denise, Kathy, Lauren, Megan M., Parrish, Andi, Jenny, Andrea T., Sidse, and Lesa. Life can throw a lot at a person, and you've been there whenever I need advice, support, or a kick in the tush. I love you all, and I feel so lucky to have you in my life!

To Jerry, the man who agreed to spend his life with a writer, probably without fully realizing what he was getting himself into.

It's not easy, especially when one adds a child to the mix, and I realize I often put you last on my list of priorities because it's too easy to take a marriage for granted. But I know full well that you're the most important part of my life, and there's no way I could do any of this without you. Thank you so much for sacrificing your limited free time by taking care of Anna nights and weekends while I work, and for reading my manuscripts and giving fresh, incredibly intuitive insights. I love you so much and am forever grateful, even when I forget to show it.

Most of all, I want to thank my wonderful, creative, cuddly, hysterically funny, sweet, and loving daughter, Anna. (So thrilled that you're already a bookworm. We spend hours at a time cuddling on the couch reading about talking animals, and pirates, and boys with purple crayons. And as I wrote this novel I found myself imagining how fun it'll be to introduce you to all my childhood favorites. I just can't wait!) Anna, you are my heart, you make me laugh every day and see the world in a brand-new way. We are both so blessed to have you in our lives.

The BOOK *of* SECRETS

ELIZABETH JOY ARNOLD

A READER'S GUIDE

1. Our childhoods can impact us in far-reaching ways, as seen in Nate's and Chloe's lives. Can you think of any childhood experiences or relationships that have greatly impacted you?

2. Nate uses books to communicate with Chloe and their son, Gabriel. What children's books do you still refer to in times of sadness or trouble? Why? What do you get out of them? If you had to create a treasure hunt/secret code using books, which ones would you choose?

3. Nate and Chloe play together first as small children acting out Narnia books and then as teenagers daring each other to do things for badges. In both scenarios, they use their imaginations heavily. Do you think using one's imagination can ever be dangerous, as Mr. Sinclair seemed to believe? What was different from their play acting as children and their pretending as adults?

4. Loyalty plays a big role in this story, whether in the romantic relationship between Nate and Chloe or the parental one between Mr. Sinclair and Grace. What are the consequences of betrayal? In this novel? In your own life?

5. Though they grew up in the same home, Grace, Cecilia, and Nate lead very different lives in part because of their very different personalities. How did the same experiences shape them? Compare their reactions to grief and crisis.

6. Religious fervor drives many of the disastrous things in this novel, but so does love. What do you think the author is trying to say about both things? What similarities do they bear to one another?

7. Forgiveness features heavily in each character's life. Do you think these characters are better or weaker for forgiving their loved one's failings? How do you think you would act in Nate's shoes? Chloe's? Cecilia's? Grace's?

8. How important a role does class play in this novel? If Chloe had been wealthier, how do you think the story would have changed? What about if Nate, Grace, and Cecilia had been from the wrong side of the tracks like Chloe?

9. The author touches on the effects of loneliness in several places in the novel. How does Chloe's loneliness affect her throughout her life? How does she finally come to peace with it? Do you agree with the Thomas Wolfe quote Chloe cites that loneliness is an inevitable fact of human existence?

10. Do you think the secrets Nate kept from Chloe were justified? Why do you think he hid so much of his childhood from her, even after they were adults? How did those secrets impact their relationship? Are there secrets in your own past that you wouldn't share with those closest to you?

11. Chloe muses that one might be able to judge a potential partner's compatibility based on favorite books. Do you think the types of books you're drawn to say something about your personality?

12. What impact do you think Mrs. Sinclair's death had on the lives of the other characters? Do you think things would have turned out differently if she had lived?

13. Grace chooses her own happiness over Nate and Chloe's. How do you think she justifies this? And is she able to hold on to her faith while doing this? What would you have done in the same situation?

"WHAT do you mean, you're busy?" Kylie asked me. She'd come next door to play as she did every day, the two of us passing lazy, amiable afternoons filling pages of my Disney coloring book, and playing endless games of Crazy Eights or dress up.

I gave her an apologetic smile and tried to explain. "It's just . . . there's this book I'm reading."

I felt awful when I saw her face. "All you ever want to do is read books," she said, and then she spun away, toward home. She never came back. But what could I do? A giant caterpillar had just bitten through the stem of a giant peach, sending it rolling down a hill. Aunts Spiker and Sponge were squashed, the peach was still on the move with James inside, and most of me was still rolling through town with them when I answered the door. Kylie was no competition. And so it was that Roald Dahl cost me a friendship.

What is it that makes some children readers while others would rather do anything else? It was one of the many questions I was trying to explore in *The Book of Secrets,* and for Chloe at least it seems to have been a mix of life circumstances, personality, and something as simple as having found the right books, all of which were factors in making stories an essential part of my own life as well.

When people describe their childhoods as magical, I'd guess they're usually referring to backyard ball games, a lack of responsibilities, or a belief in Santa. But when I think back on the magic of my own childhood, the first thing I think of are books. I don't think I was a particularly happy child; I was lonely in spite of my friends, sure that I was different from them somehow, and I thought I should be more than I actually was, stronger, prettier, more heroic. But when I entered books, I became the person I wished I could be. I'm guessing it's what all children wish for at times, and it's a theme so many popular children's books seem to have in common, from *Huckleberry Finn* to *Harry Potter*, the discovery of something fascinating that can transform you.

I think *The Book of Secrets* is the book I've always wanted to write. Partly because I got to revisit my childhood favorites while writing about them, and partly because it has the fairytale structure of those favorites: a lonely girl with a difficult childhood who discovers a new, enchanting, and disquieting world. But I also feel close to this book because as a child I was Chloe in a way, full of a kind of chaotic energy and longing for somewhere epic to direct it. So writing this novel, becoming Chloe and entering the world of the Sinclair children, I was reliving those days when I still believed finding that transforming new world was possible.

I was one of those kids who took books everywhere, along to dentist appointments to read while being fluoridated (I still do this), on car rides where I'd read for as long as the accompanying nausea let me, on walks down our street where I somehow managed to avoid bumping into trees.

We lived in a smallish town with a smallish library. The children's section was in the basement, with blue fluorescent lights and only one high, rectangular window, and I recognized the crazy incongruity of it, that there was so much life hidden in such a completely lifeless room. My mother took my sister and me every Saturday, and I don't remember ever seeing other children. Thinking back on it, I'm guessing Miss Sue, the librarian (yes, I remember her name), must have loved having me there, the kind of kid she was probably envisioning when she decided to take her job. She'd sometimes set books aside for me that she thought I'd like, and I can still see the expectant look on her face when she described them. (Do librarians ever do that sort of thing nowadays? It was such an amazing gift she gave me, especially since this was before the days of the Internet and "Customers who bought this item also bought" links. I actually could use someone like that now, somebody who understands my tastes and has the ability to magically spin through the now infinite rows of shelves to find what I don't even realize I'm looking for.)

We were allowed to check out seven books at a time, one for each day till the next week's trip, and I'd start reading on the drive home, as excited as if I was carrying armfuls of new toys. I remember standing in that small basement room worrying that I might finish every book in existence, and then what would I do? Until I was taken to a huge bookstore in Manhattan, seemingly endless shelves stacked so full they were straining, and the predicament became even more urgent. How was I possibly going to read them all?

I knew they couldn't all be great books; of the hundreds of novels I read in those years, there were far fewer that resonated, and only about twenty books that changed me. But how could you possibly find the Joan Aiken or J. R. R. Tolkien needles in that impossibly huge haystack? I started getting stressed over what I might be missing, in the way I get stressed now when I don't get a chance to see the news for a week, that sense that there might be something momentous out there that I need to know but have no idea about. It's another thing that makes books so powerful for kids; they realize there's so much for them still to learn, and getting to meet people very different from themselves, in circumstances very different from their own, gives them a sense of how huge the world is and how much they still don't understand.

Of course children don't just use books to learn about the world outside their own small circle. When they're old enough to read carefully, they also learn about themselves. And that was one of the main themes in *The Book of Secrets*, the power of books to change not only the events in Chloe's and the Sinclairs' lives, but also the people they became.

I brought many of the books that changed me into this novel, most notably *The Lion, the Witch and the Wardrobe,* the book that really turned me, at eight, into a "reader," just like it was the book that also first lured eight-year-old Chloe into reading. My aunt sent me a boxed set of Narnia books, and I remember looking at the covers, their muted foggy romance-novelish colors, and being unimpressed. But of course that all changed when I started reading.

I'd read quite a bit before that; I was an early reader, starting when a broken leg kept me from being able to do much else, and throughout childhood my parents made sure there were always books available. We moved to the UK when I was six, a country that at the time had only three TV channels, and we brought hardly any toys with us, so I spent the vast majority of my free time curled up in the living room with a book. I'd discovered the Little House series, L. Frank Baum, and Francis Hodgson Burnett, and I lost myself in a gorgeously illustrated volume of *Heidi,* and *The Annotated Alice*. But as much as I loved those books, there was something completely different about Narnia, and re-reading it as an adult last year, I felt exactly the same awe.

I think it's more than just the story, it's the way Lewis writes; he's like a kind grandfather in the way he explains without being condescending. He talks directly to you and develops a relationship. I think he makes children feel respected. And somehow that gentle, everyday language and the very human characters and struggles make everything he writes feel more authentic, like he's talking about this magical world with real, firsthand knowledge. You believe him.

I knew immediately that I'd use Narnia in my story to lure Chloe into reading, and pretty much everything she wrote about the experience was autobiographical. I devoured those books, a drug addiction; there was no sleep, barely time to eat or shower, and for the next three or four years (until adolescence changed my priorities), I stayed gripped by the addiction, looking for the next high.

I wasn't all that hopeful when I asked Miss Sue whether she could find anything even remotely similar, but she introduced me to Edith Nesbit's *The Enchanted Castle,* and then *The House with a Clock in Its Walls, The Wolves of Willoughby Chase,* and *The Phantom Tollbooth.* Even thinking about those books now makes me feel a jolt of electricity. I had a love affair with each of them—that heady, hungry, won't-sleep-till-I-see–you-again kind of romance. It took me over, reading, in a way I haven't experienced since, and I'd feel devastated and desperate when each book ended. I wrote scripts for some of my favorites, the way Chloe and the Sinclairs do for Narnia, acting them out with friends, with my sister, or even alone, all in an attempt to keep the story going and get even closer to it by experiencing it firsthand.

And then came *A Wrinkle in Time,* which still obsesses me so much that it appears in two of my novels. So many books seemed to enter my life at exactly the right time. I think it happens to all of us, but especially in childhood, and the book becomes part of us in a way. It might be the reason I can remember so much about the plots and characters from books I read before the age of ten, when I can hardly remember even the names of the books I've read over the past year.

I was nine years old when I first discovered L'Engle. The image that sticks with me most is of the town on Camazotz with every house the same size, shape, and color, each with children bouncing balls and jumping rope to the same rhythm, not allowed independent thought. It's one of the main lessons from the book, the importance of uniqueness and creativity, and I'd been struggling with exactly that worry, of how different I felt from my friends. Maybe everybody goes through it at that age; it's the age fitting in starts to become more important, but it really used to worry me. I had a sense that if people really knew who I was they'd completely alienate me. I was a daydreamer, shy and overly sensitive to other people's issues and emotions (in retrospect, all qualities that fit with becoming a writer!) I'd been trying all year to pretend I was cooler, somebody I wasn't, and it was when I got to know Meg, even quirkier than me, and realized I really, really liked her, that I stopped worrying so much that the way I saw the world was often different from the people around me.

And isn't that one of the best things about books, that we can get inside people's minds in a way we rarely do in life, and see that we aren't alone? That everything we've stressed over or been embarrassed about, every unusual thought we have, isn't quite as unusual as we'd worried it might be? It stretches the boundaries of what we judge as acceptable inside us. (As an aside, *A Wrinkle in Time* also made me realize how extremely awesome science could be, and made me certain that I wanted to grow up to be either a scientist or an author. I ended up doing both!)

Of all the books Chloe and the Sinclairs read, it's their conflicting interpretations of the Bible that affect them most throughout the story. In my own life, since we weren't an especially religious family, when my mother read the Bible to us it was much as she would've read any collection of bedtime stories, not trying to make us believe it was real, but still explaining the lessons in morality that the stories were trying to teach. The Bible fascinated me as much as any book I read throughout my childhood. Despite my upbringing, I wanted to believe it was real life magic written by a higher power, its creation over the centuries like a story behind a story. It was full of heroes and hardships, as many plot twists and as much magic as any epic. Like I was saying earlier about all the best books, the Bible's stories tell us about the world and about ourselves, with all the same archetypes and plot motifs that are in the novels we're reading now.

I liked Bible stories because I've always been driven to find order in the world. Life and the people around you don't usually turn out the way you think they should, even though you know deep down that bad should be punished and good should be rewarded. The Bible is full of absolutes, and children like absolutes— for people and events to be internally consistent.

Maybe that's why I'm driven to write, because I want that kind of control. I know it's stretching metaphors too far, but when I'm first creating a story I feel like I imagine God might, inventing a new Earth and adding characters, giving them more or less free will, only reining them in when I absolutely have to, and they usually get what they deserve and come out stronger from the struggles. Maybe in the end that's the real reason people are drawn to stories, because they make sense in a way life never does, and even when bad things happen to good people, by the end we usually understand that it's led to something necessary.

Now I'm seeing proof of how innate the love of story is in my daughter's pretend play, as imaginative as science fiction, where a lost baby puzzle piece finds his mommy puzzle piece and the two rejoice, animals fly kites to the moon, and a plastic teacup helps a rubber duck who's gotten stuck inside an underwater Lego village. I'm doing whatever I can to make sure her love of story continues.

In reference books on furthering your child's development they mainly talk about the value of stories in enhancing vocabulary, but in my mind there are so many other subtler but more important benefits to a child's future. I have no idea who I'd be now without hundreds of books behind me, but I'm pretty sure I'd be more two-dimensional, less empathetic, and much less informed about the world. So I sit with my daughter to read *The Big Blue Truck*, a picture book centered around friendship, and imagine introducing her to *The Outsiders* in ten years. I think about the books waiting to be written that she'll introduce to me. And I imagine her face lighting up when she talks about her favorites, the way I think mine still does. I just can't wait.

ABOUT THE AUTHOR

ELIZABETH JOY ARNOLD is also the author of *Pieces of My Sister's Life, Promise the Moon,* and *When We Were Friends.* She was raised in New York, and lives with her husband and daughter in Hopewell, New Jersey, where she is at work on her next novel.

elizabethjoyarnold.com